THE SPHINX EMERALD

H . BEDFORD-JONES

THE SPHINX
EMERALD

H. BEDFORD-JONES

ILLUSTRATIONS BY

MAURICE BOWER

ALTUS PRESS • 2014

EDITED AND DESIGNED BY
Matthew Moring

PUBLISHING HISTORY
"The Sphinx Emerald" originally appeared in June 1946 issue of *Blue Book* magazine.
"Red Sky Over Thebes" originally appeared in July 1946 issue of *Blue Book* magazine.
"The Last Pharaoh" originally appeared in August 1946 issue of *Blue Book* magazine.
"Master of the World" originally appeared in September 1946 issue of *Blue Book* magazine.
"The Son of Julius Caesar" originally appeared in October 1946 issue of *Blue Book* magazine.
"The Eye of the Sun" originally appeared in November 1946 issue of *Blue Book* magazine.
"Assassination at Christmas" originally appeared in December 1946 issue of *Blue Book* magazine.
"The Justice of Amru" originally appeared in January 1947 issue of *Blue Book* magazine.
"Swordsmen of Saladin" originally appeared in February 1947 issue of *Blue Book* magazine.
"Leopards Are for England" originally appeared in March 1947 issue of *Blue Book* magazine.
"The King's Jewel" originally appeared in April 1947 issue of *Blue Book* magazine.
"A Task for Leonardo" originally appeared in May 1947 issue of *Blue Book* magazine.
"The Reward of Nostradamus" originally appeared in June 1947 issue of *Blue Book* magazine.
"Richelieu Raids a Tomb" originally appeared in July 1947 issue of *Blue Book* magazine.
"Jewels Have a Long Life" originally appeared in August 1947 issue of *Blue Book* magazine.
"Lady in Chain Mail" originally appeared in September 1947 issue of *Blue Book* magazine.
"The Bride of the Sphinx" originally appeared in October 1947 issue of *Blue Book* magazine.
"The Passing of the Sphinx Emerald" originally appeared in November 1947 issue of *Blue Book* magazine.

THANKS TO
Everard P. Digges LaTouche and Gerd Pircher

TABLE OF CONTENTS

The Sphinx Emerald 1

Red Sky Over Thebes 33

The Last Pharaoh 63

Master of the World 95

The Son of Julius Caesar 125

The Eye of the Sun 155

Assassination at Christmas 187

The Justice of Amru 219

Swordsmen of Saladin 247

Leopards Are for England 277

The King's Jewel 307

A Task for Leonardo 337

The Reward of Nostradamus 363

Richelieu Raids a Tomb 395

Jewels Have a Long Life 429

Lady in Chain Mail 459

The Bride of the Sphinx 493

The Passing of the Sphinx Emerald 529

About the Author 594

I

THE SPHINX EMERALD

A strange jewel that wrought mischief and magic as it passed from hand to hand down the ages starts its strange eventful dramatic history here in Ancient Egypt....

S OME PEOPLE would have said—and did say—that Nefer was a graceless scoundrel, and their say has gone unchallenged for some thirty-five hundred years. Our reply is that he was nothing of the sort. We find him in his thirties, a thorough cynic and skeptic, polished, sophisticated, extremely charming, a very able and engaging fellow indeed, not unlike many a Wall Street operator of our own day. He was notable for his warm, kindly impulses and for his defiance of accepted conventions—two highly perilous traits of character in any age, chiefly so in his own.

Nefer was the first historical person known to have been connected with that inexplicable jewel known as the Sphinx emerald. The enormous advance in the science of Egyptology made in our own time allows the origin of this famous stone to be traced and its connection with Nefer made clear, also its impact. Curious as it may seem, this emerald did have a real or fancied impact upon those in contact with it—and not always for good, either. Historic jewels are said to have a personality; perhaps they have.

One day during the festivities of the Nile flood, Nefer was exchanging jokes with the officials at the Board of Public Works in Thebes, while his scribe Ho-quac was copying certain records. Nefer spent much time here. He was a delver into the archaeology of Egypt, whose known records at this time—1510 B.C.— went back three thousand years, and more vaguely far beyond that.

Handsome, bronzed, a twinkle in his eye, Nefer capped stories with the officials over a cup of wine and kept them in a roar of laughter. Rich and great though he was, a relative of the old King Thothmes IV, and a court noble, it was not wise to be known as a friend of Nefer. Still, his charm was great. Ordinary men liked him; he had a frank, eager way with him that went to the heart. A great pity that the priests meant to destroy him.

Nefer was of the same opinion. He knew that his fate was resolved upon, and had been desperately seeking for some way of saving himself. His rank and influence had thus far kept him alive, but that rope was chafing thin; he had gone too far. Only

recently his suit for the hand of Asena, daughter of the chief high priest of Amon-Ra, had been sloughed off by her father with some very hard words.

"You fellows will have a different laugh when my book is finished," he said to the chuckling officials. "Oh, it won't do you any harm, but it will certainly turn all the old bureaucrats upside down!"

"What's it about?" queried one. "A story of magic or adventure?"

"No, a tale of thieves in high places, and a true one. That's all I'll say now. You boys wait and see."

"Then you'd better get it approved by the priests of Horus as truthful," said someone.

Nefer caught at the word. "Horus? What do you chuckleheads know about that god of truth? Mighty little! In the ancient days Thoth was the god of truth, and Horus got mixed up with him and superseded him. Why, look at the Great Sphinx, up north across the Nile! The temple of Horus of the rising sun, it's called now; but when it was built, Thoth was worshiped there, and I can cite your own records in proof!"

"My father has learned that you are writing a book of blasphemy against the Kings proving them to be thieves and rascals," Asena whispered. "Is that true?" "I fear it may be so construed," Nefer admitted.

*The Great Sphinx, almost forgotten by people in
general, leaped into life and legend on all sides.*

No one could contradict him. Nothing much was known
about the Sphinx, which was now nearly buried by blowing
sand. This was the 18th Dynasty of kings in Egypt, and the
Sphinx had been standing there before the first dynasty began.
No one cared much about the relics of antiquity. They had
served their day.

The gathering was interrupted by the arrival of a messenger
for Nefer—a dusty, gaunt, brown desert runner who came to
him, saluted him, and gave him a packet and a folded letter.
"From your cousin Senefer, my lord, in the eastern hills."

"Very well." Nefer gave him some coins. "Rest, refresh yourself, and this evening come to my house for a reply."

The packet, wrapped in linen cloth, was sealed. Something
important, then. He made his farewells, sent for his scribe Ho-
quac, and set out for home, the letter tucked out of sight in his

girdle. His cousin Senefer was in charge of the mines in the eastern mountains near the Red Sea, where gold and stones were found—a man entirely in sympathy with him.

"SOMETHING'S UP," thought Nefer, as the scribe came running and caught up with him. "Did you get those records copied?" he asked.

"All but the last, my lord," said the brown, clever man.

Nefer looked at him with shrewd eyes. "You're a rascal," he said. "I hear that you've taken bribes."

"True, my lord," said the scribe imperturbably. "Why not?"

Nefer laughed and clapped him on the shoulder.

"Take their money and tell them lies—good man!" he said. "I'm having the papers made out to give you freedom; the stones under my feet are getting slippery, and I don't want you to be lost with me."

"I'd sooner serve you as a slave than any other man freely," said Ho-quac.

"Don't be a fool. You know well enough that these damned priests intend my ruin."

"I know you'll go down fighting," said the faithful fellow. "And I'll go with you."

"Fighting? Who can fight the priests in this land of ours?"

"You, if you would. I don't know how, but you could."

Nefer laughed, yet the words struck a spark in his brain. Fight them—these haughty priests of Ra and the other gods, these interlinked despots who ruled Egypt with iron superstition? They were not fools; they were intellectual aristocrats. Fight them? He was willing enough to do that—but how? With what weapons?

"By Horus—perhaps with their own weapons!" came the sharp prick of thought. "By yielding instead of contending, by craft instead of valor! Why not? Open your eyes, fool! Use your wits, use your head before they smack it off!'"

All very well to say; but to fight them—how? The King

himself had to take his orders from them. Thothmes liked Nefer, favored him—but dared not make him viceroy and governor of a city—Nefer, whom the priests termed a dangerous man. As for marriage with Asena, daughter of the great Ra-priest Seker, that was nonsense. Yet upon these two things Nefer had set his mind and will.

TRAINED AS a soldier, he was indolent during the peaceful reign of Thothmes, whose father and grandfather had carried Egyptian arms from Nubia to the Euphrates and the Red Sea countries. Egypt was richer than ever before, greater; there was no use for soldiers now. The sly men of peace ruled the land. Everyone had money; the treasury was overflowing; temples and monuments were being erected on all sides.

The powerful priesthood profited vastly. In the nearly four thousand years since the dawn of written history, the gods had changed enormously, many being confused and run together under one name; a number of the ruling dynasties had been barbarians with their own gods, and now the hierarchy of priests was headed by Seker, high priest of Amon-Ra, with whom were incorporated other deities. To Nefer, who knew how most of these gods had begun, the system was rather amusing; but now it had become threatening.

Upon reaching his own house at the river's edge, a small former palace of King Aahmes, he hurried to the seclusion of his study, dropped into a chair, and opened the letter from his cousin. For safety's sake it had been written in neat Babylonian characters, which he could read perfectly. It was brief but significant:

> "To Lord Nefer, beloved of Amon, greetings! I send you a gift from the gods, hoping you can put it to use. No one else knows of it. I have myself polished it in secret. Health and long life."

Nefer held the papyrus over a lamp and burned it. He took up the little packet. To open it took a knife, for the linen had been dipped in gum. Curious, he cut away the outer wrapping, pulled the rest apart, and into his palm fell a bit of green beryl, uneven in shape, and which by later standards would weigh some twelve carats.

He smiled; at first, he thought his cousin had merely found a huge emerald, for such stones did come from the mines. It was not a good one; the color was uneven and pale. Then, as he held up the partially polished stone, he caught his breath. His gaze focused. Excitement grew within him.

Emeralds, even large ones such as this, were no novelty in court circles; but this one was little short of a miracle. Like all emeralds it was somewhat flawed. These flaws came together in one place, and there formed a distinct image, a shape, so sharply clear-cut as to be incredible. It was the shape of the Great Sphinx that stood near the pyramid of Chephren. It was a perfect and exact figure of the Sphinx in profile.

Time ceased to exist as Nefer sat examining the emerald. Being an initiate of the Mysteries, he had access to all records, and he had made a special study of the Sphinx, which now stood forgotten in the desert, covered almost to its head with sand. He had dug out mentions of it in the ancient writings: He knew who had built it, and why; he knew also that there was a second one like it, of the same size, built from the same plans. These things were not secret—they were just forgotten matters anyone could get out of the books.

There was something more than this to the emerald, however. Beyond the open and visible wonder lay something else, hidden and intangible. Nefer was a long time comprehending it. He even got out his greatest treasure, the secret of the Chaldean priests, which the Egyptian priests had borrowed from them— the round, curved crystal used for studying the stars—and inspected the emerald through it.

This glass magnified the stone and showed the Sphinx more clearly, but gave no clue to the intangible power of it. So at last Nefer knew that it was an effect produced upon the mind of the observer. Those shining green expanses in which the little

Sphinx was set, those crags and fields of green, exerted an almost hypnotic effect. He felt it as a keen and tremendous urge to treasure this green beryl above all things.

"The emerald of desire!" he muttered. "An effect produced by the diffused lights in the stone—ha! A dangerous thing. One must be master or be mastered; very well. Away you go into darkness, emerald of desire! I could sit looking into your heart for hours; but I choose to remain your master."

He wrapped the stone in a cloth and hid it away, then summoned the scribe Ho-quac and dictated a letter to his cousin, carefully phrased. That evening he gave the letter and great rewards to the faithful messenger to bear back to the mines.

During the next three days he sat often with the Sphinx emerald, studying it, gazing into its depths, letting himself be lost in the waking trance it induced; but at no time did he lose his head over it. A superstitious or credulous person might well do this, he readily perceived. The uncanny influence of the stone was strong—whether for good or for evil, he was by no means sure.

On the third evening he went to his meeting with Asena.

Divesting himself of rings and seals and fine garments, he left his fine house garbed in the dirty white robe of a workman, on his head a longhaired wig, smears of dirt blurring his features. He strode into the city, to the great temple of Amon-Ra; this was the final night of the Nile-overflow ceremonies, and Asena herself had fixed the rendezvous at their last meeting. For them to attain privacy was impossible, but at least they could meet and speak together. Safety could be found only in a crowd.

Tonight the crowd was tremendous, for after a long series of prayers and hymns, the largesse of the god would be distributed, in money and cakes, to all. A good thing, thought Nefer as he merged with the throngs, that Amon-Ra represented half a dozen deities merged into one; all his powers would be needed to give largesse to such a crowd. He made his way slowly through the temple courts until he reached that of Horus, then sought out the pillar she had identified—a very poor place from which to hear and see, but so much the less crowded for them.

AH! THERE Asena was, with a single slave-girl attendant, and no throng about. Nefer gained her very side, unhurried, and prostrated himself in unison with those around.

"Greetings, beloved of Mut!" he murmured, under cover of the ritual jabber that was going on. Her voice came clear enough in reply.

"Mut the mother-goddess has served us ill, my prince. I have sad news."

"On your lips all news is blessed," he said. "Say it quickly."

"My father has learned that you are writing a book of blasphemy against the kings, proving them to be thieves and rascals," she rejoined. "Is that true?"

"I fear it may be so construed," he admitted. The blow hit him hard.

"Dear man, have you lost your wits?" Her words came with a dismayed groan. "He is taking the matter to the King next month. He says it will destroy you at once."

"He's not far wrong, at that," muttered Nefer to himself; but she heard him.

"Why must you do such things, beloved? He says you are his bitter enemy, that you must suffer lest you cause us all sharp harm—"

The ritual ended. The silence cut her short. They rose with the others, and Nefer stood close beside her. But while one of the priests was chanting, he listened not.

In this instant, something clicked in his brain, perhaps provoked by her words. He touched her hand, as it hung, with his own fingers, slipping into it the love-letter he had written her; then, as the crowd lifted multitudinous voice in the long stanzas of the Hymn to Amon-Ra, he spoke swiftly:

"My dear, all's not lost! Tell me where I can obtain private speech with your father—I must see him."

"You can't. He'll have nothing to do with you."

"Tell me."

Presently she made answer.

"The fifth day from this, he sits on the throne of Amon and may be reached by any supplicant for justice. You might go to him then—"

"Good! The wit of a woman surpasses all the brains of man!" he exclaimed eagerly. "I'll do it. All I need is half an hour to talk—ha! It comes clear at last. By the gods, I have him! Now smile, and make a sacrifice to Queen Mut, mother of the gods! Within the week, you'll have news to make your heart rejoice!"

This was all they could say; the danger necessitated an early parting. Nefer went home hurriedly, changed his clothes, and sent for the slave Ho-quac, the ugly scribe. The latter came to the study, just as Nefer was applying his seal to a papyrus sheet.

"These are your papers of freedom, scribe," said Nefer. "Before

*"The god Horus appeared to me in a dream and
ordered me to give certain instructions to Seker, high
priest od Amon-Ra," said Nefer, still kneeling.*

you get them, talk! Did you tell the high priest of Amon-Ra
that I was writing a book regarding the thefts of the kings?"

"Certainly," the scribe coolly admitted. "He knew it already,
so I verified it to earn his bribes. I said that it also dealt with
blasphemy, which it does not."

"You're a man after my own heart," said Nefer with his cynic
smile. "Now earn your freedom and more bribes. Four days
from today—not five and not three, but four—go to him with
this story: The god Horus came to me by night and gave me
an immense emerald, in which was set the image of the
Sphinx—you know, that antique relic near the Pyramids, mostly
covered with sand. He gave, with this, certain instructions also
for our King Thothmes. This is all you know. Wait—look at the
emerald, so you can say you yourself saw it."

He got out the hidden jewel and displayed it to the scribe.

"Now get me the book of the Thefts of the Kings of Egypt, as far as it's completed, and then leave me. Here, take your freedom."

He gave Ho-quac the papyrus; the scribe thanked him, then got the scroll of papyrus on which the unfinished book was written, and departed.

Nefer sat for a long while looking over the writing, which dealt with half the great temples and monuments of Egypt. Here was the fruit of long research; now it must go by the board if he was to save his own life and win Asena. The section dealing with the Sphinx and its fellow in the eastern hills was typical. Built in the dim dawn of history by a king named Raferses, the attached shrine to each was dedicated to the god Thoth, with whom Horus, a later divinity, was now associated; the eastern-facing Sphinx was the temple of Horus of the sunrise, that facing westward was in honor of Horus of the sunset, the gods of morning and evening.

These great stone figures, half carved from natural rock, half built, were over a thousand years old in the day when Chephren ruled Egypt. This king cleared away the sand nearly covering them, repaired the temples, destroyed all inscriptions of the actual builder, and replaced them with others, taking credit for the building. It was now about two thousand years since his reign.

"And high time that our good Thothmes yielded to similar temptation," Nefer observed to himself. "They all did it—they chipped off the names of the real builders and replaced them with their own names. Stealers of credit! And now—what? Do I risk the play?"

He fell into reflection. If brought to trial before the King on the charge of writing this book, it meant death. Thothmes had done a bit of the same thieving, and thieves protect one another. The high priest Seker now had his hand on a sure weapon. He would use it mercilessly; there was no possible escape.

"But no matter how high a man is, he seeks always to be a trifle higher," thought Nefer cynically. "And if he thinks it worth while, he can finish me. But if I can outwit the big windbag— well, try it, try it! Play the game. I can no more than lose. I've made a fool of myself, and there's only a slim chance that I can retrieve it—but I may. True, the book would make me famous, but I'd sooner eat three good meals a day and remain obscure. Not to mention marriage to the finest girl in Egypt!"

It was a long chance. Not only did the high priest have power, but he deserved it. He had won his place by dint of great mental ability, shrewd diplomacy, and administrative skill. If the scheme that had popped into Nefer's head failed, nothing could save him. However, he was done for anyhow—why not try to win everything at one stroke? With a shrug, he dismissed the chances. He was resolved. That queer emerald might pull him out of his dilemma.

During the intervening days, he schooled himself rigidly in what he would say to Seker. Everything depended on how he handled that gentleman; one word wrong, and he was lost. Seker knew him for what he was, and feared him, and disliked him heartily. Well, he must trust to arrogance and blasphemy against the gods—and to the emerald! To be honest about it, Nefer was a bit afraid of his own scheme. That emerald must have been created by the gods themselves.

ON THE fourth evening Nefer was glancing over a new book he had purchased, a beautifully written copy of the Book of the Dead, according to the rite of Hieropolis, when the scribe Ho-quac—the name meant "Adept"—appeared. Nefer laid aside the book.

"Well? You've seen him?"

Grinning, the scribe jingled a fat purse. "Aye, lord. At first he said nothing. When I said I had seen the emerald myself, he snorted that it was all a put-up hoax, that nobody in Egypt was less liable to be visited by a god than you. I made no effort to convince him; and when I left, he was troubled. He paid well."

"Well done. Now go your ways, a free man. By this time tomorrow night I may be dead. I gave you freedom so you'd be safe."

"I gave you service, lord, for love of you," stoutly said the scribe. "I stay."

Nefer smiled at him. "Stay, then, fool! Now listen carefully, for I'm putting my very life into your hands."

He spoke low-voiced, slowly; the scribe listened with shining eyes and bated breath, an ugly fellow but of great intelligence.

"You understand?" Nefer finished.

"Yes, lord. You take a great and needless risk—"

"I must win all or lose all. Go find the man tonight. Instruct him. If he wills to serve me, bring him here and I'll talk with him."

For a long while, that night, Nefer sat with the Sphinx emerald unveiled before him, gazing into its flawed depths with unblinking eyes. He had bitter need of all he might gain from the jewel—inspiration, mental stimulus, call it what you will; for on the morrow he was about to pit his own supple trickery against the greatest master of trickery in all Egypt, and without the help of the emerald he had no chance whatever....

Next morning the chief priest of Amon-Ra took his seat on the dais in the court of Horus. He was a man of fifty, gifted with blessings or curses; a hard, indomitable and flinty-eyed man, grudgingly fulfilling an ancient ritual that no longer had meaning. His head was shaven. A false beard, part of the antique custom, graced his firm chin; he held the ankh, the cross-shaped emblem of Thoth, god of truth, in his hand.

Heralds proclaimed that the god Amon sat upon his throne to hear and redress the grievances of any mortal who might seek his aid. Those who came were few. Ordinary folk were slow to drag their troubles into public gaze; those of the better class knew this ritual was only a relic of ancient days. Half a dozen persons, no more, were gathered in the outer court to apply, and four of these had been planted by the priests. One was a woman, injured by some noble. The last was Nefer, in his bedraggled wig and artisan's robe. He carried a scroll, and in his girdle cuddled the great emerald. He gave a false name, and only his scroll drew any attention. Ordinary people seldom carried books.

One by one the prearranged cases were heard and judged, the council of lesser priests and scribes applauding. Then the woman was admitted, told her story, and Seker the high priest issued a summons for the noble to appear later. Then at last Nefer was brought in.

He crossed the court, prostrated himself humbly before Seker, and was told to speak freely and without fear. Still kneeling, he placed before him the scroll, slipped the emerald from his girdle, and placed it on top of the papyrus.

"Lord Amon, I seek only simple justice," he said, knowing that the hard eyes were prying at him and had probably pierced his disguise. "The god Horus appeared to me in a dream and ordered me to give certain instructions to Seker, high priest of Amon-Ra, lord of the city of Thebes. These instructions were to be given privately and alone. How could I, an humble artisan, seek private audience with so great a person? Give him, said the god, the two things I leave with you, and he will grant you audience, for the ways of the gods are known to the priests of Amon-Ra. So, Lord Amon, I have dared to ask your help."

THERE WAS an eager stir among the watchers, a wave of cynical mutters. But Seker was looking at the green stone, and knew it to be the wondrous emerald of which the scribe had reported. He motioned an attendant, who came forth, picked up the emerald and the scroll, and gave them to him. For a little he sat in silence, looking at the green lump of beryl; then his voice was lifted upon the court.

"My help is given you," he said. "Come tonight, at the second

*His trip ended, Nefer was chained and made
free of a solitary cell at the royal prisons.*

hour, to the Karnak temple. At the obelisks erected by Queen
Hatshepset in honor of Father Amon, a priest will be waiting;
he will guide you to the presence of Seker the chief priest. Do
you know what these two objects are?"

Nefer prostrated himself anew.

"Lord Amon, what should a poor artisan know of such

things? The one, I believe, is some kind of book. The other I took to the shop of the great jewel-merchant, the Phœnician Kra, and was there told it was a lump of glass formed about some object."

Seker nodded and dismissed him, and there was craning of necks to look after him as he departed. That last question, as Nefer well knew, showed he had won his point—the interest and keen curiosity of Seker were now aroused.

This was quite true. Even before the siesta hour began, the high priest was sitting in his dwelling, on the Karnak temple grounds near the sacred lake, when two of the temple guards ushered into his presence a much-frightened man. Kra, the Phœnician jeweler of Thebes, had little to expect and much to apprehend from any summons to attend the high priest of Amon-Ra. He was a swarthy, hooknosed man, but sharp and shrewd enough.

"I sent for you," said Seker, "to ask your opinion regarding a pretended jewel. Have you ever seen this before?"

So saying, he displayed the lumpish emerald.

Kra, reassured, inspected it. "No, my lord, I never saw it before," he stated.

"Was it not taken to your shop and there declared to be a bit of glass?"

"That might be, without my knowledge," said Kra; "but any fool apprentice would know that it is not glass. It is an emerald, poor in color, but genuine."

"So you say," Seker said with open suspicion. "How to prove it?"

From his pouch the jeweler took a flat bit of wood, painted a brilliant white.

"If your excellency will come to the window yonder where the sun enters, and will get me a piece of glass, a lump or any such piece, I'll quickly show you."

Seker was not long in finding the object; he handed over, in fact, the double convex lens through which he had been examining the emerald. Kra smiled slightly, for he too knew this priestly secret of Chaldea. He put the emerald and the glass in the ray of sunlight at the window, and to sunward of them the small bit of wood, upon which fell the backward-thrown reflection of each.

"Here is an infallible test used by merchants of jewels," he said. "Look at these reflections. That of the glass is a single sheen of light. That of the other shows a faint double refraction, greenish and yellowish. Were each subject cut and faceted, the difference would stand out clearly, emerald always throwing two colors and glass but one. This is true emerald, my lord, polished, but little used or handled."

He had not discerned, or recognized, the Sphinx within the stone. Seker, satisfied, paid him and sent him away, and sat absorbed in watching the play of light in the emerald's heart. He, at least, knew this Sphinx for what it was, and marveled.

AT THE second hour that night Nefer, in his disguise, met his guide at the obelisks of Queen Hatshepset and was conducted to the presence of the high priest. Two guards stood at the door, beyond earshot.

"Well, my lord, what means this mummery?" said Seker in harsh greeting. Nefer smiled and laid aside the wig, and took the chair indicated.

"I had to see you in private. You would have refused any other approach."

"Very likely," admitted the high priest. "You are no friend of mine."

"You mistake, Seker. I've been a scoffer, yes, but not an enemy. And it's rather silly for us not to be friends and allies, as has been brought to my attention by the god Horus himself—in dream, of course, but with certain evidential circumstances that have greatly impressed me."

"One can never be sure of you, Lord Nefer."

"True. Be sure of me now, at least. Seker, we've both passed the veil of Isis and know the secrets of the Mysteries; let me speak to you as a brother initiate," said Nefer quietly and easily. "You know those bleak hills about five hundred miles north of here, east of the Nile and nearly opposite the Great Pyramid and Sphinx? They used to be called the hills of Semes by the ancient people, according to the legends I've unearthed—Semes being one of their gods. Well, you probably know that the King Raferses, who built the well-known Sphinx, also built a second Sphinx in those hills. It and its temple are both nearly covered with sand these days, as is the first."

Seker nodded warily. "They were sacred to Thoth in the ancient time," he said.

"And Thoth is now Horus. Odd, wasn't it, how our deities developed?" Nefer smiled as he spoke, musingly. "Look at Isis—a woman in far-off Karia who was kind to our men when a fleet touched there. They bore her fame home to Egypt; later she herself came, and in time was worshiped as a goddess of kindly actions. Or Horus, the hawk-headed. He was a beloved man in Nubia, greatly mourned after his death—and gradually the story of Horus as we know it was built around his memory. Or take Set, a rascally fellow in Bubastis who discovered iron and the use of forges.... Well, well, you see I've unfortunately learned too much of ancient times, my lord. Horus said as much in my dream."

Seker smiled—a thin, sinister smile.

"He was a trifle late saying it, Lord Nefer."

"Perhaps; that depends on you," said Nefer, and did not miss the swift glint these words brought into the probing flint-eyes. "You behold me a greatly changed person, my lord. As a token of my change, I have put into your hands the only existing copy of a book on which I have spent much time and study."

"That book!" exclaimed Seker. "I looked it over; I never read so insulting and blasphemous a writ in all my life! The very thesis is an insult to Egypt. The statements that our greatest kings have been so petty and vain as to steal from their fathers the credit for building monuments and temples—why, it's absurd!"

"But it's true," said Nefer. "The evidence is there, in each case. The records of the Board of Public Works also state plainly when and how the work was done."

"None the less, it's an impious and abominable book. You, my lord, are no less than criminal in writing such a work and casting shame upon our great rulers!"

Nefer nodded, dejectedly, and gave surprising assent.

"Almost precisely the words spoken by the god Horus," he said. "I call, he added that I was a dangerous person, a heretic, who deserved to be killed. That's why I placed the book in your hands, Lord Seker. That's why I've become a changed man. You see, he laid upon me a certain penance for my crimes. I've come to consult you about it. No one else can help me—and also gain for himself immense credit."

"Do you realize your life would be forfeit were the evidence of your own writing laid before the King?"

"Lord, my life is in your hands: I gave you the book in evidence of my sincerity, as I am about to give you everything. In my dream I asked the god Horus to give me some proof, upon wakening, that his visit to me was real. He said to look under my pillow when I wakened. Well, I did so—and there was the emerald with the image of the Sphinx in its heart. You and I, Seker, have seen many wondrous jewels, but never one so wondrous or beautiful as this. In the King's treasury is none to match it."

THE HIGH priest composed himself. His keen nose had already sniffed something important in the air. Anything connected with this emerald, distinctly a jewel of kings, must be important.

"So," he observed shrewdly. "And the penance Lord Horus laid upon you?"

"That I tell my story to King Thothmes, and give him the god's request that these two Sphinxes and their temples be cleared of sand, restored and repaired, and put to service as his sanctuaries."

Nefer paused briefly. "Naturally," he went on, "I am in poor position to undertake the task. I have never scoffed at the gods—merely at the antics of their servants. Yet I am known as the scoffer, the heretic—you just called me this—the enemy of religion. King Thothmes would laugh heartily did I prefer the request of Horus to him. That is why I now seek your assistance, noble Seker."

The high priest regarded him arrogantly, coldly.

"What have I to do with you and your dreams, my lord?"

"Give the emerald to the king, and the message of Horus. Say that it came to you, that the god appeared to you; the emerald is proof of this. Leave me out of it entirely. I have put my book in your hands; destroy it if you like. I have changed my ways. I am going to seek the rule of some far city from the King, where I may end my days doing good, as a conservative official. If it please you to further my request, do so. That is why I have sought you, Lord Seker, offering my friendship and seeking your blessing."

UPON HEARING this the high priest sat in tense thought. Regardless of the doubtful sincerity of Nefer, here was a chance to seize enormous prestige. As the bearer of such a message from the gods, his fame would go down in history. He would be given new honors and added abundance. He could see instantly that the emerald itself was proof in all eyes of his story; this marvelous stone, inset by divine hands with the Sphinx image, was obviously a supernatural thing.

"It is hard to imagine you as a conservative official, my lord," he said dryly. "And yet the gods, in their wisdom, rule the hearts of men. Take my blessing and the assurance of my friendly interest. Regarding your plea, I shall take it under advisement and pray that Lord Amon will enlighten me as to my course."

Nefer saluted him and departed.

Upon reaching home, he summoned the scribe to his study.

Ho-quac came, and at a gesture seated himself at the table bearing papyrus, reed pens and other writing-materials. Nefer did not speak at once; he sat in thought, then broke the silence, musingly.

"You know the city of On, my friend? Far north of here."

"One of the great cities of the realm? Naturally."

"Draw up a memorial to the King, and sign it with my private seal, tomorrow. I wish to apply for the post of governor of On, which at the moment is vacant. My desire is to retire from all public affairs and from the court and to devote myself to the good of others. See that this petition is forwarded to the King; then leave my house forever."

The scribe gave him a sharp glance of inquiry. Nefer smiled.

"What you have to do, cannot be done under my roof. I've had a talk with the high priest Seker. I believe that within the next few days he'll attempt to put me in security where I can't talk. Once he has me safe it'll be too late to talk. So, take this letter now, as I dictate it, and keep it in your care. When you find that I'm arrested or have disappeared, send it to him—and keep out of his sight."

Nefer dictated the letter slowly, carefully framing each phrase; here was the very hub of his whole scheme, and his life hung on its effect—more than his life, in fact. He laid the papyrus aside, read it over next morning, approved and sealed it, and then wiped the affair from his mind. His own part was done.

That afternoon he went to the large jewelry shop of Kra the Phœnician, talked for some time with the swarthy merchant, gave him a fat wallet, and departed. Later, he set free certain of his personal slaves.

That same night, toward midnight, an officer and half a dozen men of the Royal Guards came to the house, arrested him, and bore him away in a closed litter. This was done by order of King Thothmes. His trip ended at the royal prisons on the western bank of the Nile, where he was chained and made free of a solitary cell. And in Thebes no more was heard of Nefer, prince of the royal house and cousin of the king....

Now the story goes to Seker, high priest of Amon-Ra. Strange news spread from court circles to the city. The god Horus, it was said, had appeared to King Thothmes and ordered certain ancient temples cleared of sand and repaired, in return assuring him of favor and prosperity.

Far from being denied, this story was affirmed and detailed by court scribes. Forces of slaves were being gathered and sent downriver, and officials of the Board of Public Works were placed in charge of the task. The Great Sphinx, almost forgotten by people in general, leaped into life and legend on all sides; so did his mate in the desolate eastern hills.

The work itself was given to the direction of the high priest Seker, beloved of Ra. Great blessings to the country were to come of it. The King's son and heir, Amenhotep, was at present hunting lions on the Mesopotamian frontier, and would return to inaugurate the restored temples of the Sphinxes to the worship of Horus, when the work was completed. Some said the King himself would go downriver for the ceremonies.

All this welter of news caused a great stir in Thebes, whose peaceful and even slothful existence was seldom so greatly disturbed. The Board of Public Works was already drawing up finely sculptured tablets to be placed within the restored temples, giving the story exactly as it had occurred. (One was dug up 3500 years afterward.) Upon Seker, and other priests, were loaded honors and royal favors without number. In the temple of Amon-Ra and his associate deities there was publicly displayed a token given the King by Horus himself, a marvelous huge emerald in which was miraculously set an image of the Sphinx. It was placed on the altar of Horus and guarded day and night.

The hubbub created was simply fantastic. Amulets in the shape of sphinxes became all the rage. A number of stone sphinxes were on order for royal presentation to various temples. Sphinxes appeared everywhere as good-luck emblems.

And just as all this popular furor came to its height, Seker the high priest returned one afternoon from a conference with the King to be informed that in the temple had been found a letter addressed to him. No one had dared to open the sealed missive; at his order it was brought to him. He looked at the seal which closed it, and saw it to be that of Nefer. His lips tight-clenched, he opened the missive and read:

> *To Seker. High Priest of Amon-Ra.*
> *Greetings and friendship!*
> *The god Horus promises to send you this word for me. I await your friendly offices with my royal cousin, whom may Amon preserve! Advise him to create me governor of the city of On, and give me the hand of your daughter Asena in marriage; we love each other.*
> *It is important that these things be done immediately. If they are not done by next week, letters now held by several prominent court officials will then be opened. The actual provenance of the Sphinx emerald—which you do not know—will then be made public, together with its history. The god Horus, who is the god of truth, sends you his greetings with those of*
> *Nefer.*

With a mutter of words, which luckily no one overheard, the high priest of Amon-Ra crushed the papyrus in his hand and sat motionless, silent, his agile brain swiftly at work.

NEFER COULD of course be executed for the book he had written; but this would not stop the laughter that would sweep Egypt from end to end when it was learned how the priests and the king had concocted a fine supernatural yarn about that emerald. The very fact that Seker actually did not know its origin, increased the value of the threat.

More—people were already too disposed to scoff at the deities and to belittle the hierarchy of priests; there were rumors of actual revolt against the old gods, in some quarters. Although he did not guess it, a few short years would see the grandson of King Thothmes sweep away all the old divinities and replace them with the one god of cosmic energy. Seker could sense that something of this sort was imminent, and devoutly hoped it would not come in his own day.

And here he was trapped, neatly caught in a snare from which there was only one way of escape! Trust that damned clever Nefer—he would have some actual proof where the emerald had come from, some verified facts that would knock in the head the story about the god Horus giving it to the King—and would send Egypt into a roar of laughter. Under no circumstances must that be permitted to happen.

On the other hand, this cynical rascal offered friendship—as a son-in-law he might be valuable—and besides, that manuscript book about the royal thefts had not been destroyed, but lay carefully locked away. This thought was very pleasant. Seker the high priest smoothed his ruffled front and even smiled over it, wolfishly.

NEXT MORNING his priestly litter threaded the streets to the royal palace. He was instantly conducted to the apartments of King Thothmes. This divine ruler, who had a cold in the head and a badly running nose, received him in private.

"Divine son of Amon," said Seker in his impressive way, "last night the god Horus appeared to me and issued certain orders. I have come to transmit them to you, since they deal with your relative, the noble Nefer."

Thothmes scowled, wiped his nose, and shook his head regretfully.

"Ah! I've been afraid of this. I always liked Nefer, myself. I don't see why the gods are so eager to take his life—"

"But they are not, royal child of heaven!" Seker exclaimed. His shrewd nostrils now scented favor; since the King was so fond of Nefer, this errand of his was going to result very happily for himself. Decidedly, he had chosen well.

"Our gracious Lord Horus," he went on smoothly, "expressed

his desire that the evidence against Lord Nefer be destroyed; therefore I have done it. Further, he ordered me to beg of you not only to free him and restore him to rank, but also to honor him with your favor and make him viceroy of the city of On, if it so pleased you."

"Ha!" exclaimed Thothmes, brightening. "Praise be to Horus! I'll do it at once!"

"Further, Lord Horus ordered me to give him my own daughter in marriage," went on Seker blandly, "and said that you would do well to honor him with the title 'Friend of the King,' if this is pleasing in your sight."

"Indeed it is—and I can do no less to his father-in-law, holy Seker!" Thothmes said warmly. "Yours be the same cherished title, and my eternal gratitude, which shall be expressed in practical terms within a few days, I assure you. Here—take my personal scarab—go to the prison yourself and free Nefer. Take him royal robes and perfumes—take my own royal litter for his transport—embrace him for me!"

So, with much state, the high priest betook himself to the prison, and sight of the royal token opened all doors. When Nefer was led forth, Seker embraced him despite his dirt, and in the royal litter took him to the baths, and later to his own house. On the way, they paused to hear the heralds proclaiming that Nefer, Friend of the King, had been appointed viceroy of the great trading city of On, in the north, and would go to his charge as soon as his marriage with the daughter of Amon's high priest was solemnized. And if Nefer smiled at this, Seker also smiled thinly.

In this manner was concluded the story of Nefer and the Sphinx emerald. Yet there was a further chapter and one deeply significant.

At his first private interview with his bride, Nefer found Asena brimming with eager warning. She was a devout little creature, and he was careful never to offend her with any cynic words.

"Careful, Nefer—you must be careful!" she said at his ear, as she clung to him. "My father does not trust you. He said to tell you that the book still exists, and it will be put to use if you commit any offense against the gods!"

"Meaning their priests, eh?" Nefer smiled. "Fear not, my love. I am going to be a very careful government official, and nothing else. I shall offend no one."

"Good!" she cried. "Perhaps that's what the god Horus meant all along!"

"Eh? What's this?" Smiling, he pinched her ear. "You've been talking with the gods, have you?"

"No, silly," she retorted. "I mean, about leaving that emerald with my father for the King, his strange appearances and so on. Oh, I know the divine Horus wanted his temples restored, true; still, a god from the other world would probably have greater things in his head than sweeping out sand. And what greater than to effect a change in you, and turn you from a cynical scoffer into a true servitor of the gods?"

Nefer was struck by this view of the affair. It brought into sudden focus that first line of instruction from the Greater Mysteries: The hierophant who seeks to serve the gods, must first learn to serve man.

"Upon my word, little princess," he said thoughtfully, "you may be right about it! You may, indeed. Our first task upon reaching On will be to sacrifice to Horus, asking his aid in our work there."

Now, little is known further of Nefer, whose tomb was discovered and opened in 1927, except that as governor of On, City of the Sun, he made a record for conservative and wise rule. In his tomb was found that fragmentary papyrus which he himself must have dictated, since it was written by the scribe Ho-quac. One of its few decipherable portions is translated:

"...formulas and tenets of the gods are merely chains for young or untrained minds. The wise man wears such chains lightly, knowing that in suffering them he performs a worthy action for

the good of others. The highest wisdom is tolerance and freedom for others as well as for self."

No scoundrel could have written those words.

Hail and farewell, Nefer!

I I

RED SKY OVER THEBES

*The Sphinx Emerald passed into other
hands—to reappear centuries later when
conquering Cambyses came storming into
Egypt with his Persian legions....*

NEKHT WAS his name. With a wooden-fork plow and a bullock, he was tilling his field outside the tiny Nile village of peasants, when the Greek captain came from Thebes with the news. An odd fellow, Nekht—tall, thewy, bronzed as any other farmer in the village, but with a hawk-nose and quick eyes of striking intelligence. He usually kept them half shut, and in the village itself passed for a fool. No one here knew or suspected his secret.

He lived alone with his mother, who told the Greek, named Peleus, where to find him. Nekht saw him coming along the edge of the fields, and recognized him; for although the soldier wore a tunic over his armor, the proud lift of the head and the step of authority could not be hidden.

"The captain of the temple guards," Nekht said, and pulled the bullock out of the furrow. "That means a message for me. What now, friend Peleus?"

"Greetings," said the other, who knew him well, "and news. I have a boat waiting; the high priest of Amon wants you."

"And the news?"

"If the Nile ran the other way, the water would be red. There's hell to pay, but the news must keep until we're afloat."

"I'll take the bullock home, and go," Nekht said simply. "Come along."

He unyoked the bullock from the plow, and they started back to the village. As to the news, Nekht had heard enough to guess

*"If the Nile ran
the other way, the
water would be red.
There's hell to pay!"*

what it must be; he was already seeking beyond the words,
mentally. He, of all people, needed no telling that Egypt was a
leaky boat in a bad storm shaking the world. During the past
two hundred years the great country had been gradually disin-
tegrating. Still powerful, still crammed with all the looted riches
of the earth, it had been ruled by Assyrians, Ethiopians,
Greeks—anyone strong enough to seize the throne and defend
the desert frontiers. The present Pharaoh, Samthek, was the
grandson of an army general who had done just this, bringing
Egypt up to a fragment of its former greatness, with Greek
help.

THE LAST native dynasty, that of the great Ramses, had
conquered practically the known world, pouring into Egypt an
enormous flood of treasure and slaves. Softened, slothful, the
old hard Egyptian race became easy-going. Now, in this fateful

year of 528 B.C., Egypt still existed intact, like soft ripe fruit
ready for the taker. Greeks had flooded in like a swarm of
summer flies. The army was composed of Greeks—and the
Persians were coming. During the past two years, the Persian
ruler Cambyses had been pushing armies across the northern
deserts, intent upon plucking this ripe fruit.

Yet one faint breath of hope lingered; somewhere in this
great land, unknown, was a descendant of the last royal Egyptian
line. Who? Where? Nobody knew. But the chief priests of the
gods had announced it as fact. Prophecy said that some day all
foreigners would be expelled, and the royal line of Pharaohs

would again lift Egypt to greatness. When? Perhaps this year, perhaps a hundred years hence; but the hope lingered.

Four soldiers in the boat, Greeks like Peleus, saluted as he and Nekht appeared and got in; the boat pushed off, swung out into the current, and was on its way to Thebes, still the greatest city on earth. Nekht and Peleus sat together in the stern.

"The news?"

"The worst," said Peleus. "Cambyses has captured Pelusium and is marching up the Nile. The army is completely destroyed, the Pharaoh a prisoner. Phanes of Halicarnassus, commander of the Greek troops, went over to the Persians. They'll be in Thebes in two or three days. They're coming up by ship."

Nekht caught his breath. The worst, indeed! Egypt was no more.

Like a symbol, the shapes of ruined buildings along the riverbanks caught his eye. Once barracks had stood here every few miles, each post holding two hundred iron chariots and equipment. Now all were empty, ruined, forgotten. Egypt was forgotten too. The blow was crushing.

"What—what hope for the city, for Thebes the glorious?" he asked, dry-lipped.

"None," Peleus replied. "No army there, except for a few of us guards—and we're Greeks. A huge, sprawling, unkempt city like Thebes can't be defended. Already refugees are pouring out. Cambyses, we hear, has given the loot of the city to his Persian legions. The gods are dead, Nekht. Egypt's dead."

"I'm not dead," said Nekht. "And there's a girl—I must see her."

"You and your girls!" jeered the soldier. "You may be a student, a friend of the chief priest of Amon—but you're a peasant, a villager, food for Persian steel. Your girl is one of thousands destined for Persian couches. We Greeks are safe enough, as allies and friends of the conqueror; but you Egyptians are as dirt under Persian sandals."

Nekht said nothing. It was bitterly true. To Peleus, he was

only a farmer, a mere nothing, like all his people—grass doomed to the fire.

He himself knew better. He was one of a few hundreds chosen from those people—chosen for descent, for character, for vigor—and secretly given most careful training, as soldiers and rulers; being made initiates of the Mysteries and heritors of all the higher learning preserved in the priestly castes. Men in each generation were thus chosen and made ready for the day when Egypt should rise again—and one among them all was the heir of the royal line, his secret guarded in bitter darkness for his own safety.

"We hear that Memphis is already taken and looted," Peleus went on. "Until the King and army arrive, we serve as we are; then, naturally, we join our fellows. If you want to get your girl out of the city, Nekht, I'll lend you a hand. Call on me. Some of us have our eyes on the temple treasury—we'll stick together."

NEKHT BROKE into soft, bitterly ironic laughter; the temple guards meant to loot it! Everything was falling to pieces. Yet he liked this Peleus—a strong, tough Greek from Samos, highly intelligent and famed as a soldier.

"Not a bad idea, Peleus," he said, watching the river reaches. "Perhaps I can tell you a thing or two about the temple treasury that you don't know, too."

The Greek gave him one lightning-swift glance. Well he knew there were temple secrets known to no guard—and this brown fellow educated in the temple of Amon might well be aware of them. He drew closer.

"A trade, friend Nekht! You and me alone—not now, but when the need comes. Keep it in mind."

Nekht gave him a nod, and said no more. The river below them was covered with all manner of boats; the panic flight from Thebes was under way. Escape? There was none, yet the wild thousands fled in terror of the coming wrath—fled to starve, to wander into the southern deserts; and chariots raised clouds of dust on the highways in desperate hope of reaching the Nubian frontier.

So they came to the vast city of Amon-Ra, whose temples and palaces surpassed anything in the world—the "hundred-gated," so the marveling Greeks called it, because of the countless and enormous gateways of these gigantic structures. In the temple quarter along the Nile was little confusion, the guards from Karnak and Luxor keeping fair order here. From the remainder of the city, smoke rose in places, denoting that the mob was looting and burning; but no one cared—no one except Nekht. He, catching the arm of Peleus, spoke rapidly.

"Friend, I'll take you up on your bargain. Whether I'll be detained an hour or a day with the chief priest, I don't know. The afternoon's at an end. When it gets dark, send word to the house of the Royal Architect that I'll come when free—get the message to the hands of the Lady Amenartis. Will you?"

Peleus nodded. "Take it myself," he said. "Come along, and I'll turn you over to the beloved of Amon, who'll taste Persian steel before he knows it."

A tough, cynical fellow, this Greek, but a good man in his way, with a laugh often in his eye. Nekht did not hesitate to trust him—a little.

The two men made their way to the towering Karnak temple, where the high priest of Amon lived. They passed the guards and crossed the vast, almost empty courts where thousands had once worshiped; but few believed in the gods these days. The lofty columns and long walls, sculptured and painted gloriously, flitted past, and they came to the innermost court. Here, said the guards, a conference of priests was under way, and Peleus pushed on into the holy of holies—a high-pillared chamber where sat a dozen priests. A mere dozen, out of the thousands in Thebes, and these all high priests of various gods.

"Here is the man you wanted, my lord," called Peleus, standing on no ceremony. Then, giving Nekht a clap on the shoulder, he went his way.

A N O L D man, wrinkled, shaven-headed, left the others and came to Nekht. This was Amon's high priest, greatest man in Thebes.

"Greetings, my son," he said. "Go into my study. You'll find wine and food there; help yourself. I'll join you immediately. You know the way."

Nekht obeyed, passing into a small room holding only the tables of scribes and that of the priest. Obviously the temple service had broken down: wine and food were set on the tables haphazard; clothes were scattered about; documents and letters were strewn on the floor. Being hungry, Nekht helped himself to the food, poured a goblet of wine, and was gulping it when the high priest joined him.

"Well, the end has come," said the old man abruptly. "Peleus gave you the news?"

"Such as he had, yes."

"Worse has arrived. The Persians are on the way upriver; they may be here tonight. They're killing, looting everything. Memphis was put to the flames. Cambyses himself is with the vanguard—a drunken despot now maddened by triumph, who hates our gods and us. Those of us not murdered will become slaves. No mercy at all."

"And your plans?"

The old man gestured hopelessly. "We have none, except to die. Everything's ended. Egypt is lost.... I didn't get you here merely to rail at fate, however. The time foreseen has come. You will live while others, all of us, perish; you'll have the traditions, the written scripts, the secrets, to revive Egypt once more, you or your descendants. I must show you how to reach the things that have been put aside for that day."

"What about the temple treasures?" queried Nekht.

A thin, horrible laugh came from the high priest, who poured some wine and drained the cup. "Let the gods protect their own gold and silver—the treasure is too huge to be moved, anyway.

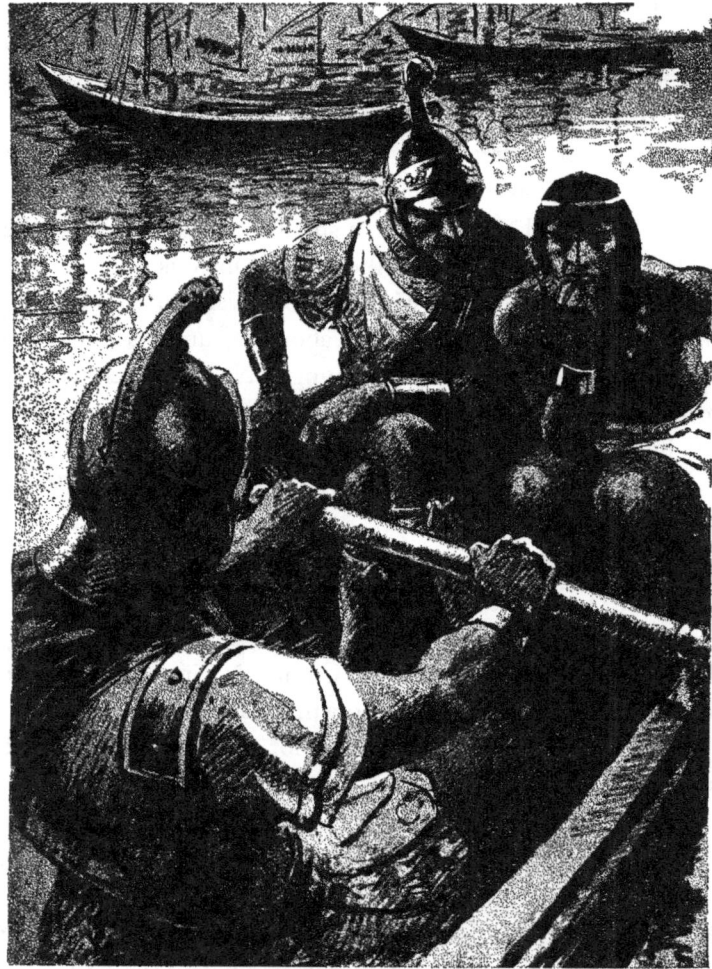

"We hear that Memphis is already taken and looted,"
Peleus went on. "If you want to get your girl—"

But now, listen well! You know the underwater chambers, the
secret rooms I showed you when last here?"

Nekht assented with a nod.

"They hold the crowns of Upper and Lower Egypt, the
records, the chief relics, and all the treasure that can be packed
in to fill the place; and the river has been turned in. The slaves

who did the work are dead; I soon will be dead; this leaves you as the only person who can reach that hidden treasure in case of need—you and your children. Some day it will serve to rebuild Egypt. Were this entire temple destroyed, the cache would remain intact to serve its purpose."

Again Nekht silently assented, and waited.

"You," said the old man, "are the last Egyptian, last of the blood of the great Ramses; tell your sons these secrets, that they may tell their sons, and some day Egypt will have a Pharaoh of the ancient blood. Go back to your village. Be a simple farmer. That is your one chance of salvation, Egypt's one future hope. Nothing of your existence as such is known, but there may be danger from these Greeks who for so long have been a part of Egyptian life. They may have picked up rumors. Now—what are your plans?"

"To get out of the city with Lady Amenartis, the daughter of the Royal Architect. We love each other. If we can get to my village, we'll be safe."

Nekht spoke simply and to the point. The old man peered at him.

"Good. I can help you a little. The maddened people are fighting up and down the wharves for the boats. I'll show you where one is hidden safely, and how to reach it. But first I have a gift for you, left in keeping of the high priest by the last Ramses, twelfth of the kings thus named."

So saying, he took from his table a small wooden box, and from the box a little object wrapped in cloth—two objects, in fact. One was a doubly convex glass, used by Chaldean priests in studying the stars,* and inherited from them as a deep secret by the priests of Egypt. The other was a lumpish green stone, such as Nekht had never seen.

"A bit of glass, and an emerald," said the old man. "The one will enlarge the other. No time now for lengthy explanations...."

---

* One such glass, dug up at Ur, is now in the British Museum.

But tuck them away and use them at leisure. Now we must go, and I'll show you the secret of the boat. A long way to go."

"Wait!" exclaimed Nekht. "An emerald, you say?"

"Yes, from the crown jewels, originally. A wondrous thing, too; guard it well, but for the present put it out of sight. We must go."

The old man was impatient, anxious, filled with fears, as well he might be.

Two hours later Nekht made his exit from the temple, free; in his girdle was knotted the Sphinx emerald and the glass. He paused at the entrance, seeing Peleus, and spoke to him. The Greek took his arm.

"Hello! You still here? By Zeus, man, but you can't get away now—no horses left, no boat obtainable without a savage fight! I hear the Persians are already at the city outskirts. Where's your girl? I left the message for her."

"I'm going for her now. I'll be back here. You'll be here?"

"Probably. We want to get into the temple treasury before the Persians arrive."

"I can help you to that," said Nekht. "Wait for me."

"Well, perhaps," agreed the other doubtfully. "You'd better get hold of a Greek outfit—the Greeks are safe. Look at the sky! Damn the fools!"

It was now full night, and red flares from blazing houses dotted the horizon. Nekht broke away and departed. He had some distance to go into the residential quarter, but at first found everything deserted and quiet here, though northward lifted a far, thin, terrible sound—distant screaming that ceased not. He hurried faster. If the Persians were already at hand, there was bitter need for haste.

Flitting shapes suddenly were in the dark street—fugitives. Stone buildings were few here. Only temples and palaces were of stone. The great mass of structures were of wood, perhaps with stone fronts; many were of fire-resistant palm trunks, towering high. An abrupt torrent of screams and shouts turned the corner ahead as a chariot and two horses came tearing madly into the crowd—some noble or priest trying for a belated escape. Blood flowed blackly on the stones. Horses and drivers were stabbed; the whole street was blocked by the uproar of ferocity; corpses or wounded lay everywhere.

Nekht somehow got past the tumultuous, heaving blockade. Light came from the flaring sky ahead. He swung into a street where frantic swarming crowds were threaded by killers of the mob or by slaves, striking and tearing like wolves. Lights flickered through the houses. The sound of screaming voices began to dull everything else. Yet all this was merely a beginning, a symptom of the flood of death which was to come.

Thankful for the plain cotton robe that did not single him out for attack, he hastened on his way; nearly there now—but from northward was increasing momentarily a thunderous dull roar mounting athwart the sky. He knew what it meant; Persians pouring in from the suburban districts, driving before them a furious, helpless mob of many thousands, killing as they came, looting houses, going to every extreme of rapine. The greatest city in the world was going down in flames and blood. All the northern sky was now a ruddy conflagration that threw the streets into plain sight with its reflected glare.

ARRIVED AT last, and the house dark, apparently deserted.

Nekht went to the side entrance, and a voice spoke—that of a slave. Recognized, he was led inside. In the central patio he found Amenartis, dark and cool and composed. She gave him her hand, then turned to the crowd of slaves grouped at one side.

"You are free," she said. "I cannot help you. Go where you like; take whatever pleases you. Well, Nekht! Thanks for the message. Where my father is, I don't know. The family left this afternoon. I knew you would come."

"We'd better be gone too, and lose no time about it," he said.

"Why? What good?" She looked at him in the ruddy glare.

Soldiers came driving along, killing any in their path.

"Everything's gone. The old order's dead, my dear. Do we just walk out—into nothingness?"

"Hardly that. Life in a village up the Nile, as a farmer's wife, providing we can get there. I have a way, if you are willing."

"Certainly," she said. "A new order, eh? Well, I'm confused, bewildered, helpless. It's like the end of the world, in very truth. So I'll trust to you."

"Things are pretty tough in the streets, and we must reach the temple. Find me a weapon of some kind; leave your jewelry and fine gown and get a cheap robe and a shawl to cover your head. Smear your face with dirt. Do it fast. I'll wait here."

She vanished into the house. The slaves came up and crowded

*Nekht drew Amenartis away from one
furious rush, holding her against a wall.*

around Nekht. He spoke frankly to them, told them that order, law and government were gone; the Persians were looting the city—they had best go, be free, try to save themselves. Inane, useless words, but all he could offer. They melted away like shadows and left him waiting, alone, while into the reddened sky lifted the sounds of hell. The wild roar was everywhere now, closer, filled with horror and ferocity.

The end of an order—a people, a civilization! She had spoken aright. Beauty and knowledge were being trampled into a mire of blood and tears this night. The Persian and his gods had come to destroy Egypt and her ancient deities—no mercy, no pity.

She came, wrapped in a common blue robe, hair streaming, face and hands smeared with ashes; yet she was calm enough. She put a belt and sword into Nekht's hand.

"This was my father's greatest treasure, Nekht; it belonged to the great Ramses."

With fumbling fingers he buckled on the belt, then took her hand. They went out by the side entrance, and were caught in a whirlwind of screaming, running and fighting humanity pressed by mailed figures—Persians and Greeks, cutting a way through to reach the houses. Nekht drew her to one side, coolly waiting a clear space, then seizing it and darting ahead. They were on their way. No force could avail here; coolness could get them through—and did.

They watched incredible scenes—the helpless fleeing mob had gone stark mad. Soldiers came driving along, laughing, singing, killing any in their path, smashing into houses, seeking loot everywhere. Nekht drew Amenartis away from one furious rush, holding her against a house-wall, waiting.

"Why the temple?" she breathed at his ear. "Will it be spared?"

"No!" he said. "But we'll find safety there, can we reach it."

Like a ravening force of wind, the fury was in all the houses. Beautiful inlaid ivory was trampled on in the streets; delicate screens were smashed; rich broideries were underfoot; figures of gods and men were flung down from the windows; rare furniture was hurled afar—the loot of the world, here stored for centuries, was given over to savage destruction, and corpses were piled up in the highways. Syrians, Chaldeans, Carians, desert Arabs, Iraki, Greeks of the islands and from all the Greek cities—this flood from the north was avenging the woes and fulfilling the hatreds of thousands of years upon the once proud and mighty mistress of the world; and after the looting came fire.

THROUGH THE madness Nekht and Amenartis worked their way—the two persons in all this horror who knew whither they were going. Half a dozen times Nekht had to use his sword;

once a running burst of insensate Greeks sent them rolling amid the corpses, but passed on; at length they came into comparative quiet, and in the glare saw the great high gateways of the Karnak temple, barred and silent, before them. Nekht sent a shout pealing up; he heard a reply from Peleus, and led Amenartis forward to the tiny door in the gate. It was opened, and they were inside.

"Well done," said Peleus. "The end's getting close here—they'll come in from the sides and back. The priests are all in the temple, awaiting the decree of the fates."

Nekht rubbed splashes of blood from his face.

"I can offer you sure hiding, and your will of the temple treasures, which no one else can find," he said. "The only condition is that you and your friends remain safely until we can get away—perhaps a few days. I can supply a boat, also."

"By the gods, you do better miracles than the priests!" cried Peleus. "How many of us? There are six of us in my own crowd."

"Get them, and let's be going. I'm about done in."

Peleus swung away.

Amenartis came close, with a low, awed word.

"But Nekht—the temple treasures! What are you about to do?"

"What the high priest instructed me to do, to insure our safety. The priests know that for them it's the end.... Here, I've got a couple of bad slashes on my right arm. Bind them up, will you? Take a bit of my robe—"

Before she had the cuts bandaged, Peleus came back hastily, with five others of the mailed guards.

"Hurry, if you've some place to go!" he exclaimed. "They're coming in the back now!"

Nekht led the way straight back through the temple courts. In one court they came on a number of Persian and Greek soldiers wandering, sword in hand, staring aimlessly at the magnificent sculptured walls. These paid them no attention, and Nekht turned out into the side courts, the glare in the sky making everything bright as day. He came to the spot indicated by the high priest, counted the pillars, and behind one of these pointed to a tall slab of stone.

"Peleus! Push, all of you, on the right side of this slab."

The Greeks obeyed with a will. The great slab moved on a pivot; one end swung out, and an opening was disclosed.

"In, everyone!" ordered Nekht, as a sudden burst of voices rose. "Quickly! We'll find lamps inside—"

INSIDE WITH the men Nekht felt in the darkness until he found the rope attached to the counter-weights. He attacked it with his sword, cut it, and there was a heavy clash as the slab swung shut. The Greeks cursed in alarm.

"It's all right," said Nekht. "I couldn't trust you fellows—but there's another way out, fear not. Now we're safe. Feel around for a shelf with lamps on it."

This was found, and presently a lamp was alight. The silence here was profound; the ray of light showed a down-sloping passage. This led to a number of rooms furnished for living; one was stacked with food of all sorts. Nekht stopped at a door and held up his lamp.

"There you are, Peleus," he said. "That goes to the temple treasury. Run along and help yourselves; it can't get away. I'm for a wash-up and rest. Come back to the rooms when you're ready."

He turned away, wearily, and went back to rejoin Amenartis, who had waited in one of the living-chambers.

AN ODD, and in some ways a dreadful place, these deep underground rooms constructed to hide treasures and priests from passing dangers; now there were no priests here—for above was no passing danger, but the end of everything.

Any small party could remain here undiscovered for a long time. Food, a running current of water, vents for air, an access to the Nile—everything needed was here. Nekht washed, showed Amenartis where to bathe, then dropped on a couch, and was asleep in two minutes, while overhead, Thebes was dying horribly.

When Nekht wakened at long last, Amenartis was asleep and the lamp burning low. He took it and went to the water-clock in another chamber. Ten hours had passed. Peleus and his friends, exhausted by frantic looting, lay snoring with treasures of gold and precious things heaped around them. His lamp refilled, Nekht returned to Amenartis, who was sitting up, yawning. He had to tell her the whole truth about himself, and did so.

"You and I, my dear, are less than the dust; look at the larger pattern of things," he concluded. "Egypt, the country, the nation, is prostrate under Persia today. Her gods are being destroyed, her civilization wiped out. But a hundred, two, three hundred years from now, she will rise again as a nation; the priests have taught me this. And when she does, one of our children's children will be at her head. The greatest treasures, the records of the gods and of the people, are safely hidden away beyond any discovery, to serve her in that day."

The hand of Amenartis tightened on his; her luminous dark eyes flashed and glowed under the emotion of his words.

"Truly magnificent, Nekht!" she exclaimed.

He shook his head. "No; for us, quite the contrary. You must realize what it means before making your choice. I can take you to safety and leave you, to work out your own future; or you can remain with me. What will this mean? Life as a farmer's wife in a little village. Entire sacrifice of your past, of the future you dreamed. Careful hiding from any discovery of the secret. Poverty, work, no more soft easy living. Make no hasty choice. Here, see what the high priest gave me, his last gift. There is deep reason, but I know it not."

He unknotted the little packet from his girdle and got out the glass and the emerald. They looked at the stone together, beside the lamp.

As a precious object, the emerald was disappointing—a

rather shapeless lump of beryl, pale in color, poorly polished.
Under the glass, all this changed. The flaws and angular bubbles
of the crystal came together in one place to form a distinct,
clearly cut image of the Sphinx. Under this, on the bottom of
the stone, had been cut a single hieroglyphic—that showing
the human eye, emblem of Thoth or Horus, the god of truth.
This, at first look, was all. Wonderful as it was, this was all.

*Amenartis said,
"Look into this
stone a while. See
what it tells you."*

"Why did he give me this?" Nekht mused thoughtfully. "Far more beautiful and wonderful things were his, by the thousand. Why this?"

"Perhaps—for me," said Amenartis. "Let me keep the thing a while."

"Gladly. An odd toy," he said carelessly. "Well, you see the difficulties ahead?"

"Yes. They terrify me," she said frankly. "I can't be hasty, impulsive; what you say frightens me. The sacrifice of so much, Nekht! Never to have any hope, any ambition, of better things for ourselves—that's terrible, hard even to realize."

"I know. I was brought up to it from boyhood, as my children must be." A smile touched his thin, hard lips. "I'm a good farmer, Amenartis."

"I can't be a farmer's wife," she said flatly. "Not for ever. I warn you!"

"Take your time, my dear. There's no hurry," he said. "It's not what you can, but what you will. That's one of the great lessons of the Mysteries—the use of man's free will. We're not just puppets of fate, you know."

She grimaced. "The Mysteries are gone. Everything's gone!"

"True. We have to begin anew the task of building—everything. A slow, sorry job."

"Then why do it?" she flashed. "Because your own fathers began it? Because you were trained to it? Because the priests told you to do so?"

"No. I could go off and be a soldier with Peleus if I chose—and I'd much sooner do that, too." He smiled at her. "A matter of decision, I suppose. Duty, perhaps. I must do what is given me to do, for I've so decided, my dear. As you must, without compulsion."

"I was a fool ever to fall in love with you," she said gloomily.

THE GREEKS were stirring amid their gold, and so the conservation ended.

Now began a strangely unreal period when, as the Greeks said, they were like people stranded beyond the world's end: These Greeks were hardy, tough, decent fellows; their contempt for Nekht as an Egyptian changed into respect ere long. The food was coarse but sufficient; there was wine, and water to mix with it. The inner chambers were crammed with a vast, incalculable treasure of all kinds, gathered over centuries.

"But you can't carry it all away," said Nekht, when Peleus called him into conference with them later that day. "Whether some of you come back later, if you can find your way, is of no consequence. I advise you to take your time and make bundles of what each one can carry."

"And you know how to get out of here?" questioned one man.

Nekht assented. "I, and I alone."

"Then when do we depart?" Peleus demanded. "They'll be sacking the city, up above, for days to come."

"That's what I fear," Nekht answered. "When we leave, I want to reach safety, not run into madness. You agreed to land me upriver at my village."

"The promise holds, my friend. But when?"

Nekht pointed to the clepsydra—the water-clock.

"That marks the hours; I'm keeping track. On the seventh night of our stay, I think it will be safe to leave."

They consulted about this, and all agreed. The Greeks went off to play with the treasure.

NEKHT REJOINED Amenartis, and found her beside the lamp, examining the great emerald with help of the enlarging glass.

She looked up to ask:

"Have you given this stone any close examination?"

"No."

"Do it, then." She gave him the glass. "Look into it for a while. See what it tells you."

To humor her whim, he complied, smiling.

He knew rather vaguely that the Great Sphinx by the Pyramids, and its mate, over in the eastern hills, had been erected by the Ancient People in the days before any dynasties began, and were accompanied by shrines to Thoth, or Horus. It was obvious that the little figure composed of flaws and bubbles was a freak of nature—yet this shape in the emerald was so exact, so perfect, as to awaken superstition. It was an impossibility—yet here it was before his eyes.

And to his surprise, there was something further in the beryl, something unseen but felt distinctly. He searched those greenish depths with growing intensity, becoming more aware of this intangible something. Then he sat back and reflected. Acquainted as he was with the inner secrets of the Mysteries and the curiously involved instruction of the priesthood, he perceived that here was some manner of hypnosis induced by looking into the heart of the crystalline beryl—a mental effect, not a trick or contrivance.

This fascinated him; and he pored anew, glass in hand. What he could distinctly sense was a feeling of radiant happiness, a pleasant strength and heartening. He looked up as Amenartis returned.

"I see what you mean, my dear. Tell me what it says to you."

"Peace," she replied, cool and composed as ever. "Assurance, firmness—oh, I hardly know! It just gives one the feeling—does it do that to you?"

"Yes, but in another way," he said thoughtfully. "I think the secret is that it says no one thing to all, but something different to everyone. It makes some mystic appeal to the mind, the physical brain. Perhaps it wakens what is latent within the mind. Those who see it only as an emerald, a jewel, might go mad over its beauty. To one with deeper knowledge, it might say other things. You're naturally a composed person; it may well bring you a feeling of quietness, of firm balance. That's only a guess. Well, I'll have to drop it for the present—the day's getting along. We must keep exact hours for eating and sleeping."

Even in nothingness there was no lack of things to do....

A week? At the first that looked tiny, a mere nothing; but after a couple of days it began to loom with appalling heaviness. Once the pleasure of toying with such treasure as they had never even imagined, began to pall on them, the Greeks had nothing to do. From this they went to gambling; but with sacks of gold-dust under the door, the stakes presented no allure. They came at last to songs and storytelling. Nekht sat in at these, and traded Egyptian tales of magic and adventure for those of Greek heroes.

He learned from these gatherings, also. Cambyses, leader of the Persians, was a madman, drunk most of the time and given over to strange Persian vices; he had even murdered his own brother to gain the throne, and the Greeks said the gods had doomed him to be harried by the Furies, in consequence.

Nekht, however, devoted much of his time to the strange Sphinx emerald, whenever he could get it away from Amenartis. He liked the auto-hypnosis it induced; he divined that the effects were good. It gave him a surer grip on himself. After spending an hour gazing into those green expanses and shimmering depths, he felt a stimulation, a fresh strength and assurance, a quickened vitality—and a new peace within himself. This never ceased to amaze him.

He even tried out the effect of the stone on Peleus, getting the Greek captain to sit and look into the emerald for a half-hour. The result was entirely different. Peleus sat clutching at his sword-grip, keen eyes dilated, his breath coming rapidly, excitement bringing color into his cheeks.

"Hey!" A sudden ringing shout burst from him and he leaped to his feet. "By Ares, Egyptian! Can your damned magic lift a man out of this underground hell to the windy plains of Troy? The clash of chariots at the gallop—the ringing rattle of arrows on the war shields of heroes—oh, madness, madness—the glorious madness of battle—"

He broke off, staring and shamed by his own outburst; then tears streamed out on his face, and he went striding away.

So Nekht was satisfied that he had divined the truth. In Peleus, the mesmeric power of those green depths evoked battle-lust and a heroic ecstasy; with every person would come a different result, as imagination wakened the dominant impulses of the individual mind. He saw now why that eye, the symbol of truth, had been cut in the beryl—truth indeed! Whatever was in the man would be brought forth, however hidden.

"Blessings on you for this gift, old priest!" he murmured, awe in his heart. "A very talisman of the gods, indeed; you could have given me nothing more wonderful, nothing more deeply calculated to give me strength and resolution when they were most needed."

But what of Amenartis? He could not tell; he did not question her, but noted well that she spent long hours with the silent emerald. He could give her no hope at all. He knew with sad assurance that there was none to give. If she stuck to him, there was life ahead, with luck—a life of drudgery in a peasant's humble hut, with never any change, never any higher ambition; complete submission of self to an indefinite and vague formula of some dimly guessed good to come in future generations— why, it was absurd to expect such things of a woman brimming with young life, a woman high-placed, wealthy, proud! And yet her whole world had come to an end.

PELEUS SAID this very thing, as they talked after a meal.

"Where are you going, lady?" he asked bluntly. "Greatness is gone; show your face in the world, and some Persian will drag you off to his harem. Your entire social system has gone crash…. Have you some refuge?"

"Yes," she said. "Hiding. Playing the part of a farmer's handmaid."

Nekht caught the bitterness in her tone.

"Oh, bah!" cried Peleus. "Get out of here, you two—come to Samos, to any Greek city where beauty is worshiped and intelligence given place! Why waste yourselves on some petty farm? Nekht, you could be a great captain if you would!"

"But I wouldn't," said Nekht, smiling. "My world's gone. Some day I'll help to build it up again, in my own fashion. Not as I would like, but as I must."

Amenartis gave him a look. "There's no reason why you couldn't go to Greece."

"Yes," he said. "My own choice. My own free will."

On the last evening but one, Nekht found her on the couch in tears that could not be checked. He sat beside her, holding her hand.

"It's not any lack of love for you, my dear," she sobbed. "It's just the life—the life of slavery, of hopelessness! Condemned to a patch of mud all my life—me! A patch of mud! I can't face it."

Nekht laughed softly. "Yes, that's one way of looking at it, true. Well, I'm not trying to persuade you; this choice must be yours alone, without interference. Once we're in the open air, there's no turning back, no changing. One decision is final, to be endured or made the best of, my heart! A patch of mud—yes. But a patch of mud with love might be better than a palace in Samos without love. What we think a bitter hard thing, may turn out otherwise—I don't say it will, but it may."

"You're hard," she said angrily. "You're stone—cruel stone."

"Yes, I think so," he agreed thoughtfully. "Stone, inflexible. Tears don't soften stone, but water does, across the long years; water blends with it, softens it, wears it gradually down to some mutual end. And love is like water, sometimes."

"Go away," she said. "I want to be alone."

He complied. He saw that she was clutching the emerald; he left her to herself, and to the curious, silent conversation of the little Sphinx.

NEXT DAY the Greeks made ready—polishing weapons and armor, rubbing their bodies with oil, getting their final selection of treasure bundled securely, shaving and preparing to face the world once more. They had supreme confidence in Nekht's promise of boat and safe egress; their trust in him was almost pathetic. He had set the hour of midnight for departure, and those last hours were hard waiting, and even harder as the end approached.

Amenartis had shut herself up alone after their final meal, and he left her undisturbed. Of the treasure he took none, wanted none. Peasants had no business with gold-dust and gauds. He kept the sword she had given him—and he would keep the emerald, if she decided against going with him. He divined easily that the trusty lion-hearted Peleus would be glad to make her a princess in some Greek city, did she so desire.

He waited, in silence. The time dragged on; eleven o'clock came and passed. At a sound, he looked up, and saw her coming to him. She had laid aside her fine garments and wore the simple blue robe in which she had come here. He sprang up.

"Amenartis—we can leave now, any minute. Have you decided?"

She looked at him, a queer little shadowy smile twisting her lips.

"Yes. I'm cruel, Nekht. I have to be. There's no other way."

His heart sank. "Oh! I—I'm sorry, bitterly sorry—"

"You don't understand," she broke in. "I mean cruel, as you're cruel. Strong, resolved, firmly decided at last. I think the emerald helped me to it. I'll not fail you, dear Nekht. A farmer's wife—yes. But *your* wife! That makes all the difference. The water that softens the stone, over long years. We can do this, together. We can do anything—together. And there's gladness in it, Nekht."

He took the hand she held to him, and lifted it to his lips. Then his arms went around her for a long moment, and they stood silently.

Peleus came in, looked at them, and grinned.

"Pardon the interruption," he said. "I came to inquire how long we must wait, but by the looks of things—"

"We go now," said Nekht, and he kissed the woman in his arms, and laughed.

The emerald knotted in his girdle, he led them—into the treasure chamber, out by a secret door, along an interminable passage adrip with dampness, and finally into open air at the river's edge, amid long reeds and trees. Here Nekht showed them where a boat was hidden securely.

THE STARS were misty; over the river drifted a pall of smoke from the city. The moon hung high and white. The boat was dipped, soaked, put afloat. They climbed in, and the oars began to bite the water. Ships were black on the river; Cambyses was here.

The Greeks rowed carefully, silently, upstream, then dipped more deeply. They were safely away, without alarm, their bundles of treasure weighting the slim craft. On and on, Peleus watching the water and shores ahead.

He put in at last, just below the dark village. Nekht stepped ashore, took the hand of Amenartis, and she joined him. There was a low chorus of farewells.

"May the gods be kind to you!" said Peleus.

"And to you, friends," said Nekht.

The boat pushed out. Peleus, looking back, saw them standing there in the moonlight, hand in hand. He raised an arm in silent salute.

One of the men grunted. "What, Cap'n? Saluting a brown native?"

"No," said Peleus. "A bit of green stone. I almost wish I were staying!"

III

THE LAST PHARAOH

*That strange bewitching jewel, the Sphinx
Emerald, plays another part in world drama
when a Mata Hari betrays the Egyptians, and
Artaxerxes of Persia storms up the Nile to take
over the ancient kingdom of the Pharaohs.*

I HAVE BEEN called a commercial-minded Greek, a sour, money-mad curmudgeon and other such names, and probably with some truth. However, it is safe to say that I am the only person who really understands what lay behind those events in Egypt. I was part of the show myself, and my firm had a finger in the events.

Full thirty years previously, my father had emigrated from Greece, when King Agesilaus of Sparta sailed from Greece to join Nekht Horu-heb, Pharaoh of Egypt, and inflicted a crushing defeat on the Persians. Our contracting firm was founded then, and I carried it on in my own day as the biggest concern of its kind in the world. Our headquarters were in Memphis, of course. This was in the time of Nekht-nebf, whom we Greeks called Nektanebos,* the greatest king Egypt had known for generations. The Hebrews gave him that silly title of Pharaoh, deriving it from the Egyptian title per aa or Great House, one of the many oddments that dangled on royalty's mantle.

We were doing very nicely in those days. Nektanebos was a great soldier and builder and civilizer. There was always war with Persia, which looked upon Egypt as a revolted province; but in fact our king belonged to an actual native dynasty tracing its blood back to the great Ramses. Our firm, Archias & Co., prospered heavily because Greeks were everywhere. The armies were largely Greek mercenaries. Greeks had settled heavily in

---

* 340 B.C.

Egypt and Persia and Asia Minor; they vied with the Hebrews
in business and commerce—indeed, my chief competitor was
a fellow named Saul, who headed a Hebrew contracting firm.

Nekht had been king for about eighteen years when that odd
business of the Sphinx emerald came to my attention. I was
getting on in years, being in my fifties; my wife was dead, and
my boy Archias was in Tyre, handling the foreign angles of the
business, while I ran the head office in Memphis.

Being on fairly intimate terms with the King helped the
bank-account but kept me on the jump. He had made me one
of the council, too, which was onerous work at times. He was
forty-five or so—easy-going, rather credulous and superstitious,
but a fine sort of man just the same. He had one son, who was
in charge of the army at Pelusium, on the Syrian frontier. The
crack troops were there because of the Persian danger. The
prince was not up to much, however, and I said so frankly to
Nekht.

"THAT BOY of yours needs a bit of stiffening," I said one
evening at the palace. "He's giving his time to women and hard

drinking. Give him a job at that new quarry you've opened at Tura—hard work there!"

"I may, when this present crisis is over," he said, stroking his oval, deeply lined features. "At the moment, he's needed where he is, as a figurehead. The army—"

"Oh, I know!" I broke in. "You should be there in place of him. You're a real soldier. You licked the Persians before; you can do it again. I've had letters from my son in Tyre. He thinks

Guards ordered me forth from my prison cell and set me in a long column of trampling wretches—slaves going to their labor at the Sphinxes.

the Persians are secretly on the move—the betting is that Ochus will be King of Egypt inside of six months."

He grunted. "That fellow's no soldier—an old man, worn out, faded! The stars say he hasn't two years to live, Archias."

"Are you still steeping yourself in astrology?" I snorted. "That's absurd."

A chamberlain came in, muttering hurried words. The King nodded.

"Bring her in, now," he ordered, then turned to me. "My friend, I'd like your opinion of this woman, and her errand. The stars predicted her coming, you know—"

"Pardon me," I broke in. "The stars don't predict anything. If I were in cahoots with one of your astrologers, I'd make predictions too, and bring 'em about."

"You're a hard-headed old skeptic," he shot out. "Don't you believe in anything?"

"Depends on how much I have to lose," I told him. "You have a good deal—Egypt. Can't you realize that these astrologers you support are taking you for a sucker?"

"No," he said, half-angrily. "The secrets of the stars, their influence on our lives and destinies, is an ancient science. We inherited it from Chaldea. Try now to control your cynic mind, and don't snap so readily at other men's beliefs. Here, while I'm talking with her, you can look at this—it's been handed down in the family from ancient days."

He passed me a green bauble. I took it but disregarded it.

"Wait," I said. "Tell me where she came from?"

"Out of the eastern mountains, with a message from the gods," he said, just as a woman and two guards came in. He motioned them forward.

I relaxed and looked at what he had given me. It was a lumpy emerald set in a ring or circlet of gold—a poor emerald of wretched color, badly flawed, sadly in need of cutting and shaping. This, for the moment, was all I saw in it, for I looked up at the woman as she came forward and sank in prostration before the King, with the two-armed royal salute. Then she rose and threw back her veil and handed him a small scroll.

"The god Horus gave me this scroll for you, O King," she said. "He came to me in dream, left this in token of his coming, ordered me to bring it myself to you. It is sealed with his own seal."

"Who are you?" Nekht asked her; and at the look in his face I suppressed a groan. Some people will believe anything, with superstition to prod them.

"I am named Merti," she said. "In the ancient days my fathers were priests of Horus at the shrine of the Sphinx."

"Oh!" said he. "The Great Sphinx by the Pyramids?"

"No, lord," she replied. "Its fellow, in the eastern hills, that faces westward."

He said no more, but began to read the scroll. She waited, her eyes downcast. She was a pretty thing in a way—beautiful, if you like the word. I prefer women with sense to those with outward beauty, and I glanced at the emerald in my hand. It startled me, and I held it up and looked again, doubting my own eyes.

BY ZEUS! It was true—within the stone was a tiny Sphinx! Some sort of trick, I thought, till I discerned the truth: Flaws and bubbles in the stone had come together to make the figure—not a mere rough shape, but exact, perfect, clearly cut— set in the very heart of the crystal. No man could have made this; it was supernatural, from the hands of the gods. I am not superstitious. I do not waste good money buying birds and bulls for sacrifice on the altars that the lazy priests may feast. Still, for one moment I did have a sharply uneasy thrill at sight of this Sphinx. Bad luck, I told myself, with a bit of Greek instinct; we Greeks never worshiped sphinxes.

"An interesting communication, superbly written," said the King, turning to me. "You read Egyptian—look at it." He passed the scroll to me and looked at the woman. "I shall probably obey the commands of the god Horus, Lady Merti. Anciently, each great Sphinx had an attached temple where Horus was worshiped; we have today forgotten those shrines, which are almost completely buried under the sand. To clear them will be a great labor. To do it myself, as the god desires—well, I shall think about it."

"Horus will reward you, O King," she murmured.

He looked pleased. "Do you remain in Memphis, lady?" he asked.

"Until I receive your answer, yes," she replied. "I have one or two other errands here. I must see a Greek named Archias, and one or two other lords, before returning."

Nekht gave me a glance, but I remained silent, and he took the hint.

"Return, then, in a week," he said, "and receive my answer. You shall be lodged with the priestesses of Isis as a royal guest; see whom you will. Gifts worthy of your beauty will be brought you in the morning."

SHE WITHDREW. She had never so much as looked at me; yet I had an idea she knew all about me. When we were alone again, Nekht turned to me.

"Well, Archias, what do you think of this?"

"Are you asking as the King of Egypt?" I demanded.

He chuckled. "No, confound you! As a friend in need of advice."

"Then it has a bad smell," I said bluntly. "As for Horus and the dream, that's just so much stale cheese. Who actually sent this beauty? Where did she come from? Why are you wanted to do such a job, one that will require thousands of slaves and baskets of money, and do it yourself?"

"Come," he said, smiling. "For once give the gods their due, Archias—"

"I'll do that," I said, "but the gods don't deal with sand, and beautiful women and rummy yarns like this one. No god wrote that letter. I tell you what: Give me three days to think this over. That girl is going to see me, for some reason, and it isn't to make love back of a pillar, either. She'll probably turn up at my office tomorrow. The day after, I'll be able to give you a line on her."

He nodded. "All right. Come and have dinner here that night—day after tomorrow."

"You're shortening me one day, but I'll agree," said I, and held up the emerald. "Where did you get this—part of the ancient royal treasure, you say?"

"Yes. A fascinating thing, Archias. Take it with you and bring it back when you come to dinner. Meantime, sit and look into it, and tell me what the stone says to you."

"Does the Sphinx speak, then?" I asked ironically. "Very well. And I advise you to send a good excavator to look at those Sphinxes and get an estimate on the cost of cleaning them up, before you give her a reply."

This amused him, and he was still laughing when I departed....

On my way out, I stopped for a word with Tii. He was a minor palace official who had a genius for undercover things; I had used him frequently, and knew him to be devoted to Nekht. I spoke frankly with him about Lady Merti.

"You have her shadowed," I said. "What's more, find out if you can, where she's from and who she is. She didn't just walk into town from the eastern hills, that's sure. If there's a plot against the King, I want to know it, and know it fast. Spare no expense."

Tii was an energetic fellow, and promised to get on the job at once.

I went home, lighted a couple of oil lamps and sat gazing at the emerald. What with reports from our agents all over Syria and beyond, I could guess at a few things myself, and why somebody wanted Nekht held right here in Memphis by a crackpot job while the army remained away up north at Pelusium.

Ochus, as they called Artaxerxes, ruler of Persia, was up to mischief. He might be old and outworn, but he had some mighty good moments and was capable of anything. The Persian army had smashed everything in the world, because it was a magnificent long-distance weapon—practically all bowmen, splendid archers who could wipe out an opposing force before it could reach them. Nekht had hammered those Persians,

The letter was brief and terrible: "Greetings, my father. I am in Persian hands. Do as they demand.... Refuse and I shall be slain."

however. He was a tactician, and had figured out how to oppose the archers and smash them, and had done it. They were afraid of him. If they could keep him occupied here, and then jump on our army at Pelusium, they would have a good chance—this might be a key to the riddle.

Having figured this out so easily, I forgot it and watched the emerald.

The cursed stone fascinated me. It sharpened my wits while I looked into it and studied the little Sphinx—complete to its head-dress and forepaws. Something about it really did seem to speak to me, as Nekht had said it would—but not nice things at all. To a Greek like me, Sphinxes were not friends; they were Egyptian inventions and they meant trouble. This emerald was in its way a wonderful jewel. Properly cut and polished, it might well suit a royal owner; an eye, the ancient symbol of Thoth or Horus, was cut on the bottom. Still, the more I looked at it, the less I liked it. I sat back and cursed the thing, and could swear that it winked back at me.

"There's evil in you," I said at last. "You're bad luck, and a lot of it. If you were mine, I'd get rid of you mighty quick! Still, given the proper cutting, you'd become a very handsome cabochon. Easy enough to see why the King—poor fool—thinks you are such a wonder."

Poor Nekht! Friend as he was, fine soldier, builder and kindhearted man, I felt sorry for him. He had no practical sense at all. He had rebuilt the great old temples and got nothing in return. He really believed in the gods. Worse, he believed in the stars and kept half a dozen astrologers living in luxury by his credulity.

What the stars are, I neither know nor care; but I'm well convinced they have nothing to do with my contracting business or with my own life. Nekht swallowed all the jabber these astrologers poured into him, and credited their deductions and ciphering to boot. I have known him to put off visits of inspection because of some fancied evil influence from the stars.

So, before I rolled up for the night, I wrapped the emerald in a cloth and put it away tightly. I wanted no more of it and its bad luck. I was right about the bad luck, too: About five in the morning they wakened me to receive a courier from Tyre. The company had its own fast courier service; sometimes we even used carrier pigeons, as the Persians did, but in important matters preferred actual couriers. This man had come from the Nile mouth by fast boat, bringing me a letter from the office manager at Tyre. The news in this letter could not have been worse—for me. It read:

> *"Your son, the noble Archias, left for Sidon three weeks ago to arrange details of supply for the fleet from Cyprus. I have just now received word from the Sidon office of his disappearance. More, I know not. I am making every effort to investigate, and shall send you further news as I receive it. May the gods bring him back safe and well!"*

This was a facer, and knocked everything else out of my head. My son was getting on to thirty, and nobody's fool. Indeed, I was proud of his level head and was hoping to turn the company over to him in another year or two. And now—this! He was the only son I had, too.

TWENTY YEARS earlier I would have started hotfoot for Tyre. Now I could only sit here and curse the distance, and wait. The company branch managers were good men; they would do what anyone could. Yet to think of him lost in Sidon, that accursed city of slave-dealers, was frightful; those rascally Sidonians thought nothing of knocking some stranger on the head one day and putting him up in the slave-market the next day.

I told no one the news, but grimly went through my usual morning's routine at the office. Absolutely nothing to do! That hurt. To think of business was hard. Pyrrhus, that old idiot of a money-lender from Samos, dropped in with a fantastic scheme of buying Egyptian manuscripts up and down the Nile. The Persians, he said, intended to conquer Egypt sooner or later, and had announced that they meant to destroy every bit of civilization here; therefore in the future such books would be of great value. Ordinarily I might have gone in with him on the deal, but this morning I turned him out savagely, with my worry about Archias in mind.

Instead of going home for lunch and siesta, I stayed in the office writing letters. Tii popped in without warning.

"I've found out a thing or two," he said. "First, this woman got here several days ago. She came by boat up the Nile. Yesterday she was in the bazaars and bought two pigeons from a bird-dealer named Pharses; probably carrier pigeons. Pharses is a Persian, if that means anything to you. She has the birds with her now at the temple of Isis."

"Who is she?" I demanded.

He shook his head. "Can't say, yet. Let you know later what we pick up."

He slipped off. I was still cursing him when a clerk came in to say that a Lady Merti had arrived in a litter, and would I see her. Naturally, I ordered her brought in, and ordered a scribe to sit behind the partition and take down our conversation—a useful little trick in many a business deal.

She came in and positively took my breath away—it was a hot day, and her only robes were those filmy gauze things women usually wear around the house that reveal every line and wrinkle of them. She was beautiful, as I have said, and well made too. She put on no airs, but took the chair I held for her, and smiled at me.

"Greetings, Archias," she said in excellent Greek. "This is an admirable place you have—quite imposing, in fact. These offices and storage-houses are larger than many a temple."

She was no demure and simple hill maiden now—far from it! Jeweled necklaces and rings adorned her; perfume scented her black hair; kohl rimmed her eyes; she was bending smiles and attention upon me—me, old Archias, who had tired of women before she was born!

*"Have that bird-dealer watched," I had said; "we
may want to take him into custody suddenly."*

"What's your errand with me?" I demanded curtly.

"A pleasant one, noble Archias, that will delight your heart,"
she said gayly. "But first—suppose that the gods overthrew
Egypt and gave this land into Persian hands. How would it
affect your enterprises, this vast company of yours?"

"Not at all," I replied. "Our branches in Tyre, Syria, Persia are larger than this one; we serve Persians as well as Egyptians. We have no concern with politics."

She eyed me laughingly. "Indeed? But you have a high place in Egypt. The King trusts you, depends largely upon your wisdom. Suppose I said that my errand here was to win you to the Persian cause—eh?"

"You'd have less sense than I credit you with," I grunted.

"The first day of the new moon is three weeks from now," she said slowly. "On that day, noble Archias, it is vitally necessary that King Nekht-nebf be occupied here, or at the labor on the two Great Sphinxes. You can readily persuade him to undertake that labor and superintend it himself. Will you do this for me?"

"Why for you?" I asked, mindful of the scribe taking down notes, and hoping to make her talk freely. "I could do this, yes; but why should I?"

SHE LEFT her chair and came to me. Oh, she was a sly puss, with her perfume and her pretty body and guileful ways!

"For more than one reason, dear Archias," she murmured. "First, because you like me a little, and secondly because I can give you all your heart's desire."

"You flatter yourself, sweetheart," I said ironically. "My heart's desire is far from here, and far from any power of yours."

She smiled, put hand to girdle, and drew forth a small sealed scroll.

"You think so? Then read this."

I took the scroll, and saw the seal of my son Archias. I broke it, opened the papyrus, saw his writing. The letter was brief and clear and terrible:

> *Greetings, my father. I am in Persian hands. Do as they demand, and I shall be set free. Refuse, and I shall be slain. However, do as may seem best to you, and may the gods protect you!*

Yes, Archias had written it. The Greek letters had the little twist of the pen that was the private code of the firm indicating personally written words, with no ulterior meaning. He had been seized in Sidon and the Persians had him! I stared at the letter, thankful that he was at least alive. Lady Merti pressed close to me, her fingers caressing my cheek.

"He is the one thing in this world whom you love, and for whom you live," she was saying. "He is everything to you; his future, his success and happiness, are twined about your heart. We know this. Do what I ask, then, for his sake; he will be given the favor of the Great King, Ochus; his days shall be bright, prosperity shall crown his work! This is a promise. Surely it is better than causing him to be killed and sent into hell—"

I groaned. They had me, and she knew it. King Nekht and Egypt and the whole wide world were nothing to me, as compared with that curly-haired son of mine. To save him I would betray the gods themselves—if there are any gods, which I doubt.

She caressed my cheek once more. "Agree, dear Archias," she said. "He is a handsome young man, well worth saving; I have seen a good deal of him lately. Now, look! I have the magic power of the god Horus to aid me. Agree, and at this time tomorrow he shall be set free, though he is far away! Refuse, and at this time tomorrow he dies. The choice is yours. His fate is in your hands."

Magic power? Those carrier-pigeons, of course. They had been planted here in Memphis, well in advance of her coming. The whole damnable scheme had been plotted out far ahead. It was good, excellent work.

"Very well, my dear; I agree," I said, looking up at her. "So you were the one who betrayed him into Persian hands, eh? You're working for the Persians. Well, all this does not make me love you. H'm—free him tomorrow. A courier can reach here in two weeks from Tyre, with word to that effect. If it doesn't come, I can still halt any labor on the two Sphinx-temples, a week ahead of the new moon."

"Admirable! I like you even better than your handsome son,"

she said. "He'll be freed tomorrow. But you must swear an oath
to make every effort to keep the King at work on those
temples—we could do without you, since we have other means
of gaining our end, but it must be made certain."

There was an oath, and this accursed spy knew it. For thirty
years the oath of an Archias has been sacred, when sworn upon
his father's beard and honor; by that oath, the company has
contracted with kings and generals and politicians. It holds the
honor of the firm, the personal honor of the Archias who heads
the firm, and from Thebes to Babylon it has become a byword
for security—and this woman knew it. No Archias has ever
broken that oath, nor would I break it—and she knew it.

So she dictated the oath, and to it she added the clause that
I would say nothing to any living person of my dealings with
her, which effectually stopped my tongue. So she was the one
who had lured my son into the trap, eh? Yes, I swore the oath,
but to myself I added the clause that she would not live to trap
him a second time. She laughed lightly, told me to await the
courier with word of my son's freedom and honor at the court
of Ochus, and took her departure.

Now, you must understand that to us Greeks, murder is a
crime, especially the murder of a woman. It was not always so.
The Egyptians held it to be a wrong, but no crime. When the
great Ramses killed his sister, this was a wrong but nothing
more serious. Either the Greeks or the Hebrews, I know not
which, brought in a new code of laws. Murder this woman, I
could not; but justice was another matter.

When she had gone, I summoned the scribe from behind
the partition and looked at his notes; they were full and complete. At their end, I added an attestation of their veracity, and
placed my seal, then returned them to him.

"Guard them well," I ordered, "and be ready to produce them
when ordered."

I went home and shut myself up to think this out, all of it.
Impelled by some inner prompting, I took out the Sphinx

"And I'm not the idle fool you think me," the King said.

emerald, set it in the light, and looked at it for a while; hatred had gathered within me, but those green depths wiled it away. Instead came caution, and craft, a feeling of immense and deadly subtlety. It was as though whispers came to me from the very lips of Odysseus, most crafty and cunning of all men.

Lady Merti had snared me, yes. I was committed beyond recall; I must advise the King to proceed with the work and free the Sphinxes of sand; I must betray him. Free or not, my son would be held by some string until this was done. Very well; but Archias, son of Archias, had not lived fifty-odd years for nothing. I had not outsmarted Jew and Tyrian and Egyptian in business, I had not built up Archias & Co. into a worldwide firm, to be caught in a net by a woman. The old fox could eat his way out of any net.

*"I know something is stirring. I've
sent my son strict orders—"*

A fine bit of brag; and quite false. I was nipped. There was
no way out. Yet, as I looked at the tiny Sphinx in the emerald,
I told myself that there must be some way, if I could only find
it or make it. From those green vistas, flash upon tiny flash
seemed to leap through my mind. A word, a thought, took
shape; "Wait. Keep your oath you must—but wait! When something turns up, be ready."

The emerald did not say this to me, but I think it did cause
the thought to rise in my head. I wrapped the stone up and laid
it aside, and sat thinking. I must betray the King, the man whom
I respected and even loved, him who trusted me; the life of my
son was more to me than he or his throne could be, or all the
splendor of Egypt. To this course I was bound. By my action
the Persians would sweep over Egypt like a plague of locusts

and reduce the fat country to the status of a desert. This was hard to realize.

The upshot was that I made up my mind to it; the only thing I could do was to wait for what might turn up. Until a courier came with definite word that my son was free, I must do nothing. So I relaxed, and sent out a code letter to the company branch managers, ordering that all funds of the firm be collected and securely hidden because of anticipated political changes.

THAT NIGHT, Tii came to my house. We sat behind closed doors.

"Lord Archias, the woman has been busy," he reported. "She visited your office this morning and was there an hour."

"Think I don't know it?" I snapped.

He grinned at me.

"She also visited the Persian bird-dealer and bought two more pigeons."

"Oh! Make a note to have that fellow watched; we may want to take him into custody suddenly."

"Right, my lord. This afternoon she visited two of the astrologers who serve the King, spending half an hour with each. She bought some woman's gear in the bazaars—henna and such things, and new sandals."

From my desk I took a string of gold rings and tossed it to him.

"So far, good, Tii. Watch the woman; she is to see the King next week, and then will leave—how, I know not. Let her leave, then stop her, catch her, cage her somewhere close to the palace. I may want to get at her in a hurry. Do it quietly, of course."

He assented. "So far I've learned nothing about her. One of the palace guards, that fellow Antenor from Samos, swears that he saw her in Sidon a year ago, and that she was a fine lady riding in a litter."

"He may be, and probably is, telling the truth," I said. "At least she came here from Sidon. Well, make sure of her when she leaves, then report."

So Lady Merti was probably leaving in a week; another two weeks would bring the new moon and some sort of crisis. And my lips were sealed. Two weeks should bring a courier in regard to my son, and this, at the moment, was all that mattered to me.

Next day I started a campaign to collect all funds due Archias & Co., with a heavy discount for immediate settlement; also to close outstanding contracts where possible. Word came in from our upriver agents that royal orders had gone forth for a mass movement of public slaves downstream at once; some ten thousand were affected. This meant that Nekht had resolved to do the work on the two Sphinxes.

He said as much that evening when I went to dine at the palace.

"The estimate is that it will require five thousand men at each Sphinx," he said, "working from thirty to ninety days, to clear them. I expect you to kick in with a food contract, my friend."

I nodded. "Gladly, my lord."

"And I'm not the idle fool you think me. I know something's stirring. I've sent my son strict orders to keep on the lookout, and officers are on the way upriver to raise a force of five thousand Nubian archers, to join him."

"Better," I said gloomily, "if you'd pack off those lazy astrologers to Pelusium or to hell. Sitting all night on their hind ends studying the stars!"

He laughed at this with hearty amusement.

"No. Great things are going to take place on the first night of the new moon," he affirmed. "Certain of the planets will then be in conjunction; there's to be a meeting of the astrologers, at which I'll be present. It's expected that the destiny of Egypt itself will be affected, and we must take advantage of the indications at once."

No use at all talking to him; he was besotted by his superstition. He asked if I were against undertaking the work on the Sphinxes.

"No; quite the contrary," I said, thus keeping my vow. "In fact, an astrologer has made the astonishing prediction that in two weeks I'll receive a vitally important message from my son, who's up in Syria somewhere. If it comes true, I'll withdraw my objections to star-gazing."

He laughed and thumped his golden wine-cup on the table.

"Ho! That'll be worth a celebration!" he cried. "See here, Archias—if it does come to pass, let me know and I'll give a banquet in your honor! To be rid of your croaking would be well worth it. What's more, I'll grant any request you may make of me—my word upon it! What do you say?"

THEN AND there the idea flashed over me. I demurred, to make him more eager, until he swore by the gods to keep his word. I said that my son had disappeared, and foul play was feared, but that the astrologer had declared word of his safety would come in the fortnight. He became keenly interested and repeated his great oath to do as he had said. So it was settled.

He mentioned the emerald, and asked if it had exerted any effect upon me.

"Yes. I don't like it," I said, and taking it from my pouch, I handed it to him. "I dislike the thing, in fact, distinctly. It brings queer thoughts into my head."

"It does that to everyone, Archias," he said soberly. "I used to gaze into it frequently, and do you know what it made me think of? An oasis in the desert—I could even see the place distinctly in all details. I've been told that it's the oasis of Sekhet-amit, the 'field of palm-trees' where Amen-Ra is worshiped; but I've never been there."

Superstition had him again; and he babbled on about this oasis of Siwa, as we Greeks knew it, but I paid him no further attention. Oracles, priests, oases and gods did not interest me, except where Archias & Co. might be concerned. Besides, I had eaten too much of the delicious duck that was served, and knew I was in for a spell of indigestion. I was, too, and it bothered me for the next three days.

I was not present when Lady Merti saw the King again, and learned he was already preparing for the work, and took her leave of him. Tii informed me about it. She was loaded down with royal gifts and was taking a small boat down the Nile, no doubt to connect with a Sidonian galley below town. She did not connect, because Tii's men bagged her neatly.

Nekht was in earnest about clearing the Sphinxes of sand, and huge batches of slaves came downriver and established camps. The Sphinx in the eastern hills was difficult of access, out of the way, practically forgotten in those wild desert regions; we had taken the food contracts and it was a job getting stores shipped there.

Every day now a palace chamberlain came to see whether any news of my son had arrived. None came; I grew worried and anxious, though the fortnight was not yet up. Everything was quiet on the frontier, and it really looked as though the Persians did not mean to make trouble after all. I even began to think I had made a mistake in having Lady Merti put into a cell close by the palace; everything was uncertain, insecure, trembling in the balance. I wished vainly that I could again look into that Sphinx emerald, for reassurance and its calming effect on the nerves, but this was impossible.

Day after day, and no news; that accursed woman had been caged for nearly a week now and Tii reported she was troublesome—trying to buy a guard, trying a dozen stratagems. I waited, desperately hoping against hope. Then, early one morning, one of our river captains sent up word that a light galley from Tyre, flying our house-flag, had just been sighted coming up the Nile. Word at last!

I sat there fidgeting, until steps sounded and the clerk showed one of our couriers into my private office. The man saluted me.

"He lives, lord—he is safe!" he cried, and handed me a scroll.

Evidently the whole firm, up north, had been on tenterhooks. "He is safe, and has taken one of our ships for Samos."

This pleased me intensely. The boy had been freed, and had kept his head, getting completely out of Persian hands at once.

His letter confirmed this. It was not only guarded but also in code, and went into few details. He was well. He had been released, had been given great gifts by the Persians, and promises that Archias & Co. would receive honor and employment from Ochus. "But," he added, "look out for a storm, and quickly. I will write fully from Samos."

S O H E was safe, out of their reach! This keen intelligence of his pleased me intensely; a true Archias, that boy! Further, it opened to me the path of action that I needed. How true had been the advice inspired by the Sphinx emerald: *Wait!* I had waited, and now had come my reward. Break the oath I had sworn? No, that was impossible; besides, it would do no good. Nekht was chained in his own superstitious folly. However—

I sent out my servants—one to bear this news to the King, another to seek Tii, another to summon all company officers to a conference at once. A storm, and quickly—this meant war, and Archias & Co. must be in shape to meet it.

However, when a palace chamberlain came with a message of congratulation and delight from Nekht, and invitation to a banquet in the evening, I accepted. Then came Tii in haste. I gave him my orders.

"Attend the banquet at the palace tonight and be ready for what happens. Watch that bird-seller in the bazaars—Pharses. I may want to reach him swiftly tonight. Guard the woman well. That is all."

Last came the scribe who had taken down my conversation with Lady Merti. I ordered him to have the scrolls ready and to attend me at the banquet. After this, I was free for the company conference, which occupied most of the afternoon. I told them the truth: "Gentlemen, I am uncertain of the future. I am taking steps to hand over Archias & Co. to my son; I want him elected general manager here and now. My only concern is to insure his future and that of the company. Tomorrow I may not be here; therefore, a deputy must be elected to fill my sandals if I turn up missing. Business is business; the company must go ahead regardless. As to his personal future, I shall take charge of that myself."

It was a hot session, but nobody was giving me any back talk and things were done as I directed.

Then I climbed into my litter and proceeded to the palace.

I shall pass over needless minutiæ; the banquet was a grand one, and I was heartily congratulated by all on my son's safety. Nekht honored me with the ancient title, *"Friend of the King"* and in his speech stated that within a day or so he was leaving for a temporary camp near one of the great Sphinxes, where he would inaugurate the beginning of the reparation work. Then he turned to me.

"Now, Archias! I promised you that if things turned out well with your son, I would grant whatever request you might make. I reaffirm that promise now. Ask whatever you will; it shall be granted."

I rose and thanked him. "I do have a wish, my lord; it is that for one hour I may sit upon your throne in the great audience hall and be for that hour the unquestioned King of Egypt, with all your power."

There was a terrific outcry from council and nobles and princes; they called me upstart Greek, sacrilegious blasphemer, and all the usual things. Nekht commanded silence and said:

"Friends, Archias is an honest man and one whom I would trust with more than life. My word is given and shall be kept. Bring out the double crown of Upper and Lower Egypt. For the hour he wears those crowns, Archias shall be King of Egypt in name and fact. Come, everyone—to the great hall!"

Off we trooped, palace guards leading the way, and the looks on some of the faces made me chuckle. More than one man there had reason to fear old Archias; however, I had no concern with them. In the great hall of audience, Nekht handed me to the golden throne-seat, took the heavy double crown, and placed it upon my head, then saluted me.

"Hail, King of Egypt!" The salute was repeated after him. The moment had come; for an instant I sat with fear shaking me; then I summoned Tii and the captain of the guards.

"Take men," I told them, "and bring before me the woman you are keeping confined. Also, send and arrest Pharses the bird-seller and bring him here. Let him be the first led before me. My friends, I am going to deal with certain enemies of Egypt in my hour of rule; but let none of you be troubled. Where is my scribe?"

HE CAME forward and saluted me. I indicated him to Nekht.

"Royal Nekht-nebf, it is my command that you withdraw to some private room with this scribe, and peruse the scroll he carries. Perhaps you have some fear?"

Nekht smiled. "This is the thirtieth dynasty that has ruled Egypt, Archias, and never has a truer man sat upon that throne. I obey your command. Come, scribe."

They strode away. What had first looked like some wild jest to the courtiers now became sober fact. One nitwit princeling essayed a comic role, requesting of me the fit reward for his many services to the throne; I ordered him dipped in the lily-pond in the great courtyard, and the guards took him—and there was no further comedy. At last guards walked in, dragging the trembling bird-seller.

I spoke sternly:

"Pharses, you're a Persian agent, a spy. You were planted here in Memphis to do certain work, and you've done it. From you the woman known as Lady Merti obtained carrier-pigeons that would take her reports to Persian emissaries in Sidon. She has confessed her share in this work. Now, if you tell the truth, you'll be set free, but if you lie, you shall be killed at once. Speak."

The poor devil was shaking like a leaf. In an access of terror, he flung himself on his face and babbled out everything. Lady Merti? She was actually the lady friend of a Persian general, one Memnon, chosen for this work because she spoke Egyptian fluently. Yes, the fellow had been a spy here for the year past, sending reports each month.

"Take him outside and set him free," I told the guards.

Lady Merti was brought in, walking proudly enough until she saw who sat on the throne; then she wilted, staring with great dark eyes. I was anxious to get finished with her before Nekht returned, lest he interfere, so I wasted no time.

"Lady," I said, "you have served the Persians well. You have acted as their agent here, under a false name. You imposed upon the royal Nekht and beguiled him to do your will, but now I am king. Have you aught to say before I sentence you?"

"A lie!" she cried out. "A lie! An outrage—you are not king!"

"And you are not Lady Merti, but the concubine of General Memnon," I said, and motioned to the guards. "Strip her."

THEY TORE the rich garments from her—holding her helpless, naked, for all to see.

"This is madness, Archias!" she cried. "Your son loves me, and I love him—"

"You may possibly speak the truth in that," I said, "but I am not minded to let my son marry the concubine of a Persian general. If he has lost his senses, I still have mine about me." I beckoned the guard captain. "Take her out to the gates and execute her there with the sword, as a spy of the Persians."

She shrieked, and there was a stir in the crowd, but the guards were already in motion and no one dared interfere. They had her out of the hall and away before Nekht came striding in at the side entrance.

"By the gods, Archias!" he cried out. "An amazing conversation, that! Did the woman actually force you to betray me, as she thought?"

"You've just read the record," I replied. "It's all true."

He broke out into a laugh. "It's also true that the stars have predicted great events for the night of the new moon! My astrologers are going to meet there at my camp near the Sphinx— not the one by the pyramids, but the other one, in the eastern hills—and watch the amazing conjunction of the planets. That Lady Merti did me a good turn after all, it seems."

"Then it's a good thing I caught her, and not you," I said.

"Who? What?" He broke into perplexed questions that gained ready enough answer from nobles and courtiers. I let them babble and leaned back. What was done was done. Nekht, listening to what was told him, went white with rage, called a guard, and learned that the woman was dead. This overbore everything else in his mind and threw him into a fit of fury. Spy or not, he never would have killed her, as I well knew.

"I've had my way, and I'm wearied." Taking off the heavy double crown, I held it out to Nekht. "Take it; I've had enough. If any remains of the hour, I resign it. I've done my best, not for you, but for my son and his future."

"Aye," he said, "as I have for mine, the last of the princes of Egypt! But you killed her, Archias—you murdered her, that woman sent by the gods, that glorious woman! I can't forgive that. Guards! Here—this man is a king no more. Into the royal prison with him, at once."

Sent by the gods—why, the man was so besotted by superstition he hardly knew what he said! They led me out, the courtiers jeering at me. I cared not. Nothing mattered; in the prison cell I dropped to the mat with exhaustion, and slept. My work was done....

Two days, three—how long I lay there, I know not. I saw no one, ate what was shoved at me, paid no heed to anything; then guards ordered me forth and set me in a long column of tramping wretches—slaves marching down to the ships. Once aboard, we went down the mighty river, slaves going to their labor at the Sphinxes. We disembarked at the east bank and were lashed up through the hills, past the forests of trees turned to stone in ancient times, and so at last to the camp near the huge westward-facing Sphinx, buried to the neck in blown sands.

From my quarters in the slave camp I could see this great image of stone; it was like looking at the tiny image in the emerald. I looked at it a while before falling into exhausted slumber, and wondering at its meaning; then closed my eyes. This was the end, and I had no regrets. I could not survive the labor and the whips, and I knew it.

With morning, one of the overseers came when the slaves were being turned out to work, and took me aside.

"Lord Archias, I used to work for your company," he said. "Give me an order on your head office for a gold ring, and I'll see to it that you need not labor. Eh?"

I gave him an order for a dozen rings, and went back to my mat and lay there. Age and the journey here had broken me; I could scarcely move. A day passed, two days, and I began to feel more like myself. With the next night, I looked at the sky and saw the faint, thin horn of the new moon hanging there. This was the time of crisis foretold by the astrologers. At this thought, I cackled with ironic amusement, and rolled up to sleep.

Morning came. We were fed, and the slaves filed out to their work. I sat on my mat, looking out westward to the Nile valley, and the shadowy tips of the Pyramids against the sky. A short quarter-mile from the slave camp stood the gorgeous tents of the King's encampment. From these tents a single figure was approaching—a horseman wearing a common blue robe and turban, but riding one of the King's magnificent chargers.

He came straight to the barracks, came to where I sat, and dismounted. Not until he walked over to me and I saw his face, did I recognize Nekht.

"Greetings, lord of the two worlds!" I saluted him ceremoniously.

He said nothing, but sat down. His face was gray and haggard.

"Archias," he said at last, "my son is dead. You know what that means."

The words gave me a shock; yes, I knew what that meant to him.

"An hour ago a courier reached me," he went on. "Night before last, Ochus himself suddenly appeared with his army, and stormed Pelusium, then wiped out our whole army. My son was killed." He lifted his head and looked at me. "You think I wronged you, Archias; but I could not. I arranged that you should do no labor. I meant to free you. I do it now. Take this, get a horse from the tents yonder, and get off to Memphis before the news is known generally."

From his finger he twisted the big blue scarab ring that was his royal signet, and held it to me. I took it.

"But my lord, I cannot desert you!"

He laughed harshly. "It is I who am deserting. The astrologers met last night. I listened to their patter and learned the truth. You were right, Archias; they are a pack of fools, and I am the greatest fool of all. My superstition has lost Egypt. My son is dead; my house has come to an end. The thirtieth dynasty is finished. Go, make your peace with Ochus, and prosper. The gods be good to you!"

He stood up.

"But where go you?" I demanded. "There is still hope—"

"For me there is nothing." He took something from his girdle and I saw a flash of green. It was the Sphinx emerald. "I take this, Archias; I ride into the western desert, to the Siwa oasis or beyond. I've sent a courier to Ochus, abandoning the kingdom to him. I shall never return again to Egypt. Would to the gods I had listened more to you and less to my proud foolish heart! Farewell."

He mounted his horse, and rode away—the last of the house of Nekht, nevermore to be seen among men.

AS for me—well, Archias & Co. flourishes under Persian rule, and my son is high in favor with the present Great King,

Darius. So I should be happy in my old age. Perhaps I would be, did not my heart turn so often to the vast, empty western desert where a lonely man vanished forever with the Sphinx emerald. Like him, I have but one last word to give—

Farewell!

IV

MASTER OF THE WORLD

Alexander of Macedon had conquered most of the world, and his legions were rolling toward Carthage when—a wily little priest strangely presented to him the Sphinx Emerald.

THE EGYPTIANS called it Sekhet-Amit, meaning "field of palm trees;" to the Romans, it was the Oasis of Jupiter Amon; we know it as Siwa Oasis, one of the ancient and sacredly renowned spots in the world, in the Sahara Desert, three hundred and fifty miles west from Memphis.

It is, and always has been, extremely difficult of access. In the old days before the practical Romans put that Asiatic beast, the camel, to work as a means of desert transport, to reach Siwa was almost impossible; and yet, from the earliest prehistoric time, kings and generals and many lesser men made the pilgrimage hither, and desert caravans from Mid-Africa to Carthage. For the oasis was sacred to Amon, father of the gods, and the oracle of Amon told the future to those who asked, and gave wisdom. So suppliants came to worship the god and seek the aid of the oracle.

In this February of 331 B.C., the spot was an area of about ten square miles, abundantly watered by springs and wells, with about a hundred thousand date palms and a luxuriant growth of olives, figs and other trees. One of the chief wells was accounted miraculous, because it was warm by night and cold by day, and still is so. Under the trees crouched a weird little old temple, home of the god Amon, the Zeus of the Greeks and Jupiter of the Romans.

To this far-famed spot was coming the even more renowned Alexander as a suppliant, a regal suppliant, for he had conquered

*If the great world-conqueror got
this far west of Egypt, he would
assuredly go on to loot Carthage.*

Persia and Asia Minor and Egypt with his barbarous Macedonian army, and was now rumored to be marching on Carthage and Rome in order to complete his world-conquest and to pillage the West as he had pillaged the East. This rumor had run insistently for months, as Psammon was well aware.

Psammon, they called him; "Little Amon," or more politely "The Little One." He bore a Carthaginian name but only the priests knew it. This oasis was nominally Egyptian, but was at the edge of territory ruled by Carthage, and Egypt had fallen to pieces so the Carthaginian power was largely felt hereabouts.

With the whole Western world atremble at thought of Alexander and his tough Macedonians, who met all opposition by slaughtering the men and raping the women, it was natural that Carthage should have an agent here at Siwa. Psammon had been here a long time. If the great world-conqueror got this far west of Egypt, he would assuredly go on to loot Carthage

and Sicily and Rome, and nobody westward enjoyed the prospect.

Psammon was not happy about it either, and with far greater reason. As agent of Carthage, he had been ordered to perform a task so utterly impossible as to appear almost ludicrous, were it not so tragic—one at which kings and empires had failed and gone down to dusty ruin. How, then, could he hope to fulfill it, seeing what he was?

He was a cheerful, sharp-eyed little man of incredible agility;

not deformed in any way but merely small—a trifle over three feet in height. His features were aquiline, finely chiseled, mellow as old ivory; his eyes were a very keen and bright blue, usually laughing and sparkling with life.

But now, as he sat talking with the high priest of the temple, they were vexed and gravely helpless. He spoke without reserve, for he could be quite frank with this one person.

"Tell me, help me!" His voice was musical, deep in timbre. "I am ordered to stop this Alexander, to turn him away from Carthage, to avert his destroying legions. How can I hope to do such a thing? The very thought is absurd. Darius, the king of kings, with all his satraps and legions, could not do it. Yet the Suffetes, the rulers of Carthage, order me—me!—to do it. Tell me how!"

His slender-fingered, deft hands, which had been playing with a green stone, fell motionless. He peered at the gentle old priest in perplexity.

"Little One, you touch upon a mystery," said the older man in kindly accents. He liked this dwarf. "If the gods desire a thing done, they inspire men to do it—how, we can never tell in advance. I advise you to pray to them."

"Pray? Bosh! Something better than prayer is needed," snapped the little man. "What I need is some practical help."

"Where can you seek it, except from the gods?" said the old priest. "As to Alexander, we have been kept fully informed by couriers. He comes with his staff and a few guards, not many. Why? Because he fully believes himself to be the son of Zeus or Amon, and wishes this confirmed by our oracle, which is respected by the whole world—"

"Everyone knows he's the son of Philip, King of Macedon," blurted Psammon.

The priest smiled. "His mother Olympias is a woman given to wild, ecstatic furies at times. King Philip called the boy a bastard. She announced that the god had visited her on her wedding-night. Alexander has believed this, always."

*"By the horns of Amon, my son! It
is worth uncounted gold!"*

"And if you know what's good for you, you'd better confirm
it!"

"My son, the priests of the oracle say only what the god puts
into their minds. We're honest fellows; but I grant you we would
never ask a thunderbolt to hit us. This Alexander is a proud,
haughty young man, the greatest today living on this earth: yet
he is given to gentle and noble impulses, like all men truly
great."

"He, the greatest upon earth, and I the least," murmured Psammon unhappily. "And how am I to turn him from his course of conquest, with all the wealth of Carthage almost in his hand?"

"That I know not, my son; only the gods could tell you," said the old priest frankly. "We must favor this man when he comes, for his heart is noble and honest. Little One, I'll help you in any way possible. Yet every man must seek within his own heart how to accomplish his work in this world; the discovery adds to his merit. What is that green stone you've been juggling?"

The stone seemed to vanish of itself and was tucked into Psammon's girdle.

"That? Oh, an emerald, of a sort," he replied. "You remember the Egyptian who died here last year—the queer fellow Nekht, who lived like a hermit? He gave it to me when he was dying. Well, I must get a letter written to give the courier you're sending, so I'd best get home and write it.... Just when does Alexander get here?"

"Within two or three days, if storms don't detain him on this desert. This is the season of south winds, which bring sand."

Psammon left the temple, looking like a small boy as he flitted among the thick trees, making for his own hut on the outskirts of the village. He had been here some years and was held in great respect by the natives and priests alike. He himself liked the oasis far better than noisy Carthage; what with caravans and visitors, there was no loneliness here, yet the desert nights and days held a mystic peace, the very sunlight was different. It was a simple life, and none despised him for being a dwarf.

IN HIS hut, he made fire, lighted his palm-oil lamp, dipped a reed pen and wrote a brief report, which he signed and sealed. This done, he composed himself, took from his girdle the green stone and set it close to the lamp so that light was diffused through it. Then he sat motionless, looking into the lump of beryl.

An emerald, yes, a huge stone from the Egyptian mines, not of good color. The Egyptian wanderer, the man Nekht who had settled here as a hermit, had given it to him before dying, and Psammon found the thing precious and wonderful beyond belief.

In itself, it was marvelous, for the flaws and bubbles which all beryl contains had settled together at one point, forming an image. Not a fancied shape but a real and perfect semblance of the Great Sphinx, so real it seemed supernatural—a miniature Sphinx sitting there within the gem! Whence had the stone come? A royal jewel, the dying wanderer had said, a relic of the ancient Egyptian kings—well, no matter. Egypt was a Greek country now.

NOT THAT Psammon cared about Egypt; he was a Carthaginian, heart and soul. Having long ago accepted his small stature as a thing beyond help or cure, he gave to his city a fierce allegiance of spirit, serving it as secret agent with a pure devotion. He had nothing else in life to serve. Such single-mindedness had given him a sharp perception of men and agile mental powers beyond the normal. Perhaps this was why he found something else, and far more wonderful, in this emerald than the mere tiny Sphinx.

In the flashing sunlight, or beside the lamp, intent study of the stone rewarded him with strange thoughts, strange mental effects; those green depths of beryl inspired him with nameless but ecstatic beauties, intangible sensations. He imagined pictures of Eastern lands he had never seen, of glorious regal cities and buildings, of vast horizons and marching armies and magnificent panoplies of war by land and sea—he, who would never bear arms, dreamed of such things.

He was no fool. He knew that this ecstasy was due to the jewel, and that it was a sort of auto-hypnosis. It was like a hashish dream, but he never used hashish. The green scintillating depths of the emerald suggested such visions to him and left his brain happily content, fed with aspirations and ambitions he could never know in real life.

He heard a step at his door. Swift as a cat, he reached out, clawed the emerald from sight, and looked up as a man stepped into the hut. It was the courier who had come with the last news of Alexander, and who was leaving shortly for Carthage.

"Greetings, Little One," he said. "Have you a letter for me to take to the Suffetes?"

"Aye," replied Psammon. "Sit and rest. I want to ask a thing or two."

They sat talking of the greatest present subject on earth—the Macedonian. The courier told of his occupation of Egypt—an incredibly young man filled with flaming energy and convinced that a god, the greatest of the gods, had sired him. He was generous to a fault, lived the divine madness of youth to its full, had conquered half the known world and was reaching for the rest.

For some centuries past, Greece and its ideas had gradually molded the thought and politics and religion of all the eastern lands. The gods of various countries and peoples had melted together. In Macedonia, the great Amon of Egypt was worshiped, being identified with Zeus and with Min and other gods. Even here at Siwa, where in the temple was preserved a huge supposed meteorite, Amon was worshiped as the god of meteorites. To any simple soul this theology was a very confusing matter. But Alexander, as the courier made clear, was coming hither not as a conqueror but as a suppliant for the god's favor.

"Some say he'll go on to Carthage and Rome," said the courier. "Others that he'll return to Egypt, then lead his army east to India. Nobody knows. I doubt if he himself knows yet just what he'll do. He's a young man, impressionable, unformed. He has marched a hundred and forty miles west along the coast, then has headed on the hundred-and-eighty-mile march south to this oasis, and the gods have protected him."

"Well, here's my letter." Psammon gave him the sealed scroll.

"Whatever happens here, word will be sent on by another courier without delay."

A little more talk, and the courier departed. The Little One did not resume his play with the emerald. He went out into the chill February night and walked to the miraculous well. This had a constant temperature, which made its water seem cold on hot days and warm on chill nights. Psammon made his ablutions, and then took his way to the odd little temple, more ancient than man's memory. A few lights burned there. It was not guarded; there was nothing to steal and no one to steal anything in this sacred place. Passing through the courts and chambers, he came to the very sanctuary of the god, and there made his prayer for light and guidance. His perplexed, helpless mind was in sore need of it.

A queer, dim, ghostly place, this sanctuary. Seventy years earlier, Lysander the great king of Sparta had come hither, seeking the words of the oracle. An army of Cambyses the Persian had perished on the way hither; kings and wanderers had come from all parts of the earth, and had left votive offerings which were hung about the walls. In the depth of the chamber was the god himself.

A portable ceremonial boat stood there, covered with gold leaf; and in this boat or ark stood the figure of Amon, unlike that of any other known god. It was a long, shield-shaped slab of green stone set with precious stones. In the center was a circular hollow, in which stood the tiny figure of Amon himself. This peculiar object was a relic of the most ancient times in Egypt, before the dynasties of kings began; in those primitive days the shield-shaped slabs were supposed to have fallen from heaven as meteorites—and perhaps one had done so, originally. In this ancient temple, aloof from all the world, had lingered the primitive form of worship. The great green stone slab and the tiny figure of Amon in its center were relics of prehistoric days. Both were sacred objects.

Psammon, staring at the thing, felt a sudden catch of the breath. An odd notion had jumped into his head—a notion startling him with its daring, with its breadth and scope. As though Amon himself had answered his prayer! This thought awed him.

Yes, the thing was possible, but to face it took courage. He knelt, eyes wide on the dim golden boat, trying to recapture the threads of that fleeting visionary idea. His own share in the business troubled him not at all. Alexander was one enigma; but the conqueror's character was well known. That courier had painted him aright. He was coming here, a rapt young mystic, an honest believer in the oracle; he would credit anything.

The priests of Amon here were honest too; this might be an even greater problem. They honestly believed that the oracle was the inspiration of the god. None of them would indulge in any sacrilege or falsity.

"Well, that's not necessary," thought the Little One excitedly. "I can do that myself; let them give forth their own oracles! The high priest, however, is wiser than the rest, and he's in command. He has a broader outlook, too; he's keenly anxious to make a friend of this Macedonian. Hm! I think he'll listen to reason—at least, in part. I'll be the one who'll take the chances—the littlest man in the world against the greatest!"

THE NOTION took shape in his head. Fantastic as it was, his shrewd brain saw its possibilities, realized fully the queer powers instinct in the Sphinx emerald, and how those powers might well affect Alexander—if properly guided. Yes, it might be done. He knew everyone in the village, he knew women who would help him with their clever fingers. First, he must make sure of the high priest—and the less the priest knew about his scheme, the better.

He bowed before Amon, thanked him for inspiration and help, and went back home, where he lay awake a long time, thinking about the idea.

Next morning he sought the presence of the high priest. The whole oasis was in a hubbub of work and excitement. It was February, and the last of the date crop had long since been gathered from the hundred thousand date trees scattered over the oasis; but now these had to be cleaned up—the old spathes and bunches removed, the dead leaves cut away. Everyone was at it, and the smoke of the burning hung like a cloud against the sunlight. Even the temple precincts were being cleaned up a bit.

THE MORNING sacrifice was long over, and the old high priest was breakfasting when the little shape of Psammon settled down respectfully before him.

"Well, Little One? Have you thought of something?"

"Yes, master. You will show this great man the sanctuary of Amon?"

"Naturally."

"He is a conqueror, the son of the god," said Psammon. "He is a taker, master. He will see the little figure of Amon—he will take it."

"Eh?" The priest started. "No, no! He would not dare such a sacrilege here—"

"It is no sacrilege for a son to take his father's image," said Psammon. "But I have thought of something far better. First, hide the image in a corner somewhere. Replace it in the green slab with something you can offer him as a gift—something so evidently made by the gods themselves that it will satisfy and delight him."

The priest frowned at him uncertainly.

"Your words are full of wisdom, Psammon. But we have no such sacred object."

The Little One took from his girdle the Sphinx emerald, and gave it to the priest.

"Look at this carefully, master. It is a great emerald. That fellow Nekht said it had been made by the gods themselves and once belonged to the royal treasure of Egypt. Such a gift would delight even Alexander, greatest of men. I think Lord Amon himself made me think of this last night, when I was praying to him."

The high priest, naturally, was one who took nothing for granted. He looked at the emerald and saw the Sphinx set far inside it. With an exclamation, he took it to the morning sunlight and gave it a minute examination, seeking any possible cleavage. But there was none. That marvelous figure was obviously formed by the flaws in the beryl itself.

He came back, sat down, scratched his shaven pate and stared at Psammon in awe.

"By the horns of Amon, my son! This is a wonderful thing; I never saw anything like it. Why, it is worth uncounted gold! It would make you rich!"

"Gold is of small worth to me," said the Little One almost sadly. "I shall hate to part with it, true; one becomes attached to the stone. But, in the service of Amon, I must do what I must. If you will use it for this purpose, I give it freely."

The high priest looked into those strange blue eyes, intently. His grave features relaxed and smoothed; perhaps some deep and silent intelligence passed between the two men.

"Come to the sacrifice in the morning," said the priest. "I shall give you the special blessing of Amon, my son. And, whenever you have need of gold, I'll gladly supply it. I am asking no questions. I know there is no evil in your heart. No one else here knows that this emerald belonged to you?"

"No one. I have never shown it to a person, except yourself."

"Very well. I shall do as you suggest; it is quite obvious that Amon himself sent the emerald here for this purpose, so I shall tell no lies in saying it is a gift to Alexander from the god his father—"

He checked himself quickly. Psammon made no sign, and the priest smiled. This odd dwarf was a fellow to be trusted more than most; it would be quite safe to make use of the emerald as suggested, and save the precious little image from

*Lights sprang up; armed guards came. Alexander led
search of the whole place. No one, of course, thought to
look up at the palm trees leaning against the house-top.*

possible confiscation by the great visitor. The image, like the
huge green stone slab, was thousands of years old, and
priceless.

That Alexander intended coming to Siwa, was no secret; it
had been openly announced for many months. No preparation
had been made against his coming; no one knew what to do.

He had taken Egypt and was now its king, and this was
Egyptian territory. The wily businessmen of Carthage had
Psammon here for agent, as they had agents everywhere, but
they, too, had done nothing except give hopeless commands.
Everyone was helpless and paralyzed before this young man
and his tough, killing, raping Macedonians before whom no
army, no city, could stand.

The Little One was bitterly conscious of his own abject in-
feriority as a person; but now he was far too busy to think about
it. At the sacrifice of the emerald, which really hurt, he had
started something which he had to finish, and this he himself
must accomplish with none to aid. Now it was the littlest man
against the greatest—person to person, in a battle not of force
but of strategy.

The temple had no guest accommodations. One of the larger
houses in the village was being prepared for Alexander and his
suite; the troops with him could camp in the open. He would
be here on the morrow; a runner had just come in with the
news. Beds, lights, food—everything had to be conjured out of
nothing.

Amid this bustle, Psammon glided with agility, seeing now
one person, now another; he had to have certain things made,
he had to make others himself, and time lacked. It would have
been much nicer, he muttered, if the god had sent his inspiration
a little earlier. Alexander would be here only a couple of days,
just long enough to make the usual sacrifices and consult the
oracle. It was certain that in Egypt he would have seen the huge
Sphinx near the Pyramids, with its great red-painted face and
gay head gear, facing toward the rising sun—indeed, it represented Ra-Harmachis, the sun-god. Upon this fact, and upon
his own judgment of the hero's mental reaction to the emerald,
the Little One was founding his entire plan of campaign.

By afternoon, he had everything under way, and made a trip
to the house being prepared for the royal guest. He studied it
carefully. He himself could clamber about on these mud houses,
with their jutting beams, like a fly, but in this instance he dared

risk no error—just one mistake would ruin him most terribly.
Then he sat himself down to a barber and had his head shaved
completely, like that of a priest, amid many scurrilous jests flung
at him from all sides. He made no response and the jesters,
disappointed, went their ways.

That night he labored late, completing what he was making,
and early in the morning picked up the sandals and robe the
women had made for him—taking no more sewing than a
child's dress. He got the dark stain he needed, too; with his
white skin, this was imperative.

WHILE THE excited village buzzed and labored that day,
Psammous sat and looked at these things, and at the false little
stubby beard he had made; and growing fear sat clammily upon
him. Such an easy little thing to talk about and plan—but as it
drew closer, he became bitterly afraid. He began to count the
cost of one mistake, and it terrified him. He spoke Greek, of
course, and there was no reason to fear any mistake—yet he
feared. Alexander, after all, was the greatest man in the world.
When he left here he would be a god.

The Little One wished vainly that he could have the emerald
again, even for an hour. To sit and look into it would restore
his confidence and hearten him beyond measure; but this was
impossible. In the heat of the day, he stole away to the temple,
as the next best thing. He could not get into the sanctuary; all
were barred from it. He bowed himself in prayer to Amon for
help and went back to his hut.

Here he stripped and applied the darkening juice to his whole
body, head and face. With this darker skin, his bright blue eyes
made even more startling contrast, as he knew. Then he slept
away the afternoon, until the trumpets called him.

Alexander would have trumpets, of course. The Little One,
peering from openings in his hut of thatched palm-fronds, saw
the march come in from the northern highway. No camels—the
animal was as yet unknown in Africa. Men who marched afoot,
with the swinging march-step of veterans, donkeys following

with the baggage. Iron men, these, but none of them the equal of their leader, who led the way with his staff around him. The eye went to him as to a magnet.

Clean-shaven among the bearded Greeks, wearing no armor because of the desert sun, the golden fillet of a king about his hair, Alexander looked what he was—young, impetuous, gawking about in curiosity at the great oasis, waving his hand in return to the shouts of acclaim from the people. He looked unwearied, fresh, in contrast to the fagged officers and men around. His eager laugh was dazzling; he radiated youth, energy, ardent expectancy. He was the greatest man in the world, and knew it, and played up to the role with almost boyish delight. Then they were past.

THE LITTLE ONE sat on his mat, breathing hard, chewing dates from a wooden bowl. He had seen the Macedonian! The priests were greeting him now, making him welcome. The lord of two worlds, king of Upper and Lower Egypt, of Macedonia, of Tyre, of countless other lands afar, Alexander, third of the name, son of Philip—now to be proclaimed son of the god Amon, like many another potentate. The swift twilight died into darkness, the sun was gone.

Presently came one of the villagers who had promised to make report. He sat on the mat with the Little One, excitement in him, and spoke.

"They've been bathing at the holy well. The priests put him and his staff in the house. They would take nothing but a few dates. They say he eats the rations of the other Greeks. It's been a hard march; tonight they rest. They are soldiers—a few guards have been placed already. Tomorrow there'll be ceremonies in the temple, and a feast. Ha! Those Greeks have iron feet, Little One—not one of them even limps! And they say birds guided them across the desert after a sandstorm, when the guides lost the way."

Presently the villager departed and the Little One sat, alone and afraid.

That man, like the sun in splendor—Psammon could not help being afraid. How could he hope to impose upon that splendid being with his silly little story? Yet, as he thought about those Greek faces and their look of awe at everything around them, a faint hope revived in him. Alexander was a man—no more. He had marched these hundreds of miles afoot because of credulity. His belief in his own greatness and divinity was mere credulity. Greatest man in the world—yes, from the physical, the material viewpoint. But his own vast credulity and superstition would tend the more to make him credit the words of the Little One.

"The one difficulty now is to reach him, because of the guards," Psammon told himself, his shrewd brain wakening. "They'll be weary. After an hour or so they'll relax. There's a full moon, but it comes up late—so much the better. Moonlight is always more deceptive than darkness, thanks to the gods!"

Waiting was hard. He went outside and sat in the darkness, listening to a distant howling of jackals. Here in the village, everything was silent. Alexander and his trumpets and his guards had gone to rest. Strange, how few men he had brought with him on this long march! Still, that was just good sense, thought Psammon; the fewer men, the less food and water to transport.

Across the mind of the Little One crept a wandering thought that startled him. If he could reach this greatest man in the world alone, asleep, as he purposed—if he could do this, then why not with a knife? Not impossible at all. The thought held a peculiar and almost deadly allure that tempted him. His own hand, tiny, feeble, might send to hell this man at the summit of all earthly grandeur....

He laughed at himself, mockingly.

"You were not made for murder, Little One!" he muttered. "Besides, if you accomplish your design, then you are greater than he, far greater. And, above all, he is a handsome, superb, magnificent creature—such a creature as you might have been but for the accident of birth! Admire him, worship him, but harm him not. Preserve your own greatness, your own integrity—for it's all you have, Little One."

The high palm fronds were silvering. He rose and went into the hut. He laid out the robe that the women had made for him, and on it put the other articles. He rolled it all up into small compass, then slung the bundle about his neck and let it fall over his shoulders, so as not to impede him. He dared not stop now to think. He must go now—now—without pause!

He stole forth, a shadowy figure no larger than a child, stripped to his loincloth, feet bare, weaponless.

Moonlight struck athwart the high trees, with their platforms whence the spathes were pollenized and the dates plucked. Everything beneath was dark. Down the haphazard village street slipped the Little One; the dogs knew him and barked not. There ahead was the large house given over to the royal guest. He approached cautiously; yes, he might have known it. Guards walked up and down. He froze, watching them. Here and there about the house lifted high, leaning palms that overhung the roof. Little by little, he moved toward the one of these he had previously chosen.

Like a gliding shadow, he gained it. No smooth-barked tree, this. The stubs of old branches, cut off year by year across a century of life, protruded all along the thick trunk, forming it, giving secure hold for agile feet and hands. He moved like a dim nightshade up the leaning trunk, came abreast of the flat bare roof where no one slept tonight, and paused. All empty here. No alarm from the sentries on the ground—the worst lay behind him!

Heart leaping, he let himself hang, and dropped. He was on the house-roof.

The night was chill, with a keen wind out of the north. No sleeping in the patio on such a night; the rooms would be used, and he knew which the hero would occupy. He opened his bundle and spread it out on the mud roof, and began to work with the articles in it. He had gained confidence now; as the moment neared to meet the greatest man in the world face to face, his heart quieted, his nerves relaxed.

IN a room prepared for him with such splendor as the oasis afforded, Alexander lay sprawled upon the couch, sleeping heavily. His scanty baggage was on the floor; beside his pillow lay baldric and sword. The chamber was dimly lighted by a night-lamp that burned on a pedestal; also, a wide ray of moonlight struck down through an unshuttered window.

This young man, literally the master of the world, stirred a little in his sleep as a whisper sounded in the room. It was repeated again and again, very softly, the Greek words stealing through the veil of slumber. Perhaps he had been dreaming those very words in ecstatic forecasting of the morrow when the oracle of the god would confirm them.

"Son of Amon! … Son of Amon!"

The sleeper turned, threw out an arm. Once again that soft, quiet whisper stole upon the room and penetrated to the drowsy brain. The eyes of the sleeper opened a little, his head moved. Then, as he caught sight of the figure standing close beside him, his eyes flew wide open.

A queer figure, standing motionless in the ray of moonlight— a small, yet perfect figure.

A priest of Amon, or perhaps even Amon himself. The shaven head denoted a priest, as did the priestly robe, the ornamented sandals. His beautifully formed features wore the stubby short beard of a priest. He held the scepter of rule and the little "Tau cross" of life. His eyes were striking in the moonlight, blue and luminous as the eyes of a painted priest sculptured in some temple wall.

A slight gasp escaped Alexander. With a sudden movement he came to one elbow.

"Am I dreaming—is there some one here?" he muttered.

"You are dreaming, son of Amon, lord of the two worlds,"

came the gentle reply. "I have come to you in dream with a message of great importance. Can you hear me?"

"Yes, yes," assented the young man, eagerly. "I want you to answer my questions—"

"What you want, Alexander of Macedon, does not concern me. Save your questions for the temple oracle," came the gentle voice, with more definite rebuke than Alexander had heard in many a year. "Attune your ears to what I have to say. You must remember the words. You must act upon them, for now I am pointing you toward your greatest destiny—if you read my words aright."

To Alexander this apparition certainly seemed real, as does many a vagrant dream of night; it had, indeed, an appalling reality. The small size of this priest or god was astonishing in the extreme, and must be supernatural. Then there was the broad ray of moonlight that heightened the mystic appearance, surrounding it with an ineffable majesty. Assuredly no harm was intended.

"Very well," said Alexander. "I listen."

"Within the sanctuary of the temple," came the strange message, "lies a gift which Father Amon, the lord of gods and men, has sent for your acceptance. Take it and fear not, but use it aright. This sacred and precious object is god-given. Sit with it alone and look into its heart, where you will see a Sphinx. Study it, listen to what it says to you. Bear in mind that the Great Sphinx faces ever to the east, whence comes all light. In the east lies your destiny, your greatness. Remember this, my son. Your destiny lies in the east with the springing sun, Ra-Horus of the morning strength."

"I hear and obey," murmured Alexander in accents of awe.

"The truth of my words will become evident to you," went on the unearthly visitor. "Son of Amon, greatest of mankind, turn your face ever eastward toward the light! Hold these words in your heart. Remember them when you gaze into the depths of the green stone, the sacred gift of the gods...."

The voice lessened, the figure of the speaker receded—it was gone from the moonray. Alexander leaped upright. He fancied a rustle of robes. One instant he hesitated, then went darting from the room, his voice pealing out to the guards, calling at them to stop anyone who tried to pass, to guard all exits from the house.

LIGHTS SPRANG up, weapons were bared, armed guards came running. No one had passed out below, said the guards, nor had anyone entered. Alexander led a search of the whole place, curious rather than perturbed, found no one at all, and finally admitted that he had had a dream of a ghostly visitor. No one, of course, thought to look up at the palm trees leaning against the house-top. But the search quickly died out at news that it was only because of a dream. In this sacred spot, with visitors invariably rapt and ecstatic, dreams were a shekel a dozen. The startled alarm died out in carefree laughter....

Later next day, Alexander and his staff officers made the ritual visit to the temple and were received by the priests in solemn ceremony. In due time he was conducted alone into the holy of holies by the high priest, who made him welcome in the name of his father Amon-Ra.

The boat or ark, shimmering in its gold-leaf coating, was displayed to him. He gazed curiously at the immense, shield-shaped slab of green stone and at the cavity in its center, now occupied by the lumpish, poorly shaped emerald. This, announced the high priest impressively, was a gift for him that had been sent by the gods in token of their favor. Alexander took the emerald. When he looked carefully at it and saw the image of the Sphinx inside the beryl, he knew what the dream had meant.

He said nothing of the dream, however.

Now came the great thing for which he had tramped these hundreds of miles across desert wastes—his consultation of the oracle. He asked the questions he had prepared, and the priest replied, with the usual ritual, nor was there any trickery considered. The one man had come hither at cost of much hardship in the implicit belief that the god Amon would answer him. The other man undoubtedly believed, with equal firmness, that his replies were inspired by Amon.

The hero was definitely acknowledged as the son of Amon, his career being the best proof of this. He would continue victorious in the coming years, for Amon had conferred upon him the dominion of the known world. Later, Alexander wrote his mother Olympias a full detailed account of his visit to the shrine; and added, in a certain naïve manner, that he had also asked some highly secret questions, promising to retail the god's answers next time he saw her. This statement, in view of her admittedly peculiar share in the whole business, must have left the haughty Queen of Macedonia in considerable suspense.

His errand was finished, and after making his gifts to the shrine, he departed and his staff officers consulted the oracle in turn. To this, Alexander paid scant attention. He went back

*"Within the sanctuary of the temple," came
the strange message, "lies a gift which
Father Amon sent for your acceptance."*

to his quarters and there remained most of the afternoon, clos-
eted with the great emerald given him by the gods.

During the next two days, no more, the illustrious visitor
remained at Siwa, then departed as he had come. His plans
were not secret; his guards knew them and discussed them. His
new city of Alexandria was being laid out; he was anxious to
get back for the foundation ceremony. Also, he had to organize
the rule of Egypt, and having already marched his troops four

thousand miles from home, was anxious to see Greece again. So, with his bearded warriors, he marched away on the northern highway.

F O R A long while Alexander kept the Sphinx emerald beside him, and when across the Euphrates in the Far East, one day gave it to his veteran general, Ptolemy—who was destined to become in later days the King of Egypt.

All this had nothing to do with the dwarf, Psammon. He kept sedulously to his hut while the Greeks were here, not venturing abroad lest he be seen. On the evening after the departure, he came to the temple quarters of the high priest, accepted a glass of wine, and handed over a sealed scroll.

"Send this to Carthage by the next courier, if you will," he said. "That ends it. My task is done. The great man will move his armies eastward, not westward."

The high priest studied him curiously.

"You seem very sure, my son. However, I ask no questions; I well know that your mind is nimbler and deeper than mine. The great man was charmed with the gift given him; it delighted him beyond measure."

"As well it might," said the Little One, a trifle bitterly. "I regret the loss of that emerald, selfishly. It was a wonderful thing. Still, it served its purpose. I am sure that Father Amon put it into my heart to use in that manner."

"And now, I suppose that you'll go to Carthage and some great reward?" asked the high priest.

Psammon sipped at his wine and grunted.

"I? What am I—not even a man!"

"Nonsense. You were greater than the king of kings who was just here, my son."

"True, in one sense. But what rewards can mean anything to me? In the cities, among normal men, I have no place. Money means little or nothing to me; I cannot buy myself a new body, I cannot find a place into which I can fit," said the Little One earnestly. "The only peace and happiness I've ever known has been in this holy place devoted to the service of Amon."

"Then stay here, where you are welcome." The high priest spoke slowly, thoughtfully, watching the agile little face with its queer blue eyes. "These Berber people who live here know you, like you, respect you. The temple is greatly in your debt."

"Yes?" Psammon peered at him sharply. "What is in your mind?"

The high priest smiled. "The priests here with me are good men, but few in number and not particularly blessed with brains, my son. Under Persian rule, the whole priestly organization has fallen to pieces; now the Greeks have taken over Egypt and no one knows what will happen. Did you see those Berbers—light-skinned folk, like you—who came here last week from that oasis to the south?"

Psammon nodded. "I remember a party came, yes."

"They brought with them a young woman; they came seeking help for her. She was twenty years of age, yet no larger than a child—a sweet thing, kind, gentle. Suppose I sent to them, telling them to return here with her? Suppose I arranged for you, as for my own son, a marriage with her. Suppose that you were to remain here, not as a useless visitor, but as a servant of Amon, a temple attendant, a novice priest—I merely show you facets of what is in my mind. You can sketch the rest for yourself."

The priest rose. "Stay, finish your wine, think it over. I must go and see that the temple lights are extinguished. I'll be back soon."

Psammon set down the cup, folded his hands, stared at the lamp as he sat alone.

It was real—incredible, but real. He had never even dreamed of such a thing. A novice priest—a temple attendant! A wife—physically cursed of the gods, like himself, yet like himself perfect and infinitely blessed in spirit—why not? This high priest, he well knew, was never hasty or ill-considered in any matter; if he favored the match, it might be accounted a favor-able one.

No one in gaudy, cheap, self-seeking Carthage had ever breathed such kindness to him; and Psammon gulped a little at the thought of it. Then the big thing took hold of him.

A NOVICE priest in the temple service—his whole life given to the worship of Amon here in this spot of sanctity so far removed from the noisy world! The mere mention of such a possibility by the high priest showed that it must have been well weighed and approved beforehand. Size meant nothing in a priest. A lifetime of peaceful service, of useful living—why, the prospect was breathtaking! In those words was offered a future, such a future as Psammon had never envisioned or hoped for!

Presently the high priest returned, seated himself, and looked at his visitor. Psammon sat silent, rapt, unmoving. The lamplight sparkled on tears stealing out upon his cheeks.

"Well, my son? Have you thought about it?"

"There is something—I must tell you," said the Little One unsteadily. "Something that I did the other night—"

"Wait." The priest lifted a hand to check the words. "Did your action bring harm to anyone, to yourself?"

"No."

"Then it was not wrong. A thing is wrong only if it brings harm. This is no excuse for crime, my son; indeed, the prospect of how our actions may bring harm is appalling. Tell me nothing; the less I know the better. I am quite certain that the gods work their will in singular ways past our understanding. Someone mentioned a dream that came to the great Alexander while he slept here—a very odd dream about the god Amon in most unusual form. I made no inquiries; it was not my affair. None the less, Father Amon is quite able to work out the lives of those who trust in him. You have a firm, superior type of mind, my son. I shall be glad to welcome you to our little circle of life, here in the desert."

Psammon lifted his head, brushed the tears from his cheeks and smiled.

"I—I would not trade places now," he said, "with the greatest man in the world!"

V

THE SON OF JULIUS CAESAR

These Sphinx Emerald stories are a veritable
Outline of History. Here the tragic young
Cæsarion dominates the scene.

THE FINEST house in Berenice—not so very fine, at that—stood on the sands above the harbor, looking out to sea: the Red Sea, blistering hot in this midsummer. Behind the town the desert mountains reached back to mid-Egypt. The caravan trail came from Coptos on the Nile here to Berenice, the route of all commerce between Egypt and the Far East. Here in the shallow harbor of Berenice ships were crowded, awaiting the July change of monsoon. Then for six months the winds would blow eastward, the merchant traders coursing before it to far India, whence they would return when the monsoon changed again and blew westward for another six months.

The house was stocked with luxuries for the boy, his tutors and his guards, who stayed here waiting for the ships to move. The tutor Rhodon was a pleasant, amiable weakling of forty-five, a Greek; the soldiers who guarded the house had small respect for him. These soldiers were Romans, men who had served Marc Antony; and they were blindly devoted to the boy. He was seventeen; he had passed the ceremonies of manhood, and had been crowned as co-ruler of Egypt with his mother Cleopatra; but to these hardened legionaries, he was "the boy." When they saw him pass, they stiffly saluted, and the murmured Roman words came to their lips:

"Son of the god!"

For Julius Cæsar had been deified and was worshiped as a

"Have you a letter for me?" the lad asked.

*"No," replied Chandra Ghose. "Only a
message—of three words: Trust no one!"*

god. This boy was like him in every way. He was, in fact Cæsar, the son of Julius Cæsar, though he was usually known by the affectionate diminutive of the name, Cæsarion.

Yet, though Cæsarion was son of the divine Julius, and King of Egypt, with many another shadowy title, it was the tutor Rhodon who was nominally in command here. Cleopatra and Antony were in Alexandria, besieged by the vindictive and ambitious Octavian; in desperation Cleopatra had sent her son here, with immense treasures, to join the fleet for India, and to seek refuge in Hindustan, where there were no ambitious Romans. They had come. The ships were ready, with the treasure on board—but until the monsoon broke, could not move....

"We never spoke of this in Alexandria, so I don't understand it very well," said Cæsarion. He and Rhodon sat in the patio of the house, nominally reading Homer. "You say that Octavian is the nephew and the son of my father?"

"Your father adopted him in the Roman fashion, yes," said Rhodon, "but acknowledged you as his son before he died. So Antony is dead! Poor Antony—he was a noble fellow in his day."

A courier had come that morning with the dread news from Alexandria.

"Will Octavian harm my mother?" Cæsarion asked. "She always said he was a vicious beast. They called him 'the Executioner' in Rome."

"No, he'll not harm her; she's perfectly safe." Rhodon stretched leisurely. "He's not a bad sort, really. He's Cæsar now, of course."

"But I'm Cæsar!"

"Yes. And you're King of Egypt; but Octavian has Egypt, and you haven't. We'll make up for that in India. I have letters from your mother to all the princes there, if you decide to go there."

"If?" Cæsarion looked keenly at the Greek, who smiled.

"Yes. It's for you to say, of course. We'll know by the next courier what's taken place in Alexandria."

"I'm going down to the shore and think. I want to be alone," said Cæsarion.

He rose and left the palace, bidding the guards stay where they were. Trudging through the hot sand, he went down to the beach, where the tide was out, and sat by the water, looking out at the listless ships.

Indeed he was like his father, finely carven of features, hard-limbed, driven by a fierce will and resolution; yet at the moment he was bewildered by destiny. He knew that he was the dream of his mother's life. For him Cleopatra had plundered Egypt, had gathered this fleet, had made certain that by her defiance of the conquering Octavian he might safely get away to the Far East, with followers and treasure fitting to a king.

But now—this news about Antony's death was grave. It would be days ere the monsoon broke, and days might count heavily. Nor was Cæsarion at all sure that flight was his wisest course. He did not know fear. Assuredly he had no fear of Octavian, the money-lender's son who had wormed his way into the family of Cæsar by marriage and by adoption, a cold, cheaply conniving rascal, and a coward. Such a man could not hurt the son of the divine Julius. According to the philosophers, a man was the only person who could harm himself; no other could.

So, thought Cæsarion, it was odd that Rhodon seemed to think Octavian a great and splendid person. Rhodon, whom his mother trusted, ought to know the truth. With a sigh, Cæsarion stirred, took from his girdle a gem that flashed with pale green fire in the sunlight, and holding it in his palm, began to study it.

The gem was an emerald that Cleopatra had given to him when he was made co-ruler of Egypt with her. Some said it was from the ancient crown jewels. There was no other like it in the world. It was a natural cabochon, of second-rate shape and color. Poor heroic, foolish Antony had said it was accursed; but Cleopatra had loved it, and so did Cæsarion. But not for itself, nor for the thing in it.

Amazingly, when one gazed into the great gem through an enlarging glass, a shape appeared in it, clear-cut and distinct. The flaws and bubbles contained in this, as in all emeralds, came together at one point and assumed the exact shape of the Sphinx. Cæsarion had heard there were two identical Sphinxes, one by the Pyramids, and another, almost forgotten, in the desert hills east of the Nile, near the petrified forest. This bit of beryl was a freak of nature—but it had also something more, something that fascinated him and gripped him in steely hands. It had a power.

HE STARED at the stone now, as always, with a fearful and complete absorption. It stirred him out of himself; it wakened strange, wonderful things within him, caught at his imagination like a blast of clarion trumpets. Antony had cursed it furiously. A priest had said that it held the magic of the gods. His mother had called it most beautiful, as in fact it was. But to Cæsar's son it was magnificent and splendid beyond words. It awed him, enthralled him, brought majestic thoughts and fantasies to his mind. It spoke to him of the great father he had never known in the flesh—the man who was now worshiped as a god.

In sheer sober fact, this Sphinx emerald had been famed in history for its hypnotic power, which was never twice alike. It stripped the beholder of poses and drew from him the secrets of his inmost being, whether noble, glorious, base or cowardly. It called to the surface the real person, the character at bottom. To the son of Cæsar, it whispered of grandeur and authority and command, shaming him bitterly for being the fugitive that he now was....

When he had gazed into the great green stone for a lengthy while, he tucked it away and rose, and returned to the hilltop house. When he came back to the courtyard, where his tutor sat writing, there was a glory in his face that made the guards stare after him, astonished.

"Rhodon!" His voice held a bite—it was the voice of Julius. He sat and caressed the cat which had joined him. It was an enormous sacred cat such as was worshiped at Bubastis in Lower Egypt, and had been given him there as they passed through. The animal had some affection for him.

"Tell me something: My mother—Antony—all of them hate and fear Octavian terribly. They said Egypt was not safe for me, that he would pursue me to the world's end, that only in India could I find refuge, that he means to kill me because I am the real Cæsar, son of Julius. Now that we're far from Alexandria, ready to depart for India with the ships—I ask you, are these things true?"

Rhodon, troubled by this appeal, fingered his chin thoughtfully. He was an honest fellow in his own way.

"Well, Cæsar, at least they thought them true," he responded. "Antony fought this man for the world—and lost. Until he began to grow old and dull, he had every talent and gift and ability, and the greatest luck in everything. Your mother had the one thing he lacked—something which most men lack; and that is loyalty. In her eyes Octavian was what they called him in Rome—the Executioner, who slew everyone in his road to power. He was a real friend to Cæsar, who adopted him in return. Your mother saw him only as a rascal, a cheap and merciless cheat from the gutter. She told the truth, as she saw it…. I'm trying to be quite honest, you see."

"Then try harder," snapped Cæsarion. "I know what they said and thought. I'm asking now what you yourself think, regardless of prejudice? Do you hold this man Octavian to be a scoundrel?"

Rhodon smiled uneasily.

"No scoundrel is such, Cæsar, entirely. The vilest gutter-rat may show charity or kindness. The noblest prince may be guilty of the lowest deeds at times. This man has great luck, great ambition, and a certain hard ability. You, as the true heir of Julius, stand in his way; a dangerous place indeed. However, since you're thinking about such matters, show me your mind. What do you yourself think about him?"

"I'll tell you," said Cæsarion, a flash in his eye. "Octavian has won his way to the top in Rome. He has mastered Antony and my mother; he has Egypt. A man can't get to such position by being a fool or a coward or rascal. He must have character, strength, nobility of a sort. Luck alone can't make or break a man."

"True, yes," murmured Rhodon. Perhaps he was conscious of his own weakness as compared with the vibrant energy of this young man.

"And am I, Cæsar, to run away from the shadow of this false Cæsar?" Scorn and anger blazed in the words. "Did my father, Julius, earn his fame by running and hiding his head like an ostrich? I've no ambition to fight him, of course—I've nothing with which to fight him, and no reason for it either. If I thought he'd grant me some small place of my own where I could live and study in peace, I'd take it gladly."

RHODON LOOKED startled. "Careful, my son! Octavian has no loyalty to anything, I warn you! No loyalty to the gods, to family ties, to anything at all!"

"And can you tell me such a man rules the world? I don't believe it. Such a thing is in itself a contradiction," snapped Cæsarion.

Rhodon gave him an uneasy glance. "I wish you'd stop playing with that accursed emerald," he grunted. "I agree with Antony that the stone has a devil in it."

Cæsarion's features softened.

"I agree with my mother that it has a high nobility in it that neither you nor Antony could ever comprehend," he said with flat finality.... "No word yet from the ship captains about sailing?"

"We can't sail till the monsoon breaks."

*When these hardened legionaries saw
him pass they saluted, and the words
came to their lips: "Son of the god!"*

"Even if we want to sail! I'm not sure that I'm sailing, Rhodon.
You may yet learn to your surprise that your pupil has Cæsar's
will, no less than his name," said Cæsarion abruptly, and turned
into the house. Rhodon looked after him with eyes of fear. This
young fellow had a mind of his own, certainly, and might kick
over the traces....

Next morning came, with never a wisp of cloud to break the
heat-filled coppery sky. Cæsarion and a number of the guards
took to the water, shark-knives at their waists, and swam out
to the ships among them; but the water itself was warm and
lifeless, and the sport palled on them. They came ashore, slipped
into cool garments, and then, hearing the shouts of arrival,

turned to the town, where a caravan was just coming in from
Coptos, on the Nile below Thebes. Such caravans arrived almost
every day with goods and lading for the ships.

In the marketplace of the hot, sun-smitten little town, they
found it. With the horses and asses and men there was one
camel—a strange beast of burden, almost unknown as yet in
Egypt; and everyone was gathered to stare at him. The rider
was a tall, one-eyed, dark man. He smiled when Cæsarion came
up to stare curiously at the camel, and spoke in very good Greek.

"So, young sir, you stare at the strange beast? Well, they're
common in other lands; and the Romans, I hear, mean to put
them to work in Egypt. Ugly, eh?"

"Hideous," agreed Cæsarion; "yet somehow attractive, like
ugly men."

"Quite true." The one eye peered sharply. "Perhaps you can
tell me where to find in this town a certain party to whom I
have an errand. I have goods to go aboard the ships yonder,
before I return to Coptos, and also have a letter to deliver to
one Rhodon, a Greek. It is a letter from some person at court—
the former court."

Cæsarion turned and met the one sparkling, glinting eye.
His own eyes were very bright and quick. He pointed to the
villa on the hill above town.

"That's his house, for the moment. He's my tutor."

"Oh! Indeed!" The dark man's tone changed. Astonishment
came into his one eye.

"A negligent tutor, to let his pupil wander about the place
thus," he said, in his voice a subtle play of meaning. "Sir, my
name is Chandra Ghose. I am a trader of Alexandria, though
I was born in farther India." His voice dropped almost to a
whisper. "Should I salute you as do the Egyptians, with both
palms down?"

Cæsarion met the one firm, glinting eye. He caught the al-
lusion instantly. Only a Pharaoh was saluted in that

fashion—and he himself was a Pharaoh, the last Pharaoh of Egypt. He gathered that this Indian was a friend.

"You certainly should not," he replied, laughing a little. A slight stutter crept into his words. It came only at excited moments, an inheritance from his long-dead father. "It would make people stare. Have you a letter for me also?" the lad asked.

"No," replied Chandra Ghose. "Only a message—a little one of three words: *Trust no one*. A woman gave me the message, and repeated the two last words—*no one!*"

Cæsarion met the one glinting eye and nodded.

"Thank you," he said. "I'll take you to Rhodon, if you like."

The Hindu joined him.

"Careless guards, careless tutor," he said, low-voiced.

"What need to be careful?"

"I'll tell you. When first I came to Alexandria, a year or more ago, I fell in with a retired Roman soldier. He was an old fellow who had served with Julius Cæsar in Gaul, wherever that is, and had been invalided. Well, we went to a ceremony not many months ago. We saw the crowning of young Cæsarion. This old fellow—his name was Aulus something—nearly had a fit. He gripped my arm and panted. He had known Julius intimately, he told me, and then pointed to the new co-ruler. 'That is no boy yonder,' said he; 'it is the divine Julius himself, in person!' The story might interest you."

The story not only interested Cæsarion; it delighted him beyond measure; it complimented and excited him, as did any intimate little story about the famed father he had never known. He took the arm of the tall brown man and pressed it.

"Thank you, thank you," he said. "I am pleased, of course! Tell me—a courier came yesterday with the sad news about Antony. Tell me—"

He paused as though unable to form the question.

Chandra Ghose nodded. "I was still at Alexandria when it happened, then took a fast boat upriver to join my caravan at Coptos. Yes, he is dead. Why do you call it sad to die? In my

This news about Anthony's death was
grave.... Nor was Cæsarion at all sure
that flight was his wisest course.

country, we know that death is an easy thing; it is birth which
is hard. Of course, no one likes to die; but after all, it is a natural,
an inevitable thing, a kind thing like Karma."

"What is that? I never heard of it."

"Some call it Fate, though we know it to be far more than
fate—not a blind thing, but one of old purpose," said the Hindu.
"The will of the gods, which is never blind or meaningless.
Destiny were a better word."

"Oh, I understand that, of course!" exclaimed Cæsarion. "A
kind thing, you say?"

"Precisely, young sir. The Autocrator"—this was the title by
which Antony had been known in Egypt—"is dead, and far
better so. Is it not better to die at the height of fame, like the
Greek hero Achilles, than to live on through old age in shame?

Die, face the judgment of the gods, face the future in the other world—why, that's a little thing! A brave thing, perhaps, yet a little thing to us folk of India."

While thus talking, they had come to the house occupied by Rhodon. Cæsarion halted.

"Wait, before we go in," he said. "I started to ask you about the queen. She gave you that message?"

"No, it came through one of her faithful women," said Chandra Ghose. He hesitated, then went on: "I understand that she departed by her own choice, rather than face the shame which Octavian destined for her."

"Departed?" Cæsarion had turned quickly. "Departed? Oh, surely—"

The dark man nodded. "It is hard to be born; it is easy to die," he repeated.

For one moment Cæsarion stood as though paralyzed; then he came to life, and beckoned one of the guards, who approached.

"Take this man to Rhodon," he ordered, then turned and strode away into the house.

It was the bitterest moment of his life. The little queen, his mother, was dead. She had gone, after assuring his safety and future. Those ships in harbor held what treasures of Egypt she could gather for him—everything for him. The little laughing queen whom everyone loved, was gone—gone into the darkness.

He locked himself in his room. The cat Ptah came and sat at his door, unblinking, but no one sought to disturb him. The unexpected sharp news from Alexandria left everyone stupefied. The impossible had happened: Cleopatra the queen, last of the Ptolemy line, was dead.

Rhodon, at first stunned, quickly recovered and kept Chandra Ghose in talk, kept him for the noon meal, kept him afterward, rather drawn to him. A peculiar fellow, this Rhodon, and not a forceful man. He had won many prizes at school, had taken up tutoring, and because of his command of the ancient Greek tongue had been given the post of tutor to Cæsarion. He had known the queen very well.

"I think," Chandra Ghose told him, "you'll have a visit from a fellow named Aurone. I don't know if he's a Greek or not, but I fancy he's a rascal; he has a bad reputation. He was with our caravan, and was heartily inquisitive about everyone here at Berenice, asking me if it were true that Cæsar's son were here, and so forth. He smells in my nostrils, and I warn you to be careful."

"May the gods repay your kindness!" said Rhodon. "Do you sail with the ships?"

"Certainly not," replied the Hindu. "I put my goods aboard,

check everything with my supercargo, and in three days shall return to Coptos, where my boat awaits me for Alexandria. What is that little tiger I saw when I arrived?"

"A cat. These Egyptians worship certain cats at a place called Bubastis. This one is of the sacred breed, and was presented to my pupil there. The animal is furred, and suffers here from the heat."

Chandra Ghose pressed for information about the cat-worship. Rhodon could not give it; he knew almost nothing of the Egyptians or their involved religion. No Greek did. Alexandria, its rulers, its general population, all were pure Greek. The city was cut off from Egypt and had few contacts with the land it ruled....

Late in the afternoon, when the siesta hour had passed, Aurone came to the house and asked for Rhodon. He was confident, assured, rather sly, and frankly stated that he was no Greek but a Cilician. Rhodon disliked and distrusted him at sight.

"What business do you have with me?" he demanded.

"Lord, I need your signature and that of Lord Cæsar to a receipt," Aurone responded, with a wink. "It was suspected that you were here. I was sent to give you certain epistles. The receipt must bear your two signatures. The letters are to you both."

Rhodon was startled. Letters? More letters? Did bad news have no end?

"Who sent you?" he inquired.

"My lord, I was not paid to talk, but to deliver the letters, which will speak for themselves. In fact, I saw them written and signed."

"Wait here," said Rhodon. They were in the cool courtyard. "I'll go and find my pupil."

On the way, he found and girded on his sword, a leaf-shaped Egyptian weapon. He was no swordsman, but anyone could use this cruelly efficient blade. He saw Ptah at the door of Cæsarion, tail curled about feet, and knocked.

Cæsarion opened the door. He was pale; his usually bright and burning eyes were dull and swollen.

"There is a caller, a fellow named Aurone, a Cilician," said Rhodon. "He bears letters but will not deliver them without our signatures. Are you able to come and see him?"

"Able? I'm a man, not a child," said Cæsarion calmly. "Letters from whom?"

"The fellow won't say. Chandra Ghose warned me against him; we must have a care. It may be some trick. He may be an assassin, or a spy sent to discover your whereabouts."

Cæsarion smiled scornfully. "Poor Rhodon: you look flushed and ill, and no wonder. Don't you think I'm capable of dealing with any Roman agent or assassin? So the trader from India warned you? Good. I like that dark man. He rings true; his one eye has an honest spark of flame in it. Come along, and we'll see this Cilician. Who could be sending us letters, if *she* is gone?"

Rhodon was startled by the change in the speaker. The boy had become a man; grief had worked a hardening change in him. His voice had firmed and deepened, his manner had become imperious. At the door he stooped and touched the cat Ptah, who rubbed head against his leg.

"Too hot for you here," he said. "I know it. You're another reason."

"Reason?" Rhodon caught at the word. "For what?"

"For what I intend to see you about in the morning, when we've slept over this news. Come along."

Cæsarion led the way back to the patio. Rhodon followed, wondering at the change in him. Aurone was sprawled in a chair, lazily. He glanced up at their approach, looking at Cæsarion with quick sly gaze.

Cæsarion halted. "You are the messenger?" His voice almost crackled. "Do you want a whip over your back to teach you respect, fellow?"

Aurone sprang up and made respectful salute.

"Now hand over the letters, if you bear any," snapped Cæsarion. "You shall have your receipt if I choose to give it."

Aurone, looking like a whipped dog, humbly saluted and produced a small scroll. Cæsarion took it, saw that it was addressed to himself and Rhodon, and broke the seal that tied it. He opened it and glanced at the Greek writing, looked again, and read it through. Then he handed it to Rhodon and gave his attention to the messenger.

"Where did you get the epistle? Speak fully."

Aurone cringed. "Lord, at the Lochias palace. I was taken there. I saw the letter written. The general sealed it—"

"What general?"

"I do not know. He had the red cloak of a Roman general. They called him Octavian."

Cæsarion exchanged a glance with Rhodon. Octavian, or Cæsar, would naturally be dwelling in the Lochias palace, that ancient regal palace of the Ptolemies.

Cæsarion called a guard, and pointed to Aurone.

"Take this man to a scribe. When he gets his receipt written, bring him back and we will put our seals to it."

AURONE WAS led away. Rhodon, having read the letter, turned to Cæsarion, his flushed features excited. He did look ill; fever, perhaps.

"It's from Cæsar, yes," he exclaimed. "Yet I can't believe it."

"He calls me Cæsar!" broke out Cæsarion. "Did you note that? Return in safety, and I can have my heritage—my heritage! It's a safe-conduct, Rhodon! It promises everything I want!"

"Promises are cheap," murmured Rhodon. "Don't believe him. Rather, credit the last message that came: *Trust no one.* That way lies safety."

"Safety! Caution! Prudence! Security! By the gods, who wants to live a life of security!" burst forth Cæsarion with impetuous force, passion in his face. "Well enough for you—you're a Greek. I'm a Roman, the son of Julius Cæsar! Security? Hell

*Rhodon rode like a madman. He knew that emissaries
of Octavian must even now be seeking him.*

take it! Life isn't won by cowards who seek only security—it
must be won by overcoming obstacles! It's no end in itself. My
mother's dead. I'm my own master now, with my own life to
live. I obeyed her. Now I obey my own heart."

"Sleep on it," weakly advised the Greek.

"Right. We'll do that. I want nothing to eat, anyway—I'm
off for a walk, then to bed and seek what counsel the gods will
send.... Oh, here's our man."

Aurone was brought in with his receipt. Rhodon and
Cæsarion applied their seals to it, and the messenger
departed.

So did Cæsarion, with the "little tiger" stalking after him,

tail a-twitch. He went to the lonely shore and sat there through the twilight, with the cat in his arms—the only thing that loved him now. He sat until the far sea darkened, and the stars twinkled above, and lights sprang in the town; then he rose and went striding up toward the lights and came to where animals and bales of goods stood about campfires while men ate. He looked for the one-eyed man and found him, and came and sat beside him.

"When," he asked, "do you return to Alexandria? Or do you return?"

"Yes. I have a boat waiting at Coptos," said Chandra Ghose. "I leave here in three days. Because of the desert heat, we leave at sunset and travel at night."

"Leave tomorrow night instead. I and my guards go with you. Name any price you desire. It can be done; so do it. We'll need horses."

Chandra Ghose sat motionless. "I have an agent; I can leave things to him, yes. It can be done," he said slowly. "But this letter-carrier saw you only this afternoon. Now you suddenly decide to change plans and go back. I distrust that man; I distrust your wisdom."

"Do you refuse?"

"No. Ask me the same thing in the morning, and I'll agree. In sleep the gods give counsel."

Cæsarion understood. The man was a true friend; he wanted only to be certain.

"Thank you." He stood up. "I shall come to you in the morning. You speak truth."

He turned away and went to the house on the high sands. He spoke with one of the guards; Rhodon, he learned, was shaking with fever and shock. He got a lighted lamp, went to his own room, and lighted the larger lamp here. The cat Ptah came in after him and curled up in a chair.

Cæsarion sat at the table. He got out the queer emerald with the Sphinx-figure inside it, and placed it under the lamp to catch the full glow of light. From a chest he took a doubly convex glass which enlarged objects, and began to study the emerald through this. He saw, not a little stone he could hold in his palm, but a huge expanse of shimmering green spaces, and his breath began to come faster as he looked.

No hint here of grief. They were dead—his mother and the Autocrator both—but of this nothing came into his brain. An easy thing, death, the Hindu trader had said. In the green depths gathered other senses, waking very different thoughts in him, appealing to different phases of him. He was the son of the divine Julius. Octavian, if made aware that he sought nothing except his heritage from that Julius, could not refuse it; had not the man promised him safe-conduct?

The shameful sense of flight, of hiding, completely left him. In its stead came the grateful idea of dealing with the greatest man in the world, Octavian. This was his right. He was not destined to treat with little people, with lesser men. The son of Cæsar must meet with Cæsar himself, face to face, as with an equal. There lay justice for one who sought only equity and his

Roman heritage. Octavian undoubtedly realized this himself, and in consequence had promised him safety if he returned. The greatest man on earth could not be a cheap and petty rascal!

Thus spake the stone, the glinting depths of beryl, as though the Sphinx within it had found tongue. Cæsarion had never felt the power so firmly, so surely; the rush of thoughts swept over him and roused him out of himself. He leaped up and went to Rhodon's room, close by. He saw Rhodon reading by a night lamp, and went to him.

"Not asleep? Feeling better? Good. Do you want to return with me to Alexandria?"

Rhodon laid aside the scroll. "I cannot, my son. My old fever has come back. I'm frightfully weak tonight. Have you decided to go back, despite everything?"

"Because of everything." Cæsarion spoke crisply, decisively, yet calmly. "I know now that my mind will be the same tomorrow, Rhodon."

"I can't prevent you or forbid you."

"No. That safe-conduct from Octavian changes all our plans. I'll go to him and see what he has to say. I'll claim my heritage from him. With my little mother dead, I'm the sole King of Egypt. He can have Egypt. I want no more than some little quiet corner of the world, and recognition by Rome as Cæsar's son."

"It's not a great thing to ask," Rhodon said. "Yet is it wise? Think of this tonight, my son. Here you have escape assured, immense treasures, a clear future—"

"And shame," said Cæsarion, smiling. "A heavy burden to bear! No. I am Cæsar, I shall act as Cæsar would have acted in my place. Besides, think of Ptah! The poor cat suffers here in this hamlet at the world's edge. I shall take him and leave him at Bubastis, where the Nile tempers the heat."

Rhodon made a helpless gesture.

"She is dead; Antony is dead—does anything matter now?"

"Cheer up! Guard the treasure. If I don't return, take of it what you like, and go whither you like. I leave tomorrow evening with Chandra Ghose. See you tomorrow," said Cæsarion cheerfully. "And I'll leave you a gift, old friend. You may not like it, yet it will serve to remind you of me, and of my mother. Good night."

FEVER CAME back on Rhodon full force that night, and with morning he was tossing in delirium. With the following morning it had passed, leaving him clear-headed but quite weak. In the afternoon the captain of the guards came to him, anxiously.

"Lord, I cannot keep it from you," he said. "Cæsarion took Plancus and Caius with him, ordered the rest of us to remain here with you, and departed with that one-eyed trader, the other night. He took the cat with him also."

"Then it cannot be helped," said Rhodon. "But he had a letter from Octavian, promising him safety."

The soldier spat. "A promise from the Executioner is a bag of empty wind. We can still mount and ride after them, if you order it."

"He is Cæsar, and King of Egypt," said Rhodon. "Let the gods who caused this happening look to their own work."

Two days later Rhodon was up and around, when one of the guards reported that he had just seen in the village the Cilician, Aurone, who had brought the letters. He summoned the captain to go with him, girt on his sword, and they went into the town. Sure enough, they came upon Aurone at the tavern, deep in wine. Rhodon bared the leaf-shaped sword, and the fellow shrank from him in fear.

"Spare me, lord, spare me!" he cried. "I have repented the ill I did—"

"What ill? Name it." Rhodon spoke coldly. "Was that letter false?"

"I know not," replied Aurone, trembling and spilling his wine. "The Roman general who paid me to bring it—he ordered me to wait here; if the letter brought the boy to him, I would receive double pay. He is—he is sending soldiers—"

Rhodon drew back his sword for the thrust, then checked himself.

"Vile dog that you are," he said, sheathing the weapon, "your death would not undo it. I leave you to the gods and your own sorry conscience."

He beckoned the captain, went out, and covered his face. But the captain, who was a veteran of Cæsar's 37th Legion, stepped quickly back into the tavern, and presently returned, wiping his sword. He, at least, indulged no scruples.

OCTAVIAN SENDING soldiers here? Fear seized the tutor at this information. He went home sweating. They gave him a little packet Cæsarion had left for him. In his own room, Rhodon unwrapped it, and the Sphinx emerald fell into his hand. He looked at it a long while; he was afraid to die. At last he rose, trembling, filled a purse with money, stole out of the house, went into the town and secured a horse.

He rode like a madman along the caravan road to Coptos and the Nile.

He reached Coptos, a haggard wreck, and took passage on a boat bound downstream for Alexandria. He let his beard grow, took another name, kept to himself. The good river air banished his illness. He tried to get news of Cæsarion, but could learn nothing at all. In fact, he was almost afraid to ask. He knew that emissaries of Octavian must even now be seeking him.

At Alexandria he was astounded by the flood of propaganda going around, spread by the Romans. Calumny of every sort was being heaped upon Cleopatra and upon Antony. The good, the virtuous, the noble Octavian was the hope of Egypt, the savior of the world; Augustus, they were already calling him.

Rhodon lingered not. Under his new name he got passage with a caravan bound for Syria. It was leaving on the morrow, And then, as he walked down the great Canopus Avenue that bisected the city like a sword, he came face to face with Chandra Ghose.

Despite the beard, the entire disguise, the one-eyed Hindu knew him instantly, and crooked a finger.

"Come along to my bazaar. There's a huge reward offered for you. With me you're safe."

Rhodon obeyed in miserable terror; his nerves were cracking up. Chandra Ghose sat with him in the cool rear room of the bazaar, dimly lit, and food and wine were brought. They ate and drank; upon Rhodon's lips trembled the one question which had no answer. The Hindu nodded.

"Yes. I know. I witnessed everything. I'll tell you about it."

This is what he told:

Upon reaching Alexandria, Cæsarion made no secret of his presence but went straight to the Lochias Palace and demanded audience with Octavian. There was a delay, and finally he was led to the audience hall. Upon the throne at the far end sat a man pallid and spotted of skin, a man who shunned sunlight and cold water alike. He kept his guards close.

A murmur passed through the ranks of soldiers and officers as Cæsarion walked toward the throne on the dais, where he himself had sat as King of Egypt. For he held his head high; his eyes were bright and sparkling; there was a slight confident smile upon his lips, and many of those present had intimately known another like him.

"The divine Julius himself!" went the awed whisper.

Octavian also had known that other. As he watched the approaching figure, his cold eyes became touched with fear and his cheeks grew more sallow. He must have known that this was a moment when anything might happen; one word from the boy, and half these Romans would draw sword for him in hysteric ecstasy.

Cæsarion halted at the edge of the dais and threw up a hand in salute. There was something gayly boyish about his looks, his words.

"Ave, Cæsar!" he cried. "I, who am also Cæsar, salute you! I have come to accept your promised protection, and to claim my heritage from the divine Julius my father!"

A stillness had settled upon the hall; in it was distinctly heard the uneven, sniffling breath of Octavian as the Roman tried to make reply, and could not. With an effort, his chill voice at last managed slow words.

"It—it is dangerous for two Cæsars to be in the world at the same time."

The cold eyes, the cold voice, seemed to shock Cæsarion with disillusion. In this instant he must have seen the whole truth. His shoulders squared, his features changed and hardened. He looked at the sallow, pimply man before him. Scorn and contempt glittered in his bright eyes, and bitter understanding.

Octavian, fearing a word too many, crooked a shaky finger at the guards.

"Quickly! Do it now—quickly!" he croaked—and they obeyed him.

THIS WAS the tale Chandra Ghose told. Rhodon put his pallid face in his hands, and his shoulders shook as broken words came to his lips. Then he gulped wine and tried to pull himself together.

"Let me—let me show you something." He made a pitiful effort to change the subject and tugged at his girdle. "He left it for me—his mother had given it to him. Look."

He brought out the emerald and tumbled it on the table. The one eye of Chandra Ghose swooped upon it. A look, a swift examination....

"By the thunderbolt of Indra!" exclaimed the trader in awe. "This is a wonder of the world! It will make you wealthy—I can give you a huge sum for it—"

Rhodon shivered.

"Be quiet," he said. "I am going to hide myself in Syria. What good is money to me? This is a memory of those whom I loved and served. I do not like it, but I shall cherish it while I live. And when I come to die, perhaps I shall return to Egypt with it."

His words died away. He took back the emerald, wrapped it in its cloth, and put it into his girdle again. He gulped more wine. The tension was broken now, and he began to speak of Cæsarion's death. A frightful thing, he said, a sad thing.

"Don't be absurd," struck in Chandra Ghose, almost in contempt. His voice firmed and echoed in the little room. "Nothing of the sort. The boy would have lived amid wars and tumults; he would have suffered spiritually. Our plans are human and fallible; those of Karma have a hidden purpose, one wiser than we realize."

He paused briefly, sipped his wine, then continued in words that Rhodon was to carry with him into Syria and obscurity:

"A sad tale, at first glance. Yet in reality it is one of those things we cannot explain, which work for good in a way we cannot see. There lies the truth."

In later days Rhodon wrote down all these things; but the Romans got wind of the manuscript and destroyed it. So they thought, at least; yet a copy survived.

VI

THE EYE OF THE SUN

This series about the Sphinx Emerald constitutes,
as has been said, a veritable Outline of History—
or perhaps "Highlights of History" would be more
accurate. For this reason the greatest event in
all history could not be left out. Here, then, we
see the Holy Family during the exile in Egypt.

I N T H E time when Cnæus Gabinius ruled Egypt as Prefect for Augustus, you might have noticed an old man with white hair and tattered garments, who drove a skinny donkey along the trail. This was in Lower Egypt, some twelve miles from the fortress of Babylon on the Nile. Not on the river itself, but on the great canal which connected the Nile with the sea—part of the great maze of channels and canals cutting up the lower country. One could float down by boat to Alexandria and the Bitter Lakes from almost anywhere here.

The old wanderer came to a strange spot, where sandy mounds, half-buried buildings and statues denoted a former city of the Egyptians, its ruins spreading for miles around. A miserable little native huddle of huts stood by the water, but this offered no asylum for a weary old man.

Something else, luckily, caught his eye. Ahead showed two obelisks of fine Aswan granite topped with copper caps. Near them was a sycamore of light tender green; by its gnarled surface roots a spring showed. Beside this stood the tent of some vagrants, an ass staked out close by.

With a grunt of relief the old man, feeble and barely able to totter along, turned to this spring. His animal carried empty water-skins and a packet of food, nothing else. They had evidently come in by the Syrian Desert trail. The old man himself carried a jewel that was one of the world's great gems, but no one would have suspected it. Upon nearing the spring he saw a woman and her baby sitting under the tree. Her husband, a bearded man who wore Jewish dress, was making repairs to a saddle.

At the scent of water, the skinny donkey quickened pace. The old man stumbled, caught at the animal, and fell. He tried to rise and could not, merely clawing the sand in futile effort. The Jew came hastening to his side and helped him gain his feet. A kindly fellow, this Jew, with cheerful smile.

"Here y'are, Father," he said encouragingly. "Come over to the shade and rest. I'll bring you water. Had a bit too much sun, haven't you?"

To one who had come through the burning desert afoot, water meant life; but shade answered a terrible heart-craving. The old man sank down beside the mother and child, and his eyes closed; he was weak and pallid and spent. The Jew brought a gourd with water; and his wife, a young and extremely pretty woman, held it to the old man's lips. He swallowed, and after a little sat up and looked around.

"May the gods give you blessings for your kindness," he said.

"The gods?" The Jew spoke in surprise. "Then you are not a Hebrew?"

"No, my friend. I am a Greek, Rhodon by name. Thirty years ago, when Queen Cleopatra died and the Romans took Egypt, I lived not far from here. I know this place well—one of the famous ancient cities of the world."

The Jew laughed shortly. "This heap of sand, a city? You jest. Those Egyptians in the huts yonder are barbarous, incivil folk."

*Rufus met a detachment of soldiers. "My lord,"
said the apologetic officer, "the commandant
desires speech with you at once."*

The old man lifted a shriveled hand to point at the closer obelisk.

"That was erected twenty-five hundred years ago by the Pharaoh Usertsen I, to mark this great city of Heliopolis, the center of sun-worship. It was the city where Joseph lived; in your scriptures it is named On. And today the Bedawin call this spring Ain el Shams—the Eye of the Sun."

The three fell into general talk. The Jew was named Yusef and his wife Miriam; they were simple, kindly folk, and greatly admired this learned old Greek who had lived so long in their own country. He had been at Jerusalem for many years, a scribe, supporting himself by reading and writing and teaching. Neither he nor they had any good words for King Herod, who was a mere Roman puppet.

Old Rhodon took a great fancy to the child, a bright-eyed, laughing babe of some months. The infant played with his finger, and he smiled.

"A fine boy," he said. "I could show him something that would make him chuckle! But a fine boy—that doesn't mean a fine man!"

"Why not, good sir?" demanded the mother challengingly.

"I was thinking of another fine boy, whom I knew long ago," said Rhodon. "He became a man—and died abruptly. Perhaps the gods were jealous."

"So you've lived among us for thirty years, and still don't believe in one god?" she asked.

Rhodon smiled at her, then waved his hand around.

"Look, woman: Before the memory of man, this was the most ancient and holy city in Egypt—the city of the sun. Now it is a few hovels, a spring, and ruins; but it is still the city of the sun, and ever will be. Strange," he went on musingly, "about that name—the Eye of the Sun! In so many countries, in so many tongues, a spring is called an eye! The association of well and eye and sun is found among many peoples. Well, Yusef, what do you mean to do here in Egypt?"

"Oh. I suppose to reach a city and go to work," said the bearded man. "I'm a carpenter, and there's always work for a man who can use tools, so I'm not worrying. And you—I suppose you'll be carrying a scribe's inkpot?"

"No," replied Rhodon calmly. "I'm finished. I came back here to die, and I think I'm about at the end."

THEY LOOKED at him in astonishment and awe. He shook his head.

"No use blinking it," he went on. "I remember what a wise man once said to me long ago, about death: It is one of those things we cannot explain, which work for good in a way we cannot see. True words, my friends. Nothing sad about it, when you come to my age; rather, it's a relief. I doubt if I'll last out the night."

"Well, just now you're exhausted," said Miriam kindly. "We've cheese and dates and other things to eat; share them with us, and take a corner of our tent for tonight. In the morning you may feel better."

Rhodon thanked them. "You are kind people. This is a beautiful child. I've never seen a finer baby. By Hathor, there's something in his eyes like intelligence! A rare thing. Most babies are like puppies."

"Shame! No such thing!" Miriam cried indignantly; then they all fell to laughing together, and the baby chortled and cooed, and Rhodon took him into his arms. The afternoon waned; and the old man, looking out across the ruins, spoke of the former city here.

"In ancient days it was the city of all learning. It inspired the King Akhnaton to form a new worship of one god alone, the sun. It sheltered your olden hero Yusef or Joseph, and gave him a wife. It is the immortal City of the Sun, as that obelisk of Usertsen still proclaims. I could have no better place in which to depart and go into the dark future—"

His voice died away and he plucked at his girdle, then looked down at the boy and smiled again. But the boy began to cry; his mother took him and disappeared within the tent, saying it was time to nurse him. Yusef came and sat with the old man, chewing at a stem of grass.

"You have learning, wisdom," he said reflectively. "You know your way around, I don't. I'm just a common fellow from a small town. Now that we're getting into Egypt, I'm worried. There's a Roman garrison just ahead, upriver a few miles. Will these Romans ask us for any papers?"

Rhodon grunted. "They will. Anyone coming from Syria had better have a passport. You have one, surely?"

"Well, no. To tell the truth, we started out in a hurry. Oh, there's nothing wrong with us!" added Yusef quickly. "Only, I had some reason to fear Herod's men."

Rhodon pondered this. "Then you're out of luck, my friend. These damned Romans are all for red tape and so forth. Let's see, now—I'll get my passport."

"May gods give you blessings for your kindness."

HE FUMBLED under his rags, produced a wallet, and from it took a folded bit of papyrus which he opened. The passport or travel permit was fairly written in Latin, the blank was filled in with his own name and description, and it was duly sealed.

"I got this at Jericho, from the Roman soldier in charge," said he, and laughed softly. "Yes, I can manage—I am not a scribe

for nothing! Get me a small reed so I can cut a pen. I'll erase this writing and fill it in with your own names—no one will question it—do it fast, before the sun sinks! Hurry! Get some ink at the village yonder. Here's money. Quickly!"

From the wallet he dumped some gold and silver, thrusting the coins at Yusef. Then he fell to work with his knife, scraping off the writing delicately and afterward rubbing smooth the papyrus with his knife-haft. When Yusef came back with reed and ink, he went at the writing and finished it before the sunset gold was gone.

"It will do," he said, examining the job with satisfaction. "I did not name the infant—no matter. He might be the Messias of Israel, for all the Romans know or care. There—now you are prepared, my friend. And I am very tired. Here, wait! This is for the boy. Let him have it to play with—leave me to sleep in the sand. I like it."

Yusef took the papyrus and something wrapped in a bit of cloth. He helped old Rhodon to scoop out sand and get comfortable, gave him another drink, and threw a coat over him.

They found him lying there in the morning, dead.

Yusef got men from the hamlet to dig a grave, paying them with coins from Rhodon's wallet, and the old man was laid to rest near the obelisk. The gift left for the baby boy proved to be a lump of green glass with a peculiar object inside it whose shape conveyed nothing to the Israelite or his wife—a pretty toy which the boy fondled. They had no conception that it could be anything but glass, of course....

That same afternoon a party came riding on horses downstream from the old fortress of Babylon, a few miles south, where a legion was now encamped. There was a tax-gatherer who wanted a report from the hamlet here; there were half a dozen Roman soldiers, guards; with them rode Decimus Rufus, a wealthy young Roman sight-seer touring Egypt, and his friend Aulus Gellius, who was making the grand tour with him.

Rufus was a hard-eyed, handsome fellow with yellow hair and a hearty laugh; Gellius, son of the immensely wealthy contractor who had helped Augustus turn Rome into a city of marble, was a careful genius with an agile brain and dark nimble eyes, always planning some great enterprise on which to employ his father's money. They had been up the Nile as far as the cataracts. Rufus loved the country; Gellius found it boring.

Finding that the tax-gatherer was in for a lengthy session at the hamlet, they went with the decurion or sergeant to see the obelisks and spring and the nomads camped there. Both of them spoke Greek and the Aramaic usually employed by Jews.

At their approach Miriam and the baby, who had been sitting under the sycamore, whipped out of sight into the tent. Yusef went on repairing the saddle. The three dismounted; and the decurion, as a matter of routine, asked Yusef if he had a permit to travel about.

Yusef showed his papyrus.

"Oh! A Jew, eh?" The decurion nodded. "Right. Everything in order, my friend. So you've come from Syria! A long road afoot."

"There are longer," said Yusef, and they chatted of Roman roads.

RUFUS DRANK from the spring, saw something green lying under the sycamore, and picked it up. Surprise leaped into his eyes, and he beckoned Gellius.

"Here, look at this. It was lying just here. It can't be true...."

By the gods! What's in the thing? Hold it in the sunlight and look. Is it real?"

Gellius complied. He showed no excitement, but his dark eyes flashed. He turned to Yusef with a question.

"What is this thing, my friend?"

"That? Oh, it belongs to the baby—a toy. An odd bit of glass."

"I'd like to buy it from you. Set a price on it."

Yusef shook his head. Just then the decurion intervened.

"See here, my traveled gentleman, I know you Jews keep your women close and all that. Still, the permit mentions a woman and a baby. For form's sake, I'd like a look at them. You might have a band of assassins in that tent, for all I know."

Barter was forgotten. Used to Roman authority, Yusef made no protest, but called, and Miriam came out, carrying the baby.

"Talk to my wife, gentlemen," said Yusef, "if you want the pretty glass. It's her affair, not mine."

GELLIUS FELL into talk with her. Rufus looked at her, noted her beauty, met her eyes and was struck by their intelligence.

Then he perceived that Gellius was offering a few copper coins for the glass, and that she was wavering. This angered him. He stepped forward impetuously, took from his pouch half a dozen gold coins, and held them out to her.

"The thing may have value," he said. "Take these instead."

Gellius stepped back, darkly flushed and furious. Yusef, at the sight of gold, came pushing forward, beginning an impassioned harangue. Miriam, who had none of the meek subservience of the Oriental woman, calmly ignored him and took the money from Rufus.

"Very well," she said. "We cannot afford to refuse your kindness. You may have the toy. You think it has some value?"

"I think so," replied Rufus. "I may be wrong. If I'm right, I'll pay you as much again to complete the transaction."

She smiled at this. The baby cooed and put out an arm. Rufus gravely took his tiny hand and looked at him.

"A nest-egg for you, pretty boy," he said, and left another coin in his tiny palm. "I may be back in a couple of days, should the thing have any worth. We'll be here for a week or so, packing and awaiting our ship to Alexandria."

Yusef said they would be here for some days still, recuperating from the desert journey.

A shout came from the village. The decurion replied. The three returned to their horses, and Rufus mounted and waved at the family. Then he fell in beside Gellius.

"A fair price to those poor devils," he said, laughing. "Let's see the thing."

Gellius yielded it. "You're a fool. She'd have sold for a few coppers. I had it bought when you interfered, curse you!"

"Hello! Ruffled you, did I?" Rufus chuckled. "My dear fellow, you're dealing in emeralds now, not in marble."

This thrust drove Gellius into an even darker fury. "I don't throw money away like a drunken soldier," he snapped.

"No," retorted Rufus, himself angry. "A soldier has earned the right."

Gellius, who had bought his way out of military service, spurred away furiously. They did not speak again all the way back to the fort. This really brought to a head a long-term division between them which had been slowly increasing. However, Rufus made an effort at compromise that evening.

"Look here, Aulus, let's patch this thing up: We might hold the green stone as joint property—"

"Keep it and be damned," broke out Gellius. "I want nothing to do with it, and no more to do with you either."

"As you prefer," said Rufus. "I'll be glad enough to part company."

It was more than that, however. Gellius had seen what was in the stone; a few words with the old fort commandant, who was something of an antiquary, told him what the thing really was—an emerald from the Egyptian crown jewels, unique and famous in the history of the land; and after that the heady wine of Cyprus worked evilly upon him.

Rufus had an old Greek servant, a freedman named Herakles, who knew everything. In the lamplight that evening, he showed Herakles the green stone.

"There's a sphinx inside it," he said. "Look for yourself. It may be a lump of glass formed about the image—"

Herakles, examining the green gem through a small glass such as jewelers used, shook his head gravely.

"No, my lord. It is beryl—an emerald from the ancient Egyptian mines. The image is natural, made by the flaws in the stone, a perfect Sphinx. I've heard of it, for it's famous in legend and story. Cleopatra owned it, and the kings before her. It is filled with magic powers for both good and evil. For the love of the gods, keep it secret!"

Rufus examined the gem attentively next day, and saw Herakles had told the truth about it; the Sphinx was indeed made by flaws coming together in a certain spot. Having, like many Romans, scant reverence for the old gods, and no belief in their powers, he saw that this was no more than a natural freak—a poor thing as an emerald, but rare as a curiosity.

During the afternoon he roved about the bazaars and purchased a number of trifling objects for gifts, and the following morning had his horse saddled and went off riding by himself. The truth was that he could not get the face of the Jewish woman out of his mind; she had impressed him deeply. So had the spot, the Eye of the Sun, with its obelisks and its ancient memories.

When he got there, he found Yusef being interrogated by a centurion and two soldiers of the garrison, while a scribe took down his replies. With the arrogance bred of his consular rank and position, Rufus intervened sharply.

"Lord," said the centurion, "this wandering rascal has found some great treasure of gems and gold, and we were sent to question him, at the instance of your friend Aulus Gellius, who will presently be here."

"Indeed!" said Rufus.

"Aye, and the fellow has the gold, indeed."

"Let me tell you a thing or two," said Rufus calmly. "The other day I purchased from this man, who is an honest fellow, a gem which he had found. The gold he now has is what I gave him, and I have brought more to complete the purchase. I'll answer for him. What's more, I'll see your commander when I return to the fort. Now, shall I speak of you in friendly terms, or have you demoted for bothering honest people who are friends of mine? Suit yourself, but do it quickly."

The centurion was a shrewd fellow. He snapped commands at his men. The gold-pieces taken from Yusef were returned instantly and the intruders marched away. Rufus questioned Yusef, learned the origin of the green stone, and laughed.

"You shan't be bothered again," he promised. "I'll have a safe-conduct sent you from the commander at Babylon, so fear not. Now I have some little gifts for you, so bring out your family and forget your troubles."

Miriam appeared with the baby. Rufus distributed his presents and gave her a dozen more gold-pieces. Later he went with Yusef to look at the carvings on the obelisks, and being entirely honest, made no secret of his thoughts.

"You'll be safe enough after this. But frankly, it's no safe place for so lovely a woman as your wife, my friend. If I were you, I'd get along and reach some city, perhaps Memphis. She's a remarkable young woman, glorious as the dawn!"

YUSEF LIKED the young Roman and he smiled now, pleased.

"I think so myself, lord," he said. "She's got more to her than most women. Of course she's a bit above me—comes from our ancient King David's family. But I understand what you mean— she's not just a pretty creature. There are strange depths and abilities in her. After you had gone, the other day, she said you

*"We started out in a hurry.... I had
some reason to fear Herod's men."*

were a person to be trusted, and your friend had a heart as dark
as his face. She's usually dead right in sizing up people."

"I am flattered," Rufus said gravely, and was.

They came back to the spring and ate. Knowing that these
Orientals had peculiar rules about eating with any not of their
race, Rufus had brought along some victuals for himself. He
enjoyed himself thoroughly. He liked these honest common

folk who made no pretensions. They talked about Syria and Roman rule and living conditions, and he got some inkling of the Jewish religion, which he thought had much in common with the one-god religion of the ancient King Akhnaton here in Egypt.

THEN GELLIUS came riding down the trail, dark and intent as usual. As he dismounted, Rufus approached him with a pleasant word, to which the other replied with a quick angry look.

"Interfering again, eh? You seem to have taken upon yourself the protection of these people, according to the centurion."

Rufus lost his smile. "What if I have? Should that anger you?"

"Not anger; mere irritation," said Gellius, loftily. "It had occurred to me that this bearded rascal must have uncovered some great treasure—"

"Not at all. A dying vagrant came along and gave him the green lump—rather, gave it to the baby as a plaything."

"As though anyone would credit such a yarn!"

"I credit it," said Rufus flatly. "And I like them. And I'll not have them bothered any further. Is that clear?"

"Admirably so." Gellius met his eyes and smiled. "It appears that this emerald is a famous stone, my dear fellow, formerly belonging to Queen Cleopatra."

"What of that?"

Gellius turned to his horse, still smiling.

"Our divine Octavian, now called Augustus, conquered her and took Egypt—not for Rome, but for himself. Her entire wealth was turned into his private purse, which sadly needed it. He now sits in Rome, master of the world, and his grandson Lucius is at present in Armenia as pro-consul."

"I don't know what you're getting at," said Rufus, frowning.

"You will, soon enough." Gellius mounted and gathered his

reins. "You and your pretty bright-eyes—ha! Give her my love, though I don't think she has much use for me."

He rode away, chuckling. Rufus frowned after him, then turned back to the others under the sycamore tree. Miriam gave him an odd glance.

"Small love in that man's heart," she said.

"Right," said Rufus. "See here, Yusef—I think you know I'm a friend?"

The bearded man nodded and smiled. "You honor us, lord."

"Well, something's wrong. I don't know what it is, but I don't like that man's words and looks. I can't be harmed by him, but you can be. I'd advise you to pack here and now, and get out of here. Take the road north to Alexandria; plenty of your people are there, and you can be lost among them."

Yusef, looking astonished, glanced at his wife.

She nodded. "I was about to suggest the same thing," she said. "I can feel it is wise."

"Oh! All right, then." Yusef stood up. "We have two animals now. I can pack up in half an hour, and we can travel all night. I know better than to distrust your judgment, good wife."

"But we don't want to leave here in the heat of the day," she put in quietly. "Best to wait an hour—"

"Best not," intervened Rufus. "I'm uneasy. Better get away now, while no one will be on the roads. Best of all, buy a boat from the villagers yonder and float downriver. I'll see to that, while you pack, Yusef."

Catching assent in the face of Miriam, he went to his horses, saddled and mounted, and cantered over to the hovels. There a gold coin did the business. He picked out a small but stout little craft, concluded the bargain and rode back. Yusef was already getting the tent down and rolled up. Rufus liked the way in which the man had accepted the situation without protest or argument, calmly going to work.

He lent a hand loading the tent on the little donkey and getting it over to the boat. Miriam and the baby followed, with a bundle of scanty belongings. Rufus, used to a retinue of servants and luxury in travel, was astonished at how little these people owned. He got them loaded into the boat, saw them off, then directed his horse upstream again for the fortress.

Babylon, an old outpost, stood at the edge of the Mokattam hills, almost opposite the Sphinx and Pyramids on the west side of the Nile. Rufus was almost there when he met a detachment of half a dozen soldiers, who reined in at sight of him.

"My lord," said the apologetic officer, "the commandant sent us for you—he desires speech with you at once."

Rufus assented silently, asking no questions. Arrest? Hard to say. A Roman of consular rank was not to be handled like an ordinary tourist. Gellius had definitely started some sort of trouble, however.

Not until Rufus reached the presence of the commandant, a tough old veteran of the Parthian campaigns, did he learn the truth. The veteran was dictating to a scribe and spewing out oaths on the side. He dismissed the scribe and barked at Rufus:

"Ha! By Hercules, this is a devil of a thing to have broken loose in my district! Look at this!" He pointed to the Sphinx emerald lying on a table. "Information laid by that damned Gellius against you—now I have to take official action against you—technical arrest and so forth. Worse, I've got to take up the case with the Prefect, put it into his hands—"

Rufus smiled. "My dear chap, suppose you tell me what it's all about? Since you've made free with my effects. I presume my servants are under restraint."

"Of course they are—oh, it's damnable! Why hasn't someone cut the throat of that fellow Gellius? Well, here's the thing in a nutshell: Some wandering Parthians or Jews or Bedawin located a huge hoard of buried treasure laid away by Queen Cleopatra. Gellius recognized it for what it was, and tried to get hold of it for Augustus. You interfered, overbid him, and got it for yourself—and that emerald is the proof. Property of Cæsar—see what a damned jam I'm in?"

Rufus broke out laughing. Then his laughter died, but he kept it up as a pose, assuming a light-hearted confidence to mask his real inward alarm.

"Has Gellius actually laid a charge against me?" he asked.

"Aye—of sequestering the rightful property of Cæsar. That emerald, if it is an emerald as he says, is actual proof. How much more of the Egyptian crown jewels you have, I don't know or care."

"Where's the virtuous Gellius now?"

"Hopped a down boat half an hour ago for Alexandria. And now I suppose you'll want to make a statement answering the charges, which means scribes and translators and no end of nonsense, but it's your due."

"Wait a minute," Rufus put in. "What's your procedure in the case?"

"Nominally, I'd send you along to Alexandria and chuck the whole thing into the lap of the Prefect to be rid of it. We'll have commissions and investigators and the gods only know what else piling along here. However, you're Decimus Rufus and a good guy. I'll play ball with you—do anything you like that I can do."

RUFUS THOUGHT fast, realizing his position was extremely serious. Ridiculous as were the charges and the whole story, Octavian was Augustus Cæsar, head of the Empire; anyone who controverted his position in any way was out of luck, as every official well knew. Everyone connected with the case would bend over backward, in self-protection. If Yusef and Miriam were picked up, they would get handled in a tough way, treated as criminals, given no trial.

"Never mind any statement," he said slowly. "What actually happened is this: We came upon some wanderers by a spring downstream and got this green stone from them. It had been given to their baby the previous day by a passing stranger. I bought it for a decent price after Gellius tried to get it for a few coppers. There's the whole thing."

The commandant looked disgusted. "Is the stone really an emerald?"

"Gellius thinks it is."

"That's why he tried to get hold of it, eh? I kept it as evidence. About these people who had it—"

"Oh, they've gone long ago. Nobody knows them."

"That's usually the way in this damned country. However, Cæsar's name is now in the case, and I can't hush it up."

"I'm a Roman citizen. Suppose I appeal to Cæsar's judgment?"

"Don't, for the love of the gods! Now, see here: I can slough the whole thing off on the Prefect. Lucius, proconsul of Armenia and grandson of Cæsar, will be in Alexandria next week on a visit. Do you know him?"

"Very well." Rufus smiled. "We shared the same tutors as boys."

"Fine, then. Here's what I'll do—pass the buck to the Prefect. Send you down on the next boat with word that the other parties have disappeared, and the whole story seems to be a pack of nonsense. Gabinius, the Prefect, is a decent fellow for a politician. You appeal to his judgment—maybe slip him a fat bribe—and everything may possibly be jake. What say?"

"Done with you," said Rufus. The Jewish family was forgotten.

"Mind, I don't say it's finished. That Gellius can still raise hell with the right sort of lies," warned the kindly commandant. "If it was my business, I'd see that he got stopped with a bit of steel in the ribs. Easily done here."

Rufus chuckled. "I'm not that scared, thanks."

"All right. I'll turn you and your servants loose on your pledge of honor—and take that emerald or glass or whatever it is with you. I'll place it in your charge. That suit you?"

Considerably less worried now, Rufus sought his own quarters, only to get bad news from Herakles. The two other servants had vanished completely. When Rufus had put the whole matter before his faithful old freedman, the Greek shook his head.

"Plain enough now where those two rascals went, master. With Gellius, of course. You'll have them as witnesses against you, eh?"

"I don't get it at all," said Rufus. "What's his object?"

"Damage, master. A mighty lawsuit can be started on less evidence. I've guessed for a long time that he bore you no love. Every rich man is a target for arrows."

Rufus shook his head. It all seemed ridiculous and far-fetched. So, in truth, did his own solicitude for that Jewish family. He wondered if he had been a fool....

That evening he sat for a long while examining the emerald with the little glass of Herakles. As a natural curiosity it had value. As an emerald, it was of poor color and cut and polish.

It was shrewd old Herakles, a great delver in legend and story, who tipped him off to what else lay in the bit of beryl. The stone had, or was supposed to have, a hypnotic effect upon the beholder. Rufus, who took no stock whatever in the mystic or supernatural, found a certain fascination in the stone but nothing more. Finally he tucked it up and stowed it away, laughing.

"All nonsense," he exclaimed. "I see nothing in it. I'm not a dreamer or a poet, so put it down to my loss."

"It holds the magic of the gods, master," Herakles said reprovingly.

"Bosh! What gods? They're all a pack of lies," snapped Rufus. "Get me a cup of wine and go to bed."

NEXT DAY a downriver boat halted at the fortress signal. Rufus was put aboard, with Herakles and a soldier as nominal guard, to report to the Prefect. As the lazy craft dropped down the river, Rufus stood watching the eastern bank, and presently descried the native hamlet, and beyond it the twin obelisks that marked the Eye of the Sun, their copper caps greenish against the sky.

Evening found them at Alexandria, coming in by the Lake Mareotis approach to the river-boat harbor at the Gate of the Sun in the south wall. These lake docks were vaster and more crowded even than the maritime wharves at the seaward side of the city; the whole traffic of Egypt was pouring in here.

Here, quartered as a guest-prisoner in the royal buildings near the northern Gate of the Moon, Rufus found himself entirely out of Egypt. This was a Greek city, the most splendid in the world, and was thoroughly European; the buildings of the Jewish quarter were noted for magnificence, but from the towering six hundred-foot Pharos or lighthouse, to the enormous marble bulk of the Serapeum behind the city, everything

*These lake docks were vaster even than
the maritime wharves; the whole traffic
of Egypt was pouring in here.*

was marble, Grecian, with no hint of Egypt. Legionaries
tramped the wide avenues, as symbol of Rome.

As for his own business, Rufus found it delayed. The Prefect,
Gabinius, lay ill in the palace—very ill, by all accounts; until
his recovery, nothing could be done. So, for a couple of days,
Rufus saw the sights of the city—until one evening Gellius
came walking in upon him, coolly insolent but apparently
friendly.

"Business, my dear Rufus, business!" he said amiably. "The
illness of Gabinius is not at all bad for us, and the visit of Lucius
next week—proconsul and heir to the empire—has thrown

everything else into confusion. Our little affair can end without any further publicity, if you say the word."

"I? I've nothing to do with it," said Rufus. "You're the one whose deviltry has stirred things up—you and your fantastic lies."

"Not so fantastic if supported by witnesses. I have a couple, at least. However, suppose we get down to business: I know you don't want this affair to go farther. It has perilous angles, if pushed—highly perilous."

Rufus was puzzled but wary of a trap. Gellius regarded him smilingly.

"Noble Roman of the old school, aren't you! I'd wager you even believe in virtue and honesty, eh? Well, look at this. I've been over on the glass market—here."

On the table by the lamp he set a glowing green lump, cut and polished like a great jewel.

"Glass, pure glass," he said, chuckling. "Made to order. No doubt you get the idea?"

"No," replied Rufus.

"Very simple. Hand over the emerald; I want it, and mean to have it. I'll pay you any price you set. Then we go to the Prefect with this bit of glass in place of it. He's damned sick and will be happy to be rid of this affair quickly. What we thought was emerald, proves upon examination to be a lump of glass—all an unfortunate mistake; I withdraw my story on the spot. You see? My witnesses will swear to it that this is the thing we found. They'll swear to anything I say, for or against you. The mountain turns out to be an anthill; Gabinius is delighted to be rid of the case; all is well. Eh? Clever, eh?"

"Clever," repeated Rufus, admiring the simplicity of the thing. "So you really want the emerald, do you? Might have had it for nothing, if you'd said so in the beginning."

"I want it. I mean to have it." Gellius waved his hand. "It's a turn of the dice, Rufus—one side serious and dangerous, the other a light nothing. It's for you to say."

"Oh, I haven't thought particularly about it," Rufus said.

"By the way, who do you think I saw today in this city of three hundred thousand souls? No other than your Jewish friends from the Eye of the Sun. A painter was doing a painting of them—that Greek artist Diomedes. He has a good feeling for line, too. Well, I presume you've no objection to my solution of our affair? Hand over the real emerald, and the thing's done."

"You tempt me strangely," said Rufus. "Let me think about it."

"Think fast, then," said Gellius, rising. "I'll come back for your answer tomorrow evening about this time."

He strode out. Rufus looked at the glass jewel reflectively. Presently he reached out, touched the bell, and Herakles came in.

"Somewhere in this city," said Rufus, "is a Greek artist named Diomedes, I think of some renown. Locate him. Spare no expense. I must see him tomorrow without fail."

Why? He hardly knew, unless it were that Gellius spelled danger.

In the morning Herakles showed up with the information. Diomedes was a well-known artist and he lived in a street near the Library. Rufus set off at once, and his freedman located the house without trouble.

Diomedes was an elderly man, famed for his funeral portraits, which he despised. What good, he would say, to paint portraits that were buried with a corpse? However, it was the fashion and paid excellently. He greeted his caller, and replied to the queries of Rufus with a laugh.

"Oh, those Jews! Yes, yes, come in and see them if you like. I'm doing a sketch of them just as they are—it's for a painting."

So Rufus walked into the studio. Miriam and Yusef greeted him with delight; even the baby cooed at him in apparent recognition. Warn them? Alarm them? He could not. Instead, he took the artist aside.

"I have a commission for you," he said, and described the Eye of the Sun and its location. Diomedes knew of it. "All right. Take a boat, load this family in, go there and paint the three of them sitting by that sycamore tree. Do it at once. I'll be here for a week or more. Eh?"

Diomedes was more than willing, named a good price, and Rufus agreed. Before his departure, the Roman went over and shook hands with the babe.

"Your dark friend was here yesterday," said Miriam to him. He met her eyes, read the question in them, and smiled.

"That's why I came today. I think you'll have no more trouble from him. I want Diomedes to make a painting of you three—I'd like to have it. Especially the baby. His eyes stay in my mind. You'll be paid, so I trust you won't mind going with him back to the Eye of the Sun. I want that in the picture too."

Miriam and Yusef laughed happily. For an instant, Miriam detained him.

"Be careful," she said quietly. "Do you still have the green stone?"

He assented. "I may not keep it. I don't like it particularly."

"Then don't. Here's a gift for you—there's a good deal of fever about. Three drops in a cup of water." She put a tiny glass vial in his hand. Yusef nodded at him; the baby cooed again.

Rufus took his departure rather hurriedly.

"*Then don't.*" Don't keep it, she had meant. This stuck in his mind. In fact, it must have largely decided him. After all, he did not want the emerald. He had not intended to yield to Gellius, but when the latter walked in that evening, Rufus brought out the bit of beryl and handed it over without a word. Gellius seized it, his eyes alight.

"Good! I thought you would. Come along, bring the bit of glass—we'll see the sub-prefect now. He's agreed to handle the matter. Gabinius is dying, they say. We'll have the affair out of the way and done with in half an hour."

STILL RUFUS only shrugged and went along, agreeably. He did not understand his own compliance, yet it gave him cynical amusement. "Then don't." The two words had a fund of meaning. Give it up. Part with it. Give Gellius his way. Why? He did not know. He was almost tempted to think that some god dwelt in that woman....

He was astonished at the way everything went off. His two former servants swore to the green stone. An expert in jewels was waiting, and with a laugh pronounced it glass. The whole bubble was pricked in a moment or two, with laughter and huge relief. The case was dismissed. Gellius went his way.

The sub-prefect halted Rufus.

"Wait. Gabinius knows you're here, wants to see you as a courtesy. He knew your father well. Will you see him?"

"Oh, of course!" Rufus was astonished. "I thought he was dying!"

"He is; he's clear-headed about it, though—the fever will recur, but no one knows much about it. Something he picked up on shipboard. If you'll have a word with him, come along. From what they say, he won't last out the night."

They went to the palace—the Lochias Palace, home of the former royal family—and were admitted to an antechamber where guards stood about, and half a dozen physicians pulled long faces and conferred. Yes, the Prefect could see them; he was conscious but would not live through the night. Witchcraft, they called it.

They passed in to the great airy bedroom overlooking the sea—now fast closed, with incense burning. Gabinius, unshaven and a mere shadow of himself, lay on the huge bed. He looked at them and feebly raised a hand in salutation. Rufus went to him quickly, took his hand, smiled down at him.

"Knew—your father well," whispered Gabinius. "Glad to see you. Not long left."

"Nonsense," said Rufus. Something pressed at his girdle. He

slipped a hand under his toga—the little vial Miriam had given him. Well, why not? For fevers, she had said....

"See here, Gabinius," he spoke out, fetching the vial into sight, "I have a remedy—might do you some good. Will you try it?"

The Prefect laughed at him, horribly, a ghastly mockery of laughter.

"They've tried everything," he croaked. "A lot you know! Well, why not? I'm past harming. Let's have it."

A slave knelt close by. Rufus told him to fetch a small cup of water. His impulse past, he felt like a fool. The sub-prefect looked on, cynically. The water came. Into it Rufus measured three drops from the vial, whose stopper came out readily. He tasted it; just water, no taste at all. He lifted the head of Gabinius.

"Here, now—put it down. Can't hurt you, and might help."

The dying man gulped obediently. "See you—across the Styx," he murmured.

They stayed a few moments more, then departed. Gabinius was falling into coma.

THAT NIGHT Rufus fell asleep upon angry self-recrimination. He had played the fool, had made an ass of himself— they might even say he had poisoned the Prefect! When he wakened to daylight, the thought recurred to him, and he groaned. Then he found Herakles at his side, shaking him.

"Master! Master—wake up! They found him—in the water—"

Rufus sat up. "Eh? What? Who?"

"Gellius. He was picked out of the water this morning, a knife-wound through his heart. He had been robbed and stripped."

Gellius! Rufus understood, and laughed harshly. So the rascal had talked, and had been knifed and robbed! No loss. Well, so much for the emerald—gone for good now.

He shaved, bathed, and was dressing when the sub-prefect

burst into his room like a madman, babbling and cursing and laughing.

"Rufus! A miracle!" he broke out. "You did it."

"I know nothing about it," said Rufus. "I didn't see Gellius after he left us—"

"Gellius be damned! I'm talking about the Prefect. Gabinius woke up sane and sound this morning—fever gone, head clear! That remedy of yours, man—it did the work!"

Incredible, amazing—but quite true. Overnight, Gabinius was out of the toils. The day passed; another came—the invalid was gaining health and strength. He saw Rufus, thanked him warmly, offered sacrifices of thanks to the gods. Yet another day, and he was on his feet.

Rufus sat staring at the tiny glass vial. That woman Miriam— had she told the truth about the remedy? He could believe nothing else. Here was the proof. He was besieged by a flood of physicians and quacks, all begging for information about the wondrous remedy. Vast sums were offered him in return. Gabinius was appearing publicly, preparing the reception for the coming pro-consul, Lucius.

Amid all this confusion and hubbub, here came the Greek painter Diomedes, with a carefully wrapped wooden plaque under his arm.

Rufus received him delightedly. "Finished?" he asked.

"Of course, my lord," said the artist. "Here it is. Those people went on up the Nile, bound for Memphis. I think this is rather good, myself."

He opened up the painting, placed it in the proper light, and Rufus inspected it.

Nothing but the spring, the tree and roots, the family and in the background a shadowy obelisk. It was the family, the Eye of the Sun, yes. The features of Miriam were well caught. Those of the baby seemed to sparkle. Good work, and Rufus said so.

"Excellent. I'll take it home to Rome with me."

"By the way, I have a message." Diomedes, laughing, held

out a small vial. "You remember, that day in my studio, Miriam gave you a fever-cure? Well, she said to tell you it was a sad mistake. Here's the real cure—she hopes it may be useful some day."

Rufus stared. "Eh? You're mad! I have the vial she gave me."

"Nothing but water in it, she says." The artist chuckled. "Water from the Eye of the Sun—she had been keeping it as a memento and gave it to you in error. Tourist mementoes! Just like a woman, eh?"

BEWILDERED, RUFUS thanked him, paid him, sent him away, then sat down to look at the painting and collect his confused senses.

Water from the spring—nothing else. A keepsake. He himself had tasted it—just plain water. Then it had effected no cure whatever. But by the gods, Gabinius was well again! There could be no mystery; there was no wonderful cure at all.

"You can't get away from plain hard facts." Rufus sighed. "Gellius robbed and murdered by waterfront thieves: The emerald lost forever, and good riddance. The Prefect on his feet—he must have recovered naturally, then. And I sit here with this picture—all because of the Eye of the Sun! Funny how things turn out. All of it perfectly natural, entirely normal, in fact. And yet—and yet—"

And yet....

ASSASSINATION AT CHRISTMAS

*Steel clashed and bugles blared in the Antioch
of December 362.... and the strange Sphinx
Emerald flashed again to potent life.*

"**F**EAR," PHILIP thoughtfully observed, "is the keynote of everything here in this room, in this city of Antioch, in this part of the world. Insensate panic—"

"At this season? At Christmas itself?" broke in Lady Glendufa. "But that is wrong. It is wicked!" Her challenging eyes swept the circle of faces. "Nothing will happen. We're wasting our time. Nothing can happen, I tell you!"

Philip shrugged, seeing how the others exchanged glances.

"Anything *can* happen, Glendufa. Fear is contagious. We fear them, and perhaps they fear us. Reason says it's preposterous, but we won't believe reason. We're afraid. We trust neither our rulers nor ourselves. We're afraid, afraid—"

"And why not?" quavered a voice, with excited thrust. "Everything's been overthrown. Around us is pagan, heathen Asia: Soldiers gathering by the thousand. Force that hates us, would love to destroy us. We may well seek some protection—"

A sound crept into the room and hushed the words. The score of people sitting here in conference shivered at it; hands jerked; eyes rolled. Voices screamed thinly like the yapping of wild beasts. Steel clashed; a tumultuous uproar resounded along the city streets and ended in a distant bugle-blare.

"The soldiers are out," growled old farmer Paulus, gnarled hands clenching, shaggy whiskers bristling. "There'll be looting and killing and burning all over the place!"

In a leap of voices others spoke their fears.

Philip glanced at them curiously. Himself a Roman, he had served in the cavalry. Here in Antioch, third greatest city of the Empire and capital of Syria, he found everything strange. Take these Galileans, for example—first named Christians here in Antioch, they still called themselves Galileans—what a queer company they made! The bishop, Meletius, was a good but inefficient fellow. Nearly all the others present belonged to the Gothic colony planted here by Constantine. They had relatives in the Legions, and consequently were the most influential of the community, since the whole army of the eastern provinces was gathering here to march into Parthia in the spring. This Christmas season of the year 362 was one of terror and fear and increasing panic on all sides.

Glendufa was quite calm, he noted; she was always calm, perfectly poised. Her husband was a centurion in the 59th Legion, now in camp just down the river. The Emperor himself was living in the old Roman fortress that dominated the city. No Christmas festival for him or his court! Uncle Constantine had made the empire Christian; his nephew Julian had reversed this, proclaiming tolerance for all religious sects— and thereby loosing the hounds of terror.

Julian was newly come to power; no one was sure of his intent; religious hatreds blazed on all sides. The Christians feared a new persecution; the pagans bitterly feared a Christian revolt—and now blood was running in the streets!

Startled movement swept the room as pounding footsteps sounded on the stairs. The door was flung open. In upon the company broke a deacon, stammering, panting and white-faced. Voices blabbed at him. He threw out both hands.

"No, no danger! There's fighting in the streets, yes. Food riots, that's all."

A surge of relief. From Philip came a strong, hearty laugh.

"Well, we're gathered here to devise some system of protection for Galileans," he said. "So we'd best get about it, instead of shaking in our boots at riot noises."

His caustic words bit into them; quiet settled on the room. Paulus, the craggy old farmer who owned the great olive orchards above the city, began to talk and talk. Philip listened with a sneer in his eyes. He dared not look at Glendufa, lest he break out laughing. She was a fine lissome woman, golden-haired, as sensible as beautiful. He could not blame himself for having fallen in love with her.

Paulus droned on. Antioch, four separate cities forming one,

had become the gateway to Far Eastern commerce. Merchants from Parthia, from farther India and all the coasts between, were established here; in some quarters the city was wholly Oriental. More peril there, said the farmer; these people who worshiped strange gods would be quick to slay Christians.

Knowing these Asiatics to be gentle people, Philip listened cynically. He wondered what these good folk would say if they knew the truth about him. Suddenly his eye caught a movement at the door. It opened a little. A face looked in; a hand signaled. He came to his feet abruptly.

"Sorry, friends; I've been sent for; I must leave you," he said. "Let me say just one word: If we Christians want protection, there's only one sensible way of getting it. Send to the Emperor and ask for it! With that advice, I say good night."

He caught a slight smile on Glendufa's lips, and hurried out. On the stairs a man waited—his friend Crates, like himself a member of the Imperial secret service.

"Well, my honest Galilean wolf," jested Crates, "are these sheep of yours plotting to cut all our throats? What weapons have they ready?"

"Droning tongues," Philip rejoined, laughing. "All talk. What brought you here?"

"Urgency. There's been some killing in the riots. I've got a dying man who wants you. A Parthian jewel-merchant. He's dying, so hurry!"

"Wants me? A Parthian merchant? By Hercules, are you crazy?"

"Well, he wants some court official—news for the Emperor, secret, urgent news! So I came for you; may be profitable," replied Crates, who was a shrewd fellow with an eye for the main chance. "He knows he's dying, so he'll tell the truth. He's in the street just ahead—I have a couple of soldiers guarding him. He was stabbed during the riot.... So you're having no luck with the Galileans?"

"They're not planning revolt at all. All they want is protection. They're scared."

Crates chuckled as he strode along. "And if they knew you were an imperial spy, they'd tear you limb from limb! Frightened people are always dangerous. Still, your job has compensations. You've quarters in the house of the most beautiful woman in Antioch."

"Bosh! Her husband's a centurion," snapped Philip. The other laughed softly. They swung around a corner and came into one of the two great colonnaded avenues of the city.

Afar lifted the darkly massive bulk of the enormous cathedral Constantine had built here. Close by, a smoky torch was blazing under the colonnades. Two soldiers stood guard. A dark figure lay on the stones, a bearded elderly Parthian. He spoke, as Philip knelt and raised his head.

"Are you—of the court? Are you a Roman?"

"Aye, a Roman." Philip spoke the truth for once. "Aulus Gentius of the imperial household."

The other clasped his arm, came to one elbow, and thrust something into his hand.

"Take this—reward. Swear—swear by the gods to give me burial!"

"I swear by the gods," Philip said gravely. "You shall have fit burial."

"Ah! Tigranes had me murdered—he's behind it—the Emperor will be killed." The gasping voice faltered, then resumed: "Eighth day before the Kalends of January—at the inspection of the troops. Tigranes replaces the driver of the royal elephant—with John of Iconium—to stab—"

The voice failed; the gripping fingers relaxed. Philip looked at the lolling head, put it down, and rose. He turned to the two soldiers and passed them some coins.

"Take care of this man's body. Have it decently buried tomorrow."

"More fool, you," said Crates.

"I promised; therefore it must be done. You hear what he said?"

"Yes. I know a wineshop that's open. Come along."

Philip fell into step, with an ironic smile. The eighth day before the Kalends—why, that would be Christmas itself! And Julian was to be assassinated that day, eh? Blame the Christians, of course; turn loose the legions to loot and massacre....

They found the wineshop, ordered wine. Crates was small, slender, vulpine, a good man. Philip was stocky, dark, with strong features well carven, level dark eyes. Barely thirty, he had won an enviable position as the best of the secret household servants of the Emperor.

He set to work delving in the camel camp.
By noontime he began to think half the
population must be named Tigranes.

"Ha! We've rung the bell," said Crates. "What to do about it? Denounce this Tigranes, whoever he is? That's folly; he'd slip out of it. Might squeeze him for a fat sum."

"Be damned to him—just some Parthian agent," Philip grunted. "This John of Iconium is the actual assassin. Who is he?"

"The name's vaguely familiar, but I can't finger him."

Philip gulped his wine. "Well, there's no rush. Four days before it comes off. Suppose we cast about for information tomorrow, and meet tomorrow night?"

"Agreed." Crates gave him a sharp look. "Suppose we just kept quiet?"

A startling thought, tempting too. Philip half smiled as he pictured it: the streets filled with savagely rejoicing men; the

Emperor dead, the bearded Julian upon whom the clean-shaven Antiocheans heaped ridicule; whispers spreading that Christians had killed him; and then the Legions let loose upon the city in merciless fury. That was how history was made. Then his smile faded.

"Scratch it," he said. "I was a soldier. I keep my oaths."

Crates sighed. "Yes, you have old-fashioned notions about honor and so forth. Well, we have the chance of a lifetime to line our pockets."

"Right. Can't afford to miss it. Sleep on it, then. Where do we meet?"

"Why not here, an hour after dark?"

So agreed, they went their ways; the evening was still young. Philip had said nothing about the hard little cloth-wrapped object given him by the dying Parthian. He went home and sought his room. The house was large, sheltering Glendufa and her husband, her elder sister and family, and a brace of lodgers.

Lighting his lamp, Philip sat down and produced the mysterious gift. He unfolded the cloth and stared at the green thing revealed. An emerald? That Parthian had been a jewel-merchant. Emerald it must be, yet it was incredible. This stone was enormous, and of cabochon shape. Smears of oil showed it was newly cut and polished, still uncleaned. The color was poor, denoting an Egyptian stone, but—but—

The Roman gripped his fists as he stared, then moved the lamp closer and bent to look more sharply. Inside the stone were flaws that came together, forming a shape. He had been in Egypt and seen the Great Sphinx; some said there was a second like unto it, up in the desert hills east of the Nile. Here was the image of it made by the flaws—no vague shape but a distinct and clear-cut Sphinx! A jewel unique, a freak of nature!

Then his thoughts strayed, though he found a certain fascination in looking into the stone. Fortune had this night given him and Crates a tremendous chance at gain, provided they did not muff it. Philip had been raised in a hard army school;

he was no angel. The old Roman conception of duty had perished hundreds of years ago; and now, with the breakdown of morality and ethics that had engulfed the Empire, duty was a joke. A thing was right, these days, if it paid. Do whatever you liked, if you could get away with it. Betray anyone, if it was to your interest.

THE SECRET bequeathed by the dying Parthian could yield untold wealth, with proper manipulation. The Emperor was a good soldier, had won great victories; he was a brawny big man, well intentioned, straightforward, simple in mind; but he had only been a year on the throne. The sons of Constantine had murdered his father and all other relatives. He did not love the Christians, for he clung to the old gods. Were he to die suddenly, anyone in the secret could cash in heavily. Philip had sworn fealty; should he keep his oath, or no?

The light falling across the huge emerald wakened odd fancies in him. Queerly enough, he found himself thinking about his father. Aulus—this was the real family name—had died long ago in the wars of Constantine. A veteran cavalry officer, he had been a hard, grim man, winning nothing except a soldier's fame. Things he had said, things he had done, came flooding into Philip's mind. Why? He could not say; perhaps the emerald had bewitched him. A long while he sat, until sounds from below told him Glendufa was back.

He went down and found her warming before the fire in the main room. It was a chill, rainy night. Her broidered woolen garments sparkled with the wet.

"What's happened?" she exclaimed. "Philip! You look as if you'd been seeing angels!"

"Sit down," he said, unsmiling, and held a chair for her, then put the pottery lamp on the table close by. "Did they reach any decision?"

"Yes. They took your advice. They chose you and Paulus to go to the Emperor."

"Very well," he said carelessly. "Glendufa, you're a lovely woman, and wiser than any I ever knew."

"You had a mother," she said significantly.

"She died when I was a child. Tonight I need your help and advice. The gods have dropped fortune into my lap."

"The gods?" Her brows lifted. "Strange words for a Galilean to use."

"I'm no Christian; there's the truth for you," he said calmly. "I'm an officer of the imperial service. My present task is to spy on the Christians here and learn if they mean to revolt. Well, I'm tired of lies. You've nothing to fear from me."

She smiled a little. She could read the trouble in his eyes, the strange conflict in his heart. She put out her hand, and he took it.

"I think a great deal of you," he said. "You like me a little."

"With much affection, Philip," she said simply. "That is not your real name, of course, and I knew you were not a Christian."

This caught him up with a jerk. "What? You knew?"

She pressed his hand. "Yes. The 59th was in Macedonia three years ago; my husband saw you then, and recognized you here."

Philip flushed. The quiet words shamed him.

"I'm a fool," he said.

"On the contrary, a very fine man, my dear. What's that in your hands?"

He gave her the emerald and told how he had come by it. She held it to the lamp-glow and caught her breath, and sat looking at it. In the silence, he got himself in hand. Love or no love, he was not a fool. His very love for her told him that her quiet poise and strength held her above any intrigue.

"There's a plot to kill the Emperor," he went on presently. "Christians would like nothing better than to see him dead. I can profit tremendously by it—if I keep silence."

She turned from the emerald to look at him—completely,

intently, studying his hard, strong features, and waiting. Her waiting compelled him to go on.

"The Christians could profit. Or the blame might be cast on them. Anything—"

"Anything is possible, even honor," she said quietly.

He started. His eyes lifted to her amazedly.

"Why, that's the very thing my—my father said! They were caught in a trap, some of the 23rd—his Legion. Some said to surrender; some said to fly. Anything, said he, was possible, even honor. They stayed. He died there. Were your words mere accident?"

She nodded. "Yes. I give them to you as my answer, my advice. Now I'm off to bed; there's all the housework for early morning. Pleasant dreams!"

She was gone. Dazedly, Philip pocketed the emerald, covered the fire, picked up the light and went back to his own room. There, he put the emerald on the table between the two lamps, and sat down, looking at it again, looking into it.

To do him justice, he had been lifted out of any love-making intent, though he did love her. She was not the sort of woman for that. She had twice shocked him; the second time with the very words of his long-dead father. Now, again fascinated by the emerald depths, thoughts of his father recurred. He had always venerated the memory of that man. Why the emerald should bring him to mind, Philip did not know; but so it did. Gradually a change crept into his entire mental makeup. The cynical, grasping, hardened promptings died away; whether the memories of his father wakened them, or whether it were some magic in the glittering green beryl acting upon his mind, a train of glowing fancies came like a procession of splendor-flashes that hinted at such old, half-forgotten things as soldierly honor, manly virtues, unpleasant actions done because duty demanded.

Perhaps, he thought later as he lay abed, Glendufa had started this train of thought. "Anything is possible, even honor"—words applicable to herself also. She too might be fighting off some temptation.

NEXT MORNING he slipped out of the house early. He had to see the Emperor sometime this day to make report; he had to see Paulus and arrange with him the visit to ask for protection; more important, he had to look up John of Iconium and Tigranes—find out who they were. Tigranes was a common Parthian name and must belong to some merchant.

He set to work searching bazaars, talking with lesser spies of the Intelligence Bureau, delving into the camel camp outside the city walls, drinking at the caravanserais which catered to Oriental custom. By noontime, he began to think half the population of Parthia must be named Tigranes, and he found no one who knew anything of a John of Iconium. Antioch the Golden, as it was named, gave his searchings no reward. And, since it contained nearly a quarter-million souls, this was small wonder.

With afternoon, he took his way to the castle and was at once admitted to the presence of the Emperor. Julian dismissed his scribes, who were taking down his dictation on a book against the Christian sect, and welcomed the visitor warmly.

"Well, Aulus, have you any information on these Galileans?"

"Plenty," rejoined Philip. "It all boils down to one word. They're honest."

Julian laughed. "Good! In Alexandria they're pestilent philosophers, in Constantinople braggarts and fighters—and here in Antioch, honest. And no plots at work?"

"Only one. They're frightened of persecution and have decided to send two deputies to beg your protection. I'm one of the two. When will it please you to receive us?"

Julian broke into hearty laughter.

"A beautifully ironic game, eh? You, an imperial spy, one of the delegates! By all means—let's see, now. Make it the feast they celebrate—Christmas. Come to me here in the morning before I leave to inspect the troops. That's the eighth day before the Kalends of January. I'll have a decree of protection all written out and sealed for you."

Philip, smiling, thanked him and turned in a detailed report previously written out. The Emperor discussed with him the idea of quartering certain legions in the city.

"Food riots like that of last night are disturbing," he said. "And there's a sense of fear, almost of panic, spreading. Where fear grows, we seldom find reason. It impels fantastic things; the greater the fear, the more fantastic are its effects.

"Quite true," said Philip. "A good many of the city folk have relatives in the 59th—move it into the city and they'd feel safer. That is, in the Gothic quarter."

Julian nodded approval and made a note. This fantasy of panic, as he termed it, disturbed him. Nineteen different rumors of plots against his life had come in: he laughed at them, but not at their cause. Hence, for the coming inspection, he had ordered out the full equipment of forty war-elephants and would use one of them himself, to make an impressive show. The narrow citadel gate was now being widened to admit this imperial chariot on four legs.

Philip departed thoughtfully. Here was corroboration of the story told by the dying Parthian. John of Iconium would be the driver of that elephant, no doubt.

That evening came a more abrupt crisis than he had anticipated. He reached the wineshop early, got a corner table, and sipped his wine reflectively. The sort of work he was doing disgusted him. Only today Julian had called him an imperial spy; quite true, and it put him to shame. It was not easy to leave the imperial household service, however. He had taken it as a stopgap and found himself bridled.

Nice if he could get out of it now—and could pick up some money. There was an opening in Alexandria with a construction firm, Romans like himself. Just then he glanced up and saw Crates coming in the door. Behind him followed two armed men, Parthians by their looks, who went to the bar. Crates had nothing to do with them, of course—but Philip sensed a sudden tautness. His nerves jumped; he became alert, wary. He knew that Crates was capable of anything. Here, indeed, anything was possible—except honor.

They shook hands. Crates ordered wine, sighed and relaxed.

"Well, any luck?"

"Not a stroke," confessed Philip.

Crates laughed.

"Ha! I've a different tale to tell—vastly different. I was approached. Our talk with the fellow last night was noted. I've had an offer. Oh, they felt me out carefully, delicately! It was beautiful work, and I played up to it."

"He's not sure of me," thought Philip, and veiled his eyes, looking down at his cup. Something smelly here; those two fellows were with him, all right. "I'll be in a pinch if I don't watch my step!" he reflected.

"I don't get it," he answered. "What sort of offer?"

"Money. Heaps of it. Parthia has gold to burn, you know, and is afraid of Julian. Well, the point is that I stalled, said I'd have to play ball with you, and so forth. If you say the word, we can get taken here and now to Tigranes. I don't know who he is, but suspect he's merely a Parthian agent. The offer is ten thousand gold-pieces to each of us, for silence. Paid tonight on the nail, if we accept."

"Oh." A fat sum, thought Philip. "And if we refuse?"

"I don't know. Didn't ask, in fact. Tonight is the deadline. I suspect some of the court officials are in the game, because the fellow who talked with me knew all about you and me both, and the offer includes a good position at court later on."

Philip sipped his wine. A pinch, sure enough. Crates had accepted the bribe; those Parthians had come along to silence Philip with their weapons if he refused.

"You tempt me," he said slowly. "It's a big sum. And, you say, in cash?"

"I saw the gold coins."

"You're a strange man," Glendufa breathed softly.
"I'll carry out the errand, be sure of that."

Damning words; he must have seen Tigranes as well, then. A short laugh escaped Philip, and he emptied his cup.

"If you think my old-fashioned honor, Roman virtue and so forth, are proof against that sum, think again! Get your guide. Let's go. I want to see the money myself."

Crates started up. "You're for it?"

"Definitely."

Crates spoke to one of the Parthians, who accompanied them outside and then set forth at a brisk stride. They followed him through the dark streets and came into the bazaar quarter of little shops and Asiatic faces, and ended at a dark entry to a rug shop. The guide knocked and spoke, the door was opened, he slipped inside. Crates followed, then Philip. A lamp glimmered on a dark passage; then a curtain was pulled aside and they stepped into a lighted room heaped with piles of rugs, where a man sat at a desk.

He was a dark, clean-shaven, alert man with jet eyes, and a strong, sure smile.

"Greetings," he said, calling them by name as though an old friend. His gaze settled on Philip. "So you found no trace of me today, eh? You sought earnestly enough."

"You seem oddly aware of my doings," Philip replied.

"You Roman spies are like children," said Tigranes. Philip bit his lip. "We need not waste words. Your friend has told you the terms. Are they agreeable?"

"Yes, with a slight change. Give me five hundred pieces of gold, to pay my debts, and the balance in an order on Lazar Brothers, the banking-house with branches everywhere." Philip spoke calmly. "And you have no assurance that I will not take your money and then betray you."

Tigranes smiled at him. "No? My friend, you are welcome to try, if you like. We have friends everywhere in the imperial household. We would know it immediately; you would die very quickly—and that is all. You would not like to lose a promising future?"

PHILIP CHUCKLED. He rather liked this fellow who called him a spy. An efficient man.

"Assuredly not," he said. "Together with another deputy from the Christians here, I'm to visit the Emperor just before he leaves for the inspection."

"Yes. You made the appointment today, I understand," Tigranes said carelessly, and Philip felt cold sweat on his palms. Probably a secretary of Julian was in the plot. "When the thing is done, the blame will be thrown on the Christians, so you had better sever your connections with them quickly. It is agreed, then?"

"Agreed." Philip nodded coolly. "I admire your efficiency."

Tigranes smiled. "The tribute is appreciated." He touched a small bell. A slave entered, received instructions, and went out. "The money will be brought. The sum promised you, Crates, will be delivered in the morning at your quarters. Satisfactory?"

"Entirely," said Crates, beaming. "About the positions to be given us later—"

"That will be arranged by the officials in concert with us," said Tigranes. "They will approach you in the matter, so fear not. Ah, here is the money."

The slave reëntered, and placed on the desk a leather bag. Tigranes waved to it and smiled at Philip.

"Yours, my friend. You will find the sum exact. Anything else?"

"Nothing, except my thanks." Philip took the heavy little bag. "May the gods favor us all! In case I need to reach you—"

"This is the shop of Permanes the rug-merchant."

A WORD of farewell, and the two friends departed. Out in the street again, Crates laughed in relief.

"Good, good! I'm glad you became sensible."

"Perhaps it's my throat," said Philip. "I've had a bit of fever—the damp nights here have hit my throat. At any rate, the money

will help cure me! Well, good night, and take care of
yourself!"

They separated and Philip went straight home. Glendufa
met him—farmer Paulus had been here to see him and was
highly nervous about the visit to the Emperor.

Philip laughed.

"Dear lady, that comes the third day from now—and a lot
more comes then, too. Send him word to come here tomorrow;
I'll be here all day. In fact, I'll be very ill. Make no secret of my
illness. Send for a couple of physicians. Arrange to give me an
hour in the morning, and to visit your husband in the camp
downriver tomorrow afternoon."

She eyed him sharply. "Have you been drinking?"

"Yes. Drinking treachery and betrayal, of which this bag of
gold is proof." He slapped the leather bag blithely. "Now I'm
going to drink common sense and good counsel for an hour,
before turning in."

"I want to talk to you," she said.

"Not tonight. I have sore need of advice from my father, God
rest him!"

He left her staring after him and went to his own room. The
very sight of her, the sound of her voice, tempted him. He was
afraid of himself.

When his lamp was lighted, he sat down at the table, got
out the emerald, and settled down to look into it and study it.
He had made vague, tentative plans; he forgot them, a sense of
composure gradually settled on his mind. Those green reaches
within the beryl wrought their enthralling spell and shut away
everything else. Across his thoughts drifted his last sight of his
father, sword-girt, cuirass-clad; it seemed the older man gave
him a smile, a penetrating look, a nod. Sheer hallucination, of
course. He had sense enough to know as much; still, one always
likes to pretend.

Queer how his father had lived and died, a plain, ordinary
army man, getting nothing out of it. Uncompromising, too;

either a thing was right or it was wrong. Few men could live that simple philosophy! It was hard to live, at times.

"Like me with Glendufa," reflected Philip. "I love her. I want her with all of me; want to live this life with her, give her everything that centurion can't give her. I don't give a damn if it's wrong—but she does. Therefore I must too. And therefore all I can do is to clear out—unless I take the easy, selfish course. But I'll have to clear out. Tigranes called me a spy; he was right. I've come down far. I'll have to climb back up again."

He thought his father was laughing grimly. He looked a while longer, then put out the light, stretched himself on the bed, and fell asleep.

SUNLIGHT WOKE him. He rose, dressed, opened the bag of gold and shoved a handful of coins into his pocket—heavy, broad pieces. He went down to the kitchen and breakfasted. In an hour, said Glendufa, she would be ready to talk. He nodded and returned to his room and there, very carefully, covered a scrap of vellum with writing. He had just finished when a servant came to tell him that Paulus was here asking for him.

"Bring him up here."

Paulus climbed up and came in. Philip shook hands, gave him a chair, and started in.

"Look, my brother. I have been given an appointment with the Emperor. We're to see him Christmas morning, just before he leaves the castle to inspect the troops. That means we meet here at eleven. That suit you?"

"Of course," said the craggy farmer. "Whatever you say will suit me."

"Then come with a horse for each of us. We must ride, as befitting the dignity of delegates. Here, take this." Into the horny palm Philip put a dozen gold pieces. "That farm of yours is just outside town in the upper valley, I think?"

"Aye, where there's no lack of water for the olives."

"Good. I want you to get two good fast horses for me and

have them at the farm. Also water-skins and an outfit of simple white robes such as the desert men wear. I may have to leave here in haste and must neglect nothing. There are rumors of plots and killings. You'll be safe, but I may be in danger."

Paulus scratched his whiskers nervously. The idea of seeing the Emperor face to face was exciting; the supposed peril of the interview disturbed him terribly. He was jumping with alarm and anxiety.

"Oh, aye, about the horses—well and good. Nothing easier," said he. "And shall I wear my best clothes to the interview?"

"The best you have," said Philip. "Horses for it, remember. And two horses for me out at your farm. We'll go there from the castle. Is that enough money?"

"Enough and double," said Paulus, and departed.

Now Philip sought Glendufa, found her awaiting him, and closed the door. He gave her two of the gold pieces.

"For the physicians when they come. Keep them a little and dismiss them. I merely want to make sure that the people watching me think I'm ill."

"Very well. I can see my husband this afternoon. Now what's it all about?"

"The assassination of the Emperor, for which the Galileans are to be blamed," said Philip, watching her. "I'm very much tempted to let it go through and seize the opportunity to carry you off. Unfortunately, my father would disagree, and I doubt whether you would welcome a new life under such auspices, so I've decided on something else."

She went from white to red as she met his eyes. "You're serious?"

"Deadly serious, my dear," he rejoined. "I'm helpless to avert the killing. My companion Crates is in the plot. So are others of the imperial household, who are conniving with certain Parthians. No one can save Julian except the army officers. They must take action at the last minute—short, sharp, decisive action. Give your husband this information; here are the salient points written down for him."

He gave her the vellum, then launched into a description of the plot as he knew it and told where Tigranes was located.

"He must be seized. There must be no errors, no time wasted," he went on. "I myself will take the assassin in hand, because this will be a sop to my pride—a bit of action that will restore my self-respect, as it were." He smiled whimsically as he spoke. "All the rest, I leave to your husband. Other officers will be glad to join him. Julian is the idol of the army. And, I may say, he has promised that when Paulus and I see him he'll give us an edict of protection for the Christians here. Paulus doesn't know it yet."

"He—the Emperor—has promised you?" she said. "You know him?"

"Of course. Now, you understand—the action must be taken at the last minute, at noon, Christmas. It must be sweeping and complete, so far as possible. Not a soul can be trusted. Let your husband take full credit—I want none."

A servant knocked. There was a man here asking for Philip, he said. Glendufa went to see him and came back with a strip of vellum, saying that when she said Philip was ill, the man left this for him. It was the promised order on Lazar Brothers or their agents for the balance of the gold. Philip read it, laughed, and tucked it away.

As he stood up, Glendufa came to him, looking at him.

"I don't know what to say," she breathed softly. "You're a strange man, a remarkable man, and I like you. I'll carry out the errand, be sure of that."

She leaned forward and kissed him frankly and unskimpingly, perhaps secure in the feeling that he would understand.

Philip went to his own room and stayed there all afternoon. He had excellent company, for the sun appeared, pouring in at his window, and struck the Sphinx emerald into a glory of green depths and exquisite refractions. A long while he sat poring over the bit of beryl. As before, it left his mind composed, quiet, gratefully reassured.

Perhaps this was because he had chosen his course and there was no backing out. He knew this jewel was an exceptional, unique thing; but he had no belief in magic. Therefore he reasoned that its singular effect upon his mind must be a purely normal matter—as one sees figures in the leaping flames. Imagination, in other words. If so, very well. He was certain that the thing fascinated him beyond words. He meant to head for Alexandria, and Egypt was the land of the Sphinx.

"So, then, you go with me," he said, smiling a little. "And it may be that a new life awaits us both there, my precious emerald!"

A coruscation in the green depths winked back at him, and he laughed delightedly.

THAT EVENING he saw Glendufa briefly. All was well, she said; her husband had the matter in hand. There was no chance for private talk. The bishop, Meletius, had come to give Philip long-winded advice about approaching the Emperor and the arguments to use in seeking protection, and so forth. Philip listened blandly and said yes to everything. A saintly man, this bishop, but scarcely interesting.

The time passed draggingly, chiefly in avoidance of his hostess; to Philip, the memory of that kiss was burning temptation. When he wakened on Christmas morning, it was with a sigh of relief at the end of suspense. The day was dark, cloudy, chill with threatening rain. He made no pretence, took no part in the celebration of the Christians, but kept to his room.

AS morning advanced, he made his simple preparations. The emerald he safely pouched, together with a goodly store of gold and his precious draft on Lazar Brothers. A light cuirass of metal links, sword at waist, and a voluminous military cloak that covered these; he was ready. He watched the time carefully, went downstairs, and when Paulus came up the street on horseback, with a led horse, he stepped forth and greeted the grizzled farmer, who was in festive garb.

"Let's be gone," he said, swinging into the saddle. "To the castle!"

Paulus was excited, nervous, on edge. At the castle gates, Philip noted more guards than usual. A group of the 59th stood about, talking and laughing. Excellent; this showed that things were moving. The two were passed into the courtyard. Philip spoke softly, as they dismounted.

"I've had a tip to look out for trouble. If anything goes wrong, jump for the horses and ride out of the city. Make for your farm."

This did not reassure the farmer in the least.

At one side was the towering bulk of a huge war-elephant, his trappings bearing the imperial emblems. Soldiers and grooms and court officials were crowded around him. While elephants were no novelty, this was a magnificent beast chosen to carry Julian himself. Philip glanced at the throng. Somewhere there must be John of Iconium!

A chamberlain led him and Paulus into the antechamber of the imperial suite. Here were officers of the staff chatting in groups. There was a wait: Philip wondered how many of these fine-feathered officers were in the plot. At last came a chamberlain, and the two delegates were led into the private rooms of the Emperor.

Julian, who was dressing, greeted them affably. Paulus fumbled out some words about the Galileans and their faithful service and their apprehensions of danger. Julian took his hand and pressed it.

"Yes, yes. You're an honest man; I can see that for myself," he said. "Of course I don't know the half of what goes on in this city of yours. I've been thinking about you Galileans, however. I want to assure you of my protection. I've even drawn up an edict to that effect. Isn't this one of your religious festivals?"

*That first instant told Philip his
antagonist was a deadly swordsman;*

*he wasted no time in skill, but shifted into
the trick he had learned in Gaul.*

"It is the day we celebrate as the birthday of Christ," said Paulus.

"Ah, yes—the birthday of your god, eh? Well, you're free to worship him or anyone else." Julian beckoned a hovering secretary and took from him a folded vellum. He handed this to Philip. "Here you are, duly drawn up and sealed."

An expression of thanks, and the two delegates departed, Paulus smiling and jubilant. As they came into the courtyard, Philip took Paulus' arm.

"Go to the horses; be ready. I heard someone say we were to be stabbed before we got away. They mean to murder us. Let me see what I can do to prevent it."

He turned abruptly toward the group surrounding the elephant. Paulus, shocked and horrified, gawked after him, then started for the two horses.

Philip came briskly to the group and picked his man at once—a stranger to him, armed and holding a long elephant goad. Coming close to him, Philip tapped his shoulder.

"Are you John of Iconium?" he asked.

The other turned quickly.

"Aye—driver of the imperial elephant. What is it to you?" he replied, dark eyes stabbing suspiciously.

"You're under arrest—" Philip began, but got no farther.

The long goad dropped. Swift as light, the man's hand slid out sword and struck. Only the cuirass hidden under his cloak saved Philip from the shrewd, deadly blow, whose impact knocked him back a pace. The man was upon him with animal ferocity; but then his own sword was out and guarding. Yells went up from those around; they were quickly stilled.

That first instant told Philip that his antagonist was a deadly swordsman, but he was legion-trained, and every legion had its own tricks. He wasted no time in skill, but shifted into the trick he had learned in Gaul with the 12th Legion. A pretended slip to one knee, then up and inside the other's blade, his own point stabbing for the armpit. It took speed and skill—but it worked.

The blade drove home. John of Iconium went staggering, a gush of blood pouring from him.

In the same instant, Philip swung around. Others were closing in, steel flashing—he broke into a run and was away. Farmer Paulus was in his own saddle, staring, frightened. Philip gained the other animal and swung up. They went clattering for the gate. Men were running and shouting. The two horses broke through them.

Done! It was done, they were out in the street, clearing the way with furious voice. Paulus swept into the lead and made for the street leading to the east gate. Any pursuit dropped away long ere they reached it. There was no question as they slowed down and rode out, passing the wagons and country folk and seeking the clear road.

"Speed!" called Philip, and the other obeyed.

No pursuit. A mile, two miles, and no dust rose behind them. Paulus slewed out of the road into a track. The gray-green of olive groves lifted ahead, and a house and stables. Paulus was there first, and dismounted, his eyes goggling at Philip.

"You're hurt!" he cried, as the Roman dismounted, his cloak lifting away from him.

"Only a scratch," said Philip, with a laugh. "With that trick, the other fellow's blade usually catches your arm—you can tie it up. Here's the edict Julian gave us. You take care of it. Now for my clothes—"

"Come into the house. I'll show you, then get your horses."

No time was wasted. Paulus asked no questions. He bound up the bleeding arm, showed the heap of garments, and went out to saddle and bring forth the horses. Philip stripped, made sure of his precious pouch, and donned the new garments. When he came outside, Paulus was just leading out the horses, one for riding, the other for load of water-skins and food. Philip took his hand.

"Good man. Thanks. Now fear not—the crisis is past, you're

in no further harm. Give my love to Glendufa when you see her. Farewell!"

Queries enough now—Philip ignored them, picked up the reins and rode off. He knew already how to gain the great army highway that ran south through Syria to Paulusium and Alexandria. He was off—he was gone, with no one the wiser, none knowing where to seek him.

Yet—Glendufa had kissed him, and this was no memory to be lightly cast aside.

IT was Christmas Day these things happened. In the following June, greater things came to pass. For Julian, battling in the Parthian deserts, was struck by a shaft and killed, and most of his army destroyed. As one result of this, a new and Christian ruler was elected, to occupy Constantinople and make it capital of the Eastern Empire for a thousand years and more.

As a further result, a man in Alexandria named Aulus Gentius hastily packed and got aboard a galley leaving for Antioch. So much the record says, and ends. What became of him, whether he returned, no one knows; but I like to think that he went for a purpose and came not back to Egypt alone.

That kind of man would not.

THE JUSTICE OF AMRU

*Fanatic Followers of Mohammed stormed out
of Arabia in the seventh century to slaughter
the Greek troops of the Great Eastern Empire
and conquer Egypt... and again the strange
Sphinx Emerald came to the scene to play
its part in the unrolling historic drama.*

T H E   Y O U N G man was robbing a corpse, with perfect composure and efficiency. From the bearded shape lying in the shallows he stripped a fine camel-hair burnous and linen garments, spreading them to dry in the hot Egyptian sun. A purse, fat with gold, a saber of quality, a silver-sheathed knife, followed. A lump, wrapped in cloth and sealed with resin, was laid aside for future examination. The young man, who wore only a native white cotton gown, dirty and tattered, then removed excellent sandals from the feet of the corpse, eyed them with complacent approval, and set them also to dry. This done, he shoved the dead man out into the Nile current and sat down, wearily.

He was thin, hard, but had scant strength. The open neck of his robe revealed the start of a half-healed scar on his left chest. Another showed on his arm. A ring showed on his hand. His features were regular, unshaven for days and blurred with brownish beard; yet his gray eyes sparkled and there was a whimsical humor in his look. He had an air of cool, deft efficiency as he sat looking at the water of the Nile and the opposite shores.

"So our elegant sub-prefect of the Memphis nome now robs dead men!" said a voice.

The young man scarcely seemed to move; yet the knife on the sand beside him vanished. His whimsical look became a

wary glint. He glanced around; no one was in sight. The desolate
desert hills, the rocks and sand dunes, stretched emptily.

"A dead Arab," he observed, "may preserve the life of Gregory,
the sub-governor who has lost his district, his army and everything else. If you know me, come into sight."

A movement stirred. From the sand close behind him rose
a woman. In this waste of naked sand and rock she seemed a
dream-figure: white-clad, jeweled, golden hair knotted behind
her head, exhaling a delicious scent of perfumes. Gregory saw
her and stared.

"Impossible! Claris—or her ghost! Do ghosts appear in full
sunlight?"

"This one does," said she, coming forward. "Did you come
to save me?"

"Save you? I can't save myself," said he. "The world's gone to
pieces. I was left for dead—those Arabs smashed our troops at
the first charge. Some natives took care of me afterward. I

floated down the Nile last night on a log, crawled ashore here, and saw this dead Arab—"

"We can get to Memphis?" she queried.

"As slaves, yes. Those Arabs came straight across the desert from Arabia. They struck us at Memphis, took the city, and now they're marching downriver for Babylon and Alexandria. Nor is that the worst. But I'm famished—have you anything to eat?"

"All you want, at the villa," said she. "I've been there, ill, for two weeks. Everyone's gone now. I came to the river hoping to find a boat going downstream."

"Too late," said he. "Where's the villa?"

"A mile away, back from the river. I walked." Her tone was petulant.

"And you complain? Look, then."

He ripped away his robe, baring himself to the waist. Her lovely eyes saw the great wound-scar in front, the others about his ribs; those eyes lost their fixed blankness—they became

human. She seemed to waken from a dream. He saw she had been in a stupor of fright.

"Come. I'll take you," she said, turning. "There are no boats."

"None," he agreed dryly. "I can save you—perhaps. It's a gamble."

She struck out, led the way, spoke no word. He followed, unsteadily gathering up the Arab garments and sword; he was shaky, but clear mentally; she was physically well but cloudy and confused in mind, a person who had run slap into the world's end. Gregory knew her father must be dead with the Greek troops—few had escaped the Arab steel. Byzantium, the great Eastern Empire, had ruled Egypt; now, in this April of 640 A.D., the Arabs were taking it.

A QUEER situation, thought Gregory. Except for scattered up-country garrisons, the Greeks ruled from beautiful, impregnable Alexandria. The Egyptian country people, the Copts, were oppressed serfs. Then, a bolt from the blue, appeared Amru and his horde of desert Arabs—leaping suddenly out of the desert and capturing Memphis, nominal capital of the country. Strange men, these Arabs, fiery zealots of a new religion, enemies to the Greeks but not to Christians. The Greeks fled to Babylon or Alexandria, or were slain; the Copts fraternized with the invaders. And then—

Makokas, imperial prefect or governor of central Egypt, struck a bargain with Amru. Upon payment of one dinar per head, the Copts, who regarded the Arabs as saviors, were to be left unmolested. Grim Amru wanted converts to Mohammedanism or else a money payment. The bargain was struck; the Copts became friends; and down the Nile like a swarm of flies went the Greeks in wild panic—or else died. Babylon, an old fortress on the Mokattam hills across the Nile from the Pyramids and Great Sphinx, and Alexandria alone remained to the Greeks; and Amru was now marching upon them.

"And we happen to be in between," said Gregory, explaining

the situation as he plodded along through the sand. "Parties of Arabs have gone ahead. Amru follows with his main army—I hoped to get through, but could not make it. Any hour now, they'll be upon us."

"I can always die," she said—her only comment.

He spat out an oath. "Bosh! These Arabs are ignorant fellows, plain desert rats. They'll kill Gregory the sub-prefect like a dog. Illas the Magician they'll revere. I know their customs; I can talk their lingo—wait and see! And without a fleet they'll never take Alexandria. A fleet with aid and supplies will come from Byzantium, and they'll be helpless. Jackals baiting the moon—you'll see."

She said nothing. She appeared to be frozen inside.

They followed a road up along a wadi and came abruptly upon a house, a villa with some trees. It had water, obviously from a spring. Everything was wide open; when the slaves departed, they had looted it. Several horses showed in the stables, however Gregory fed and watered them while she looked on; then they went indoors.

"Now, Claris—wake up, move," he said abruptly. "Off with those fine clothes; put on the roughest you have. Gold? Jewels?" He shrugged. "Get what you have. I must eat, so must you."

She came to him, touched him, looked into his eyes.

"Is there hope? Can you save us?"

"Yes," he lied. "Of course. You must be my female slave, say my wife. And we've no time to lose. Eat first. Then clothes, then horses and get away from here."

"Come and look. The villa's been plundered."

The dishes, delicate glassware—everything was smashed and littered. They found food in plenty, and wine. Gregory made her eat, and did likewise. He had known her father well, and her too, in the days before the world's end. For the world had ended in Egypt, and the desert had come in.

The meal over, she disappeared. Gregory changed into his new garments. Curious, he cut open the wrappings of the hard

object taken from
the Arab. Green
caught his eye,
stopped his breath.
An emerald?
Undoubtedly.
Hastily he
wrapped it up
again. Jewels were
of no value now,
but might come in
very handy.

He roamed
about the house,
finding nothing
other persons
would value, yet
upon which he
seized with
avidity—bits of
parchment, a reed
pen, glass trinkets,
odds and ends such
as sewing materi-
als. He knew the desert people and their ways—simple, direct,
incredibly wrapped up in their new religion. These tribes had
come out of Arabia with a fierce and consuming belief, a disdain
of death, which swept away the finest legions of the Empire
like water. Nothing could stand before them. Amru had only
four thousand men, yet had already won Egypt. If Heraclius
the feeble emperor sent no help, then Amru would win
Alexandria as well.

"As for me," reflected Gregory, "I may escape—and there's
only one way. I don't pine to be a martyr. If I can use my head,
well and good. One error will get it sliced off."

Claris appeared while he was saddling two of the horses. To

A man, he wrote, had sought him, demanding that he produce gold by magic. Amru understood, and swore heartily.

his delight, she was now a different person—fine Greek raiment replaced by ordinary blue cotton garments covered with a white burnous, a dirty cloth wrapped about her head. Gregory caught her hand, touched his lips to it, and laughed.

"Excellent! Just be yourself—a Greek slave, eh? You can sew? Then mount, and let's get away from here. I need some sewing done; then we'll be ready for anything."

BY DEGREES, he perceived, she was emerging from the frozen hopelessness, and returning to her warm self. She had seen everything she knew pass as a dream; she had heard, too, that her father was dead. He could not discuss the matter now. He knew time was short and fate hard upon their heels.

She did net look back; they rode toward the river highway. When they sighted it, Gregory saw it was empty, the river empty, but high dust was rising to the south. On the north, it was not far to Babylon; indeed, across the Nile the ponderous blue masses of the Pyramids showed against the horizon, but Arabs would be riding there, skirmishers for the army. At the villa, Gregory had smeared his bearded features and hands with dust and grime. These Arabs were no darker than he, but it was imperative that he be not known for a Greek.

Within sight of the river, he halted beside a cluster of rocks.

"Time for the sewing, Claris," he said. "While you sew, I must write; and I think I'll play dumb after this. Speak with me by signs only."

She dismounted. There was no shade; they sat by the rocks in the sunlight. Gregory doffed burnous and the shirt beneath, and showed her what he wanted sewed. She went at it with nimble fingers. He had fetched a small horn of ink from the villa, and with the reed pen began to write on scraps of the parchment—not in Greek, but in queer letters without vowel signs. He had received an excellent grounding in Arabic, which was largely similar to Aramaic, the language generally used. Much of his official work had been among the nomad tribes, in consequence.

The sewing was finished, to his delighted satisfaction, and he dressed.

"Well! Now, with luck, we're ready for anything! Mount and ride."

"North?" she asked. "To Babylon?"

"No. South—toward victorious Amru, who's not far."

The dust-cloud, rising to the zenith, was close at hand now.

Gregory took the reins of the other horse, for the looks of the thing. Afternoon was wearing on. Behind him was now nothing—his career gone, family lost in the whirl of war, life itself a mere gamble. Claris remained, a relic of the past, a lovely relic…. Worth while? He could not tell, as yet. He recollected the emerald, laughed, and handed it to her.

"A gift for you, fair lady—an emerald, I believe. It may amuse you—"

She took it, then lifted her head. A cry escaped her.

"Look—steel! Coming toward us!"

He saw the party of horsemen, steel glinting in the sun.

"Very well. Remember, I'm dumb; say nothing. Use signs if you must."

They rode toward the horsemen. Behind these appeared others, extending into a great dun dust-cloud that mounted the heavens. Here was the entire Moslem army on the move. The vanguard drew near—gaunt brown, bearded figures in makeshift armor. The leader wore mail taken from a Greek. He drew rein, gaze glittering on Gregory, with harsh challenge.

GREGORY LIFTED his hand, turning down the two central fingers—an approximation of the Arabic characters for Allah. He drew rein stirrup with the warrior, pointed to his mouth, making dumb play. Arabs clustered around.

"Kill the dog!" went up growls. "Take the woman, Musa. They are Greeks."

Gregory looked at the leader and laughed. He leaned forward, and they all saw him pluck a scrap of parchment from the ear of Musa's horse. He gave this parchment to Musa, who took it, opened it, saw writing, and stared in astonishment. Amazed grunts went up. A man who could read was shoved forward. He looked at the parchment. His jaw fell.

"It is the name of Amru ibn el-Aas!" he stammered.

"Then, by Allah, this is his affair and not mine," said Musa, and beckoned a warrior. "Guide these two to the General, tell him what happened. Forward!"

Gregory and Claris followed their guide out of the road, and the vanguard pushed on. After them came the main body of the army—all horsemen or camel corps, marching by tribes, tough desert warriors. Slaves and loot had been left behind; there was no baggage convoy; they were going to fight and nothing else. Tents loaded on camels brought up the rear.

Amru with his chief leaders and finest horsemen held the center of the march—a fine vigorous man, exceptional in feature and body; simple and fanatical like them all, yet vibrant with authority and conscious power. The serried lines opened up for the guide and his two charges to gain the General's staff. Amru glanced at them, listened to what the guide said, then waved his hand.

"Everything to its time," he replied. "When the night halt is made, when the sunset prayer is said and we have eaten, I will see them. Until then, upon your head be their safety and care. Forward."

The staff, the army, moved forward. A little army, barely four thousand in all, but of such men as were rarely seen in the world.

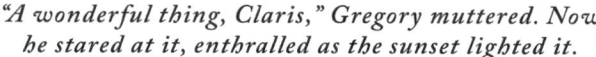

*"A wonderful thing, Claris," Gregory muttered. Now
he stared at it, enthralled as the sunset lighted it.*

Intent, fearless, utterly obedient, with a supreme confidence in heaven's aid, and superbly capable. And a leader, thought Gregory, like unto his men, worthy of them. It was no wonder these men had scattered the legions of the Empire like grass in the wind.

No convoy of luggage, except tents. No engines of war. No slaves and captives. No vast stores of food and loot. Just four thousand iron men moving to capture Babylon and Alexandria, in order to spread their faith.

Gregory played dumb and heard much talk. On the morrow they would sight the towers of Babylon and, across the Nile, the Pyramids and Sphinx. Many of these Arabs had been in Egypt previously. They knew the country. They marveled at the Sphinx above all things. One man said there was a second Great Sphinx, back in the Mokattam hills—one came first to forests of petrified trees. They told fantastic stories about the place. The Sphinx was an ancient river-beast turned to stone like the trees, they said.

The captives wakened great curiosity, and the stories of the guide; but Gregory heard nothing and spoke no word. At the afternoon prayer, when all dismounted and bowed, toward Mecca, he moved not. He was quite aware, however, of the interest roused in one man by Claris. This man, Khalid, was a warrior of renown, to judge by his arms and bearing, and was a handsome dark devil to boot. The guide, however, warned him away from the girl, and he obeyed for the moment. Gregory saw trouble there, ere long. These men amazed him and frightened him. Jackals baiting the moon? Plain desert rats? At thought of his own words, he grimaced. He was readjusting all his opinions now.

The march was halted at last. No tents were pitched. Food was given the two; the army ate. Ablutions were made. Then, as the sun touched the western sand, voices of muezzins were heard, and the army prayed as one man. After that, the guide took his two charges to the circle of captains and the presence of Amru.

Claris was left aside. Gregory came forward and sat down, face to face with the hard-eyed Amru. He made no pretence of being deaf, but made signs of writing, and in the sand drew letters with a stick. As he did so, he uncovered a bit of parchment. Everyone saw him pick it from the sand and look at it. He gave it to Amru, whose eyes glinted in astonishment. It was handed around. Grunts broke forth as the words written on it were read aloud: *"Victory. Egypt is given to Amru, the slave of Allah."*

Very careful not to cheapen his tricks, Gregory guarded all he said and did. Writing in the sand, he gave his name—Illas the Magician. Illas, of the tribe of Pent, from the country to the far west and south—the desert. Puzzled, caught by his magic powers, they followed the stick in the sand, fired in questions; Amru alone said nothing—sat watching everything. When Gregory picked up pebbles and they vanished, when he changed bits of dry stick into gold coins before their eyes, Amru spoke at last.

"Magic is from Allah or from the devils. Whence comes yours?"

Gregory took warning, and wrote: *"Who is Allah?"*

This roused instant indignation, anger and jeers. "He is an infidel—slay him!" rose the cry. Gregory wrote rapidly, and Amru read the words. He had come with his wife, in search of a new deity foretold him. This was all Amru needed.

"By Allah and Allah!" he exclaimed. "Look you! I, of the Koreish tribe, once flouted and fought against Mohammed, the prophet of Allah. May he be blessed! Now I fight for him, for the Caliph Omar, for the true faith. Was I not brought to see the light? Shall this infidel come from afar in search of Allah, whose very name he knows not, and be slain? For shame! He comes, and by his magic foretells victory. Why?"

He turned and shot the direct question at Gregory.

"Listen, infidel! Do you seek instruction in the true faith?"

Gregory nodded. An eager word escaped Amru.

"You see? That is it. Allah be praised! Cursed with dumbness, he yet speaks with us; Allah has given him some power of magic, also. Let him be given a tent, with his wife; let food be supplied them; let one of the scribes be assigned to instruct him."

Khalid, who had edged into the circle, struck in with bold words.

"Let him be shaven, also, and tested to see if he knows Greek."

"Be shaven—and shamed before all men?" said Amru acidly. "Is that how you would interpret the hospitality due to a guest— one who asks your aid and seeks your faith? When such men as you, Khalid, give orders in the Caliph's name, then will the true faith become accursed of men! Let it be done as I have ordered."

S O, U P O N the next night, within sight of the massive round towers of Babylon, and the Pyramids west across the Nile, the tents were pitched—the massive dark tent of Amru first, center of the encampment. In those days the river ran so close to Babylon's walls that a huge stone quay jutted into it from the enormous towers. Greeks were jammed into the place, but Amru's clouds of light horse swept the whole land unopposed. And amid the tents was that of Illas the Magician and his wife. When he came into the tent that afternoon and stretched out beside her, he was in deep gloom.

"There's no hope, Claris," he said under his breath. "I've just heard terrible news. They say no aid will be sent Alexandria, and that Heraclius has given up the entire province as lost."

"Is that so terrible for us?" she demanded. "We're safe. We have shelter. These Arabs give us food."

He grunted. "Yes. I hoped for escape to the fortress here, or to Alexandria. But the Greek troops are leaving the fortress, going down to occupy the island in the river, leaving the citadel empty. Treachery, of course. Amru will occupy the place tomorrow. And Alexandria will be a death-trap for all who are in it.

I hear most of the ships have already left. Well, I'll have to sleep here in the tent."

She laughed lightly. "Don't be absurd about it! All conventions are swept away; we remain alive—nothing else matters. Now come closer. I want to show you something. I've had plenty of time to study it, and it repays study."

GREGORY MADE the discovery of the Sphinx emerald, as he sat on the sand looking at it in the sunset light—the emerald he had taken from the dead Arab, the emerald at which he had scarcely glanced. Now he stared at it, enthralled, as the sunset lighted it up.

Immediately he began figuring how he could make use of it. What he had learned of news brought in by the scouts, had confirmed all his half-formed plans and schemes. He had been playing a sure thing with the Arabs; they were eager for converts above all else, and it really mattered little to him what he was. Religion had never meant much to him, anyway. With his knowledge of Egypt, of war, of the Empire, he could rise to any height he liked among them.

Sight of the Sphinx in the beryl captivated his fancy. It was a perfect, tiny Sphinx image, formed by the flaws and bubbles of the beryl, which came together, making it. The perfection of it startled him. The stone was, otherwise, rather poor in color, and had been poorly cut or trimmed in cabochon form.

"A wonderful thing? Claris," he muttered. The sunset light, entering by a chink of the tent-flap, struck athwart the stone now, straight across it. Gregory found sudden new depths and vistas opening to his fancy, and fell silent in amazed interest. The play of refracted color hushed his hurried thoughts and stilled all impulses; it was like a benison—a silent blessing upon the mind—filling him with noble and inspiring fantasies.

Not that noble thoughts were of any avail, he reflected later, when he stretched out in the sand to sleep. He and Claris were at the end of the world; anything that would save them was justified. He would be killed; she would be sent, like other golden maids of Egypt, to the bed of the Prophet, were the truth known about them. And now he knew there was no help, no escape. Alexandria and everyone left in it was lost. Noble thoughts, indeed! Poppycock!

Morning found her laughing, gay-eyed, intent upon turning the shabby tent into a home. She had changed enormously; the shock was absorbed; she was herself again. Gregory went off to watch affairs, thinking of her, marveling at her, but highly uncertain of her.

Amru and his captains were slow to occupy the great massive towers of Babylon. The Greeks had abandoned the fortress and were hurriedly entrenching upon the island; it seemed madness, and it was madness, but the Arabs scented a trap and had no men to lose. Not until evening did they seep into the fortress and finally seize it, almost without a fight. For the Greeks, who had no boats, there was no escape. Amru sent off hurried orders upriver to Memphis to bring all available craft at once.

Gregory, that day, received lessons, which he protracted with idle queries, from a scribe, touching the new faith of Mohammed. He sat long gazing at the emerald, too; he was at this when a shadow touched him. He covered the stone as Khalid appeared, dropped beside him in the sand, and grinned through spiky whiskers.

"Greetings, and peace," said the Arab. "Inside that burnous there is a patch, under the left arm, sewn with red thread. I sold the burnous to El Bokhari. Where is he?"

Gregory met the impudent grin and knew himself caught. El Bokhari had been that dead Arab whom he had tripped. It was truth about the patch. He leaned forward and wrote in the sand. Khalid squinted at the writing.

"He is bewitched—ho, you bewitched El Bokhari, did you? I'll bewitch you with my sword, infidel! That is, unless you make it worth my while. Eh? Yes or no?"

Gregory thought fast. He had the pouch of golden loot. Conversion would make his position secure, but this was still in the future. For the moment, he must buy silence or else be ruined by this rascal. Khalid, sensing his hesitation, chuckled.

"Lend me your woman for two or three days or nights. Either that or gold. Yes?"

Gregory nodded and wrote. Ten golden byzants. Good enough, said Khalid, but when? Tomorrow night. The Arab rose,

"Good; a promise. See that it is kept, or you'll be sorry."

He departed. Gregory uncovered the emerald again, and was staring at it when he heard a step. Claris, this time. She laughed lightly. Her eyes were dancing.

"Looking at the magic stone again? Well, tell me something. How far goes this game of religious instruction? Do you intend to assume the Arab faith?"

He eyed her narrowly. She seemed in extraordinarily high spirits.

"There seems to be no other prospect," he said slowly. "Yes, to be honest, I think it must be done. I suppose you'll upbraid me for a renegade Christian?"

"Not at all," she returned, to his surprise. "I didn't think you had that much common sense, Gregory. And what about me?"

"You?" He fingered his new beard, still watching her. "You? Oh, I'll manage to assure your safety—"

"I'm not worried about my safety," she said, dimpling. "That handsome Khalid tells me—well, never mind now. You've relieved me. Good luck, my dear."

She went, and Gregory returned to his emerald. She was appearing in a new and vastly different light now. No longer the dazed, hapless refugee, she was bright, cheerful, heartless, indifferent to what fate might bring, so long as she did not suffer. Aye, herself, her true self!

He growled under his breath. There must be a devil in this emerald, the way it made him see things clearly! Why, he himself was just what he had seen her to be—no whit better, assuring himself safety by any means at hand! The green stone blinked at him. A scheme had come into his head regarding those ten golden byzants, also; he had laid a pretty trap there for Khalid. He had the gold in his pouch now.

"Just like her," he thought, staring into the emerald depths. "Grabbing at any straw that may save—save what? Life? Why, it's a shabby thing, anyhow. Honor? That's lost in any case. Position? A new future? Bah!"

QUEER THOUGHTS, certainly. Did they come from the green stone? Was there something magic in it and its tiny emblem of the Sphinx? He put it away, and instantly felt relieved, once more confident and assured. Trap Khalid, yes; accept the teachings of the scribe, pronouncing the few words that would make him one of the Moslems, the enlightened—then he was safe, his future secure. So little a thing to do, so much to gain! His old wounds were healing—his strength had returned—he was himself again. He laughed a little as he fell asleep that night. Amru had the fortress now—see him tomorrow and bait the trap for Khalid!

On the morrow he turned again to the emerald; it fascinated him, though it left him troubled and ill at ease, since somehow it confused all his purposes. He took it out into the full sunlight. Far beyond, the hills and fortress and the Nile were outspread, Pyramids and Sphinx in the distance. The Greeks were entrenching feverishly. As yet, Amru had made no attack, for he was awaiting the boats due today or tomorrow.

The hot, direct sunlight wakened new depths within the green stone. Gregory was conscious, now, of the mental effect upon him. He was quieted, eased, his troubles were wiped away; his temptations were all folly. He had never heard of auto-hypnosis, yet the condition was plain enough. To him it seemed that the emerald was guiding him. That tiny Sphinx held him spellbound, was almost speaking to him. Saying what? Things he disliked and rebelled against; yet he could not forego listening and looking.

The scribe came and spoke of Mohammed and the law, the

new faith, Gregory listened, and accepted dutifully; in the sand
he wrote that he almost believed—just one or two things more
to be understood. The teacher went away rejoicing. Gregory,
having made ready his pieces of gold, went to see Amru, at the
big tent.

Seated beside the General, where his writing in the sand
could be deciphered with ease, he fell to work. A man, he wrote,
had sought him, demanding that he produce gold by magic.
Amru understood, and swore heartily.

"By Allah, produce that man, infidel!" he said. "His name!"

Gregory demurred. Charges were one thing, belief another.
Perhaps on the morrow he would make public profession of
his belief. Let Amru judge for himself. Upon this, he plucked
the first byzant out of the sand beneath Amru's foot.

One by one he produced them, one from the very hand of
Amru, while the watching captains grunted and marveled. Ten
in all. He piled them together, then wrote rapidly:

"Beloved of Allah, with your knifepoint mark each coin
secretly, so that you will know it again. Tomorrow I will summon
the man who takes the gold from me."

PERCEIVING HOW the trap was being laid, the
General chuckled, and the warriors around watched the scene
with amusement. Amru swore them to silence, then with his
knife he made faint marks upon the coins—solid coins, minted
in Byzantium, of full gold, soft to the steel point.

Gregory pouched them again. Amru said that if he were a
true believer, he might fight against the Greeks on the morrow
in the ranks of the faithful; the island would be attacked as
quickly as the boats arrived. This was a distinct shock. It had
never occurred to him that he must fight against his own people.

"Better, perhaps," spoke up someone, "to let him try a sword
against whatever warrior of the faithful he accuses."

"As Allah liveth, let it be so!" exclaimed Amru. Gregory
assented and withdrew. He had made his point, and now let
Khalid, avid of gold and women, beware the trap!

That afternoon fighting began, for the boats were coming down in swarms from upriver and the troops were eager to attack the island. It was close, hand-to-hand work, but Amru stopped it before the sunset prayer. It was obvious that the position of the Greeks was hopeless, therefore, said shrewd Amru, attack in the morning, that the remainder of the day might give time for slaughter and prisoners.

Khalid came to Gregory's tent in the evening dusk, obtained his promised gold, saluted Claris with a flourish, and went his way. Gregory made no comment. He was thinking of what must happen when he became one of the Moslems and must fight the Greeks, here or at Alexandria or elsewhere. He lay sleepless a long while that night, his mind busy, and noted that Claris laughed in her sleep. She, at least, no longer dreaded the future.

Kettledrums and trumpets wakened him. It was just after the sunrise prayer, and in swarms of boats the Arabs were at the attack. Amru sat in his tent and watched. For a space Gregory watched also, heartsick, but then turned away from the sight. The Greeks were doomed....

For a space, Gregory sat under the sunrise, gazing at the emerald, oblivious to the slaughter at the island. The green stone spoke to him, wakened bitter things in his brain. He knew that destiny was upon him now, that he could not postpone decision; action was imperative. He must go ahead with his schemes and advance the future, seize the prepared strings and go forward to fame and fortune—

"Oh, renegade! Renegade!" He started. The words actually seemed to come from the stone. He could hear them as with an inner ear. The green fields shining in the sun, the scintillant emerald depths there before him—he looked up and away with eyes that hurt, and sighted Amru sitting in his tent entrance. Amru—oh, by God, there was a man! A true man, a great man, no palpitant coward scheming and conniving to save his pitiful little life....

A groan burst from him. He shoved the emerald away and
let it lie in the sunlight, came to his feet, and going into his
tent, took the keen curved sword he had found on the dead
Arab. He flung off the heavy burnous and walked to the tent
of the General. After a moment Amru looked at him, and made
a gesture. Gregory seated himself and laid the sword before the
feet of the Arab.

"We have conquered, thanks to Allah!" said Amru.

"I too have conquered," said Gregory. The other, with startled
surprise at this speech from a dumb man, gave him a piercing
look. "Aye, Amru. I am Gregory, sub-prefect of central Egypt,
your captive. I played a dark and subtle game and I am sick of
it. I do not care for life. I am not a convert. The woman is not
my wife. I am not dumb. Call your warrior Khalid, who took
my money under threat of exposing me, and let him kill me
and end it all. I am alone and weary, and wish to die."

THE BITTER words poured out of him. Amru made no
reply, but gazed at him for a long moment, then crooked a finger
at one of the guards and ordered Khalid brought. Gregory sat,
chin drooped on chest, staring at nothing. It was done, and he
was glad.

There was a wait. One man after another came with reports—
the island was taken; the Greeks were slain or captive. The
messengers stood waiting. The captains came from the island
and the pursuit, wiping their weapons or binding their hurts.
All looked at Amru and the bowed figure before him as word
passed around of what Gregory had confessed.

Then came two men bringing Khalid. He was eager and
laughing, and wore fine Greek armor taken from an officer.
Amru cocked a finger at him and spoke to him.

"Peace to you, Khalid. You fought well. Where got you that
armor?"

Khalid laughed. "From an infidel Greek who no longer
needed it."

*Khalid pressed the attack, gaining confidence,
putting out everything he had. Suddenly, swift
as light, Gregory saw his chance coming—*

"So! Is it true that you are blessed by Allah with money of gold?"

Khalid felt beneath his armor and brought forth a pouch that hung about his neck by a thong.

"A little," said he. "I took it from the Greek who wore this same armor. He sought to buy his life with it—in vain."

Amru stretched out his hand and took the pouch. He opened it, and examined the gold coins it revealed. Khalid flung a glance at the motionless Gregory, but sensed nothing amiss—until, with a sudden violent cry, Amru threw the coins from him and scattered them afar in the sand.

"Liar! Each of those coins bears the secret mark I myself made on them. You had the gold from this infidel to buy your silence. You have taken part with infidels to betray your brethren of the faith."

Gregory looked up and uttered a harsh laugh.

"Behold justice, Khalid!" he said. "In the trap, my friend—in the trap!"

Hearing the dumb man speak, seeing the look on the faces of those who stood around, suddenly perceiving that he was lost, Khalid could find no words. Nor had he time, for Amru's voice pealed forth in deep anger.

"As I swore by Allah, so let it be done. Your sword, infidel—and you, Khalid! Up! Up and kill!"

Men came crowding forward to see. The hot, quiet sunlight was abruptly electrified by the savage words. To his feet sprang Gregory, baring the sword he had brought. There were no preliminaries. Khalid whirled upon him, snarling and furious, then leaped forward with naked blade.

But, to the amazement of all, the infidel could use his weapon. Gregory knew it was the end of everything for him, and smiled. At least he could die fighting—a soldier, not a craven! He parried the assault, unheeding the stark ferocity of the man facing him, then launched his own attack, sharply.

In those master hands the blades clashed and clashed again, slithering in and out. No quarter—a fight to the death, and both men knew it. Each put forth his skill, and for a space it seemed that little happened; but the keen watching eyes knew swordsmanship, understood each twist of muscle and stance, and yells of approval went up. A leap, a turn of the sword, a parry swift and deft as the assault, in and out, in and sideways, then they were standing almost toe to toe, blade countering blade, hot breaths panting, steel ringing as the quick chopping strokes were parried.

MORE AND more watchers gathered. The word spread: men came running; they ringed the open space a dozen deep. Wagers were laid and taken. Still the angry steel rang and clashed, blows missed by a miracle, skill countered skill. Khalid had a disadvantage in his looted armor, and Gregory was aware of it; he knew that armor; Khalid did not. He was saving himself, waiting until he could get a chance at the shoulder-chink. Both men were beginning to fail; the terrific expenditure of energy had told on them, and they were running with sweat; but Gregory gave ground more and more, waiting for the one chance that he dared not miss.

Khalid pressed the attack, gaining confidence, putting out everything he had. Suddenly, swift as light, Gregory saw his chance coming—as sure of it as though a whisper at his ear told him. Khalid drew back, poised for a blow. There was the opening, and Gregory was ready for it when it came. His steel flamed in the sunlight; the keen edge found the shoulder-chink and sheared in—in and in—down through the shoulder. Then Khalid staggered back and wrenched the haft from Gregory's sweaty palm, and stood there with the sword fastened in him and his arm almost sheared away and the blood spurting.

In that one frightful instant, Khalid reacted convulsively, almost blindly. The sword left his hand. He threw it, as he fell—flung it point first. The steel struck Gregory, who was staggering from his own effort and unsuspecting—struck him under the arm and brought him down in a sprawled heap as it pierced into him.

There they lay, as the yelling, excited watchers leaped out and huddled about them. Amru strode through the throng, looked at the dead Khalid, then turned to Gregory.

"He is not dead," said a man, examining him. "A bad hurt, but he will live."

"Slay! Slay! Kill the infidel!" went up hot voices.

Amru swung around and lifted his arms.

"In the name of Allah, the merciful!" leaped out his dominant voice. "Know ye not what is written in the Ninth Sura of al-Koran? Listen, then! If any of the infidels demand your protection, it says, give him your protection, that he may hear the word of God; and afterward let him reach the place of his security. So long as they act with fidelity toward you, do ye also act with fidelity toward them; for God loves those who fear him.

"So it is written, and I obey," he went on, amid a deep hush. "This infidel came not against us with arms, but demanding protection. Now carry him away, bind up his hurts, and when he is well let him go in peace to his own place. So this matter is settled. We have overcome the unbelieving enemy. Let the prisoners be gathered in this fortress. Let our wounded and a hundred sound men remain to hold the place. The remainder of the army marches tonight, after the evening prayer, upon Alexandria. Strike the tents and be ready!"

S O G R E G O R Y was carried away, and in the mercy of Allah passes out of the story. Yet the tale is not ended.

The Greek camp was looted. Much time was spent gathering the prisoners and finishing the pursuit of those who escaped. Amru himself had a look after many details. While he was about them, a warrior came to him saying he had found a piece of glass lying on the sand in the camp. Most of these desert men had never seen jewels.

Amru took it, perceived that it was not glass but a great emerald, and when he looked more closely he saw inside it the tiny figure of the Sphinx—like to the mighty stone Sphinx with red face and headdress across the river near the Pyramids. He stared at the emerald and marveled, and stared again; then, sighing, handed it back.

"Turn it in with the rest of the booty for later division," he ordered, "that no man may profit more than another."

So was it done. What then became of the emerald, or what became of the girl Claris, is not set down in the records. One thing, however, is known of a certainty. That is, that as the afternoon waned, Amru saw that the tents were not being struck; he demanded the reason.

It was reported that, at the very top of his own tent, a pair of doves had made a nest. The birds were shown him at their work; he was asked for the definite order to destroy their nest that the tent might be struck.

"God forbid," said he, "that any true believer should refuse protection to whatever living creature sought the shadow of his hospitality! Let those birds, who have become my guests, be respected as such. Leave my tent here where it is until we have taken Alexandria and returned here."

Thus, to this very day, Mohammedans know as Al Fustat, the Tent, the great city which rose upon this site—the city known to the rest of the world as Cairo.

IX

SWORDSMEN OF SALADIN

*In the Twelfth Century an intrigue at the court
of the great Sultan Saladin brings forth the
Sphinx Emerald to play its strange magic rôle.*

L IKE OLD WHOOSIS, the Roman poet, I sing of swords and rascals. With certain few exceptions, all men are rascals. I am, naturally, one of the exceptions. Yet my career has given me no cause of pride, unless it be the affection in which I hold my master Saladin, as he is usually called—a contraction for Sala'h-ud-Din, which means "Honoring the Faith." His given name is Yusuf or Joseph. In the Kurdish country where he came from, they use Biblical names.

Greek-born in Alexandria, I was educated as a scribe. My drunken father sold me to the Arabs as a slave, and I was named El Bahi, "The Elegant," because of my good looks. I was taken to Cairo, rapidly made my way and became secretary to Saladin when he came to Cairo, a green Kurdish country boy, with his uncle the governor. This was in the Year of the Hegira 564, or as Christians reckon it 1168, if you must have history.

Myself, I have no love for history; it is dull work. I have set out to tell the truth here, and it deals with some chancy intrigue, an honest eunuch, and a bit of hot swordplay—also with that accursed and beautiful jewel the Sphinx Emerald. This may also be history, but it is generally unknown and deserves to be told. So, with one hand upon my alleged heart, I bow gracefully; El Bahi is at your service with the truth. Salutations!

Let me skip the preludes of intrigue, treachery and struggle. Five years after coming to Cairo, Saladin's uncle was dead, and he was governor of Egypt for the Sultan Nureddin, chief ruler

of the Moslem world. As his secretary, I was doing very well
for myself. His vizier, the eunuch Karakush, ruled the city and
country, with all its emirs and captains, Mameluke slaves and
soldiers, workmen and Egyptians. Let me paint these three
men for you, since our world revolved about them:

I was rather small, stoutish, of great elegance in dress and
manners, and well accustomed to finesse—in a word, a diplomat.
I came only to the shoulder of my good friend the tall and
scrawny Karakush. He was given to violence and savage passions, but was actually secretive and highly careful. We lived in
the old palace with Saladin and his soldiers, but both of us were
too wise to cut any figure among the swaggering emirs and
great lords. Jealousy and treachery were everywhere, and throats
were swiftly cut.

Karakush had one talent; he was a gifted builder, and over a

cup of wine could dream great dreams in stone, which later took shape. He was spending Saladin's wealth, and held our master in great love. So did I, and why not? Everyone loved Saladin.

He was then thirty-five, handsome and generous, brave as a lion, so clever with arms that no warrior could stand against him. Yet he could dissimulate, worm his way amid conflicting interests, and suddenly seize an unsuspected point. We had served him well when he became governor. Perhaps Karakush suspected his ambition; I knew it, for Saladin confessed it to me one afternoon after dictating letters.

"El Bahi, the wind is stirring the trees," he said. "Sultan Nureddin—may Allah prolong his years!—is a suspicious old man. Luckily, the Crusaders in Jerusalem are keeping him too busy to molest me. What would happen if I took arms against him?"

"Things unpleasant to you," I said. I noted that he was playing with a great green stone set in a ring, but at the moment thought nothing of it. He had startled me. "Nureddin is the Commander of the Faithful, head of our religion; also, he has armies. Your emirs and captains swore fealty to him; they obey you because you govern in his name. He can depose you. He can slay you. That is, if he can reach you."

Saladin grunted. "I had a pigeon this morning. Nureddin orders me to join him with my best troops to lay siege to the Christian city of Karak, their Arabian outpost. This means he wants me under his thumb. I must either obey him or defy him."

HERE WAS evil news. Nureddin had established a very efficient pigeon-post linking all quarters of the empire. Saladin himself handled the letters that came by pigeon—one day from Damascus, two days from Bagdad. It was like magic! …. His reflective eyes dwelt upon the jewel in his hand, then rose to meet mine.

"This is highly secret news," he went on. "Give me your advice, El Bahi. Egypt is rich and powerful. Karakush is now building a citadel on the hill above the city. I am tempted. Emir El Ghazy is confident that I could defy the Sultan with impunity."

Here was worse tidings. "El Ghazy is a rogue. He'd love to ruin you. He's a good soldier but a bad guide."

"He gave me this emerald," Saladin said. "An ancient stone found in the palace treasury—one of magic power."

I CLUCKED my tongue at him and laughed. This angered him.

"Stop evading!" he snapped. "I want advice, not grins."

"Opinions are prompt, but advice comes best after sleep," I said. "In the morning, I'll give what you ask. Let me sleep upon it."

*It was an imposing procession that arrived
at the house behind the Mosque of El
Azhar. Safir, decked with a jeweled Persian
caftan, made a magnificent figure.*

He nodded, his gaze returning to the emerald, which seemed
to fascinate him.

"Very well. A splendid fellow, El Ghazy. He gives jewels like
a sultan—jewels that hold angels or devils, I'm not sure which."

He seemed dreamy and uncertain, and this worried me.

The reason? I got a hint of it that evening when I unburdened myself to Karakush, giving him the whole story. We were accustomed to such confidences; we worked together for mutual protection, highly necessary in a palace crammed with intrigue and treachery. He liked me, and I had great respect for his brains. More than once we had managed affairs behind the curtains and effected great issues.

Chewing at his eternal sweetmeats, which never put any fat on his belly, the gaunt eunuch eyed me sardonically but said nothing till I had finished.

"Our heads are very loose on our shoulders, El Bahi," he grunted abruptly. "Emir El Ghazy, may Allah blast him, is a clever fellow, a spy for Sultan Nureddin. Unless we can get our master Saladin out of this tight pinch, we'll be in a tighter one ourselves."

"No argument," I commented.

He snarled between his thin lips. "You placid cat! If I didn't know your sharp claws and keen wits, I'd throw a cushion at you! Look at the game we play! Nureddin makes the overt move to catch the eye, but he's far away. Emir El Ghazy holds the sword, unsuspected. He's the danger-point, the one to watch. Somehow he has over-reached us.... Ha! An emerald, you say! Did you examine it closely?"

"I paid it no attention."

"I've heard tales of such a stone; it bewitches men, casts a charm upon them. Hm! You have a cat's nimble jump. How would you handle the Sultan's demands on Saladin?"

I told him, and he nodded slowly.

"Well enough; but the peril is here with El Ghazy. Ten to one, there's a woman in it, too. You pry into that angle. Saladin's no prude; question him. And remember, he has terrific pride and self-esteem! I'll go after the larger game. I can reach the length of the great road, into the hell-pit of the Pyramids, and to the craggy heights above."

The sardonic demon loved to boast, but this was the simple truth. Having Saladin's entire confidence, he was pushing forward vast constructions. First in Cairo, where the citadel was building and the city walls being extended to take in the older towns of El Fostat and Babylon. Then a great army road was being built, north into Lower Egypt and south to the Cataracts, following the Nile. Canals, bridges, cisterns were being constructed with the stones of several small pyramids. Having thousands of slaves and free workmen at his own orders, Karakush was almost unlimited in power.

However, I had some abilities myself. Before midnight I had set a dozen skillful men at work, and had written a letter to the Sultan. Then I turned in to sleep. There would be trouble with El Ghazy, of course, but I was fairly sure of Saladin. He never drank, being fanatical on the subject; he had a repressed love of horseplay; his vanity and pride were solid qualities, well founded; and while he paid no heed to slaves and common girls, he did have an eagle eye for an exceptional woman. So I knew just about where to lay hold of him. And if I knew nothing about weapons and made no swaggering show, as Saladin's secretary I had an almost unlimited expense account, which was useful. Saladin had issued glass money, as a novelty, but I had a fat chest of golden dinars on which to draw; and a gold coin is worth a dozen blustering swordsmen.

NEXT MORNING Saladin came to my room after the sunrise prayer—he kept unearthly hours—and cursed me for a lazy dog on finding me still asleep. I gave him the letter I had written, and he read it with astonishment.

"So I'm an obedient slave of the Sultan, am I? Obeying his commands with devout speed ... the troops being gathered ... arranging to meet him at Karak.... In Allah's name, what means this nonsense?"

"Not nonsense; good sense," I said sleepily. "Gather the troops. It'll keep 'em busy. Seal and send the letter. It'll make

Nureddin happy. He'll go to meet you at Karak, and the Christians will trounce him soundly when you don't show up."

He folded the rice-paper thin. I saw he was pleased.

"So! El Bahi, add ten dinars a month to your salary. I'm going for a swim in the Nile.... Here—you can play with this till I come back. Guard it carefully."

He threw the ring with the green stone at me, and departed.

Wide awake now, I seized the emerald and inspected it. Bewitched? Obviously. In the stone was a tiny figure, the exact shape of the Sphinx; this was a marvel, surely. Apparently it was quite natural. The emerald was a poor one, but I found it fascinating.

Two of my own slaves appeared. I was trimmed and bathed; then my breakfast came in; and all the while I kept the ring on my finger, admiring that emerald. The masseurs came, and had just finished rubbing me, when in walked El Ghazy. We had no privacy in this old palace—that was why Saladin was building a new one with the citadel. I sent away the rubbers, saluted the Emir humbly, and he smiled at me. He had a keen face, bearded and trimmed, and his eyes were like a sword.

"My good El Bahi," he said, "I know quite well you're a damned deceitful rogue, and you love money. Eh?"

"Not glass money, my lord," I replied.

He chuckled at this. "I have a hundred golden dinars here," he said. "Do they make your nose itch?"

"By Allah, they do!" I told him. He nodded at me. He was a lordly man, well made, magnificently attired; his arms and jewels were of the finest. But I had turned the emerald inside my hand and closed my fingers over it, so he did not observe it.

"Our master Saladin, upon whom be peace, has received certain orders from the Sultan, beloved of Allah," he said. "Can you tell me what answer he returns?"

"Certainly," I said. "He honors the commands of the Sultan,

*"Let discussion
wait until later."*

and is sending troops to aid him, and will himself follow as
soon as he recovers from a fever that has smitten him sorely."

"Oh!" The Emir grinned, swallowed this lie, and pulled a
purse from his girdle, tossing it to me. "Good man. I see we
understand one another. Salaam!"

I wished him peace also, and he departed happy. I returned
to contemplation of the emerald, which was fascinating indeed,

and was at this when a slave announced Karakush. He was hot and sweaty, having been overseeing the work since sunrise.

"Oh, damned luxurious cat, may you roast in hell!" said he.

"That being likely, I prefer to be comfortable here," I retorted. "This is the emerald. Look at it."

While he did so, I told him of my late visitor and what had passed.

"You see," I finished, "El Ghazy now believes that Saladin is trying to evade the Sultan's orders, thus will press his own affair."

"By tomorrow night we should have some news. Let us meet, then, luxurious prince of deviltry," he said. "This emerald is the same of which I heard. Does Saladin know that it has bewitched him?"

"No, but he suspects something," I said. "I think he'll ask me soon."

He went away. I selected a robe of thin white silk, with a peach-blush girdle, and when dressed went to attend Saladin. He was holding morning court. When it was over, he retired with me to the secretariat.

"The letter you wrote has gone," he said. "Now take some orders regarding the troops and the gathering of supplies for the Karak expedition."

When they were done, he asked for the emerald, and I gave it to him.

"It is bewitched," I said. "Any man who wears it is bewitched. Like you."

"Me?" He snorted angrily. "Bewitched?"

"Certainly. You asked my advice; that shows. Usually you give orders, and have no need of any advice. The stone has one of those ancient Egyptian gods inside it, and it addles the wits of any person who wears it. That's why El Ghazy gave it to you."

This angered him. "The Emir is an honorable man, utterly devoted to me."

"I had a hundred dinars from him an hour ago, to get your

answer to the Sultan. He knew all about that order you
received."

HE WAS staggered. "Eh? He bribed you? And you betrayed
me?"

"No, him. I lied to him. The hundred dinars is good money
for a lie."

His lips twitched. "My elegant El Bahi, it will grieve me to
see your head hung above the gate of my new citadel! I fear it
will come to that."

"If Allah desires it, yes," I asserted. "After El Ghazy is governor of Egypt."

He patted the emerald. "When you have proof of the magic
and witchcraft you assign to this emerald, come to me with it
freely. Until then, use no more loose talk about it." He spoke
sternly. "Punishment for loose talk, rewards for proof, by Allah!"

"Then remember it is an oath by Allah's name," I said. This
startled him, for he was a devout man, but he could not eat his
own words, so the matter ended thus.

THE ORDERS went out to the troops; I knew El Ghazy
would find my words to him thus confirmed, so all was well.
The day passed in routine business. That afternoon Saladin
embarked on a boat for an inspection trip up the Nile; he would
not return for a couple of days, and I breathed more easily.
Luckily he had not taken me with him.

I had bad luck toward evening, just the same. Karakush sent
me a jar of wine, and in sampling it I spilled some on my handsome girdle. It was Cyprian wine, and the stain would not come
out; the girdle was spoiled. Strictly speaking, wine is not drunk
by the Moslem; but neither Karakush nor I cared particularly
about religious tenets, and we did like wine.

It was the following day before I began to hear from the men
I had set to work. Reports came in fast that afternoon. I got
them tabulated, and things began to look exciting. When the

time came to get together with Karakush, that evening, I really had something, too.

He had not been wasting his time, either. In his sardonic way he urged me to speak first, and set out cups and a whole beaker of his Cyprian wine. So I gave him my story, and then launched into the reports I had.

"You were right in suspecting a woman at work. A woman occupies a house in the street just behind the Mosque of El Azhar—a very beautiful woman, but rarely seen. Her servants are Persians. Gossip says she is a Persian princess. Emir El Ghazy has twice been seen to visit this house by night, in company with Saladin. A huge amount of hazy detail boils down to these facts. I am having the house watched. Carrier pigeons have been seen to arrive there; whence they come, none can say. The apparent master of the house is the Persian rug-merchant Selim whose shop is in the rug-bazaar, but this is obviously a blind; he never goes there, though his servants often do. The house is registered in his name with the police. That empties my pack, worthy Karakush."

He grinned in his tigerish way. "The woman is named Leila; she is sister to Melek, the vizier of Sultan Nureddin," he said, relishing my astonishment. "That house is a trap set to snare a lion. How do I know? Because, for the past twelve hours a man has been lying in the prison at the construction camp across the river. He happens to be one of El Ghazy's secretaries."

Chilling information, this!

"You've had him tortured?" I said.

"No. He's been kept full of hashish, and all his words recorded." Karakush smiled. "In conjunction with your reports, his babblings make everything clear. He has, however, spoken of a certain date which means nothing to me. Monday, the seventh day of the month Safar. Eh?"

I shook my head. It was the following Monday; it had no meaning to me. There was a sample of our excellent working. Without my information, Karakush would have seen nothing in the babblings of his prisoner; the two were complementary, perfectly fitting, opening the entire plot to our understanding.

"Further," went on Karakush, "the personal troops of El Ghazy are being assembled at his house in Boulak, the island near the city. They have orders to gather there the end of the week. Those of several other captains are under orders also. They are friends of El Ghazy, but he is the most prominent. Do you think something is expected to happen next Monday?"

"Probably. Let me speak with Saladin about it, and I can tell better," I said. We refilled our cups. The wine was strong, and had its usual effect on Karakush—that is, it melted his outward seeming, and drew out his real self. He sighed, rubbed his big hook of a nose, and nodded at me.

"I have an ambition," he said. "We need not be godly men to give of godly stuff. I would like to carve a great eagle upon that citadel. I have picked out the very spot, on the west façade of the wall, so that all men would see it until the end of time. But to represent any living creature is abhorrent to the true religion. Saladin would never permit it."

I regarded him curiously. "An eagle? Why?"

"My friend, I will never have children," he said, after gulping down his wine. "You do not know why I am called Karakush; it means black bird, or eagle. Once, as a child, I was named Ardzrouni, meaning eagle-bearer—the name of a royal Armenian family. I would like to put the Armenian eagle on the wall of Saladin's citadel, you see?"

"It would put your head over the gate," I told him truly. "Well, shall we warn our master or not?"

He shrugged. "Useless. He would not accept warnings; he trusts El Ghazy, probably is in love with this woman. Let us wait." He stretched out his arm, smooth as silk yet muscle-hard as iron. "I could use a sword, once. I still can, better than most men. When Saladin returns, feel him out carefully, and we shall see."

I left him, presently. So he was Armenian, of high birth! Probably taken in war and made a slave—an interesting sidelight upon his character....

Two days later Saladin returned to Cairo, full of praise for the construction work, and heaping honors upon Karakush, who heeded them not. A queer fellow, that eunuch.

I took occasion to talk with Saladin, casually. He still had the emerald, still watched and studied it by the hour; he gave me curt replies while he looked into it. On the Monday evening, said he, there was to be an entertainment by some dancing girls, to which Emir El Ghazy was going with him. A private affair.

Although it was a hot morning, I went out into the city and climbed to the construction on the hill-flank, and found Karakush at work.

"It's only too clear," I told him. "Saladin is to be killed there on Monday night."

"Naturally. Of course that's the scheme," he said, and chuckled. "Can you write Persian?"

"That's my business, isn't it?" I retorted. "Persian, Turki, Armenian or what have you. Even Bokhari. Tomorrow's Friday. What are we to do?"

"Pray to Allah," he said. "I sha'n't tell even you, my friend. Trust me. On Monday morning you shall write the letters. I'll deliver them later. There's just one thing to give you hope. Our master loves a good joke and a good sword; we'll give him both."

More he would not say. I thought the heat had addled his brain, and going home got into a tepid bath and cooled off. The nights were chill, but the days were foretastes of hell if one got into the white sunlight. How Karakush stood his architectural work I could not see.

DURING THOSE next days Saladin, in high humor, lost no chance to rail at me about the emerald. It was the very father of inspiration, said he, the fount of all good luck and virtue; a royal jewel, fit for a sultan.

"Once you depended on yourself," I told him impudently.

"Then you were a Kurdish prince, the greatest of warriors. Now you seek luck from a heathen stone."

He went into a roar of laughter, but all the same it pricked him hard. I saw him watching me, after this, with thoughtful eyes.

Saladin was nobody's fool, however. He knew those troops were concentrating about the city, so he ordered El Ghazy and the other captains to get them started on the desert road toward Karak, and sent others of his own troops along, and they had to obey him. He had me write Sultan Nureddin that the troops were moving and he would follow at once. I tried to warn him, and he shut me up with peremptory voice.

On Monday morning, Karakush looked me up at the secretariat and showed me a letter to be written out in florid Persian. I read it and choked.

"You've gone stark mad!" I said. "A letter to Leila—the noble Persian Safir, sent by the Sultan himself to consult with her—"

"Peace! Write it," he growled. "Safir arrives toward sunset, goes tonight to her house with this letter. Leave the rest to me. Get it written, and bring it to my quarters tonight after supper. And for the love of Allah, stay sober or I'll have you flayed alive!"

I wrote the letter myself, with much beard-scratching, and did a good job.

THAT EVENING I took the letter to the apartment of Karakush. I was innocent, unsuspecting, fearing nothing. A slave bowed me in, and I saw no sign of the Armenian. Then a very demon of a man appeared—a tall fellow with a curled beard, a black patch over one eye, a magnificent Persian costume, jewels on his hands. Two slaves were with him. At his command they seized me roughly, tearing off my delicate green robe of Medina weft.

"Persian dogs, Allah upon you!" I cried angrily. "You'll be flogged at the gates for this outrage—Karakush will rip the skin from your backs!"

"Strip him," said the tall Persian, and the two slaves stripped me. "Now shave his head and beard. Those curled whiskers are not necessary."

They committed this outrage while he stood looking on, gripping a cruel curved sword and laughing amusedly at my threats. When they had shaved off my beard, which required an hour's dressing and curling

At this moment came musicians and dancing-girls; our byplay was ended.

each day, they rubbed into my skin some brown stain which darkened me, clothed me in a hideous harsh, ill-cut robe of camel's hair, and about my neck set a huge rosary of beads for the ninety-nine sacred names of Allah.

The tall fellow picked up the folded letter, which had fallen in my struggles.

"Certainly no one will now recognize you, sleek cat," said he, laughing at me. "You're my honored companion, the holy man El Kahin, so don't forget to finger your beads and mutter prayers. I have numerous slaves waiting to escort us fittingly. What, the noble Safir does not please you?"

It was Karakush himself, and he was well tricked out. His

garments and belongings carried the two polo-mallets called *chugan*, heraldic arms much used in Persia, where polo is a highly popular game. The Chugandar, as he is known, is an important court official there.

I cursed him bitterly, but curses and protests were alike vain.

"Drink your wine and save your breath," he said, sipping the Cyprian they brought us. "I need you, and I need luck as well. My problem is to carry off things so that Emir El Ghazy will not call in the armed men he doubtless has ready. We must confuse him so he will be uncertain. Allah alone knows what the event will be! However, we must hope for the best, and then it may happen."

He called his slaves and set forth, dragging me along until I yielded to force and went along of myself. The slaves bore lights; some were armed; and it was an imposing procession that arrived at the house which was behind the Mosque of El Azhar. Safir, decked with a jeweled Persian caftan, made a magnificent figure.

Word was taken to the lady of the house, and we were admitted. Leaving our slaves outside, we were conducted to the presence of the lady Leila, as Safir demanded. This was in the large central chamber, open to the sky above, where fountains played, and a thousand lamps made brightness in the alcoves. She was there, sitting upon rich cushions; and there also was Saladin, and the Emir El Ghazy, both of them looking rather aghast at this intrusion. The lady herself was veiled, icy in manner, very decorous, clad in gem-spangled robes. A small monkey on a golden chain sat by her.

Safir, ignoring the other two, saluted her with the greatest courtesy, using her real name.

"Peace to you, sister of the most noble Melek!" said he, presenting his letter. "I arrived in this dog-ridden hovel they call a city barely an hour ago, and have made all haste to present myself before you and deliver this epistle from your brother, vizier to the Sultan—may Allah be kind to him!"

At this disclosure of her actual name and rank, Saladin betrayed no surprise; he was regarding us keenly.

She took the letter and spoke in an angry voice.

"I do not seem to recall your face."

Safir preened himself, and laughed.

"Lady, I am Safir el Amidi, Chugandar of the court. And this,"—he waved a hand at me—"is the holy man El Kahin, a magician, as his name implies, dweller in the desert and master of incantations and charms."

All this while Emir El Ghazy, apparently alarmed by our arrival, was in a mood of gathering black anger.

Leila glanced over the letter, then addressed Safir.

"Let discussion wait until later. Sit down, be at ease. These guests of mine are here to witness some dancing—"

She presented Emir El Ghazy, but Saladin made her a gesture of caution.

"I am Yusuf, of the Emir's suite," he said, to keep his rank from being known. He stood up and came toward us. "Peace to you," he said politely, and saluted me. "If it be true that you are a holy man, El Kahin, I ask you for your blessing."

He suspected nothing, evidently. It was perilous to jest with Saladin on religious matters, but I could not lose the opportunity.

"Take my blessing in the Prophet's name," I responded. "The more so, since you seem to need it badly. I see you are not yourself, but a man bewitched."

He started slightly, and his dark eyes flashed.

"Bewitched?" he repeated. "I?"

"Precisely." I fingered my beads. "It is proof that you are bewitched, because you are here and not in a safer place, use a name you do not generally use, and appear to trust those whom you should suspect."

AN outburst threatened, but Safir checked it by a roar of laughter.

"That's the way with him, always stirring up trouble!" said he. "Pardon him, I beseech you. El Kahin is very holy, but a bit soft in the head—you understand."

He gave me a warning kick as he spoke. It was all very bewildering to the lady and also to El Ghazy; our arrival had entirely upset their scheme of things. However, Saladin seated himself again. Slaves brought in trays of sweetmeats and the rarest sherbets.

Leila was examining the letter, and she seemed more puzzled than ever. This did not surprise me, since it bore neither signature nor seal. Emir El Ghazy paid me scant notice but fixed his attention upon Safir, and I saw trouble brooding.

Since I knew very well that Saladin was here because Leila was no ordinary person, I thought best to put trouble aside and please my master. I asked:

"Noble lady, would it please you, while awaiting entertainment, to permit me to divert your mind?"

"How would your holiness attempt such a task?" she said, none too politely.

"Oh, nothing could be simpler," I replied in the same tone. "I pray you, let me be given a brush and ink and paper, and I'll write an incantation which will astonish you. And you yourself shall be the judge."

My voice gave me away to Saladin, for I saw a twinkle come into his eye. But the lady beckoned a slave and told him to give me what I wanted. A bit of paper and writing-materials were given me.

"In the name of Allah!" I said, and began to write, making a play upon the names of El Ghazy, "The Victorious," and Saladin, *"Honoring the Faith."* It took only a moment. *"Victory,"* I wrote, *"can bring sorrow; to honor the Faith is ever wise."* I let the words dry, then handed her the paper.

"A true enchantment," I said, "that will cure all trouble in the heart."

She read it; then her hand clenched the paper into a crumpled ball.

"You are a sage," she declared, with a little silvery laugh. At this moment came musicians, and three dancing girls; drum and fifes began to play; figures began to move about the fountain before us, and our byplay was ended. But I liked her laugh. She knew now where we stood.

Safir made a noble show, blustering like a true Persian, admiring the dancers, making an ass of himself generally. On purpose, of course! His intent was to keep El Ghazy bewildered and confused, unable to strike a decisive course. Saladin, though discussing the finer points of the dancing with his hostess, kept an eye on Safir—an enjoying eye, it seemed to me. He had never suspected his tall eunuch of such histrionic art.

Saladin had been given a magnificent sherbet in a huge golden cup. He had set it down beside his cushion to speak with Leila, when Safir began to boast about some famed dancer at Erzeroum—a man who danced with his sword and did marvelous things. As he spoke, he hitched around his saber and gestured with it, and the tip of the sheath struck against the golden cup and knocked it over.

Saladin said nothing. El Ghazy flew into a passion, but Safir put on a show that struck me dumb. He apologized most humbly to Saladin, cursing his own clumsiness, asking pardon, finally taking up his own untouched cup of sherbet and asking Saladin to accept it in place of that spilled. He did this just as a slave was bringing another golden cup. Saladin took it and gave it to Safir.

"Take this, my friend," he said, "and I'll accept yours with pleasure. In Kurdistan, where I was born, a sword can do no wrong while it is sheathed."

EL GHAZY cast an angry look at Leila, and I knew that Safir had acted with intention. The cup which Saladin had given him, he kept untouched. El Ghazy, however, fingered his own jeweled hilt and scowled at Safir.

"A child should not play with the toys of men," he said significantly.

"True, beloved of Allah," said Safir. "Also, jewels become women, not warriors. Your sword-hilt is pretty; the dancing girls would like it. Mine is unadorned, but does not slip in the hand with blood and sweat of battle. A sword that slips is perilous to a man."

"Not if his hand be firm," snarled El Ghazy, quick to accept the challenge. All our attention was now centered upon the two. Leila made a gesture, and the dancing girls left the floor, and the musicians retired. El Ghazy went on speaking, with gathering anger.

"The hand is what matters. If the hand be firm, the sword bites."

"The hand cannot be firm unless it be true," said Safir with a ghastly grin. "And if hand and heart be false, victorious one, how can it be firm? The hand that betrays its master must slip, in the justice of Allah. The ambitious heart that aspires to murder its master and take his place—"

"You Persian dog!" burst forth El Ghazy, the veins swelling on his temples. "You prate fine words and dare not back them up with actions!"

Safir fingered his false beard complacently. "I have no permission," he said gently. "It is discourteous to bare sword in the house of another. If this gracious lady would give her consent, I should be most happy—"

"Oh, by all means!" spoke out Leila, clapping her hands. "Both of you are bold braggarts. Back up your loud words if you can, and let Allah favor the truest heart!"

As a serpent glides yet cannot be seen to move, Safir left his cushions. His tall shape moved out across the tiled floor, and the sword was bare in his hand. A plain sword, but the edge of the steel glittered, and I knew it must be exceeding sharp. El Ghazy rose, slipped off his embroidered coat, and the blade came naked in his grip. He stepped forth, a magnificent picture of a warrior, perfectly coordinated, his dark gaze fastened upon the tall, ornately clad Persian.

I glanced at Saladin. He was leaning forward, watching intently, excitement in his face, all else forgotten.

"Allah!" he ejaculated, his own fingers twitching for a sword-grip. "Allah! The winner shall have a purse of a thousand dinars!"

"The loser," said El Ghazy, "will have no need for it."

He laughed, as he advanced toward the tall Persian. At this moment occurred a slight interruption, although it passed almost unnoticed. A slave came hurriedly in and crossed to Leila, sank on his knee and extended something. It was a tiny pellet of paper, I observed, such as might have come from the leg of a pigeon. She took and tucked it away, and the slave departed.

Then the steel clashed.

Exciting? Not in the least. Neither man was mailed; each had a sword, to serve as weapon and shield alike. For all his proud hauteur, El Ghazy was deliberate and very careful. He crossed blades with Safir. The two men began to strike, in a methodic way; each was feeling out the other and risking nothing. Saladin, obviously, thought it was no more than a fencing game—or did he? To read that dark intent face was impossible. Leila's features were lost behind her veil, which revealed only the eyes.

I watched the fighters, thinking how cleverly Safir had gained all his objectives, drawing the Emir into this match without rousing any hidden men. He was clever now, too, his tall figure stiff and unbending before El Ghazy's attack, his footwork crude and uncertain, his pose awkward; his sword scarcely moved, but was like a wall in the air, clinging to the other blade and holding it. This was not the sinewy, willowy figure I knew so well. He was dissembling.

SUDDENLY EL GHAZY broke into movement too swift for the eye to follow. He delivered three slashing blows, ferocity whistling on his blade. Safir received each on his sword, drawing the steel slightly away as he did so; he was a little slow for the third, which caught his embroidered caftan and shore most of it away from his head; yet he avoided the keen edge. El Ghazy laughed.

"Not bad, Persian! Next time the head goes as well as the hat."

"I'll take your chain to pay for the caftan," said Safir. His long arm and long saber and long body shot forward like a steel spring. A backward leap saved El Ghazy, but the steel point caught the links of a great gold chain he wore about his neck, and the gold went clattering on the tiles. Saladin cried out admiringly.

The two men paused, breathing hard, each eying the other. El Ghazy made up his mind and moved forward craftily, apparently slashing high, for the head. The steel whistled as it came in—aimed for the long legs, a deadly stroke.

Yet before our very eyes Safir changed stance and body, it seemed. He was no longer tall and erect. He was leaning far forward, his legs well back and safe, his blade pecking threateningly for the throat. Almost in panic, El Ghazy slashed and slashed; his edge was parried each time; he fell back a step and another step; he tried to beat aside the blade before his eyes, and the haft slipped in his hand so he almost lost his sword.

At this, amazingly, Safir halted.

"What did I tell you?" he cried out. "If the hand be false, it cannot be firm!"

The bearded features of El Ghazy darkened under a rush of furious blood. He must have seen that the tall man was playing with him. The rest of us knew that we were looking on swordsmanship little less than magical. Still Safir laughed.

"The great El Ghazy, no longer simple emir, but now Governor of Egypt!" he went on tauntingly. "Hapless Saladin, bewitched by the emerald and dead of poison, El Ghazy ruler in his stead—"

His jeering almost killed him. El Ghazy came in slashing like a madman, reckless and terrible, with such furious address that Safir backed and backed and needed every last bit of skill to avoid the blows, leaping sideways, handling his blade with frantic strength, all energy intent upon defense alone. It was a marvel of attack, a marvel of defense, two masters hard at work, but Safir did not strike a blow in return. He had no chance, so incredibly swift was El Ghazy. Back almost to the fountain went Safir, then fell into that curious crouch. El Ghazy took warning and checked himself.

Saladin was in a blaze. "With two such captains, I could drive the Christians from Jerusalem!" he yelled excitedly. "Allah give me such men—"

He came to his feet and shouted incoherently—for now Safir was attacking, the first time he had really extended himself. I saw his object. He was making no brilliant assault, just a steady, close, savage attack that El Ghazy had to meet with his whole effort. He tried no tricks. His blade swung like a living streak of fire in the air, and El Ghazy had to watch like a hawk. Remembering that lissom, sinewy sword-arm of tireless steel muscle, I knew this was a deliberate attempt to sap and weary El Ghazy; but the latter was no weakling.

Thus far neither man was touched—an eloquent tribute to the matchless mastery at work on either side. Both were streaming and streaked with sweat, the magnificent garments disarrayed, their breath a panting whistle, and the false beard of Safir hung in grotesque patches about his chin; but I saw that the eyes of El Ghazy were staring and distended, and his smile had become a grotesque grimace.

Out of his deadly crouch Safir flew as from a released spring, sword a part of arm and body. The other man, with a terrific effort, parried the reaching blade, swept it aside, and cut forward. A line of scarlet leaped out along Safir's forehead—the point had barely scratched him in passing. With his left hand he whipped the blood from his eyes—and suddenly swept forward again, uncoiling that incredible length of arm.

El Ghazy parried, and as before found an opening and cut in for it, desperately. This was what Safir wanted. He came suddenly to his full height, parried the cut neatly, and slashed. The other could not recover to ward the blow. I could have sworn that it reached him; yet nothing happened. Safir lost balance a little with the force of his own stroke, and staggered away a pace.

THEN—ALLAH FORGIVE all sin! The truth is past belief—the head of El Ghazy toppled, and rolled almost to the feet of Saladin. The body was relaxed, and fell backward into the fountain, with a frightful rush of blood. The saber clattered on the tiles. We had seen an impossible thing, the thing discussed in every gathering of swordsmen and affirmed or denied blankly—we had witnessed it, and the fact stupefied us all. Even Safir, leaning on his blade and gasping for breath, merely stared and gulped and could say nothing.

"Us," did I say? Not all of us—not the veiled woman, at least. Upon the dreadful choked silence I caught a tiny rustle of paper. Unwitting that she had just now beheld the miracle possible only to a perfect sword and swordsman, she was unfolding the tiny paper message and reading its brief content. A queer strangled sound came from her—a laugh that was not a laugh. She thrust her arm toward Saladin, extending the tiny paper.

"Saladin—read, read!" Her voice was a gasp. "It came from Damascus—by pigeon. Read it!"

He snatched the paper and glanced at its message.

"By Allah—and Allah!" Amazement broke upon his lips. "Sultan Nureddin died in his sleep last night! If this be true—"

His speech failed, but the words had burned into us all.

"If this be true," I spoke up, "then he who moves quickest has the prize. That is, unless he sits mooning over an emerald while the world turns upside down—or holds his belly like a monkey who has tasted poison meant for his betters."

This made them all look quickly. Leila's little monkey lay with beady eyes winking around. He had quietly slipped to the sherbet spilled from Saladin's cup, and had been gobbling it greedily. A short laugh escaped Leila.

"You are fools, all of you," she said. "There was no poison in the cup. El Ghazy thought there was, but I replaced the poison with a narcotic drug. No harm is done."

Saladin's fierce, eager laugh broke upon the room. He gestured at me.

"I am not the fool you thought me, anyway! But there was sense in the proof you offered about the emerald. Perhaps I was bewitched; at all events, I am myself again now. El Ghazy? I was not that man's tool. Take his head, El Bahi, and have it hung over the city gates. Karakush! To me, swordsman!"

Safir moved, very wearily, and came to Saladin, who took his hand and spoke.

"Egypt is a pleasant land; this woman is true. She came to beguile me, an enemy, and Allah turned her into a friend. Take care of her, take care of Egypt, for me. I am going—now, tonight, and I shall return as Sultan. Whatever request you ask of me shall then be granted on the spot."

"Careful!" A faint laugh escaped Safir. "Careful of promises, Master!"

"I mean it. I swear by Allah that any request you make of me, even if it be to the half of my power, shall be freely granted. As for the emerald, I shall keep it—to bewitch and ruin some other man, one of these days."

THERE, MY friends, you have the story I promised. How Saladin swooped upon Damascus and in time returned home as Sultan, the greatest ever known to the world, is in the history books.

If you will some day come to Cairo, you shall see for yourselves what was the wish later made by Karakush and granted by Sultan Saladin. Look toward the west façade of the noble citadel that overhangs the town. You may see it carven there as a witness unto future ages—the royal eagle of the Armenian kings, symbol of the eunuch who, but for the will of Allah, might have worn a crown.

You ask about the veiled lady? Well, I am merely El Bahi, chief of the Sultan's secretariat, so what should I know of the harem of my master? Still, I have heard laughter at times behind the carven screens, and it was the laughter of the veiled lady Leila—may Allah bestow many sons upon her!

But as for the Sphinx Emerald—I never saw it again, for it was kept by Saladin unto his own purposes.

X

LEOPARDS ARE FOR ENGLAND

That malign and magic jewel the Sphinx
Emerald comes on the scene to play its part
in a stirring drama of the Crusades.

THE MAN in the tent was bull-necked, of massive build yet not too short, his features alight with keen intelligence. Except for a long mustache, he was clean-shaven. The fiery energy manifest in him was amazing; yet he was ill now, and had long been ill. His voice, rapidly dictating, broke now and again with impatience; he was a person of astounding power but scarcely of poise. He wore a single cool, armless garment that came to his knees and was ornamented with the heraldic device of a lion—the Lion of Flanders, in fact. Despite the afternoon breeze off the sea, the heat was intense and deadly.

"That will do," he concluded curtly. "Now I want Fitzalan—Sir James Fitzalan."

The two secretaries, one French, one Arab, departed. The man went to the tent entrance, wide open for air, and stared out. He was barely thirty-five, hard-muscled, alert. He looked at the sandy curve of shore a quarter-mile distant toward the city. Tents, huts, shelters backed it; men by the hundred were in the water or lolling naked on the sand.

Moving outside a little, the man turned and gazed in the other direction. Here was a tremendous plain running into the eastern horizon, dotted here and there with trees, with oleander bushes in gay flower, but showing hereabouts no sign of life. This was part of the historic Plain of Esdraelon, lying between Askalon and St. Jean d'Acre—a plain that had been repeatedly,

from historic times, flushed with the blood of armies, the de-
ceptively easy-looking plain that led into Palestine.

Squinting into the distance, the man found what he sought—
a mere glint of light. It was there day and night, a glint that
came from sun or moon on helm and shield; a pin-prick of
reflected radiance, cruel and terrible, merciless emblem of Asia.
This corner of naked plain was hemmed in by the united forces
of all hither Asia and Egypt. For the first time in history, the
Arab people had no divisions and were united in a *jihad,* a holy
war against the Christian, under one leader who was superb
and unconquerable.

Another man came from the horse-camp to the tent, a
younger man with worn features, deep straight eyes, hollow
cheeks. The armed guards saluted him; like them, he wore a

small cross on the right shoulder of his mantle, tokening the Crusades. The big man in the entrance smiled; with warming, kindling gaze he took the newcomer by the arm and turned into the tent with him.

"Holá, Fitzalan! Did the swim help you?"

"It put new life into me, sire. I'm practically cured of fever, anyhow."

"A many have been cured for eternity. I have an errand for you."

"As many as Your Majesty desires."

"Oh, bosh! Stop that damned formal speech. You remind me of my Arab scribe, always prating *Melek el Anketar* at me—King of Angleterre indeed! By God, I'm Richard Plantagenet, and no fancy strutting peacock! Sit down, stretch out, be comfortable."

Fitzalan complied, smiling. Four years of war had hardened him, aged him, left him very tired and hopeless. The old fine fervor had gone long ago. He was sunk in a morass of failure, treachery, death; so were they all.

Sounds of laughter and shrill vituperation brought him erect. He looked out. A boy, detained by the guards, was furiously cursing them in French, Arabic and the lingua franca commonly employed by the army. King Richard was laughing heartily at the storm of oaths.

"Yusef! Be quiet!" snapped Fitzalan. "Go away. Wait for me by the shore." He resumed his seat on the cushions. "It's that confounded town boy who plays at being my esquire. A smart lad, in truth, but a nuisance at times."

The King nodded. "Aye, I heard how you saved his life and won yourself a devoted servant. You're a lucky dog, Fitzalan. Well, what news from my coat with the new arms?"

LIGHTLY FITZALAN answered: "The ladies are finishing the broidery, sire; but everyone swears the animals are weird and unearthly. If you change your blazon from the Flanders Lion to these three nonsense creatures, your good Blondel says all the French heralds will lose their wits!"

King Richard cursed softly. Blondel was attending the Queen in the city just now. Pretending to be a minstrel, he had learned the trick. In reality he was an expert swordsman and a bodyguard.

"I know more about blazonry than all the heralds in France! So does any educated Saracen. Heraldry is purely an Eastern art; we're bringing back from the Crusades what will some day become a science…. Well, well, let it pass. If you're fit to ride, go find this infidel Sultan for me."

"Easily done." Surprised though he was, Fitzalan agreed impassively. "That Saracen outpost is in plain sight. Whether we seek single combat, friendly intercourse or diplomatic usage, the outpost is at our service."

THE BULL-NECKED man grunted. "They are the polite, soft-spoken bastards—but by my father King Harry, how they can fight, eh!" He licked his lips appreciatively. Then his mood changed. The fire died from his eyes. A sad crafty expression came into his face.

"I'm sending you because I can trust no one else. Spies watch us all day and night, so be careful. Also, it may give you a chance to investigate your brother's affairs. I have only one item of instruction for you: Speak only with Saladin himself, and speak the exact truth. No lies."

A simple knight of the royal household and no herald, Fitzalan listened in growing amazement as the King went on:

"Our supplies are about done; our money's gone; no more help is coming this year. Philip of France and Austrian Leopold have gone home. I've taken Askalon and Acre from Saladin; he's taken all the inland places from me. We hold the coast; he holds Syria. For the past year we've exchanged futile letters and messages—now I want a meeting. The truce must become a definite peace to end this shabby war. I'm going home."

"England, sire?" The word trembled. Here was news with a vengeance, news to shake all Syria!

"Aye, England! I'll raise men and money at any cost, and return here later for a better try at Jerusalem. Saladin will know only that I'm leaving, and will make excellent terms to get me gone. We must meet personally; that's imperative. I'll grant any kind of conditions, though we've already charted general terms. Get him here if possible. Tell the truth as I've just put it—except that I hope to return. He'll understand what I'm after—he's a smart devil. But, mind you, don't tell the truth to another living soul, not even to the Queen!"

Fitzalan began to understand, too. These knights and lords of Syria, who had lost Jerusalem, would like King Richard to

*"I have come, Englishman, to give you what you
deserve," said Sir Jean Menpes. A whip whistled
and Fitzalan felt the lash sting across his face.*

win it back for them—but all the same, they would trick him,
rob him, betray him and ruin him. He knew it now.

While speaking, the King had been playing with a ring, a
new one. He held it up, smiling admiringly, as Fitzalan regarded
it with curiosity.

"A present; it came three days ago from Saladin.

Sala'h-ud-Din—Honoring the Faith! Odd names these paynim bear. Well, give him his due, he's an honest fellow."

A lumpy, ill-formed, pale stone set in a gold ring. A true emerald, said Richard, who was vastly delighted with it. A messenger brought in a parchment, a mere two lines to which the royal seal had been affixed; the King gave it to Fitzalan.

"Your authority to speak for me. I must send a gift in return for this ring, too. You're for the city? Then see the Queen. Ask her to give you the jeweled dagger I took from the Persian emir at the Askalon fight, and to wrap it fittingly. Eh?"

Fitzalan assented, and picking up the boy Yusef, took his departure for Acre, the army headquarters. This seaside outpost was merely a spot where the sick could come and bathe and refresh themselves under the present truce. Richard did not get on too well with Templars, Hospitallers, the various bishops and lords of the allied forces; and despite his vast energy was bitterly ill at times. Despondent, too, seeing the Crusade a failure for all his own victories; the outpost camp was his haven from difficulties.

FITZALAN ENTERED the city, whose port was crammed with all sorts of vessels, and whose fine Arab palaces now housed the nobility of England, Cyprus, France and Provence. He sent the impudent, laughing Yusef home with the horses, telling him to have them ready for a daybreak ride, then sought the presence of Queen Berengaria, the slim Spanish princess whom Richard had carried off and married.

In the gay palace gardens, bright with the presence of troubadours, ladies, court officials and knights all gladly abandoned to idleness, he had no difficulty reaching the Queen, and presented Richard's request. Berengaria at once sent for the dagger and a proper wrapping.

"A gift for the Sultan, eh?" she said. "An edged gift is bad luck—but Richard would never think of that, poor man! No word of a return to England?"

"None, madam," lied Fitzalan, as he must—and the little Queen sighed.

"Alas, I'd like to see England! We're well into the year 1192—must we stay here all our lives? Who is going as his embassy to Saladin?"

"Your Majesty, I did not ask. The King was very bright and cheerful."

"That means trouble afoot," she said shrewdly. "Here comes the pretty gaud now."

One of her ladies brought the jeweled dagger wrapped in handsome Genoa velvet, and Fitzalan made his way to his own lodgings, the sunset light upon the city. He was a little heartsick, as always when in contact with the brilliant, sad court circle that was trying to make the best of a shabby situation. Supposedly, men served the Cross in utter self-abandon; actually, they fought one another bitterly—out for anything they could get.

Richard had stolen a bride in Spain, had rescued his sister Joan from unhappy marriage in Sicily and forced immense loot out of her former husband. He had taken Cyprus for himself and then sold it, plunging headlong into jealousies, treacheries and strife with other leaders of the Crusade. Personal bravery somewhat made up for these things, but only slightly. Fitzalan could guess that the coming peace with Saladin would under its specious cloak conceal some genial rascality. Saladin would guess it too. That Saracen was a wise man, generous, able, chivalrous, outgeneraling all the Crusading kings.

He thought of this again in the pale dim dawn, when he rode out with the eager town-boy beside him, now his esquire indeed. He wore a light helm, a light hauberk; he feared no treachery. Long Crusading years had brought Saracen and Christian together, giving them knowledge of each other, and mutual respect. Prisoners might still be slaughtered in ferocious outbursts; but in general there was a superficial veneer of chivalry and common decency.

His own affairs—this thought held Fitzalan. The Crusade had failed, and so had he. He had never found any trace of that older brother who had vanished four years ago in the fight at Ramleh. It was not from brother love alone that Fitzalan sought him, but because of the English title and estates—sordid worldly affairs, he granted bitterly.

As he rode, he chatted with the quick-witted, alert Yusef. The boy was unlike any other he knew—kings and spearmen and archers, all were weary for sight of home shores, home people, home ways. This was the fourth year in Syria. Even the kings and captains were now unspeakably weary. Richard had stuck it out longer than the others.

"Has the King given you no blazon?" the boy asked him. "You're a knight; you should have a coat of arms like the others. French knights all have them."

"He has promised, yes." Fitzalan nodded toward the sunrise. "I must learn first about my brother. If he's dead, I'll be head of the house. If he's alive, it'll be different. Keep your eye peeled for that Arab outpost. Hard to see against the sunrise."

"They say the King will marry his sister Joan to Saladin's brother," piped up the boy. "A dirty shame if he does, they all say—"

"Keep your tongue off the King's doings, or you'll get a flogging," snapped Fitzalan.

YET HE felt the same himself. Everyone did. No one could tell if such a match would happen. Richard might well be weary enough to sacrifice a sister, if that would get him home again. God—to get home! That desire was now more powerful than for loot or women. There were ships and to spare, if they could but go! It had become an obsession.

But being a king, Richard could not just turn around and go as the others had done. He must, somehow, make a show of saving face. Fitzalan knew this.

"I see them now, master. They're coming," cried the little esquire.

*Finally Fitzalan rode into a ravine where
an unexpected little town developed—*

A knot of men, dark under the sunrise, were approaching. They came nearer. Bearded men, their shields bearing odd and unknown blazonry. One rode out, saluting, and Fitzalan drew rein and spoke in the lingua franca, giving his name.

"An emissary from the King of England to Sultan Saladin. Is he anywhere near here?"

The dark man nodded. "He is camped within a three-hour ride. I'll guide you. I am the Emir Mirza."

The Saracens rode away. Mirza and one warrior rode south with Fitzalan. A pleasant, genial man, this emir, who chatted

trees and water and black tents. Men
appeared. Here was the Sultan himself.

lightly as he rode. The two men were soon laughing together like old friends. The Saracens were war-weary too; Mirza made no secret of it. He had not seen his home in two years and more, nor a son born since his leaving. Very human fellows, these Saracens, just like everyone else.

THE THREE hours under early sun passed quickly. Fitzalan had food; Mirza had dates; they shared. They met two parties of Saracens, and finally rode into a ravine where an unexpected little town of mud houses developed, and trees, and water and farther on, black tents. Men appeared. Here was the Sultan himself.

Fitzalan was taken directly to him. A slender, arrow-straight man of fifty-five, grizzled beard, aquiline features, keen eyes. He read Richard's brief missive and nodded.

"Peace to you," he said. "Bathe, rest; later we'll eat and talk. You have good horses. Ha, a gift!"

The dagger pleased him and he slipped the chain over his head so that it hung on his chest, native style. He laughed lightly.

"I send your master an emerald that will bewitch him; he sends me a dagger—a fitting exchange! Well, sir knight, take your comfort. We have good water here."

Fitzalan and the wide-eyed Yusef were taken in hand by black men, bathed, rubbed, garbed in cool silken robes, and later brought into the black tent. The sand was covered with rich rugs and cushions. Numbers of captains were here, hard, armored fighters. Fitzalan eyed one of them amazedly, narrowly, then checked himself and settled on his cushions. Amenities and news were exchanged with his host. The latter then made blunt demand.

"You bear a message for me?"

"Aye, Lord Saladin; but not for my esquire or for your emirs."

The Saracens cleared out, taking the bragging, garrulous Yusef. Fitzalan followed the one man with his gaze—a bearded, brawny captain whose garments, under his steel-linked hauberk, were adorned with the crest of a cup in a circle. Saladin noted the look, and spoke.

"You seem interested in Firuk, my cup-bearer. You know him?"

"No, but I know his hauberk, a fine Flemish piece," said Fitzalan. "It was once worn by my brother."

He briefly mentioned his unavailing search. Then, alone, he plunged into the King's business. The older man listened, heard all the messenger had to say, then sat in thoughtful silence for a space.

"I shall never understand what the truth means to you Franks," he said at length. "Some of you respect it; others deride it. If I were to ask you something—"

At the pause, Fitzalan smiled. "The King ordered me to speak the exact truth to you, but to no one else."

"Ha! He did?" Saladin slapped his thigh and broke into quick laughter. "I see, I see! Things begin to come clear. Then let my questions wait a little. I'll put them to you later, when we have eaten, and shall then send you back. A night ride will not be unpleasant. But let us see about that brother of yours."

He clapped his hands and sent for Firuk. The latter appeared, touched forehead, lips and chest in salute, eyed the visitor curiously, and exchanged a torrent of Arabic with his master.

"He says," translated Saladin, "that the hauberk was worn by a knight with yellow hair whom he captured at Ramleh. The infidel was badly wounded, was taken to Egypt a captive, and was later sold to the chief of a Sahara tribe. Alive? Dead? He knows not."

Fitzalan relaxed. The same old story—nothing certain.

"I thank you," he said. "Then I can do nothing."

"Perhaps I can." Saladin spoke anew with Firuk, who removed a ring from his hand and gave it over. Fitzalan recognized the worn old signet of his brother.

"Keep it as a gift, he says," Saladin went on. "Now behold! Tomorrow I send a pigeon, which reaches Cairo before evening. My vizier gets its message. In Cairo, at the end of this week, gather representatives of the Sahara tribes to renew their fealty to me. They are questioned. The answer comes to me by pigeon—you see? In two weeks I bring it with me to the meeting with your master. Do you wish to ransom your brother?"

"Yes, yes!" cried Fitzalan, astonished and delighted. Saladin, enjoying his wonder, laughed softly, and for the moment, the affair was ended.

O R W A S it? Fitzalan had a feeling that forces were in action which had ends unforeseen; a feeling, rather than a thought. Saladin puzzled him. Here was the Sultan of all the Muslim encamped with a few men, yet in constant touch with all parts of his vast empire. And during the frugal meal that followed, he was conscious of the interest of the emirs and captains. Why, he did not know; but they certainly discussed him.

They interested him, too. They could fight, yet had not the huge armor-breaking swords of the Crusaders. Their deadly blades were straight or curved, lithe and razor-edged. They were nimble men, quick of wit. Yusef had become a favorite among them. Watching them at prayer, one could guess them sincere and devout.

The meal over, all dispersed. Fitzalan went outside, looking at the stars. Mirza came to him.

"Later I am to accompany you back. Your horses are cared for. Give me, I pray you, your blessing."

Astonished, Fitzalan said: "You mistake; I'm no priest or holy man."

"Our master said you are the one Frank he has met who seeks nothing for himself; therefore you may be an agent of destiny and Allah. Your blessing is worth while."

Sheepishly, Fitzalan complied. Other peoples, other customs! He understood now why they had seemed interested in him. A little afterward, when they were talking alone again, Saladin said much the same thing, quite frankly.

"L E T U S speak the truth, my guest. If you do so, it may mean much to your people and mine. Suppose, for example, that I agree with your master to make my brother Sayf-ed-Din, Sword of the Faith, the King of Jerusalem; that he is to marry the sister of your King, who will bring him Acre as her dowry; that he is to give your people free access to the Holy City. Think you Melek el Anketar would wish such terms?"

"Yes." Amazed, delighted, Fitzalan began to see the point.

*"King of
Angleterre indeed!
I'm Richard
Plantagenet,
and no fancy
strutting peacock!"*

Could Richard make such a peace, his failures would be all forgotten. "I think he would."

"And would your emirs and bishops all swear obedience to a peace on such terms?"

"Our English barons, yes. The Templars, Hospitallers and Syrian bishops—no. Not unless your brother were to become a Christian."

Saladin broke into amused laughter. "Then your King talks for all Christians—but in actual reality I deal with him for himself and his army alone, eh?"

Fitzalan assented grudgingly, but the Sultan seemed delighted.

"Good! An understanding is excellent. I see why he sent you. He is an honest man. He knows the value of truth in a world of rascals. Others in your armies seek to bribe me with gold. He bribes me with the truth. By Allah, I like that man! We shall get on. I am sorry now that I sent him the emerald."

"He is overjoyed with it."

"No. Warn him. It will bewitch him." Saladin shook his head earnestly. "It is an old, famous, very evil jewel. It bewitches its owners."

Fitzalan did not argue the matter. It was now arranged that in two weeks Saladin should come to the camp outside Acre and meet Richard. Details of the escort were settled. All war was to be ended for a term of three years. A remarkable belt and straight sword, its hilt of massive carved gold, was presented to Fitzalan as a token of his host's appreciation, and the audience was finished.

Ten minutes later he and the boy Yusef were riding with Mirza under the stars. Seeking his chance, Yusef drew close and spoke in French softly to Fitzalan:

"Master, there was another Frank in that camp, a man from Acre. He has been there two days, I learned, but kept himself hidden from you. They say he was sent by the Templars to arrange financial matters dealing with tributes paid and prisoners to be ransomed."

Curious, thought Fitzalan. That was what Saladin had meant by mentioning attempts to bribe him. The matter slipped from his mind. It was none of his affair.

Mirza, as though following some unseen road, led him straight across the plain to the seaside camp. It was past midnight when Fitzalan passed the sentries. Following orders, he asked for the King and was taken to the royal pavilion. Lights sprang up, Richard, a cloak flung about him, came into the outer tent and embraced him with a bear-hug.

"You didn't reach him already—and back again? Magnificent! I'll order some wine; then we'll be alone. You had luck, eh?"

"The best," said Fitzalan, and said no more until the wine was brought and they were in private. He noted that Richard still wore the emerald ring. Then he got into his story, related everything in detail, and did not forget the curious warning of Saladin about the emerald. At this, Richard laughed heartily.

"Bewitch me? Not likely. Ha wants it back, that's all. Wait till I show you its secret…. But go ahead!"

Fitzalan complied. He spoke of his own affairs and showed the signet Firuk had given up. The King sat in a glow of utter delight, examined the gift sword, gulped his wine.

"Lucky man indeed! You've won the Sultan's favor—you must sit in the peace conference. Here, take the emerald to the lamplight, examine the figure inside the stone. Can you see it? A Sphinx, a very Sphinx, utterly exact!"

"What's a Sphinx?" queried Fitzalan, to whom the word was new.

"Look and see. A monument of ancient Egypt—lion body, man head. Whether it be magic or no, it's a marvel! And more," Richard added, "the emerald itself is tonic to the mind. Sharpens the wits, they say; I find it true. This jewel may bewitch some folk, but gazing into it provokes great thoughts of high emprise. Ah, I love the stone!"

N O U S E going on to the city at this hour, said the King. Stay here, take a couch in the tent, and enjoy a morning swim later. Fitzalan complied. He told Yusef to turn in the horses with those of the King and be ready to go into Acre on the morrow.

Morning brought details—letters from Cyprus, business to handle with the Venetians; Richard kept him busy following his early swim. When by afternoon he was ready to leave, Yusef had disappeared. He thought nothing of it. Sometimes the boy was gone for days at a time.

Before leaving camp, he did have a good look at the emerald

in full sunlight, and it astonished him. The tiny Sphinx-figure stood out distinct and clear, and there was no way for it to have been inserted in the stone. It was a true freak of nature. So upon this he had his horses saddled, and rode into Acre.

NO SIGN of Yusef here. During the next three days, Fitzalan was harried by important duties, securing contracts with half a dozen shipowners on behalf of the King, for sailing in a month's time. The Queen and court ladies had to be secured passage first of all, then lesser women, and the chief barons and captains. All these could chance the passage home via France; but whether or not Richard could, was not so sure. For him France might be unsafe.

Inevitably, word spread of a coming return to England. Possibly, said the King; it depended on whether a peace was effected. Since Fitzalan alone knew of the broad gold coin paid over, nobody was certain of Richard's intent, but rumors flew and excitement rose. And then, without warning, the boy Yusef turned up in ghastly fashion.

During this time Fitzalan had been increasingly aware of scowls and mutters. It was different when he met a French knight he knew well, and heard an angry oath.

"Perchance, monsieur, you are displeased?" he said, halting.

"With friends of heathen Saracens, yes," snapped the Frenchman. "Your ragged, comic esquire has hinted at your doings. A fine sword you're wearing—no doubt it came from England?"

Fitzalan let the sarcasm pass, let the quarrel go; abruptly uneasy, he pushed the query about Yusef and was told to visit the quay of Genoa. He went straight on to the quays, saw a crowd at the wharf of the Genoa galleys, and pushed through to find the boy Yusef just picked out of the water, dead, cut badly, a knife still in him. Fitzalan took the knife, examined it, gave orders about the body. Little grief shook him, but hot anger did. On the way home he met an official of the Hospitallers, halted him, displayed the knife, told whence it had come.

"Here in the wooden haft is burned the name of Menpes," he added. "I accuse Sir Jean Menpes as the murderer of my esquire. Since he is one of your knights, I ask justice."

"Ask and be damned," said the Hospitaller. "You're half a Saracen yourself. The boy told plenty. Go ask your friend Saladin for justice!"

Fitzalan, amazed and aghast, hotly sought advice from the King's chamberlain, who threw up his hands and groaned in despair.

"You can't bring such a charge against a knight of the Hospital! The King? He would back you in hot fury. That's what they want—an end to all amity, to all his plans—"

"And I'm to let my retainers be butchered with impunity?" snapped Fitzalan.

"If you're a great man enough to control yourself, yes. Good God, don't you know the gossip that's going around? You make secret visits to the Saracen camp, receive gifts from the Sultan—in a word, you're a recreant knight and no Christian! That's the rumor."

"Bosh!" Fitzalan was white to the lips with rage. "All done on the King's service!"

"Aye. Prove it. Let Richard come barging in, raising hell, starting a new and more savage feud with the French, with the Hospital—that's what they want! Man, we can't afford it now. Suffer in peace, for God's love!"

Fitzalan understood at last, and suffered with infuriated meekness. Yusef had been caught, tortured for information, killed. He himself was under deep suspicion—that Frank hidden in the Saracen camp had caused it all. Appeal to the King would bring instant justice. Richard would come charging into Acre like a mad bull—to what good? Another and more bitter quarrel would be under way. The Hospitallers wanted it, hoped to provoke it.

"I'll bear with it," he said at last, "for the greater good. If I can."

The days brought him ostracism, except among the English; taunts, open sneers, insults—treatment unendurable by any knight. He endured silently, kept to himself, and inwardly grew white-hot in fury. Richard had strictly forbidden private quarrels.

The situation would have drawn wide attention, but now news of the peace conference was spread, and this overwhelmed all lesser events. Saladin was coming with his emirs and relatives and captains—coming to make peace! False rumors sped on eager wing. Excitement lifted every heart. Home! Home again, the war ended!

Twice, attending the King out at the shore camp, Fitzalan saw the big emerald, saw Richard sitting gazing at it as though indeed bewitched, and wondered. He was so choked by his own bottled-up fury, however, as to give scant attention. Richard was wearing the fine mantle on which the court ladies had embroidered his new arms—three leopards, it was said. Since no one had ever seen a leopard, many fantastic heraldic arguments arose, to the vast amusement of the King.

Fitzalan had new duties that kept him busy, in preparing for the coming guests. Saladin was bringing a hundred of his chosen captains; Richard was choosing an equal number of his own knights, with the Grand Masters of the Temple and Hospital, to receive them. Pavilions had to be made ready, horse lines prepared, servants instructed, protocol settled by the heralds—a world of details.

In the midst of all, with the arrivals due on the morrow, Fitzalan came late to his lodgings in town. He dismounted, entered the courtyard, and was aware of a dark figure by the gate lantern. He heard his name called.

"Yes?" he said, turning. Then he saw who the visitor was.

"I have come, Englishman, to give you what you deserve," said Sir Jean Menpes. A whip whistled, and Fitzalan felt the lash sting across his face.

That loosed the gates. Forgetful of all knightly courtesy, aware only of the uncontrollable fury at last set free, Fitzalan stepped forward and his fists smashed in twice—terrific blows with his full weight in them, crude peasant blows, knuckles sinking into bony face. The man with the whip collapsed under those crashing fists and lay quiet.

Fitzalan went on into his lodgings, slightly appeased, but when morning came he saw that the red weal of the whip would not come from his face. He was marked. And this day Saladin would arrive—this very morning. With a shrug, he shaved and dressed, and rode out of town to the camp, and said nothing to anyone about the mark on his face.

SALADIN AND his retinue arrived, before the hot noonday. What with drums and trumpets, Richard in his gorgeous scarlet mantle with the golden leopards, the famous Saracen knights and lordly Crusaders, the slim graceful figure of Saladin, heralds and troubadours, the camp was a bedlam. No women, of course, were here—the presence of even the Queen would have affronted Arab notions. Guests were shown to quarters, horses were taken care of, and the deadly enemies made a fine pretense of fellowship.

With Richard, who took Saladin in his eager personal charge, the fellowship was very real. He was absorbed in his guest, and Fitzalan had no difficulty in keeping out of his way and his regard. Hawks had been brought, and Richard was very keen about hawking; the birds and their keepers were given into Fitzalan's charge and when, in mid-afternoon, he was abruptly summoned to the royal tent, he supposed it was on this business.

He found Richard and Saladin in eager talk; Blondel, the minstrel-swordsman, and half a dozen others were at a little distance, while crowds surged through the adjoining pavilions. This was a purely social gathering. Business would come tomorrow.

"Ha, Fitzalan—this way!" cried the King. "Or guest has asked for you!"

Fitzalan approached and saluted. The King's words had provoked a general stir of interest. Saladin smiled.

"A promise is an obligation, my friend," he said. "I brought the news as I foretold. It is not, I fear, good news. The man in question died two years ago. My secretary will give you the message to this effect."

Fitzalan thanked him; then he observed that the forehead of Richard was darkening with a flush of passion —in Richard this was a sure sign of threatening outbreak.

"What is this?" asked the King abruptly. "Your face is marked, Fitzalan. Explain it. Speak out. By my father King Harry, let's have the reason!"

In a flash, Fitzalan saw that Richard knew everything and had deliberately chosen this moment for a clearance. But it was a bad moment.

"A drunken assassin in the city last night, sire," he said lightly. "I punished him as he deserved. It was too dark to see his identity."

"So?" Perhaps Richard took warning. His gaze was stormy. Then he lifted his hand and for an instant his eyes were fastened upon the emerald. "I promised," he went on slowly, "to give you a blazon. Now that your brother is dead, you are the head of your house, so wear a leopard. Leopards are for England, or shall be. Take a leopard—my brother, you know this animal, no doubt?" He turned to Saladin, touching the leopards on his mantle.

"I do not," said Saladin, "but I shall be honored in learning from your lips. Is it an English animal?"

"No, a famed beast of far countries," said Richard. "According to the tales of travelers, a leopard is begotten in spouse-breach between the lion and the fabulous pard, and we have no exact description. Therefore we give him the aspect of his sire, as is most probable, and distinguish him from the lion by showing him full-face, gazing sideways at the beholder, a lion being usually shown in profile."

"A new animal in blazonry," said Saladin with interest. "And with your permission, may I not add a touch to the arms you give this knight? With the leopard, then, let him wear in memory of our friendship a star, drawn in whatever fashion may please your custom."

"Good! Be it so, Fitzalan!" exclaimed Richard, whose brow had cleared again.

Fitzalan was rendering the proper thanks, when a slight commotion took place outside. Blondel, a lute in his hand, stepped quickly closer to the King, his eyes vigilant. A chamberlain in some flurried haste appeared and bawled forth an announcement.

"Your Majesty, the Grand Master of the Order of the Hospital has arrived to greet Your Majesty's distinguished guest."

"Ha! An unexpected courtesy," said Richard dryly. "Let him enter."

THE GRAND MASTER was entering, a half-dozen of his knights with him, clanking in full mail. Richard's forehead was looking angry again; the proud hauteur of this distinguished order was not to his taste. Yet Fitzalan was puzzled to observe his evident effort at self-control. It was as though the King knew of threatening danger and, for once, was trying to fend it off instead of meeting it bull-fashion.

When among the party Fitzalan saw the figure of Sir Jean Menpes, with face bandaged, he scented trouble brewing, and withdrew to the side of Blondel, who gave him a swift, significant look. However, the knights saluted Richard as usual, gave Saladin friendly greeting, and the Grand Master spoke in smooth polished Arabic. All the while, Fitzalan noted, the King was fixedly looking down at the ring on his hand. It sharpened the wits, he had said. He had need of that emerald now, if ever.

Saladin spoke courteously, firmly, hinting at the desire for peace which had brought him here. He finished. The Grand Master made brief reply, then turned to Richard.

"It grieves me, Your Majesty," he said in French, "that I am compelled to seek justice at your hands, yet knowing your strong desire for equity I am confident it will be granted gladly."

Richard gave him the lion's look, threatening much.

"You are right," he replied. "But I know not the form of your complaint."

The Grand Master motioned to Sir Jean Menpes.

"One of your knights, Majesty, only last night made a strange assault with his bare hands upon this excellent gentleman of the Order, and indeed struck him senseless. Therefore I must seek from your justice a meeting between the two, in the fashion usual to knights and gentlemen."

"One moment," said Richard quietly. "Of your kindness—a moment."

In the silence, every eye except his own went to Fitzalan; but Richard was looking again at the emerald on his hand, as though seeking in the green stone some advice and counsel. So, perhaps, he was.

The purpose of this visit was now evident enough, at least to Fitzalan. Single combat between himself and Menpes—and beyond this the murder charge. Could the lion-fury of Richard be aroused, a definite breach would be made, all negotiations might well fall through; it was only too certain, in the usual course of events, that Richard would fly to the defense of his own people with a tremendous and unrecking fury. But, as he now gazed upon the emerald, the King was slightly smiling.

"Who is this knight of mine whom you accuse?" he asked.

"Sir James Fitzalan, Your Majesty."

The King looked up, looked at Menpes, and asked a question.

"Your Grand Master, who is our beloved friend and most honored ally, has stated your case, Sir Jean Menpes. I do not suggest that he is wrong. Still, error is possible to anyone, and therefore I ask whether you support his charge."

Menpes bowed as well as his armor would let him.

"Absolutely, Your Majesty. Every word which he has uttered is the exact truth."

"Good. Let all present remember the charge," said the King. "Sir James Fitzalan, I should like to hear what you have to say regarding this matter. The leopards are for England, so it seems to me that exact justice is necessary."

The leopards are for England—the words, the look accompanying them, struck deep meaning into Fitzalan's mind. A hint: The important thing was getting away for England. Nothing else mattered. Exact justice—was it possible that the lion had turned to a smooth craft as cunning as that of the Grand Master?

"I T IS very simple, sire," said Fitzalan. "The entry to my lodgings is dark. As I returned there last night, someone waiting there assaulted me with a wild cry—assaulted me, not as a gentleman, but as a footpad. So I knocked him senseless and went on to my rooms. Naturally I could not, either then or now, make use of the weapons of a knight against a mere footpad in the night."

Quickly, so quickly as to show that he meant to give the enemy no time, Richard spoke up. He seemed vastly amused.

"This is a very odd mistake! Evidently it is a mistake, as you must all admit. Fitzalan's face bears the mark of assault. A senseless man could not have struck the blow, so it is obvious that he was the first assaulted. Nor could he draw sword upon a footpad, as he says. Any man, gentle or ignoble, who makes an assault in the dark forfeits all his rights to the customs of chivalry and knighthood, including those of judicial combat. As we have today met in gentle chivalry toward all enemies, I admonish Fitzalan to forget this mistaken charge upon the part of Sir Jean, who evidently suffers from error, perhaps from too much wine. So, my honored Grand Master, since it is evident that no knight of your noble Order could play the part of footpad, it were best to pass over all charges."

Smoothly said, silkily said—why, here was a new and novel

Richard! And he had the Hospitallers where he wanted them.
Menpes dared not mention the whip, dared not admit he had
been lying in wait. The Grand Master, having failed to provoke
the lion's wrath, was helpless. That weal across Fitzalan's face
had conquered him. His whole attack had missed fire.

Bowing to the King, he accepted defeat gracefully and withdrew from a very bad situation, taking his knights with him.
The King beckoned Fitzalan, and held up his hand to display
the ring.

"You see? It counseled me, sharpened my wits, as I told you
it did," he said. "Are you satisfied or do you wish to press matters
to an end?"

"Sire, I am more than satisfied," said Fitzalan. "I am delighted. I did not know Your Majesty was aware of all the
events."

"I keep informed," said Richard, brusquely, and he turned to
Saladin. "Tomorrow we'll make that peace treaty, eh? Everything
is settled except the length of the peace."

"I think," said the Sultan, his eyes twinkling, "that three years
should be long enough. My relatives, my emirs, all will swear
to keep the peace—and you shall find that the Muslim keep
their oaths."

"Yes," said Richard. "Some Christians I know might take a
lesson from them. Well, tomorrow sees it done, then."

The morrow saw it done. What is more—and mentioned
with the greatest astonishment by the Arab chroniclers—was
that the morrow saw Saladin and Richard exchange a hearty
English handclasp upon the terms of the treaty.

NOT THAT this mattered. Before the English army was
over the sea horizon, the peace was smashed to flinders—and
not by Saracen violators either. But what of that? The emerald
had departed upon its curious way, to be lost in English fogs
and laid away and forgotten, until another king remembered it
and brought it forth to later adventure.

Like the leopards, the emerald was now for England—temporarily at least.

XI

THE KING'S JEWEL

The strange Sphinx Emerald which Richard had brought home to England from the Crusades was the property of Edward III in this year 1349—a year of triumph because of victory; of terror because of pestilence. And when a beautiful woman coveted the jewel, its tragic power came again to life.

S IR THOMAS JESSOP rode his black mare along
the roads toward Norwich with an ever-gathering blackness, blacker than his good mare, surrounding him on all sides.
The King had sent him from London; Sir Thomas wished most
devoutly that someone else had been sent here into East Anglia,
because horrible things were happening here—happening all
around and ahead of him.

It was a lovely countryside in this late spring weather, and
Norwich was the second greatest city of England, but Jessop
had no love for it. He was afraid, and he had good reason for
fear. There were no highways in those days, and he had to track
from town to town, village to village; in all of them he found
death, invisible and pitiless, and the farther he went, the more
death he found—it traveled faster than he did.

He had seen the wars in France, but this was different—a
different death, more deadly and terrible. One could not escape
it, for it struck by stealth. He was a youngish man, strong and
stalwart, a good horseman; he had strong features and fine eyes
and was said to have a brave future ahead at court. Indeed, his
present errand as King's messenger was proof of favor. Because
of his very strength, he knew he was afraid, and denied it not.
This year, as figured in the Rolls of Parliament and elsewhere,
was the twenty-third of Edward III—which is to say, the year
of our Lord 1349.

Only a few short months since, Jessop had seen the King

enter London in triumph, the greatest man in Europe. England was bursting with such glory and power as she had never before known. France had been shattered at Cressy, Calais had been taken. The King of Scotland lay a prisoner in the Tower. King Edward had been chosen as Emperor of Austria, and had refused the extra crown with contempt. Everywhere in England money burned in pockets and there was wild spending. And now, only a few days north of London, Jessop found himself in a different world, with death grinning at his very elbow.

His errand lay to the Bishop of Norwich. William Bateman, the Bishop, was in France as ambassador, but in his place had left an official named Thomas de Methwold. To this man lay Jessop's errand: to obtain a royal jewel found in the Bishop's coffers—a jewel belonging to the Crown—and to fetch it back to London. A simple errand, apparently. Now, with Norwich close ahead, fear bestrode the roads acutely. He felt it athrob in him. True, the pestilence—some sort of Oriental plague—had been bad in London before he left, and was said to be abroad in some of the shires. But this—this was worse than anyone had dreamed, and worsening daily!

A ghastly chain of death was working inland from the coast—village and town and manor linked by invisible fingers. Jessop drew up at the inn of a village just outside Norwich, and the host brought him cheese and ale and gossip. Half the folk here were gone; at Earlham and Wytton and Horsford and other villages, all within five miles of the city, it was said to be worse. Jessop shivered as he ate and gulped and rode on. The city, by all accounts, was a charnel-house. And he was going through this hell because of a jewel—a jewel for the King! The thought brought a croaking laugh from him.

Norwich at last, hovels and palaces, creaking wagons piled with corpses, all going his way, and he soon found out why. The churchyards were all full; the great cemetery was in the cathedral close. The open space between the cathedral and the Bishop's palace and the Erpingham gate on the west, was the goal all day long of wagons piled high with corpses, tilting them over

Fulk would not dismount; terror had him by the hair.
The pestilence was sweeping like a whirlwind.

into the mammoth pits made ready. Jessop, like all other comers
to the palace, must pass across this graveyard, and pass it he
did.

In the vicar-general he sought, he found a most unhappy
man. Thomas de Methwold was grim and gaunt and shaken
with horror. He received Jessop courteously, read his letter,

nodded, and ordered wine served. Then he took Jessop by the arm and led him to the window. He was quiet enough, but in him Jessop sensed frightful tension, nerve-strain almost at the breaking-point.

"It is two months since the Bishop went to France and the pestilence came," he said, pointing to the huge graveyard. "I have lived with that—with the pestilential stench filling the palace! Everyone who comes, must come this way. I'm breaking; I can stand it no longer. The Bishop has a residence in Essex, and I'm going there next week. I was told to stay here, but I'm finished. I've reached the end."

The King's jewel? Oh, yes, it was being fetched. He went on about his duty here, which was to institute new priests in the parishes as fast as they died. Twenty-three in April, seventy-four in May—they were dying faster now. Half the population was gone.

At this point a servant came in with a leather case. Methwold took it and laid it on the table—papers to sign and so forth:

"When are you leaving?" he asked.

"Just as quickly as I have your permission," Jessop said frankly.

"I don't blame you." Methwold sighed and nodded. "Will you pass by Gillingham on your way back? The Bishop's brother, Sir Bartholomew Bateman, lives there. I've certain letters and papers that should go to him; if you'll take them, it'll be a gracious favor."

JESSOP AGREED gladly. Methwold sent his servant for the letters, and for food and wine for Jessop to take with him. It should be a pleasant stop at Gillingham, he said. Sir Bartholomew was a man of great wealth and standing, had represented Norfolk in Parliament, and so forth. Here was the receipt, and it would be best for Jessop to look at the jewel. He opened the leather case, removed the silk packing, and Jessop saw the Sphinx emerald.

At the moment, it meant little to him—a huge green stone set in a ring of worn gold. Methwold said King Richard had brought it from the Crusades, some hundred and fifty years before. It had been lying in the diocesan treasury here a long time, and had but recently been discovered.

The receipt was signed. Jessop pocketed the leather case; it was not a large object. The letters for Gillingham came, and the packet of food and wine. Jessop was glad; the air here was damnable. His horse had been baited and was ready. He took his leave, and rode away with enormous relief. It was hard not to spur and get out of the plague-struck city at a gallop.

Noon was now a little past; twenty miles to go—sunset should see him at Sir Bartholomew's mansion. An overnight stop there, then on to London town. All very simple....

The day was hot. Incredibly, a village where that morning he had breakfasted, was now empty, deserted, abandoned. Reaching toward Gillingham, Jessop sighted wanderers who took to their heels at his approach, and saw frightened faces peering from among the trees in wooded stretches. Sunset brought a glimpse of church towers—Gillingham supported three churches in those fat days—and in the sprawling half-emptied town, Jessop was directed to the manor—a fine lordly mansion amid oak trees.

Death, he perceived, was here ahead of him. His shout had no answer. The doors were wide open. He dismounted and walked into the house. Just inside, he came face to face with a young woman clad in black.

"I was coming to answer your call," she said. "No one is left. I am Eleanor Bateman."

Jessop saluted her. She had an oddly sweet and gracious air, friendly, gladsome, with youthful charm.

"I have brought letters from Norwich for Sir Bartholomew," he said.

"He died last week. In two days nearly everyone died," she said calmly. "My mother, Lady Petronilla, has gone to the nunnery at Bungay. They are dying there, too. If you are not afraid, enter and welcome."

AFRAID? HE was, but scorned to show his fear; he walked in and produced the letters. She laughed, brought ale and cakes, and they talked. That the two of them were alone in a world of the dead drew them together. Jessop was delighted by her, yet alarmed for her safety.

"Not safe to be here alone," he said. "The woods are full of rascals. Houses are broken into everywhere."

"This is home," she said simply. "Indeed, I do lock up at night! The pestilence is all around, so this is safe as anywhere. Will you remain for the night? You must."

True enough. Stay here or take to the woods! Get her some

Jessop shouted repeatedly. Finally Lady Eleanor appeared, coming to his aid. "Rats must have gnawed the supports," she said.

help from the town? No one would come, she said. She was calm and well-poised. Panic and terror were everywhere, but not in her. Jessop was heartened by her quiet composure.

So he stayed, making himself useful the while.

He buckled in to help her get the place closed and locked; he put up his own horse, carried in water and wood for the cook-fire, and helped her to prepare the supper. Odd work for him, odd work for her, but she was very cheerful about it. She seemed not to mourn her lost father too heavily, and Sir Thomas Jessop found her a singularly charming woman.

They proved to have mutual friends in London, and as they chatted over the meal, he mentioned the reason for his journey. He pulled out the case, and displayed the King's jewel to her. As they inspected it, he himself really saw it for the first time.

It was Lady Eleanor who discovered the tiny Sphinx within the beryl. Jessop knew nothing whatever about jewels. He had a post in court, estates in the west country, and had served in the French wars. He had never heard of the Sphinx, and did not know an emerald from a bobstay—to him, this was a great gaud and nothing more.

Later, after he had retired within a curtained, boxed-up bed that held the day's heat most damnably, he recalled only vaguely that she had kept the pretty gaud to look at it again; then slumber took him.

NOW IT chanced Sir Bartholomew had greatly loved manuscripts and floriated initials and such things; and since his sight was not too good, had kept a huge glass that would enlarge them for his pleasure. So Lady Eleanor sat up to a late hour with two wax tapers burning, studying the emerald through the glass.

The longer Lady Eleanor examined the emerald, the more remarkable and fascinating she found the stone, and at length she put the ring aside to study by daylight.

Further, among the dead knight's treasures was a manuscript copy of the Chronicle of Raimbaut, the Provençal song telling about King Richard's escapades in his Crusade and how the Sphinx emerald had come to him from Saladin, who thought it an evil thing although most wondrous. So, before getting to sleep, the excited chatelaine got this manuscript and read it over; this was the very same stone, of course. The poem put ideas in her head, or else the emerald had done so; and, like the average high-born damsel of her day, Eleanor was not troubled by inhibitions. The King's jewel this might be, but it was certainly the Sphinx emerald as well, the most wonderful thing she had ever seen. And then and there she determined to have it.

While Sir Thomas Jessop lay late next morning in his hot but luxurious feather bed, fondly imagining himself in perfect security, Lady Eleanor was up and long at work with enlarging glass and emerald, verifying the very strange things she had discovered the previous night. There was a Sphinx within the stone, yes—a tiny yet perfect figure, formed of the angular bubbles and tiny flaws occurring in all emeralds. This was of course mere creative chance.

But, far more, this stone possessed a singular power—a power over her mind.

This was not mere imagination either. It captivated her, but this captivation was an obsession, almost a frenzy. Those green depths, those sparkling, winking vistas shown under the enlarging glass, not only appealed to her, they dominated her. She could not resist them. She felt a furious impulse to keep this ring for herself at any cost, to make it her own and jealously keep it. As the green facets sped refracted lights to her brain, the stone spoke to her. She had never heard of auto-hypnosis, but she had actually hypnotized herself with the jewel. From unknown depths of her nature, hitherto unguessed, had been wakened things that held her powerless. She must have this gem—she must!

Nothing strange or fanciful about this. The Sphinx emerald was famed in history for just such workings—perhaps because of its delicate refraction and its odd little figure, it appealed irresistibly to the imagination. Lady Eleanor was therefore scarcely to blame if she found in the stone a jeering, malignantly powerful attraction that hinted delightfully wicked ideas.

WITH THE sun came heat; the day would be a bad one.... Jessop crawled from the huge bed, shuddered at sight of his stained, dusty traveling attire, went to the window and glanced into the courtyard below. A well was there, with a stone border, a wheel and bucket, and a huge stone trough into which Lady Eleanor was drawing water. She wore a long white gown girt with a golden belt, and had her luxurious hair in two long braids.

"Good morning!" Jessop called. "That water looks attractive. If you'll go away somewhere, I'm tempted to bathe."

She laughed brightly. "All right. I'm getting some water for the kitchen. In a moment you can have the place to yourself and welcome."

Presently she filled a pan and departed, Jessop, who still had the decaying pestilential fumes of Norwich in his nostrils, flung his riding-cloak around him and found his way to the courtyard. He drew more water into the big horse-trough, then doffed his cloak and plunged in. The dip was delicious and made a new man of him. He emerged, donned his cloak, got back to his room and dressed.

He found her in the huge-beamed kitchen, setting a meal on the table there. She greeted him with a kiss on the cheek, in usual fashion; she was cheerful, even gay. She had fed and watered his horse, and the two remaining to her in the stables, she said. Since both of them were hungry and the morning was getting late, they sat down at once to the meal she had prepared.

"Well, what to do?" queried Jessop when hunger was eased. "Cannot I see you to some safe place, or will your mother and servants return?"

She shrugged. "You know as well as I do."

"Then I suggest that you collect some clothes and valuables. Load one horse, ride the other, since you have two. I'll see you safe to London or where you will. Eh?"

She reflected. "Yes, I think that will be best. But not at once—in a day or two. I must get things together, you see. You'll not mind delay?"

Jessop laughed. "Would I object to spending a day or so in this pleasant place, rather than face the hell of the countryside? Hardly. With this hot weather, the pestilence will grow worse, I fear. Can't I induce servants to come from the town?"

"No, and they're not needed," she said. "I'm capable. I don't want the poor frightened things. But I would like to have my father's strong-box. It's in the strong-room, up at the east end of the house, and I can't lift it."

"Show me the place," said Jessop.

She nodded. "Very well. Later."

"I forgot to get the King's jewel back from you last night."

She gave him an odd look. "Let me keep it while we're here. I like to play with it. Must the King have it? He has so many!"

"He's devilish intent on getting it, for some reason," Jessop replied carelessly. "And, as I'm responsible, he'll get it. But play with it if you like. It pleases you?"

"Truly, it would please anyone, Sir Thomas. Have you been to the French wars?"

They talked of many things—their lives, themselves. The house was an island that shut out the world of death and desolation; it was their own and a refuge. Jessop talked of the war in France, of London, of the court, of the west country that he loved. From her he heard much about books, of which he knew nothing, and quiet country living. She made him tell of the great Cressy battle of two years gone, and they spent the morning very pleasantly.

Now, Thomas Jessop was no fool; in fact he was a shrewd and able man; but he had no reason for the least suspicion, and he was charmed by this young woman, and more charmed the more he saw of her. That she liked him was evident. She was well-bred, had a thoughtful manner yet was merry withal, and was highly efficient. She was talking to him about getting some of her father's Flemish wine out of the cellar, and cooling it in the well, when a pounding at the front entrance drew them both. A traveler was there—a sweaty man on a sweaty horse, seeking his way to Yarmouth.

HE WOULD not dismount; terror had him by the hair. Fulk was his name—a London merchant. He bore terrible news: The pestilence was taking a third of the people there, and was sweeping all the eastern shires like a whirlwind. Fulk accepted a cup of ale, got directions, then went his way. Jessop closed the doors and looked at Lady Eleanor.

"Things are going from bad to worse," he said. "The country is perishing."

"Then stay here. The larder is stocked. Why depart?"

"I must," he said. "My errand. I cannot fail. I'll take you to the King."

"As you like," she replied. "Day after tomorrow we can leave; no hurry."

This unexpected contact with the outside world had shaken them both; she was white and horrified by Fulk's story.

"Get the wine, quickly," she said. "Come. I'll give you a pitcher and show you the way. The cellars are deep and dark."

She got a pewter pitcher and a candle and led him down into the cellars. These were dingy and crowded. The wine-cask stood near a central pillar. Close to it was a huge vat of copper-bound wood on a tall and shaky scaffolding. She put down the candle on the floor and gave him the pitcher.

"There you are—I must go feed the fowl," she said, and departed.

Jessop worked at the spigot, but it ran only with a dribble, so he set the pitcher under it and turned to examine some flitches of bacon hanging at one side. He had just reached them when he heard a scraping noise. Then came a tremendous blast of sound, and he was knocked sprawling. The candle was out.

He was hemmed in by fallen objects. He shouted repeatedly. Finally Lady Eleanor appeared, with a lighted candle, coming to his aid. He saw that the great vat had tumbled over smack upon the wine-cask. The pewter pitcher was a bent mass of metal.

"Rats must have gnawed the supports," she said, helping him to get clear. "Had you been just there—"

Jessop shivered. She was badly upset by his danger. Once out of the cellar, she lost her composure, clung to him, wept, then with shaky laughter remembered that the spigot of the wine-cask must still be turned on, and fled to take care of it. She came back with the pitcher and they got a couple of mugs of wine from the bent mass. Over this, the adventure ended in laughter. But all Jessop now remembered was how she had clung to him; it was a warming kindly memory.

"You spoke of a strong-box," he said.

She shook her head.

"Not now—let it wait." With this, she produced the ring and its great pale emerald, put it on her hand, and began to peer into it. He watched her play with it and was amused by her intent absorption. The thought began to take shape in his mind that she would be a pleasant companion, would make a good wife. She must inherit solidly from Sir Bartholomew, the family was notable, her uncle was Bishop of Norwich. It was all a very happy thought indeed, well worth considering. And it was high time, he reflected, that Tom Jessop was marrying and settling down. With her father so lately dead, however, it was not a subject to broach just now.

They ate sparingly of noon meat; the day was hot and lifeless. She showed him over part of the house: the library, a rare thing to find at that day but not interesting to him, and the armory where the mail and bows and weapons were kept. The chapel was closed. Sir Bartholomew had died there. They stood at the entrance of the room and looked in. She was close to him, almost touching him.

The high-boned turn of her cheek, the curve of her lashes, the firm lips and the white throat, held his gaze. She turned her head a little and her eyes came to his; her lips smiled, but her eyes did not, and it puzzled him. She held up her hand, and on it he saw the Sphinx emerald.

"I must have it—I must!" she murmured. "You must find a way."

One part of him was tempted terribly, so expressive was her face. She was his for the asking, he realized; with that stone, he could win her on the spot. But the hard, practical side of him rebelled. He had been raised in a stern school, and was adept at crushing down the importunities of the flesh.

"The King must have his own, sweet lady," he said.

*"Why must you be hard,
unyielding? Life could
be so rich, so sweet, if
you would let it be!"*

At his words, a flash lit her eyes, their tenderness departed, and she turned away. Her nostrils quivered, as her breath came rapidly.

"You prate too much of the King," she rejoined.

"I swore him loyalty," said Sir Thomas. "I keep my vows—that is the family motto."

"So much the worse, then, for you." She laughed a little and swung around. "Well, I must get my things together. The house is yours; be comfortable. Later, when it's cooler, we'll go to the strong-room. Really, I'm grateful for having your strength to help me. I could never handle those great weights."

She touched his arm—a massive arm, trained to swing the sword and ax—and smiled at him; again the smile was on her lips, not in her eyes. But Jessop did not notice this, for her touch quickened his pulse. On swift impulse he reached out to take her by the shoulders. She laughed merrily and slid from between his hands like a wraith, leaving him at foolish stance.

"Your chivalric training, my fair knight, is far too good," she said as she slipped away, and perhaps her words held more than one meaning. "However, you may have one more chance to reconsider—so, until later!" She kissed her hand to him and was gone.

JESSOP GRUNTED. "Truly, women are vixens until they marry and have a house full of brats!" he muttered angrily. Then, thankful for something he really understood, he swung off to the armory and began a delighted investigation of the armor and weapons, which detained him a long while. He did not pretend to understand Lady Eleanor, but all the same he found her pleasantly full of promise. She would make a good wife, he thought again.

Later he visited the stables and curried his black mare, found equipment for the two Bateman horses, and emptied a bucket of water over his head to cool him. He was shaking the water out of his hair when, without the least warning, he heard a sound he had often heard in France—the curt twang of a taut bowstring loosed.

By sheer instinct and habit, he dropped, every muscle relaxed. He heard the whir and breath of a shaft almost touching him; then the cloth-yard arrow struck the stone curbing of the well and shattered into flinders. Strength had drawn that bow! Someone was in the house, shooting at him—next instant, he was up and running, his brain working fast. No second shot; a trained bowman would have sent two more shafts through him before he had gained his feet. Some country rascal, some lout of the town, had broken in to plunder the manor! A fair shot too; that shaft would have transfixed him, but for his quick drop.

Next minute he was in the house and plunging into room after room, knife in hand. He found only emptiness. There was no sign of anyone. He reached the stairs going to the upper rooms and came face to face with Lady Eleanor.

"What's wrong?" she exclaimed. "And a knife, too—"

"Someone took a shot at me from the house; I was at the well," he said. "There's some rascal in here!"

"Then he's not upstairs," she replied. "I've been in sight of the stairs—going through my wardrobe. Have you looked in the cellars? Here, I'll lend a hand. We'll go over the place carefully."

She produced a knife of her own, a jeweled bodkin that would scarce have killed a thrush, and flung herself into the search. They found no one; but she called him suddenly and pointed to an open window in the dining-room, one used to let out fire-smoke in cold weather. And the bows in the armory were at sixes and sevens.

"There's the way he went," she declared. "His shot failed and he went in haste. Someone must have left this window un-latched. A town rascal, eh?"

Jessop agreed, but took a candle into the cellars none the less, found no one, and gave up any further search.

Lady Eleanor found some wine, and they desisted from their labors, sitting over the cups. This happening pointed up the peril to a lone woman staying here, as Jessop made plain, and she nodded soberly.

"You are right, Sir Thomas. Think you we had better leave tomorrow, instead of the day after? I can be ready if you so decide."

"It's best," he said. She laughed and held out her hand.

"Then let me borrow that stout knife of yours. I must cut some thongs that are shrunken into my chest of clothes and won't come open. Then we can look at the strong-room and get my father's money-box."

He gave her the knife. She put it down, held up her hand, and admired the emerald.

"I must give this back to you, eh?"

"I fear you must," he said, laughing.

She grimaced.

"Tyrant! Not until we actually leave, then. Will no pretty plea tempt you to give it up—no golden money?"

Smiling, Jessop shook his head. "Tempt me, yes; prevail upon me, no. As I've said, it's the King's jewel. Were it mine, you should have it and welcome."

"The King may be dead. All London may be dead—all England, for aught we know! What if we were alone and the world gone to the grave? Then you'd give it to me?"

"Possibly," said he, mock-serious. "And all the crown jewels with it!"

She laughed, picked up the knife, and pushed back her chair.

"Whew! What heat! Shall I show you the strong-room? It must be stifling in there, far too hot to get the box now, but you'll know where it is."

They came to the stairs, which had a solid carved rail of Flemish work. There she stumbled, caught at the rail, and half drooped over it. Jessop's hand stayed her; she clung to his arm.

"Sorry; perhaps it was the wine—I feel all gone," she said faintly.

"It's the heat. You probably need a good dose of greens," he said prosaically. But he did not feel at all prosaic. He held her against him and his pulses were pounding.

She twisted about slightly and looked up into his face. Her fingers touched his cheek caressingly. Her voice was low, gentle, muted.

"So strong! Why must you be hard, unyielding? Life could be so rich, so sweet, if you would let it be!"

*"Sheathe swords, lads," said Jessop. "Easy does it,
now—we'll not harm you if you're peaceful folk—"*

"I? Why, what have I done?" he said hoarsely.

"Denied me. The jewel is wonderful; it has shown me magnificent things, my dear knight. We could go to Scotland from here. No one would ever know. Probably the King is dead, and half the court. The emerald on my hand, you in my heart, life beginning anew for us—all sweet and fair. None of the ghastly death that lies all around us, that steals ahead of us in the night—"

HER VOICE wove a magic spell that weakened him. Truth was in her words. Why, she was offering him the very thing he

had been pondering: herself in marriage, away from this horrible pestilence His hands tightened upon her slim warmth. His heart pounded.

"I am so weak against you," she went on, with truth. "Yet together, with the great emerald our friend, we could be so strong!"

He came to sudden life. It was the emerald she wanted, not him.

"Don't tempt me, sweet lass," he said. "I keep my vows—aye, so I do. You don't know what you're saying. Here, now!" He lifted her a little, set her on her feet, and smiled. "Come along and we'll look at the strong-room, then step down to the garden and forget all such pretty nonsense!"

A sigh escaped her, an impatient sound. She turned, took hold of the rail, and stepped up, with a complete change of mood that astonished him.

"Very well. I have the keys here. The room's all of oak; my father built it for safety. None shall ever break in or out, said he, not the strongest!"

He followed, wondering at her. She had a bunch of huge keys that had hung at her belt. She came to a door and paused there, working at a lock. A massive bar of oak was in place, and he lifted it away at her bidding. She swung open the door, and hot air like a furnace-breath smote them.

"Such heat! No one can live there long," she murmured.

Jessop pushed past her and peered around. Here it was quite dark. The house had windows set with thinned and translucent horn; there was one such here, set up high, but it was long and narrow, not six inches wide, and closed fast. He had a vision of massive beams. The wall-studding was massive too, great oaken posts—

He heard a click as the door closed and the lock caught.

For an instant he thought nothing of it, until he heard faintly the scrape as the oak bar was settled into its socket outside. The sound reminded him of the scrape he had heard just before the vat fell. It startled him. He sprang at the door, assailed it, shouted—but only silence responded. Incredibly, she had locked him in!

He was slow to realize this, but it became evident soon enough. Already the intense heat had him in a lather of sweat. He jerked at his clothes, then assailed the door with frantic fury, cursing, shouting, promising, threatening. His spasm of violence gained him nothing save exhaustion.

He steadied, ceased his useless effort, and looked around. The little room was empty. Nothing was in it—no strong-box, nothing. The heat was intolerable; it burned his lungs. He ripped off his clothes, stripped to the buff, then approached the window. His knife—she had taken it! Clinging to the wall, he reached the window and found it nailed fast. He pounded at the thin sheets of horn with his fists, and broke one out. The breath of air was refreshing. It steadied him. He looked out, saw leaves of an oak.

His brain cooled, and he let himself down, began to think.

This had been done on purpose. She had planned it; but why, in God's name? "You may have one chance to reconsider," she had said. Was that the chance, on the stairs? Surely she would not murder him, to get that green stone?

He realized then that he had hit on the truth: that scraping sound before the vat fell—she must have drawn some cord that made it fall! That arrow—she must have been the bowman! She had no strength to cope with him, so she had used her wits, was using them now. He broke into a storm of cursing and fury, hurled himself at the door again, finally clambered up to the opening in the window and gasped in fresh air.

Get out by this window? The thought was folly; a bird might leave, but not he. A look around the little room brought despair; there was no tool, no weapon of any sort. She had him here, and he was safely stowed. Two days or three of this—the idea made him sweat. He spied the roofing: Solid beams, sheathed with lead outside. He had noticed the lead sheathing on the roof as he approached the house, he remembered.

He dropped to the floor, streaming with sweat. The afternoon had been half gone when he came here. Night would bring relief—He cocked his head at a slight brushing sound outside the window. Leaves, twigs—an oak must have grown up against this place. He could hear the branch brushing again; evidently a breeze had sprung up.

Stretching out on the dusty hot floor, he looked up at the roof and got his thoughts in order. She wanted to be rid of him, yes. This was the third attempt. The emerald would be hers, then—all this for an emerald? A wonderful stone, she had said; she was mad about it. Sometimes jewels did that to people. He had heard someone at court talking about the subject. People did go stark mad, sometimes, over jewels.

"I'll be stark mad in another day of this heat, too!" he muttered. "The damned room's an oven, no less—well, I must get out of here this night, or I'm a dead man. How to do it?"

He stared up, unseeing, trying to figure some way. The window made a break in the wall, but his hands could make no effect upon it, except to punch out the horn. The sly puss, to take his knife so coyly! She had figured craftily too: He would be accounted dead of the plague, when he did not return, and no search would be made.

What was that—a stick?

He focused upward, where something out of line caught his eye among the rafters: A short, straight line. Aye, a stick of some sort, left by the builders. Could he gain a cross-beam, he might reach it. He stood up, feeling withered and dried out by the heat. With a spring, he could get his hands to the beam.

He sprang—he got a grip, tried to pull himself up. After a struggle, he made it, but the rough oak beam was covered with splinters that dug into his chest and stomach. No matter—he was up, had his leg over the beam, then rose to his feet. A stick, nothing more—a stout two-inch stave of old hard oak. He got it down, then sought the floor again and began clawing out splinters while the daylight lasted. Already it was waning, the heat was lessening.

BEFORE DARK came, he was at the window, scanning it closely, examining every joint of the wood, getting it fixed in his mind. He looked out and saw the oak branch close to hand, a scant foot away, and fixed that in his mind, too. Thirty feet above the ground would be an unwanted fall.

Then, poised and agonized by both clinging and exerting effort, he fell to work.

He could effect nothing; this was his first sad discovery. After a long while he ceased work, rested, and then in the dark began afresh. This time he forced out the panels of horn and attacked the little cross-pieces of the window. One shattered, then another. The frame gave slightly, that was all.

Another rest. He was certain of one thing—this was the only chink in the solidly built room. Not with an ax could he hope to get through the door, for all the steely strength of his arms and shoulders. Back in his niche once more, he pried away, slowly, carefully. A creak, a slight splintering, rewarded him after a while.

He had to rest anew; not even his strength could long endure the effort.

He dressed, since it was now cool night, and returned to work. He had to be careful not to break the little stout stick; luckily, it proved stouter than the window casing. This creaked more and more, finally splintered and gave the full opening of six inches. Not enough. Another two or three inches, and being slim-built he might pinch through. But how to get that extra space?

He fingered the casing over and over, and at length his fingers discerned a slight upward give in the outer shell of oak. He set the stick to it. The board, probably loosened by rain and weather, gave a little more. He worked at it until he had to drop, exhausted, to the floor and recuperate.

WHEN AT length he returned to the work, the board gradually came loose and finally clattered off the side of the house. He explored feverishly with his hand.

The opening was no wider than before.

This was a facer; it nearly knocked him out. At length he pulled himself together and came back to the window. Nothing gained, indeed, but now he had access to another board, and gradually pried and worked at this until it gave a bit. All the sad dark work over again, endless in the night, a fumbling effort without eyes—until suddenly, just as he was on the point of giving up in blank despair, there came a great creak and the board was loose. Space! He might even get through!

This put new life into him. He finished dressing, rested a bit, climbed back to the window and made a determined effort to emerge. His head went through the gap. His shoulders followed and stuck; cloth shredded away, then he moved on. The oak leaves brushed his face. He was through to the waist, but stuck again. His hands found the oak branch. He made shift to pull his hips through, at some cost to clothes and skin, and got a grip on the main oak branch. With this safe hold, he wriggled through somehow, then had a terrific struggle to maintain his hold on the oak branch.

In the midst of this he began to laugh.

It all struck him as ludicrous. He, a veteran of the French wars accustomed to the din of ax and sword on mail, the whistle of bolts and the trumpets of battle—fighting a strife to the death with a girl, crawling about attics and skirmishing with oak trees like a farm boy! It was funny, yet it was damned serious too. He managed eventually to reach the dark tree, felt his way down, lost his hold and fell the last ten feet, but landed unhurt on the sward, scratched, breathless and triumphant.

He lay there a while beside the black bulk of the house, until a noise reached him and he sat up, incredulous. It came again, faint but distinct: a rousing fusillade of oaths in Norman-French. After this sounded a woman's quick startled cry, Lady Eleanor's voice, filled with terror; it was ended abruptly, and all was silence.

From the house, by God's wounds—from within the house! Jessop came to his feet. Everything was dark here, but he went scrambling around to the front. He was seeing his way in the starlight, now. Something black was near the entry—two horses tied fast. A dim light showed at a window upstairs, then moved away. Two horses—two men here! The front door was fast shut, but the side lattice swung open, the same which Eleanor had pointed to as the way of the supposed bowman's escape. Jessop went to it. Must be late, perhaps past midnight, he thought. Well, he could not leave her at the mercy of two rascals—and there was the King's jewel, too. He must get that.

Before anything else, he must get a weapon. No hard task.

He scrambled through into the house, listened, heard nothing. All was dark here, but he knew his way well enough, and headed for the armory. Passing the stairs, he caught a chuckling laugh and a hoarse jest from above, but paused not. He had his mind's eye on a sword he had seen, beautiful of work and balance, a gift to Sir Bartholomew from the City of London. He could put his hand right on it, dark or no dark.

The doors were closed. He made some noise but cared not. Here was the armory. Knowing the spot on the wall, he reached for the sword, but struck a helm and sent it clattering and clashing to the floor. No matter—he had his hand on the sword now, and brought it down from its perch, and bared the blade.

"Well, that's better! Now I'm myself again," he muttered.

He started out of the room, only to hear steps on the stairs and a voice.

"I tell ye there's someone about down here, Wat! Hang your lanthorn on that hook yonder. I'll keep mine."

So they had heard him. He looked and saw them at the foot of the stairs. One was hanging a lantern on a hook projecting from the wall. The other held his light. Both had swords bared; they were burly, leather-clad men, obviously army veterans out for plunder.

"Sheathe swords, lads," said Jessop. "Easy does it, now—we'll not harm you if you're peaceful folk—"

An explosion of startled oaths, as they sighted him in the hall. The one with the lantern plunged for him.

"At him, Wat!" rang out the voice. "Around back—I'll take him i' front—"

"Ah, you fool!" said Jessop, and engaged the blade reaching for him. A savage hot fury took hold of him; the sword in his hand came alive, clashed the seeking blade aside, slashed the arm that held it, slashed again at the shoulder and cut into that—then, as the man screamed and cursed and fell back, Jessop turned to meet the attack of the one called Wat, who

was in upon him from the side. Stouter work here, for Wat was
a swordsman of skill, but skill availed him little against Jessop's
trained hand and hot fury. The London sword slipped from the
leathern coat, and slipped again, but the third time it bit and
the blade sheared in, drove down once more and the keen edge
went home through neck and shoulder. Wat died there, and
Jessop looked to see the first man scrambling out past the lattice.
He let him go.

Eleanor? No sign from her. Jessop called and had no reply.
He took the fallen lantern, leaving the other on its hook, and
climbed up the stairs. The second room he glanced into proved
to be hers. She was lying across a couch—she had fainted, he
thought. He went in and held up the lantern, and his heart
stopped.

She lay in her night-shift, and the jeweled handle of her little
bodkin dagger, that would scarce kill a thrush, protruded from
her side. She was dead. Jessop looked at her for a long moment.
Realization chilled him, steadied him. She must have killed
herself with the bodkin, probably while struggling with those
two ruffians. He leaned over and touched her hand; it was still
warm. How piteously lovely she looked! She would make a
good wife, he had thought; memory of his errant urgings
spurred at him harshly. That slim fairness would delight no man
now.

ON THE couch he saw a little open leather box, and he
roused—the King's jewel! Where? He glanced around.
Everything in the room was ransacked and disordered. He came
back to her and looked; her hands were clenched, and on one
of them he saw a golden band. She had turned in the emerald,
had clenched her hand upon the stone. He reached down, and
for an instant she seemed to resist him slightly, in death as in
life. Then her fingers came open.

Gently, he removed the green-glinting jewel for which she
had schemed, for which she may have died. He put it within
the case, pocketed this, and picked up the lantern. He paused,

went to his knee, and said a short prayer. Then he kissed her hand, rose, and strode out of the room, and on out of the house, to where the black mare awaited him.

XII

A TASK FOR LEONARDO

The incomparable Leonardo da Vinci had great plans for the magic Sphinx Emerald— but though the King of France was his friend, he had also made a bitter enemy.

IN THE day when King François was young and handsome and magnificent, glorious with victories, ablaze with majesty and splendor—let us say, in the year 1517—he was a great patron of the arts, and brought the Renaissance back to France with him from Italy. Among others, he brought the famed old artist Leonardo, and gave him the manor of Cloux, a fine little property in a suburb of Amboise in Touraine, and with it seven hundred crowns a year, a princely pension. Here Leonardo da Vinci settled down happily.

The artist was not a painter alone. Having the title of Royal Architect, he planned cities, palaces and even a canal system for King François. Being an accomplished engineer, he could turn his hand nobly to any form of work or art. In doing so, he could even hide, at first, the sad fact that this hand was failing him; but after a year or so, it became evident that a form of paralysis was creeping over those fingers which had created so much loveliness, winning him renown and the whole world's respect. Finally the right hand entirely lost its use, though he could still work and sketch perfectly with the other.

The King one day came to the little square house at Cloux, embraced Leonardo warmly, and with satisfaction looked over the plans for the canal system. Then, in his restless way, he turned to something else.

"There is a little thing you can do for me, Leonardo," he said. "I love you. Men have ever loved you, for you are like a god in

*So, in due time, came the King,
splendid and laughing, with half
a dozen of his lords around him.*

all you do. You create beauty. You have the ability to look at a stone, and envision in it the statue. Well, here is a stone on which to try your fancies. Intrinsically, it is worth little, yet it has vast value. It is a stone of strange history, 'tis said. Take it, study it, and some day tell me what to do with it."

So saying, he gave the old man, whose long white hair and beard were like glistening snow, an ancient, thin-worn ring holding a great lump of green.

Leonardo looked at it, and drew down his white eyebrows.

"Is it an emerald, Sire?"

The King laughed. "Aye, by report. In the days when King Harry of England exchanged gifts with me, instead of threatening war, I had it from him. Keep it for a while, ponder how

strange a thing it is, my friend, and later advise me concerning it."

The swaggering king went his splendid way, while the old artist stayed close; and a morning came when Francesco Melzi, the devoted Milanese pupil who served him so nobly, heard a ringing cry of ecstasy from the garden, and looked to see the old artist seated there, gazing at something under a glass, an enlarging lens.

"There is a man here to speak with you, master," Melzi called. "One Messer Baldino of Florence, a cutter of gems."

"Then let him in," replied Leonardo.

Past seventy now, clear as a bell in mind, he tucked away his useless right hand and eyed the visitor from beneath the heavy white brows, so carefully tended. He was ever careful of his appearance; indeed, he was a great gentleman in every way, fastidious and never neglectful of the least detail.

This Baldino was a cocky, assured fellow with quick eye and nimble tongue, who bowed low and gave the great artist humble greeting; one felt the humility assumed. In his calm, serene way Leonardo listened. He was a good listener. Never excited, never emotional—even when Buonarotti had insulted him to his face, he only reddened and remained silent—he was serenity itself. He could feel, with those extra senses of his that felt so much, the meanness of this man Baldino; yet the words rang fair enough.

This gem-cutter had made a reputation and money and had come to join the artistic ateliers of the King of France. He was in love with a girl here in Amboise; in fact, was affianced to her, and begged that the master would sketch her—a mere sketch from the angelic genius of Leonardo! A little thing—a vastly great one. Baldino spoke well, and Leonardo, a trifle ashamed of what his intuition told him, did not refuse curtly or at all. The man did not insult him with offers of pay, but begged the favor as being himself a Florentine, from Leonardo's own fair city.

It might be, answered the old artist; he would have to see the girl. She might interest him as a model—why not? As they talked, Baldino caught sight of the ring and its great lumpy emerald. A stone of poor color, not of good deep hue, and above nine carats in weight—unevenly cut, a huge lopsided cabochon. He spoke eagerly of the stone, and Leonardo nodded at him.

"It is not mine. Look, if it pleases you."

Baldino took the ring, saw that the gold was thin-worn and done for; and then the jewel gripped him. He did not see what lay within it; yet it seized hold of him by the roots. He perceived how it might be reshaped, after a fashion, and knew it must belong to the King, who was Leonardo's patron. He asked if he might sketch it.

Leonardo assented silently, watched his work, and saw what a facile, superficial botch of an artist he was, but made no comment. Presently the sketch was done, and Baldino handed back the ring, spoke of the latest news from Florence, made an appointment for his fair Flora, and so departed. Old Leonardo got out his glass, and once again began gazing into the emerald, feeling as though some evil thing had left him. Not that poor Baldino was akin to Satan, but he was a slipshod sort of artist; and in Leonardo's sight, this was the most evil of all things.

Then he forgot the fellow, because the glowing green gem took hold of him—not on the surface but inwardly, fixedly, most amazingly.

S O M E   D A Y S later the young woman Flora came to be sketched. Francesco Melzi received her, talked with her. It was no secret that old Leonardo was a princely person of most eccentric manner. The girl was submissive, quiet, undemonstrative. To her, it was entirely fitting that she should await the genius of the artist—wait until he deigned to notice her and make the sketch. She made no objection to coming at ten each morning and waiting until noon. Melzi told her to come, sit, make herself comfortable, do whatever she liked, until Leonardo became aware of her and made the promised sketch.

This, of course, was not Leonardo's way or wish; it was the devoted apprentice painter speaking, perhaps in hope that the girl, who lived nearby, would weary of the affair. The Milanese considered it shameful that Leonardo, besought for work by kings and dukes, should sketch this unknown girl for some rascally fellow from Florence. So he said naught of it to the artist.

Until, one morning, he came round-eyed into the studio, where the old man worked with one hand at his unfinished and never-to-be-finished picture of Saint John.

"Master," he said in the soft Italian that Leonardo so loved, "there is a man come to see you, and his name is the Sieur Laforge—"

"Ha!" cried out Leonardo, putting aside his palette. "Laforge! Now the gods indeed do me honor! Bring him here, my son, and let not the King himself disturb us!"

In came the soldier, he of the merry features and large fine eyes, and knelt to kiss the hand of Leonardo; but the older man touched his fingers in the Italian fashion and embraced him. He had commanded the escort bringing Leonardo from Italy,

"Oh, to be in Milan again, and twenty years younger! Those soul-windows of yours stir sleeping things far within me."

and they had become friends, and more. They were of a kind, these two, soldier and artist; smiling, silent, aware of unseen forces, puzzled and wondering at the world around, yet touched often with quick laughter and divine thoughts.

Laforge was visiting the court at Amboise, in a brief lull before returning to the army in Italy. François, more sensual and profligate than ever, foresaw more shining victories ahead, Laforge said sadly. He himself foresaw ruin and disaster, and an end of grandeur for the King, with no way to avert it all.

"Why not?" Leonardo said calmly. "That is the human scene, my friend—progression and then retrogression. All life moves in waves. We think that our own will propels the impulses of destiny, and we are proud; but always, in the end, we are cheated."

"Pessimist!" said the soldier, smiling. "What we call ruin and disaster may be no such thing in reality! We simply cannot see the higher levels, my master."

"Or mayhap we see them and are thwarted in the execution,"

said the artist, with a glance at his useless right hand. Laforge understood and nodded. "But never mind all that, my friend. Did you come to look at pictures? I have three here—one of Saint Anne, one of John the Baptist, one of a Florentine lady. None finished yet to my taste. But I have something far greater to show you, a thing of exquisite wonder, unique in the world."

Laforge's eyes twinkled. "I've seen her already. We've been talking in the garden. She is indeed a lovely creature!"

"She?" Leonardo peered oddly at him. "A woman? I've none here!"

"Then you entertain angels unawares." Laforge told of meeting the girl Flora in the garden, where she waited to be sketched, and Leonardo nodded; some affair of Melzi's, then. Satisfied, he went to the big table, shoved aside his volumes of notes and sketches, put away his drawings, and set up the enlarging glass with the old worn ring beneath it.

"Here is a poorly colored emerald," said he, "a lumpish stone that needs proper correction. But look into its heart and see the mystery! Ah, were I thirty years younger, what things I might see there!"

LAFORGE WAS a simple and curiously medieval fellow. He sat down to look at the emerald. A cry escaped him at sight of the great flaws making up the figure of the Sphinx. He had never seen or heard of the Sphinx until Leonardo now told him of it, but the singularly powerful effect of this figure amid its green fields, precipices and sunlit glories quite pierced to his soul. It wakened strange fancies in his imagination, and even frightened him.

"Wizardry! It is bewitched!" He crossed himself hurriedly.

"Don't be childish," said Leonardo, smilingly watching him and stroking his flowing white beard. "It is bewitched like my paintings, that is all—with beauty. Touched with unseen loveliness and the mystery of art. You feel it, but cannot see it. Look again."

Laforge obeyed, marveling, and remained for a long while

looking, speaking of what he saw there, and of what he fancied. This had to do with the girl Flora, though he could not say just how; but it was all very sweet and gracious, wakening the mind to wondrous things. Leonardo smiled and nodded comprehension. He too knew the mysterious love that was not of the body, and could not be fixed down with words.

"In that very sort of thing I am slowly building here, in my own way," said he, at length. "With the reach of my art, and with this fragment of green stone, I shall achieve something great and glorious in its beauty and power. Don't ask me what; the vision comes only in its due time. It is forming, taking shape, and one of these days you shall see it."

The soldier rose, loath to depart.

"The angel in the garden is beauteous enough for me," he said, smiling. "May I come again, to see her?"

"Come when you like, as you will, and do what pleases you," said Leonardo. "Truly, all I have is yours, and it affords great pleasure to place it at your service. I know in my age that the truest and most lasting pleasure is that which we have given others; we keep only what we give away. A curious little fact, which is somehow bound up with the existence of the soul, I think."

Laforge was not given to pondering souls or metaphysics, though gentleness and beauty did attract him beyond measure. Leonardo revealed a few sketches to him, and he cried out in rapture. They showed merely the necks of children. Then came, in contrast, the wrinkled nape of an old crone, and he nodded, his eyes clouding.

"I see, Florentine," he said. "The most beautiful and the most ugly of all things! Well, we two are not unlike, although I think your eyes see deeper far than mine. If I may, I'll come again."

WITH LAFORGE gone, Leonardo gazed anew into the emerald, and forgot to ask Melzi about the girl in the garden. He felt uplifted by this visit from his friend, and worked all through the afternoon, sketching this ghostly wonder—the

Sphinx and its green fields and the things he fancied therein. It worked up into a magnificent sketch, enlarged so that one could see into it as into the very emerald, sensing the singular effect the stone had upon the imagination. A wonderful bit of work; it really satisfied the artist as he studied it that evening by candlelight.

Bedtime came. Then he remembered the girl, and spoke to Francesco Melzi, who reminded him of the gem-cutter Baldino and his promise to sketch the affianced bride. He nodded as it came back to mind.

"Very well, my son. Bring her to me whenever you like—tomorrow, perhaps. After all, I must discover what it was the gentle Laforge found in her."

It was not the morrow, but a sunny morning some days hence when Melzi brought her into the studio. The square little house of white stone and brick near the rustling brook was nestled under the wing of a hill that broke the north wind. Yet it was chilly, and Leonardo was wrapped in a great furred mantle. He peered at the girl as she stood with eyes downcast, then spoke abruptly.

"Look up, look at me! I want to see you, not your outside—look up!"

She obeyed, looked at him, caught sight of the ring on the table before him, and her gaze widened upon it. That of Leonardo softened. Tenderness crept into his voice, and youth, and all the beauty of lost dead things, as he spoke, so that she gave him a startled glance.

"That's right; look on, think—why, child, they are pure thoughts! All purity and white wings and a swan in flight.... Nay, nay, look back at the green stone! What I say is nothing. I am going to sketch you now, this moment, just as you are, a child of light … Oh, to be in Milan again, and twenty years younger! Those soul-windows of yours stir sleeping things far within me—how the light melts in your eyes! It is like the soft moist air of Milan, veritable sweetness made light—the gentle *sfumato*—I used to rub the paint with my thumb to get the effect—"

Now he was working away as he talked, uttering a flow of words that she did not in the least understand, while his left hand drew her features on the parchment with magic surety of touch.

She was beautiful, true; beautiful with a tender softness like that of a flower. One could not say how or why, or define the rapt ecstasy of her eyes—Leonardo named it purity; and so it was, something not of the flesh at all. He captured it, and got it into the sketch, vaguely aware that as he worked, someone else had entered the room—it was the gentle knight Sieur de Laforge, who stood silent and motionless, looking on.

"There, it is finished," said Leonardo. "I caught it—ha! I caught it, that look of ecstasy! Girl, tell your gem-cutter to come and get it, and defile it with his touch and take it away, this essence of sheer loveliness that will mean nothing to his dull gaze—nay, take it yourself, child, and give it the blessing of your eyes before his sight desecrates it."

Thus passing swiftly from beauty's world to bitter words and harsh, as was his wont, he gave her the sketch. As she departed, her eyes met those of Laforge, and a veil of delicate color crept up her cheeks. Laforge came to the table and looked at the first trial sketch the master had made, a brief unfinished head.

"I love this," he said softly, "as I think that I love her, too. May I have it? I am leaving in a few days for Italy."

"Ask the man she loves, not me," said Leonardo brutally.

Laforge stared, his honest features aflush with chagrin and surprise.

"But she loves no other!" he blurted out. "I've seen her often—we've talked much together."

With anyone else, Leonardo would have cackled laughter and let the game play itself out bitterly. But he loved this soldier, who was too simple to lie. He perceived instantly that Laforge and Flora understood one another, yet were helpless; they were not great nobles, but little common folk.

AS UPON some vast canvas, the scene swept before him, piteously clear. This honest soldier must go his ways, go back to Italy, his love-fancy unattained. The pure and innocent girl must go into the arms of Baldino, since this was her fate. The King, the great Valois, was heading toward ruin and disaster—there was no help for it, no avoidance whatever. Leonardo's one good hand crashed down on the table.

"I, what can I do? Am I God?" he burst forth angrily. "You, in love! The soldier, become a soft garden dove!"

Laforge, staring, abruptly changed. Purpose leaped in his eyes; his features firmed and hardened.

"I don't understand, master. But this girl I must have," said he.

"Indeed!" Leonardo stared slightly. "What was it you said the other day—ruin and disaster may not be what they seem? Look, now. You're here on the chateau grounds. This girl is destined to wed another, whom she loves not. You must go to Italy. For God's sake, then take her! Wed her or not, as you like—but take her and go. Do it rapidly—you have no other chance. Yes or no?"

"Yes, by the saints!" exploded the soldier. "But how—how?"

"Leave tonight, an hour after sunset. She'll be here. Yes?"

Laforge, comprehending now, eagerly seized his hand.

"Then, master, you are indeed God!"

"No blasphemy," said Leonardo. "Aye, for once I'll play God's part, though I think the ending may not be what we'd have. Be here an hour after sunset, with horses. I have money in plenty. I'll see to the rest."

So the soldier departed, and Leonardo sent Francesco Melzi to find the girl Flora and bid her do her part. In the dusk of evening she came, and Leonardo put money into her hands, and a jewel about her neck, and saw her go riding away with

"In the dusk of evening the girl Flora came, and Leonardo saw her go riding away with the soldier, and heard their blessings pronounced upon his head.

the soldier, and heard their softly spoken blessings pronounced upon his white head....

They went out of his life, out of his thoughts; and as the days passed, he let himself sink into the spell of the Sphinx emerald. He spent long hours gazing into that bit of green beryl, whose play of broken and refracted lights so fascinated him. He

*He displayed his colored sketch of the Monstrance
to the regal visitor. François was charmed.
"This must be made at once!" he exclaimed.*

sketched it anew, sketched the odd fancies that came into his
mind—how to make use of the jewel, how to cut it and shape
it aright, and at the last, what to do with it when it was perfectly
cut. This was his ultimate vision.

It came to him slowly, by little bursts of unfoldment, until
under his left hand grew the likeness of his ideal. The ethereal

spirit of him flowed into this work; it took him back to the youthful days when he labored in the atelier of Verocchio. For the King who owned this gem, he took no thought. It was not his way to pander to selfish principles or the delight of an owner, in his creative frenzy. He was lifted far above any such plane, just as he was uplifted beyond any petty idea of Deity.

That clear, spiritual, serene gaze of his saw far more than material ends. It was clear seeing, a pure comprehension, a perception beyond earthly words. Under his steady inspiration the sketches grew, until they became a Monstrance wherein sat the emerald in central splendor, a Monstrance for the exposition of the Lord's Body, a great jewel ablaze with rare colors and precious things, with the emerald supreme, the focal point of the whole.

There he left it, fervent and excited, yet calm in the knowledge that he had created a wondrous concept, the greatest of his entire career.

The canals had to be builded. He rode out to oversee the work; no worn-out old man of extinct fires, but a fiercely adventuring soul ready to conquer the bare gray soil with his engineering skill, able to link the Saône with the Loire, doing it. Also, he was planning a new capital city for François to build, and a new royal chateau—was he not the King's Architect?

He thought often of what that soldier had said—ruin and disaster and what men call death are not what they seem. Mortal things, yet with immortal overtones for perceiving eyes. He smiled disdainfully; such things did not exist, in reality. They were only steps to a greater beyond.

THAT MONSTRANCE laid away among his sketches was now a finished thing; the Sphinx emerald lying in his cabinet was also a finished thing—in his own mind. He had decided to do the recutting himself, for unless it were accomplished in a certain way, the lumpy jewel might be ruined.

So, while laboring at weightier matters, he made his preparations for this, the great final adventure of his art. Now and then

he took an hour off, to gaze into the green depths beneath his
glass and dream of the glory that the Monstrance would
become, one of these days, when King François remembered
about the emerald.

There was much for him to get. His facile brain saw no difficulty about recutting the gem in the usual way, with the wheel,
and retaining the huge cabochon of the stone; but his intent
was to go far beyond a mere polishing of the upper round. With
his intense perception of light, he quickly saw what brilliancy
would be given the emerald if it had a refraction of light from
the underside; so the idea of facets came to him and he played
with it. To his mind, everything was based upon mathematics,
and therefore the best geometrical disposition of these facets
to produce the ultimate effect was a matter for figuring.

As to the making of the Monstrance itself, any goldsmith
could do that. This recutting of the emerald was the great thing,
the one essential of the whole scheme, and with Francesco
Melzi's help he could do it. Little by little he procured everything he would need, even to some small and broken diamonds
to crush into dust.

This detail was, of course, something new, for he invariably
improved upon existing methods of work. Earlier gem-cutting
had been done with a sapphire point, which was laborious hand
work and uncertain. Such faceting as he proposed had sometimes been employed for rock crystal, but so much of the crystal
was lost in the process that its use upon jewels was prohibited.
Diamond dust and oil would do it perfectly.

At this point he remembered something; the owner of the
emerald had not as yet given his permission for any such work
upon it. And since much of the stone must be lost if Leonardo
had his way, even if the remainder would be enormously improved, this permission was something to think hard about.

Coming home one day from a trip of inspection over the
Romorintan canal work, Leonardo found his sketchbooks in
some disarray and called Melzi on the carpet. The Milanese

swore he had not touched them, except in dusting the table, and no one had been here—no one, that is, but Messer Baldino the gem-cutter.

He came asking for the maestro, said Melzi, to display some jewels just recut, and had waited an hour or so in the studio, looking at some of the sketches. It was no great matter, and Leonardo dismissed his first irritation. The King was soon arriving at Amboise and would be holding a conference with him—so he must remember to bring up the subject of the emerald. Leonardo brushed all thought of Baldino from his mind.

Later, however, it was not hard to see how all his troubles sprang from that one unhappy hour, when he had taken upon himself to play God.

At the moment he was occupied with experiments, cutting facets on bits of rock and quartz crystal to prove his theories; and finding them proved, he was jubilant and flushed with triumph. He knew precisely what to do with the emerald. It weighed nine carats and more; four must come off, to leave a superb cabochon with a faceted base, and the figure of the Sphinx intact.

He now made a larger and perfected sketch of the Monstrance he had conceived, and brushed in color, touching in the emerald as it would be after the recutting. Then he cut out the little circle showing the emerald, and kept it to hand, waiting until the King should come.

AND IN time the King came, after his hearty fashion. He loved to talk with Leonardo and treated him as an equal, with the deep glowing respect of a young amateur for an old maestro. His respect was genuine; but after all, François was a queer mixture of sensuous and sensual, and he was a king, proudly a king in those young days.

Had the old artist been Harry of England, François could not have met him with greater ease and courtesy. The restless royal brain plunged into canal and city plans, made quick promises of impossible things, and touched upon the subtle, beautiful sketches with eager delight. Well did the King know that no other man alive could sketch so clearly and simply, or perform more exactly, than this old man with one dead hand.

The conversation, as always when Leonardo da Vinci guided it, glistered with bravely shining conceptions. The King loved nothing more, and flung himself into it with a will. His vast, inordinate vanity, greatest and pettiest of all his qualities, was flattered by such talk, and the artist failed to perceive this glaring fact. Leonardo, indeed, was for the moment quite carried away by huge visions and far projects, until, almost at the last, recollection of the Sphinx emerald came to him.

Thereupon he got out his colored sketch of the Monstrance and displayed it to the regal visitor, without its central point. François was instantly charmed: but when Leonardo inserted the missing circlet to show the emerald in place, a cry of rapture broke from the King. So exquisitely perfect was this one touch of color, so quick and bright was the balance it gave, that the entire concept took on new glory and came alive.

"*Pardieu!* This must be made at once!" he exclaimed, kindling to the vision of beauty. "Who can do it, Leonardo?"

The artist removed the emerald circlet, and pointed at the Monstrance.

"That? Any fool of a goldsmith can do that, Sire. The great thing, as Your Majesty perceives, is the central emerald. No hand but mine own can touch this bit of daring work. Here is the old and worthless ring you lent me. I'll cut the stone in a new manner, with your permission, and if it loses half its size, the result will be inconceivably more brilliant."

Lose half its size? At these words, a slight frown touched the King's brow, then vanished. He propounded quick queries— what quantity of gold would be needed, what other stones and materials would be required, and so on. Leonardo answered with his usual careless grandeur, and set down notes of the various amounts for François to take with him. Then, a little late, it occurred to him to stir the royal vanity.

"This Monstrance for Your Majesty's chapel will be the talk of Europe," he added. "No other king will have such a gem of artistic perfection."

"A chapel?" said François, who had just—and barely—defeated the Church in heavy fight. "A chapel? And why that?"

"For the very practical reason of safety, Sire," Leonardo urged. "Such a jewel needs protection. In the royal chapel, it will be safe from impious hands."

"Hm!" mused the King. "The rule is a poor one, beloved master. When my troops took Brescia, I recall, every chapel and church was looted most thoroughly, and the same fate may yet come to other places in Italy. Well, let it rest. I shall remember this glorious thing of your creation, and shall make plans for it. Our treasurer must be consulted, of course."

He went on to speak earnestly about it, being actually deeply touched by the superb grace and loveliness of the sketch, and went away filled with rare intentions and impulse.

HOWEVER, SEDUCTION of Mme. de Chateaubriant was just then in midway career, and this occupied him keenly. And here at home, for some reason, money was getting surprisingly tight; while abroad, and chiefly in Italy, things were not going well at all. He might have to go there himself ere long to pull matters into shape.

Then there was old Leonardo himself. Supreme artist though he was, could he possibly execute the delicate task of cutting down that big emerald? After all, the man had only one hand with which to work; he might accomplish marvels with it; yet the fact remained as a disturbing element at the back of one's mind.

Still, riding one day to the hunt, François stopped briefly at the little square manor and saw Leonardo, assuring him that the affair of the Monstrance was in hand, and that the treasurer was making a report upon the monies involved.

So Leonardo went on with his experiments, the great conception remaining alive and promising to be his final and greatest work of art; and in those days Francesco Melzi learned more of gem-cutting than of palette colors. Even the great folios of sketches and notes were left idle, while Leonardo's hand busied itself with oil and diamond-dust, awaiting the word to go ahead.

One day, out walking with Melzi, he came face to face with Baldino. The latter bowed humbly, but not before Leonardo saw the flash of vivid hatred in his smooth face. This flash lit up the man like an inner light. Leonardo thought of the girl Flora and the soldier, and chuckled all the way home....

Time passed. The little manor of Cloux gathered dust, and was visited by gossip of things artistic—paintings, buildings, canals. Now and then Leonardo, gazing into the enlarged emerald, where sat the Sphinx in its green enchanted world, felt his vision upbuilded and his serene perception of beauty comforted and full fed. Until the day when Baldino came to demand the emerald from him!

Here now was a different Baldino, sleeker, fatter, eloquent of good living and hearty fees, bowing low and humble, but with a touch of hatred in his eye, a new assurance and sharp brightness in his gaze. Leonardo received him and wondered at his hintings, finally asking outright what he wanted.

"The Sphinx emerald, master," replied the man with surprising boldness. "I am to recut it and set it anew for the King. Here is the preliminary sketch I have made to show the work."

He unrolled a parchment and Leonardo looked at it with unseeing eyes. He caught the glint of hatred, and understood that too.

The emerald—*his* emerald! It was utterly incredible. He focused on the sketch and found it absurd folly. A glance showed how Baldino proposed to recut the stone, clumsily and heavily reshaping it for use as a necklace pendant. Gone, all his noble shining vision—gone! But no, that was impossible. He shoved away the sketch, his old eyes piercing into the man with sudden anger.

"Go away, fool," he said. "I think you are a madman."

"But, most excellent, I have here an order from the King's treasurer."

Leonardo burst into hot words. "Eat it! Keep it! Sleep with it! What the King gave, only the King can take away. Francesco! My dagger—quickly! Come, throw out this whining rogue!"

Baldino took to his heels and came back no more.

King François had recently come to visit a few weeks at Amboise. Leonardo dictated a note which Melzi wrote out fairly and carried to the royal chateau. He brought back a reply on the spot and Leonardo, reading the honeyed words, took heart:

> *There must be some grievous error in regard to that emerald. I have not forgotten your Monstrance, revered friend; fear not! I shall come in person to pay you my respects, very shortly, and shall then settle this vexed matter. Are the iris lilies coming out along your brook? I am eager to see them, and you.*

Leonardo folded his hands in his furred mantle. Evasions! He knew what that meant from the gay François. Yet there was still hope, there must be hope.

Yes, the iris flowers were coming in; spring was warming the trees; Lent was wearing Easterward, and a mortal hurt was piercing into his spirit. Gazing with dulled eyes across his own garden at the brook, he thought of how the red and white pomegranate blossoms must now be budding in Florence. Hope, like them, sprang ever anew. Surely the Valois could not deny the vision of splendor that was his Monstrance! Impossible!

STILL, THE uneasiness hurt—and the thought of this cheap Baldino with his coarse botched artistry. It sprawled athwart his white pure vision like an evil thing. He had mocked at destiny; was destiny catching up with him now? Was this some repayment for his playing at the ways of God? He had

given the girl Flora to Laforge, had sent them away in happiness—was he paying for that action now?

"Look you, my son," he said to Melzi, "and note well the
lesson: For the green stone I dreamed a glory, a beauty, no one
else could even imagine. And instead, the gem goes to a cheap
fate. Well, you shall see! I can still smile. What was it he said?
What we call ruin, disaster—why, it does not exist if we perceive
it aright! Yes, I can smile, for the price is bitter; yet it is a small
price after all."

"But master," pleaded the anxious Milanese, "the King is
coming in a day or two—I myself heard him say so. He will do
the right thing—"

The white-maned head lifted, the old eyes flashed once more.

"You say truth, my son; aye, always the right thing! Set out
the leaf that bears the colored sketch of the Monstrance, and
put the central bit in place, and have the emerald ring ready
against the King's coming. There is always hope, even when it
is denied. And send to tell the notary that I wish to make my
last testament on Easter Eve."

So, in due time, came the King. He came in some haste,
having been called to celebrate the birth of his second son at
Saint Germain-en-Laye, and must depart on the morrow. He
came, splendid and laughing, with half a dozen of his lords
around him; and in his train followed the sleek gem-cutter
Baldino, a pricking query in his eye. Leonardo caught this look
and smiled to himself in comprehension.

Spring was burgeoning, but a fire burned in the studio of
Leonardo, where the old man sat folded in his furred mantle
until he rose to receive King François, who embraced him lovingly and stood awhile in gallant talk of Italy and Milan. Then
the King's eye caught the sheen of the emerald on the table.
He picked it up, smiling as at an old friend.

"So, Messer Leonardo, you would pare away half of my green
jewel?" said he, with a hearty laugh. "A pity, so to waste this
loveliness!"

Leonardo pushed forward the colored sketch.

"There, Sire; look at the Monstrance. The iris bulbs must die, ere the green leaves and the flower come forth; and what men take to be waste, flowers into a mysterious beauty that speaks to the very soul."

"Ah, my master," said the King, "you are ever charming, ever a weird necromancer of words! But you propose a beauteous thing for the worship of God. Now, God already has far more beauty than I, and I need it more than He, *pardieu!* Our good craftsman Baldino has proposed a jewel to adorn our person, and therefore he shall have his own will with the emerald."

Leonardo said nothing. A cold hand was over his heart; when one beholds a vision perish, with other eyes blinded to it, only silence can make answer. Words are useless there, as so many a one has found, and thus Leonardo found now, in the bitterest of all moments.

The parchment with the colored sketch slid from his hand and soared into the fire, blazing up nobly upon the room. And when the King and his gay troop had ridden away, Leonardo leaned upon the arm of the Milanese and went to his bed, there to await the notary and make his will.

He did it slowly, carefully, said Francesco Melzi afterward; and oddly, he did it with a smile upon his lips, dying like the great gentleman he was. Perhaps his heart was broken, but his smile was that of victory.

XIII

THE REWARD OF NOSTRADAMUS

*Catherine de Medici coveted the Sphinx
Emerald. And when the King gave it as a
reward to his physician, Dr. Notredame
rode in dire peril of his life.*

THE COMTE DE VERGY, Royal Equerry, intimate friend of the King, and easily the most influential noble at court, was a handsome, swaggering, arrogant fellow—not half clever, but apt at worming himself forward. One of his methods was to pay much quiet attention to the little Italian princess Catherine de Medici, who would be Queen of France one of these days.

Catherine was extremely plain, but was clever enough to invent the sidesaddle in order to display her one beauty, a well-formed leg. She was highly superstitious, like any girl of nineteen; and having few friends at court, she welcomed the courtesies of Vergy, and ultimately made him her confidant in the matter of the Sphinx emerald.

Catherine and her husband the Dauphin were on hand because the King was believed dying. This was in the summer of 1538. King François had come to Orléans because of its healthy air, and occupied the huge Hôtel Groslot.

Incurably ill, outworn by his vices, François was doomed and accounted dying; but while he lived, he was very much King of France.

On an afternoon, Catherine sat in her apartment, sewing, her attendant ladies at a little distance, while Vergy sat with her, fingering a lute as he talked. Demure as a mouse, careful to avoid scandal, keeping herself well out of the court picture, Catherine saw everything that went on. Despised as an Italian

A maddened bellow escaped Condoulet; in
blind fury he sent his horse at Vergy.

by the incredibly haughty French nobles, she was ever on the
defensive, and was most careful to shun their jealousy and envy.

"And you, M. de Vergy, do you think the King will die?" she
was asking.

"They say his physician, Maître Guillaume Chrétien, has
given up hope," he said, pulling a sad face.

She smiled faintly as she eyed him. "If only someone would
do something for me—something wicked, perhaps," she sighed,
"he might ask any favor in his heart and find it granted—some
day."

The significance of her words could not be missed. Vergy
met her eyes—and promptly laid aside his lute.

"I am that someone, madame," he said softly. "And I can be discreet as the dead."

"An ill omen—be careful, my friend!" She frowned slightly. "You know the necklace His Majesty usually wears?"

"Certainly, madame. A gold chain made for him by Cellini; pendent on this chain is an emerald of size, but poor in color."

"The emerald, the Sphinx emerald," she breathed. "The most wondrous I ever saw!"

Vergy shrugged lightly. "One is like another, to me."

"Not to me, monsieur." Her dark eyes lit up; excitement flushed her olive cheek. "More, that stone is rightly mine, belongs to me! The King gave it to me when I came from Italy to be wedded. I wore it, came to cherish it dearly—and then he took it back. He borrowed it from me—and kept it. He refuses to part with it, and laughs at me when I beg for it back. And I must have it, monsieur—I cannot lose it—I must not, I will not!"

Vergy, scenting intrigue and high profit, was all attention. He was not a bad sort, but high-tempered, an expert swordsman, and keenly ambitious.

"Suppose," she went on under her breath, "suppose he—he should die?"

"Then you, madame, will be Queen of France."

She gestured impatiently. "I am thinking of the emerald. You know what will happen. A mad scramble for jewels, for gold, for power—his mistresses seizing what they can, his attendants grabbing at everything within reach!"

From her ladies came laughter at some jest; Vergy murmured:

"Madame, I comprehend—say no more! I shall make myself responsible for that chain and pendant. It shall be my privilege to see that it comes safely to you. Is there any person of your suite whom I can trust, in case of need?"

"Lorenzo," she breathed, and looked up. "Here he comes now."

Lorenzo approached. He was one of the few Italians left in her service, his position being too humble to attract French jealousy. He was one of the grooms—a dark-visaged fellow with crafty eyes, lean and scarred of face. He bowed profoundly to Catherine, delivered a message, and departed cringingly.

"Is that man in your confidence, madame?" Vergy asked incredulously.

She assented. "He is more than he seems, a very able Florentine. He serves me."

The ladies approached. Vergy rose, bowed, and took ceremonious leave.

"Farewell, madame. I repeat, you may rely absolutely upon me."

Catherine looked after him, hiding a smile in her dark eyes....

On the following evening Vergy stood in the royal ante-chamber with a group of courtiers. He looked at two soberly clad men who had just entered, their birettas or square bonnets proclaiming them master physicians.

"Who," demanded Vergy, "is that short red-cheeked fellow with Guillaume Chrétien, the King's physician?"

Glances were directed at the pair, and one of the group made response.

"Oh, that's a country doctor from Provence—M. de Notredame, I think the name is. Another of these rascally medicos who hopes to cure the King. I hope he pulls His Majesty together enough so that we can return to Blois; I hate this accursed rathole."

IN THOSE days France had no capital. The focal point of the realm was wherever the King happened to be, and François was ever restless, ever changing his residence. There was no royal palace at Orléans, but one place was as good as another to die in.

Chrétien, the King's physician, was famous in his own right, but no less so than his friend and colleague, with whom he stood talking. Formerly professor at Montpellier, greatest college of medicine in Europe, Michel de Notredame had thrown up his position in order to combat the fearful pestilence raging in Provence. He had come north to Orléans for a few days only, to purchase drugs of which he stood in dire need. As they talked, Chrétien handed him a small horn box.

"There's the prescription you wanted made up; I watched the job myself. But these simple herbs can have no effect, Michel. He's done for. That abdominal abscess will finish him. Why waste time with a mere salve of herbs?"

"Not being a great man like you, Guillaume, I seldom make predictions," said the visitor with a trace of irony. "I must work with simple things, not with such stuff as powdered pearls and horns of unicorns. How long do we wait here?"

"God knows! Until summoned. But have a care. They tell me

he's sadly irritable today, flying into a passion at the least excuse—a result of his melancholic humors."

"More likely from deprivation of the goddess he has so long
worshiped."

At this cynical remark, Chrétien glanced about cautiously.
One must be careful in this antechamber where so many of the
court gentlemen stood about; a loose word could destroy a man.
Life was cheap; envy, jealousy, assassination were everywhere.

"True, no doubt." Chrétien spoke now in Latin, for safety's
sake. "He sees beautiful women all around; both his natural
vanity and his insensate desires are affected by enforced virtue.
Make him no promises, I beg of you. He has tried everything
known to science, without help."

"If you rascals were any good, you'd be able to relieve the pain instead of feeding me vile concoctions which effect nothing," said the King.

"Much that was formerly known to science has been forgotten," Notredame murmured.

He was a smallish, robust man, lithe and vigorous, with broad brow, straight nose, rosy cheeks and extremely bright gray eyes above his clipped, graying beard. He had made a great name for himself fighting the plague—the same plague which had swept away his immediate family; but he did not always subscribe to the conventions of his colleagues.

"Who," he asked his friend, "is that handsome, arrogant young noble preening himself in the adulation of the throng around him?"

Chrétien looked. "That's the Comte de Vergy, present favorite of François. Rather a decent chap, but a swordsman and duelist. Why do you ask?"

"Curiosity. I have an uneasy suspicion—intuition, perhaps— that he and I are fated to be friends—or enemies.... Ah, at last!"

They turned, as the doors of the inner chamber were opened, and those who had gathered for the royal *coucher* came out.

Monluc, a scarred Gascon soldier, came to the pair and bowed.

"He's ready for you, Maître Chrétien. I was sent to summon you."

Notredame was presented to the Gascon gentleman, whose face lit up.

"Oh, I've heard of you!" he exclaimed. "You're that man Nostradamus who they say has brought the plague under control down south by his magic powers!"

"They exaggerate, monsieur," said Notredame. "But we must not keep the King waiting."

They went in. This country physician knew little of courts and their ways, but was no whit awed by his surroundings. He found himself before a great figure perched in a huge bed whose curtains were partly withdrawn for the interview. This was the Valois, center of all majesty and power in the realm, master of such profligacy and splendor as France had never known—this huge, bloated, swollen shape, this face of fringing beard and pendulous dewlap and quenched eye, whose tasseled nightcap topped it like a ludicrous mocking crown. A torrent of groans and profanity poured from the lips of François.

"So here you are, miserable charlatans who pretend to cure and can only torture! Thrice-damned angels of Satan, a pox on your whole tribe! Chrétien, where's the fellow you promised to bring? Ah, I see him…. Step forward, you! I've heard of you, a sorcerer who conquers the plague with wizardry—"

The croaking voice failed of effort. Notredame was presented and bowed profoundly.

"Notredame—yes, that's it, Nostradamus," said François. "Do you know that sorcerers are sent to the stake? All alike—doctors, sorcerers, astrologers, damn 'em!"

"Sire, M. de Notredame desires to present Your Majesty with a new remedy which may afford relief," Chrétien said smoothly. "He is one of our most accomplished physicians, notably honored by Montpellier. I am prepared to vouch for his remedy, and for him."

"*Pardieu*, well spoken!" said the King. "There are few men for whom I'd say the same. You always were an honest rascal, Chrétien. Bring lights, here! Let me have a look at this sorcerer."

A chamberlain brought a candelabrum to the bedside, and François scrutinized the visitor with suspicious gaze.

"Remedies! There are none," he said thickly, and cursed. "This damned pain has me in the sweat of purgatory. If you rascals were any good, you'd be able to relieve it instead of feeding me vile concoctions which effect nothing."

NOTREDAME CAME close, looked at the King, and smiled a little.

"Sire, my remedy is a penetrating salve, not a draught. If Your Majesty will allow me to examine your pulse, I may somewhat relieve your immediate ills."

Notredame took the huge flabby hand, held it for a moment, and motioned for the other; François complied. Quietly, Notredame began to speak of Avicenna and his theories; his musical voice flowed softly on as he discussed the Moorish savants and their ideas of art and beauty—subjects which fascinated the Valois.

"*Ma foi*, I'm resting easier, indeed!" grunted the King. "Come, lean closer! Predict how long I have to live."

"With Your Majesty's permission, I'll make a more pleasing prediction...."

Leaning over until his lips approached the ear of François, he murmured a few words quite inaudible to those around. The King's eyes opened to their fullest extent. A laugh rumbled through his ponderous expanse and came to rest upon his lips— such a laugh as he had not uttered in long days. For an instant he was his old jovial, charming self.

"You lie, you rogue, you lie!" he croaked.

"Pardon, Sire, it is the exact truth." Notredame drew back. "And now permit me to withdraw, while M. Chrétien applies the salve—"

'Wait!" came the order. "Will it cure me?"

"Sire, only the grace of God can effect a cure," Notredame said calmly, "but my belief is that the salve will afford great relief."

"Very well, I understand. Come, Chrétien! Here's the old belly you should know so well; work your will upon it."

The salve was applied, the interview ended. The two friends walked out together, donned cloaks and birettas, and passing the dour gaze of the Scots Guards on duty, gained the dark streets. Chrétien took his friend's arm, speaking softly.

"Michel, it was marvelous! He was like a bawling calf, and you cured him on the instant! What did you do?"

"I'm ashamed of you. Minor hurts irritate themselves into a fever that aggravates them; a calm presence, a few words to distract the mind, and they lessen in importance. You, so famous for your bedside manner, should know this."

"A king is very different; especially François. And what was the secret which worked a very miracle upon him?"

Notredame chuckled in his quiet way. "I told our good patient that tomorrow afternoon I'd give him a prescription of Avicenna's which, within a week's time, would enable him to taste all the delights of marriage without its drawbacks. I'll have to get the prescription made up in the morning."

The other clucked his tongue, horrified.

"Well—it's a risk. If the salve works, and you also accomplish this prediction, your fortune's made!"

"Many false prophecies are laid at my door," Notredame rejoined dryly, "but those which I myself utter are infallible, I assure you."

Notredame, an unassuming man who put on no airs, had not even a lackey to serve him. He had come to Orléans to purchase a stock of drugs that he needed, and Chrétien had insisted on dragging him to look at the King.

THE NEXT day he was out early, about his business. He meant to get away as soon as he was free of the royal patient, on the morrow if possible, and get back to the plague-stricken south where he was sorely needed.

The two thousand-odd persons of the court had filled the old city of Orléans to bursting, and amid the gay rout the gray-clad figure of Notredame drew no eyes. He finished his purchases, watched a chemist put up the secret Avicenna prescription, then started home. He was passing the hostel of the Three Emperors, when a heavy hand fell on his shoulder and a tremendous voice burst forth in the Provençal tongue.

"*Saperlipopette*—Notredame, of all people! Thunders of heaven, man, embrace me!"

He was crushed in the arms of a giant—a huge red-faced, awkward, roughly clad man, no other than Sieur Palamedes Tronc de Condoulet, seigneur and wine-grower of Salon in Provence, whom he had known for years.

Notredame freed himself, laughing. "A surprise indeed, old neighbor! What are you doing here?"

"Came with a present for the King, a cask of our best wine," declared the other, with rolling rustic oaths. "Those accursed courtiers pretend they can't understand me, and pass me from one to another and keep putting me off—"

Notredame clapped him on the back. "Listen: The King occupies the Hôtel Groslot. I'm to see him early this afternoon. Come there, ask for me or Dr. Chrétien, and we may be able to help you. Now pardon me, old friend, I must hurry to keep an appointment. We'll meet and talk later, eh? Right."

Knowing the big, kindly, somewhat dense Provençal would talk by the hour, he did not hesitate to free himself, since noon was at hand. Despite his haste, he was pleased and warmed by the meeting. A sterling fellow, Condoulet, with heart of gold.

Upon reaching home, he found Chrétien gone and no sign

of lunch. He got himself some bread and cheese, and was eating it when his host burst in upon him hurriedly, with panting speech.

"Michel! He has sent for us—one of his gentlemen came— will meet us at the Hôtel Groslot. He says the King is very cheerful this morning and much better—hurry, man, get ready!"

"I'm ready. No haste. You seem astonished that all has gone well. I should be astonished if it had not."

Chrétien bustled him off. "Ah, Michel! Not even a royal command flurries you! Where did you get your eternal poise, your amazing composure? I suppose one must be born with such a gift."

"It can always be encouraged to grow. Easy, now."

With quiet words, Notredame calmed the hurried excitement of his colleague, told of meeting his old friend from Salon; and presently they reached the royal residence. Crowds of city folk were clustered outside the line of Scots Guards to get glimpses of the great, and a gentleman of the King's suite awaited them, bowing to Notredame with surprising respect.

"His Majesty is in the garden," said he, leading them into the courtyard. "He wishes to see you at once, so come this way."

They passed through the building into the garden, and as they traversed the graveled paths, it was the turn of Notredame to be surprised. A gay awning had been spread beside a marble fountain, and here sat François, talking with Manluc, Vergy and the Comte de St. Pol, the main groups of courtiers remaining at a little distance out of earshot.

And what a François it was! The groaning hulk of last evening was gone; the nightcap was replaced by a jeweled bonnet. The puffed and enormous shape was clad in a magnificent suit of white and gold; the heavy long-nosed features were laughing and radiant. The Valois was himself once more, shrewd, jovial, great-hearted, eking out his words with rapid gesticulation.

"Good day, Maître Chrétien," he wheezed. "Ah, Notredame,

prince of magicians! Do you know that your wizard salve has banished my ills, as you promised?"

Notredame bowed. "Sire, when Dr. Chrétien approved my prescription, I knew that it could not fail."

"Neatly said, my friend. Hm! I seem to have a memory of something else, a voice whispering at my ear. An angelic voice, shall I say?"

FRANÇOIS SHOOK with laughter. Notredame advanced, and in his broad palm laid a curious little box of metal, Byzantine or Saracen work, exquisitely enameled.

"My faith!" The King, who was an excellent judge of such artistry, eyed it with quick pleasure. "What admirable enamel! Limosin himself never made better." He opened the little box and glanced at the tiny pellets it contained.

"If Your Majesty will take one pellet with each meal, or not above four a day," said Notredame, "I believe that in a week's time the prediction I made you last evening will be fulfilled."

"So?" A glint came into the shrewd, dulled old eyes. This man, like every crowned head of the period, had lived most of his life in dread of poison. "Suppose we try this noble medicine on M. de Monluc, yonder—what say you, Notredame?"

Glancing at the scarred, stalwart Gascon, Notredame smiled slightly.

"Sire, that were a pity; indeed, a very sad waste. Allow me to prove the honesty of my own medicine." So saying, he reached out, took several of the tiny pellets, and swallowed them.

François, holding his vast belly as mirth shook him, went off into a roar of laughter. Monluc grinned. The Comte de Vergy made some comment that sent the King into a fresh spasm.

"A waste, says he," came his gasping croak. "A sad waste—ha, Monluc, he has heard of your reputation among the ladies! A pity, says he.... Come hither, Provençal! You've done well. Upon my word, I love you! We must keep you here at court, make a place for you—eh?"

"Sire, you need me not; and Provence, smitten by the plague, does. Maître Chrétien has far greater skill than I."

"Ha! You scoundrelly doctors always pat one another on the back. Your pardon, Chrétien," Francis added quickly. "I meant no reflection on you. God knows you're one of the few I trust with my whole heart! Come, Notredame: You've done for me what no other could do. You promise what all the others have denied. What reward seek you?"

"I do not give my help for rewards, Sire," Notredame replied, bowing. François peered at him, saw that he really meant the words, and grunted.

"So? On your knee, fellow—on your knee!" As Notredame obediently knelt, the King snatched off a chain of beautiful gold links bearing an emerald pendant. He put it over the head of Notredame. "There, my favorite of all jewels for you, man—even if it did break the heart of Leonardo the painter. Cellini made the chain for me. Take it with my blessing—if I didn't value it so highly I'd not give it to you. Maître Chrétien," he added, taking a ring from his finger, "accept this with my thanks. Whenever you have more friends like this man, bring them to me without delay."

A S H E rose, Notredame caught a glimpse of the face of Vergy. It astonished him, so contorted was it with anger and dismay. However, thinking he must have made some mistake about it, he dismissed the matter from his mind.

Rewarded and dismissed, the two, bowing ceremoniously, backed away and left the garden, passing through the building toward the entrance courtyard.

"If you'd come to court as he wishes, you'd soon be the greatest man in France!" Chrétien said softly.

"Or the greatest rogue. More likely the latter," said Notredame, as they came into the courtyard. "Hello! Wait a bit. I have business here.... That's my friend from Salon!"

The Scottish archers of the guard were clustered about two

figures, their officer and a huge man, roughly dressed, whose words rolled on the air with a rich Provençal accent.

"But I wrote to him!" he bellowed. "I tell you, I wrote the King a letter, and he is expecting me!"

A guardsman tipped Notredame a wink.

"This fellow," he said, grinning, "has a name exactly like a Provençal oath!"

"The King will know of me," roared the visitor. "Send to him, you fools! Ask about my letter! Find his physician, or Maître Notredame, the physician of Salon—"

Notredame pushed forward and spoke loudly.

"Sieur Palamedes Tronc de Condoulet, is it not? Greetings, monsieur!"

Condoulet turned, recognized him, and beamed delightedly.

"Ha! Look there!" He pointed to a horse and cart, detained by the guards, and gesticulated frantically. "I bring the King a cask of our finest vintage, and these popinjay rascals say it might be poisoned!" He went into a storm of fantastic oaths, amid the laughter of the Scots.

Now, the King's physician was an important personage, and anyone just received in private audience was superlatively important; the name of Notredame had been on all lips. Consequently a chamberlain came bustling up, swift at the chance to curry favor.

"What is wrong, messieurs? Can I render you any assistance?"

"If you will have the kindness, yes. Have that cask of wine set down from the cart and opened," said Notredame. "Let us see if it be good wine or not." To the gentleman from Salon he spoke in Provençal, which no one else understood. "Leave this to me, friend."

Now there was brisk movement. The cask was brought from the cart and opened as Condoulet directed. A number of courtiers, attracted to the scene, looked on amusedly. The golden necklace worn by Notredame, which everyone knew for that of the King, aroused swift interest and discussion.

The chamberlain, his eye also on that mark of distinguished favor, approached with a goblet.

"You are serious, monsieur, about tasting the wine?"

"Certainly. I shall do it myself." Notredame took the goblet. Wine was poured into it from the cask. He tasted, drank, and beckoned Guillaume Chrétien. "Here, sample this admirable vintage. Have you any hesitation in recommending it to His Majesty?"

"My faith, no!" said the other, after emptying the cup. "I only wish I could get a cask of it myself!"

"Then,"—Notredame turned to the officious chamberlain— "suppose you present the gift with word that I and Maître Chrétien beg to recommend it highly. And you might present the Sieur de Condoulet also. If you can do this, pray consider me deeply in your debt."

The chamberlain was overjoyed. He departed, dragging Condoulet after him, and flinging orders about the wine-cask. Notredame, laughing, passed out of the Hôtel Groslot into the tree-shaded avenue.

His friend plucked at his sleeve.

"Why this fantastic byplay, Michel?"

"Condoulet and I are old friends and neighbors. We're country folk, we Provençals. Peasants at heart, helping a neighbor at need."

Chrétien, who had as yet eaten nothing, took his guest home, insisted upon having a bounteous meal set forth, and together they curiously examined the emerald and chain. It was one the King had always worn, said Chrétien, an odd, lumpish stone, poorly cut.

"You take it and keep it," said Notredame. "I dislike jewels."

The other gaped. "Impossible, man! The King's gift? No, no, it's yours to keep."

"I don't like to own things. I've lost my worldly ties, and desire to own nothing."

"Don't be absurd. This is a famous emerald—the Sphinx, it's called. I don't know why. There was some old scandal about it—connected with the Italian artist Leonardo, if I recall, when I was a boy. Wait till I get an enlarging-glass, and we'll have a look at the stone."

He had barely returned with the lens when Condoulet came bursting in upon them, having tracked Notredame to his lodgings here. He was excited, voluble and gesticulating—the proudest, happiest, most blithesome man in France. He embraced both physicians in a fervor of emotion.

Yes, he had been presented to the King, had kissed his hand—he, Tronc de Condoulet, bourgeois of Salon and merchant in wines—though it was true he had a right to the de of nobility, his grandfather having belonged to the petty noblesse—that is to say, his grandfather on the maternal side, who was an Auvergnat....

He talked on interminably. The King had accepted his wine, had thanked him most graciously, had accepted the loan of a few thousand crowns as a token of fealty. Massive, radiant, so overflowing with animal spirits that the room seemed too small to hold him, Condoulet at length ran down, gulped a glass of Chrétien's wine, and vowed he would send the physician a cask of the same vintage he had brought the King.

"Curious, Guillaume," said Notredame, who had been examining the emerald under the glass. "Take a look. There's actually a Sphinx in this gem!"

S O T H E R E was, indeed. Enlarged, it was plain to see—the flaws in the stone, by an odd fantasy of Nature, took the exact semblance of the Sphinx sitting in a field of glittering, flashing green. More, there was something keenly fascinating about the enlarged view thus obtained. Chrétien could not take his eyes from it.

"Magnificent, Michel," he said, awed. "There's magic in the

appeal it makes to the imagination. One sees things in the stone—"

"Glimpses of the moon," said Notredame with a careless laugh, and turned to the Provençal. "When do you return to Salon?"

"Now! Immediately! That is to say, early in the morning. I'm stopping at the Three Emperors."

"Have you a horse for me? If so, we'll travel together."

Condoulet was overjoyed. He regarded Notredame with the awe and veneration any rustic pays to a great physician; the idea of traveling home together elated him. He agreed at once to stop by here and pick up Notredame in the morning, and with this took his departure. Chrétien, who had been summoned to visit two ladies of the court who had need of his services, reluctantly handed over the chain and enlarging-glass to his friend, and went his ways.

MICHEL DE NOTREDAME took the chain into the garden and began a careful scrutiny of the emerald. The carelessness he had affected was false. In reality, this emerald affected him so acutely that he was startled and disturbed. He disliked and vividly distrusted anything which so aroused his emotions as did this jewel.

But why? That was what he meant to determine—why such an effect? He pored over the emerald for an hour, two hours. Amazement, even a species of fear, grew upon him. The more he looked into this green lump of beryl, the more he saw, or fancied that he saw, in its heart. It aroused speculation, fed the imagination, suggested singular scenes and fantasies—ah, that was it! Suggestion! As a physician far in advance of his day, he knew well the power of suggestion; he used it almost daily himself; he was thoroughly acquainted with its remarkable effects. Here was suggestion—and something else as well, something darker, more sinister. The fascination this emerald exerted was gripping, almost like that of a drug….

"A mental drug, yes," he murmured, resisting the keen

*"When the rascally doctor is overtaken,
make certain that he does not complain
to the King. Is my meaning clear?"*

temptation to look anew. "Dangerous, these fancies! One feeds the brain upon them as upon mandragora; one comes back for more, ever more; one eventually loses contact with life's realities.... Bad, very bad!"

Resolutely, uncompromisingly, he put the thing away and would have no more of it where he himself was concerned. Not that he despised it. He could well conceive cases, mental cases, where it would be of the utmost value to him. The everyday opinion about such a stone, he knew, would simply be that it was bewitched by a devil. He discounted such notions, being aware that the natural world around held marvels greater than any necromance, could one but see them.

But while Notredame was thus playing with the King's gift, a singular scene was taking place in the apartments of Catherine de Medici.

The little princess was listening to the Comte de Vergy relate the happenings of that afternoon. There was no secret about it, of course; he spoke for all to hear, Catherine's attendants hanging on his words, and bursting with laughter to hear him jest about the doctor from the back-country.

For once, however, Catherine did not share their mirth. Instead, she sat like a cat on tension of the prowl—her lips tight, her nostrils quivering, her hands clenched tight and hard. Gone! The great jewel, the marvelous Sphinx emerald, handed over to a country doctor! It was maddening. However, many things had happened to Catherine de Medici that would have maddened other people, and she was still alive and well. She lost her tension, and when able to speak privately to Vergy, nodded calmly to him.

"There is to be dancing this evening, in honor of the King's recovery," she said. "We may talk then with greater freedom."

Cautious Catherine! They talked safely that evening, under cover of the violins and the gay laughing voices. The Comte de Vergy swore he would get the emerald for her. He had found that Notredame was leaving for Provence on the morrow. He could be waylaid easily enough…. Catherine stopped him abruptly.

"We must not be rash, my friend," she said coolly. "In all justice, that emerald belongs to me; the King had no right to give it away—but he did so. If anything happened to this miserable fellow here, and the King's gift were missing, there would be a hue and cry at once. Step softly. I'll send Lorenzo to you tomorrow with horses; you'll find him an excellent lackey. Follow this doctor to a safe distance—you comprehend?"

"Perfectly, madame." Vergy kissed her hand. "We'll manage it safely. Upon my honor, we'll follow him to Provence if need be, and I'll return with your jewel!"

Next morning Catherine instructed the groom Lorenzo, in her careful way:

"Serve M. de Vergy faithfully—but remember you serve me as well. Don't let him overtake this rascally doctor too close to Orléans; and when the fellow is overtaken, make certain that he does not complain to the King. Is my meaning clear?"

Lorenzo showed his white teeth in a merry laugh, and touched his dagger.

"Perfectly, *principessa!* He shall complain to no one—I promise it!"

HAPPILY IGNORANT of perils, Notredame bade farewell to Maître Chrétien and set forth with the Sieur Condoulet for sunny Provence. Before they were over the long stone bridge across the Loire, Notredame caught sight of the barges ascending the river, and had a notable idea.

It was a long and weary road for two men on horseback—Orléans to distant Lyons, and thence down the Rhone a hundred and thirty miles to Avignon—Papal territory, not a part of France; and the rest was but a step to Salon, for which Condoulet was bound, and Aix, the capital of Provence, Notredame's destination. The weariest part of the journey was from here to Lyons—why not, then, ride aboard one of those barges toiling up-river, which could carry them and their horses to boot?

No sooner said than put into effect! And this was why the Comte de Vergy picked up no sign of his quarry until he reached Lyons, and then found himself far behind. With fresh horses, he and his lackey now spurred on desperately. But Notredame and the Sieur Condoulet jogged on together, enjoying one another and the countryside as they journeyed.

They came to Vienne, viewed the Roman remains and went on to Valence, thence on to Montelimart and St. Esprit with its magnificent bridge of twenty-six arches. They could smell Provence in the air now, and pushed ahead eagerly to Orange, with Avignon the next town on the way. Here at Orange, however, Sieur Palamedes Tronc de Condoulet overate of an enormous eel pie, and Notredame had to physick him, which delayed them a day.

They left Orange on an early morning, thinking to make the short distance to Avignon and get in early. Notredame knew the Archbishop who ruled there for the Pope—had, in fact, pulled him through the plague only the year previous—and assured his companion of a right warm welcome. The two were ambling along, a league or less this side of the Papal border, when the Comte de Vergy and his lackey at last caught up with them.

Notredame had noted the dust-spurts behind, and on making out two riders overhauling them, spoke to Condoulet, who laughed and loosened his sword in its sheath—an old and over-long rapier. Sieur Palamedes, who was more pugnacious if less witty than Sir Palamedes of Troy-town fame, looked forward hopefully to attack by brigands. However, the two pursuers overtook them amicably, called on Notredame by name, and the latter amazedly recognized the Comte de Vergy. Not bothering to dismount, the Comte went direct to business, unaware of his lackey's secret instructions, and minded to avoid trouble if possible.

"Monsieur," he said, reining in, "I have followed all the way from Orléans, trying to overtake you. His Majesty sent me after you, monsieur."

Condoulet, finding to his disappointment that it was not an affair of robbers, applied himself with noisy gulps to a large leather bottle of potent wine, which he had obtained at Orange. Notredame, although astonished by the words of Vergy, did not doubt them.

"Indeed? And for what purpose, may I inquire?"

"He has repented of the gift which he made you, monsieur," said Vergy, not caring to waste great politeness on a provincial like this fellow. "He desires you to return it to him, and to permit me, in your courtesy, to make good its value in some other fashion. I trust this will prove to your taste, good monsieur—"

Vergy's approach had been carefully weighed, and ordinarily would have succeeded perfectly; Notredame would have turned over the emerald with the greatest indifference. But the courtier's words were interrupted by Condoulet, who dropped his bottle and broke into furious oaths.

"What's all this? Do I understand you to say that the King, King François, presented M. de Notredame with a jewel and now wants to take it back again?"

"You do," coldly replied the Comte Vergy.

The Provençal exploded wrathfully. "Then, monsieur, I say to your face that you lie!" he thundered. "No one shall so basely insult the King in my presence! The King is my personal friend, and his honor is as my own. Notredame, this is all a scoundrelly plot to rob you of the jewel!"

Vergy was dead white with fury and dismay, for Condoulet was absolutely correct. Meanness or lack of generosity had never been a fault of François of Valois.

At this instant Notredame intervened, intent only upon avoiding any trouble.

"Tronc, for God's sake hold your tongue," he snapped, and turned to Vergy. "I beg you, M. de Vergy, to overlook the hastiness of my friend. The emerald, I assure you, is at His Majesty's service. I shall be glad to confide it to your care."

While speaking, he reined in his horse beside that of Vergy, and took the emerald and chain from his pouch. The Comte de Vergy accepted the jewel with a polite word of thanks—and it was here that his lackey, finding himself close behind Notredame, gave his horse a kick forward and slid out his dagger. He was in the very act of delivering the thrust, when Condoulet intervened.

There was no time to draw weapon, to cry out, to warn Notredame. The Provençal merely jerked his steed around, rose in the stirrups, leaned far over and gave the unfortunate Lorenzo one buffet with all his weight behind it. Not only was the Italian struck senseless—he was literally knocked from his saddle, sent headlong to earth and left hanging, one spur caught in his stirrup. The dagger still glittered in his grip.

The Comte de Vergy exploded in an oath, whipped out his rapier, and struck in his spurs. His startled beast lunged forward and struck against Condoulet's horse. Condoulet, nearly un-seated by the shock, was pinked in the arm by the rapier. A maddened bellow escaped him; his long weapon leaped forth; and he sent his horse at Vergy. He had no thought for any niceties of fence. In blind fury he slashed the nobleman across the face, knocked his weapon aside, and ran him through the body. The Comte de Vergy dropped his rapier and fell forward, lolling over the neck of his horse.

I T   H A D   happened swiftly, all in an instant. Condoulet was roaring at Vergy to fight on, when Notredame, who never lost his perfect composure, dismounted and went to the side of the courtier.

"Quiet," he said. "I fear you've done for him. Come, lend a hand here."

Condoulet scrambled down. "He's not dead?"

"No, but he soon will be." They stretched the senseless man on the grass. Notredame bared the wound, examined it, and fell to making a bandage and compress. "He may live a few hours if I can stop the blood. What about the other, the lackey?"

Condoulet went to Lorenzo, tried to lift him, and straight-ened up with an oath.

"*Tron de l'air!* The fool fell on his head and broke his neck! He was about to stab you in the back when I hit him—here's his stiletto."

Notredame glanced at it and nodded. He finished his work, then picked up the chain and emerald, which had fallen in the grass. With a grimace of distaste, he slipped the chain over the head of Vergy. He turned to find Condoulet standing staring at him and scratching his head, heedless of the blood dripping from his wounded arm.

Notredame made him bare the wound, and bandaged it.

"I owe you thanks for saving my life, neighbor," he said. "But this is a bad affair. This man was the King's favorite. I'd hate to see you broken on the wheel."

Condoulet eyed him in anxious perplexity.

"Maître Notredame, you know everything, so tell me what to do."

NOTREDAME LAUGHED slightly, then sighed.

"We can't let Vergy die here."

"Why not? Dead men are picked up on the roads every day."

"True, but this man is a nobleman of the court." Notredame reflected, plucking at his beard. After all, Condoulet had saved his life. And had the King really sent for the emerald? That story began to look a little extraordinary.

"We're close to Avignon—and once there, we're out of France," he said. "We'll take Vergy along to the city—and you, Sieur Palamedes, keep your mouth shut. Not a word out of you—not a word! Help me tie him in the saddle. My friend the Archbishop can help us here, providing he doesn't learn the truth."

"But the King—the jewel—"

"Devil take them both." Notredame gave him an angry look. "Not a word!"

Making himself dumb, Condoulet fell to work. With Vergy

tied in the saddle, they rode on toward the great rock towering against the sky.

Notredame gave his name at the city gates, stating that he must reach the Archbishop immediately. He was promptly passed in, and leaving his companions at the first inn they saw, hastened on to the enormous Place du Palais. At the Archbishop's palace, under the high citadel and palace of the Popes, good luck was with him. He reached the prelate at once, and was greeted with the greatest warmth, but made no delay.

"Monseigneur," he said, "my friend and I picked up and brought in an injured man, who lay by the road outside town. I think he will not live long. I can see to his hurts myself, but you might well send a priest to shrive him. Having met him recently at the King's court, I recognized him: the Comte de Vergy—"

A priest was summoned and Notredame hurried back with him to the inn. Vergy was still alive and weakly conscious. He looked at Notredame and whispered:

"Not the King wanted the jewel—it was the Dauphine, Catherine. That was her man with me. I am sorry—"

Notredame left him with the priest and stood in thought. So it was Catherine de Medici who had tried to get hold of the emerald in this way! Things were explained now, and the frowning features of Notredame cleared.

"I was right about that emerald," he reflected. "Envy—cupidity—a mad desire for it—ha! Leave it where it is, and good riddance."

He looked up as the priest appeared with a nod.

"Your friend made a good end, monsieur. That is a beautiful chain about his neck."

"It brought him to his death, so leave it where it is," said Notredame. "Come, Condoulet; to the palace, and no talk."

He took his friend back to the Archbishop and presented him. The prelate made them welcome; a secretary jotted down their report of discovering the injured man; and now arose the question of how to dispose of the body.

"My friend, Sieur Condoulet of Salon," Notredame said calmly, "desires to make a charitable offering, for the good of his soul. He wishes that this gentleman be given burial in one of the churches here, with a suitable tomb and a marble angel above it, and will gladly meet the expenses involved."

The astonished Condoulet opened his mouth, but the look he received from Notredame caused him to shut it quickly. The Archbishop was gratified by this laudable purpose of the gentleman from Salon, and nodded amiably.

"The old church of St. Martial, where is buried the Lady Laura, of the poet Petrarch's fancy—the very place!" said he. "The work can be done in two or three days, the gentleman buried, and the marble angel can come in due time."

Condoulet drew Notredame aside and got permission to speak.

"On the fountain in my garden at home," said he, "there is a marble angel. It would be the very thing, and save expense—"

"Silence," said Notredame. "An angel from Salon would not feel comfortable at all, here in Avignon. Be quiet."

The Archbishop, cautioned that Vergy's body might be robbed, undertook to have it entombed intact, and the matter was finished.

LATER IN the evening, when they were alone together, Condoulet took issue with his friend. A great shame, he said, to bury that magnificent chain and jewel with the dead man. Let alone its value, the King—

"He did not send Vergy for it." Notredame explained the case. "No, it is an evil thing. I earned it, so I've no desire to return it to the King. It is better off in the tomb, old friend. Between you and me, I'd not be surprised if that emerald were bewitched."

Condoulet hastily crossed himself. He was not in the least

superstitious, but no sensible man would have any dealings, any dealings whatever, with any ensorceled thing!

In the days that followed, one matter lingered in Notredame's mind. He often wondered what King François had meant by that singular remark about the emerald having broken the heart of the Italian artist Leonardo, now dead a score of years. Notredame was a curious man, and would have loved to know the story, if there were a story.

Yet he never tried to learn it; he felt a distrust, an actual hatred, for that green stone with a Sphinx in its heart. Better left alone, said he, and acted accordingly.

A wise man, Dr. Notredame—like most country doctors.

XIV

RICHELIEU RAIDS A TOMB

The malign magic of the Sphinx Emerald works its spell anew in one of the famous dramas of history.

A VIGNON HAD been a great and flourishing city while the Popes dwelt here. Now, although they still owned it, and across the Rhone lay the foreign territory of France, the old city was full of decay and ruin and forgotten tombs and dead memories. In this January of 1618, with winter coming on late and bitter, Avignon was a most dismal place. No one lived here who must not. The only travelers were foreigners—sight-seeing French and Germans, or beef-eating Goddams. Even the few troops who garrisoned the citadel made scant pretense of policing the desolate city below.

So it was natural that gossip should center on the young man who had come here in the preceding April, renting a house close by the Minorite convent, and living like a recluse with his cook and lackey. There was no mystery about him. A bishop, as his episcopal ring testified, he lived simply and quietly, had few or no visitors and spent his whole time in the study of theology—he was forever writing sermons. A bishop exiled from Paris, said rumor, speaking truly for once.

This young Bishop of Luçon—a bishop who had never been a priest—had been exiled by King Louis XIII personally; had he not been an ecclesiastic, he would have lost his head, since the King hated him with panicked fear. Now, as he stood on the ramparts and gazed out across the wintry Rhone to the French shores beyond, his thinly handsome hard-jawed face was set in lines of melancholy. Behind him lay complete ruin,

just when he had attained power as Secretary of State, thanks
to his influence with the Queen-mother, Marie de Medici. Now
the boy-king had clapped her into prison and seized power,
sending to death or exile or the Bastille those who served her—
chief among them the Bishop of Luçon, whom he hated
implacably.

Standing here, looking out at the French landscape, the
Bishop's manner might well be melancholy. His family held
the bishopric of Luçon in its gift, and needed to make sure of
its revenues, so he had been plucked from his university studies
at the age of twenty-one and created bishop—things were done
that way in France. And now, though still bishop, he was a man
without a future, his life ruined.

"There lies France, Cadillac; and here stand we, exiled," he
said sadly to the faithful lackey who followed him like a shadow.

*Marie de Rohan, assured that her game was won,
showed herself most adorable. When she mentioned
the deplorable intrusion of the two seminarians,
he waved his hand and dismissed it as a mere
nothing—greatly to her wicked but secret delight.*

"Monseigneur, you can mend the broken net if the chance comes," was the reply. It drew a smile from the Bishop, whose long jaw was very hard and firm.

"The broken net—well said. It is true. I can hold the lot of them netted. Yes, I can outwit the foolish, lecherous, haughty lot of them, from the King down. I can manage them, adjust their quarrels, pit one against another, and hold them in balance—control them. No one else can do this. But will the chance ever come?"

"It will come in God's good time," replied Cadillac, a sedate, devout yet surprisingly capable man.

The Bishop's thin lips curled slightly. "No doubt, but I fancy the Deity needs a nudge of the elbow. Run along, my friend, and get your marketing done. I'm for home and a warm fire."

He needed it. His health was none too good, and the wintry air provoked a frequent cough. So Cadillac went to market, and the Bishop turned back to his little house, hoping the cook would have a fire laid in his study.

It was laid, and he relaxed gratefully as it flared up and warmed him. The study was a room of fair size, with theological tomes scattered thickly all about; but the books looked singularly dusty. Sitting before the fire, the Bishop conned written sheets from his desk—a sermon, no doubt. Yet the scribbled lines looked very much like poetry, and brought a smile to his lips as he read them over.

A small table near the desk was occupied by a huge chessboard. Before it was a single chair; an accident, perhaps, though the chessmen looked unusual. Over the fireplace was a mantel in the Italian style; and on this mantel lay two handsome brass pistols and a gold-hilted rapier. The exile was obviously not pressed for funds.

NOW THE BISHOP went to the desk, opened a drawer and drew out a dozen sheets of paper. These, evidently, were letters; for one by one he read each with care, then took a quill from the holder and signed it, sometimes adding a few words, then folded and addressed it and sanded the address. When sealed, he laid it aside and went on to the next, using for seal his thumb, which he pressed into the warm soft wax after wetting it. There was a neat little pile of letters ready, when the door opened to admit Cadillac. The Bishop looked up at him.

"You're back—good. Kindly take these letters at once, before dark, to the Prior of the Gray Penitents, in the Rue des Teinturiers. I think his private courier for Paris leaves tomorrow. Give them to him personally, as usual. Ask if he has any letters for me."

"Yes, monseigneur." And the lackey came forward. "Your pardon, but—"

"Yes? There is something?"

Cadillac held out a folded bit of paper. "A man accosted me, asking me to give this to my master. Apparently he knew me—"

"Cadillac, Cadillac, for the love of God be careful!" broke in the Bishop anxiously. "You know we must beware of spies, that everything we say and do must—"

"I said nothing at all, master. The man disappeared. He wore plain black, not a livery, though he spoke with the tongue of Paris."

The Bishop opened the paper. It bore only a line or two of writing:

Come tonight at nine to the house of the notary, opposite St. Joseph College. It is on business of the Sphinx emerald.

"Unsigned—perhaps a trap," mused the Bishop. "Here, Cadillac, show this to the Prior when you give him the letters. He's close to the college, and may know the house in question."

The lackey bowed, took the note and the pile of letters, and withdrew. The Bishop sat looking into the fire, his fingers playing with the mustache and chin-tuft that lent distinction to his rather ascetic features.

The Sphinx emerald—that name jogged his memory, a memory that forgot nothing. He probed, and gradually it came clear. There was a famous jewel by that name. François I had owned it; Cellini had set it for him; there had been some public scandal at the time, a hundred years or so ago—all forgotten now. The gem had disappeared.

The most fantastic stories were told about the jewel. Whoever looked into it was bewitched with a mad fascination to have it at any cost. Reputedly it was ancient, for old writers had told of it. It was said to bless some, to curse others, and to be vaguely connected with the Sphinx.

The Bishop of Luçon grunted scornfully, and frowned. He prided himself on his mentality, which was clear and coldly factual.

These fables about jewels were utterly absurd, he reflected. Certainly, precious stones made no appeal to him; he even despised the episcopal ring on his hand, seldom wearing it. Who, then, had come from Paris to summon him on so wild a pretense? A trap, doubtless; traps were ever awaiting him.

The thought made him glance at the chessboard and the pieces on it—at first glance conventional chessmen, until one looked twice and counted. Then it proved there were two queens but only one king, several bishops, half a dozen castles, as many knights, but very few pawns—very singular, indeed.

Returning his gaze to the fire, he thought of the chaos now engulfing France. With his patron Marie de Medici, the Queen-mother, securely prisoned and the weak young King in power, the great nobles fought each other with evil rapacity; crime ran riot; assassination was common. The people themselves were half in revolt; Protestant and Catholic were cutting each other's throats again, and the country was surely headed for renewed civil war. There was no control, no central authority; the King was a figurehead.

"Yet he might become the central force of all France," mused the Bishop of Luçon, "if only the right man put him there—the right man! What might I not do, were I a cardinal and the chief of state! How I would make these rascals, these degenerate nobles, these pompous fools, move into the Bastille or lose their heads—"

A sound roused him; it was the cook, announcing his supper. He followed into the dining-room, where two candles lighted his frugal board, and had scarcely settled in his chair when in came Cadillac, crafty eyes rheumed, long nose frosty.

"Good!" said the Bishop. "Here, drink some wine—sit down. A truce to ceremony—sit down and talk, I say!"

Cadillac obeyed, wiping his nose on his cuff.

"The Prior had no letters, monseigneur," he said, "but expects daily to hear from your friend Père Joseph du Tremblay. He says the house of the notary, so-called, has been taken over by some lady who is in deep mourning and is making a pilgrimage to Rome, pausing here on the way. She has two servants, a man and a woman, and spends her whole time at prayers and devotions."

The Bishop reflected. The intrigues of women prevailed in the sorry court that now ruled France. Yet here might be some emissary of Marie de Medici, trying to get in touch with him. If the Italian Queen-mother ever got out of prison, she would set off a powder-keg under the whole country. Very well, he decided; risk it! He frequently made mistakes, but he never made the same mistake twice.

"Very well," he said; "at eight-thirty be ready to accompany me—pistols charged, warm wraps. We'll beard this female devil in her den."

At the appointed time the two men left the house, threading the dark and tortuous old streets at a rapid pace toward the College St. Joseph. Cadillac led the way to the house of the notary and knocked. The door slid open; a light was thrown on the visitors, and a servant admitted them with respectful bows.

"Madame is expecting you, monseigneur," he said, evidently recognizing the Bishop. "This way, if you please."

Hand on sword, pistols ready, the Bishop was shown into a large room where a fire blazed cheerfully. A burst of laughter greeted him.

"My faith, a walking arsenal! Good evening, M. de Richelieu. You need have no fear of me, I promise you."

TO HIS utter amazement, the visitor recognized Marie de Rohan, wife of the all-powerful Duc de Luynes—the most beautiful, reckless and courted woman in France. Intimate of the young queen Anne of Austria, heiress of the great house of Rohan, self-willed and witty as she was lovely—Marie de

Rohan, blonde, beautiful as an angel, and decked out with mocking diamonds, girl rather than woman.

"Impossible! You here—alone, unknown, in secret—"

"To see you, my dear bishop. Lay aside that armament, and enjoy the fire. Better to burn here than hereafter—isn't that good theology? You appreciate good wine—here is some admirable Chateauneuf du Pape from the vineyards by the river yonder. You look well. I am glad. I have need of your help."

"Then the saints defend me, madame, for I shall have need of theirs! I am at your pleasure, naturally."

M. de Richelieu, as the Bishop was named, made himself outwardly comfortable. Inwardly he was in a fury of uneasiness. He knew the infernal cleverness of this young woman, who had neither restraint nor morals. He knew she had a finger in all the court intrigues. He stood in real fear of her because he feared any irresponsible and impetuous person; to his methodic brain, recklessness made no appeal.

MARIE'S HALF-SECRET presence here in Avignon shouted to him that she was risking her great position and herself; therefore, he told himself, it was not secret at all to those who mattered—her husband, her lovers, perhaps the King. He sipped his wine, chatted lightly, fenced verbally with her, and sniffed danger close at hand. Presently he mentioned the Sphinx emerald, and her lovely eyes lit up.

"Oh! That is why I came! Do you know of the stone?"

"Vaguely."

"Take this." She thrust a folded parchment at him. "Sketches made by Leonardo da Vinci. I took them from the King's cabinet. Study them at leisure. That emerald is here in Avignon. You must help me get it."

"I am an exile, without influence, quite helpless—" he began.

Abruptly he found her on her knees before him, clutching his arms, face close to his, pleading and beseeching his aid. She was mad about the jewel—also, she had made a bet with the King that she could obtain it. No one knew she was here; she

Marie de Rohan—the most beautiful,
reckless and courted woman in France.

was supposed to be spending some weeks at Aix, seeking a cure
at the famed waters for a chest complaint. A plausible story, he
thought, but not very likely.

And yet, for all his freely admitted intellect, the fires of life
ran warm in the young veins of the Bishop of Luçon. Here was

the most beautiful and hotheaded woman in France on her knees to him, and closely in contact with him, presenting ravishing glimpses of a magnificent bosom—Marie de Rohan knew the full value of personal display. She, whose favors the entire court from the King to old Bellegarde sought most desperately, now sought his! A pleasant sensation, particularly as she was unreserved and quite ardent about it.

So, ere long, they were talking intimately together. The Bishop gathered that she stood ready to reveal many court secrets, and could exert the most powerful influence in his behalf; this was very pleasant hearing. Cadillac, meantime, was being entertained by Marie's faithful lackey, one Giles. Presently she summoned this fellow Giles and presented him to the Bishop.

"You must be ready at all times, Giles, to obey Monseigneur as you would me. Hold yourself at his service in any way he may desire," said she.

Giles, on bended knee, kissed the episcopal ring and swore fealty. The Bishop accepted his devotion and dismissed him, to himself thinking he would sooner have the devil for a servitor; to judge from his face, Giles was ripe for any crime.

"YOU MAY trust that man absolutely," said Marie, when they were alone again. "He is loyal. He knows about my quest, and lately has discovered the whole situation at the church."

"What church?" Richelieu asked.

"The old and ruinous church of St. Martial, now in charge of a rascally caretaker. Plutarch's Laura is buried there."

"You mean Petrarch's Laura?"

"It is all the same. Some woman he wrote verses about."

"Yes, I presume it's all the same," agreed the Bishop. "She's buried in half the churches of Avignon, by report. What has all this to do with the Sphinx emerald?"

"Why, the tomb of the Comte de Vergy is in that same church!" said Marie, wide-eyed, innocent as an angel, a slight and delicious color in her cheeks—induced perhaps by the fire, perhaps by contact of her hand with that of her guest. "The emerald was buried with him—you comprehend?"

"Not in the slightest," he replied curtly and rather coldly. "You must explain—"

From the street outside came a loud burst of furious voices— a mere drunken row, but it flung Marie into trembling fright, or an excellent imitation of it.

"I am afraid—spies may be watching me!" she exclaimed, shrinking against him. "I am in terror all the time—this house echoes strange sounds—it was folly to bring you here. You must go, go now! Tomorrow night I'll confide everything to you—I can't think or talk, with fear in my heart. Where shall I find you?"

Later, Richelieu realized that she had handled the situation quite capably, getting him away at a provocative moment, and forestalling his refusal to help her. He admired her address, thoroughly comprehended her wiles, and found them amusing. A clever young woman, well worth seeing more of—but one, he told himself, with whom every precaution was highly necessary.

So, upon reaching home, he brought Cadillac into his study.

"I am about to ask a disagreeable but vitally important service of you, Cadillac."

Cadillac bowed profoundly. "Monseigneur, it will be an honor to die for you."

"I prefer that you live. That rascal Giles looks like an arrant rogue, but stupid."

"Somewhat so. He worships his mistress, has helped to kill more than one man for her sake—he boasted of it. He did his best to pump me of information about you."

Richelieu smiled grimly, and from his desk produced a heavy purse.

"Here is gold. Spare no money in getting friendly with this Giles. Keep him drunk. Be open-handed. And specifically—" He spoke rapidly for a moment, and Cadillac nodded.

"Let me pose you a game. Look! Suppose
the Duc d'Epernon were to release Marie
de Medici from prison, then what?"

"I understand, master. I think it can be done. His mistress is not free with money."

"If anyone can do it, you can. I know your ability. That is all."

Left alone, the Bishop of Luçon sat motionless for a time, concentrating, calmly analyzing the words and actions of Marie de Rohan. The analysis was thorough, merciless and exhaustive; he was good at this sort of thing. It helped him to reach conclusions which were usually correct; in this instance they would have been very startling to the lady concerned.

Then, sighing, he took up the parchment she had given him and looked at the sketches by Leonardo—bold, assured sketches from a master hand. He looked at them more closely, moved the candles over, sat down and began to study them attentively.

"Remarkable!" he murmured in astonishment. "Can such a thing be possible?"

The sketches showed the emerald in its natural shape and size—noted as eight and a fraction carats, lumpy and very poorly cut—and also in a remarkable and most exquisitely drawn enlargement. It was this that drew the eye of Richelieu, showing what could scarcely be seen at all in the smaller sketches. This was something within the gem itself, some cluster of shadows, perhaps flaws, that took the exact shape of the Sphinx, seen in profile. As if to accentuate the marvel of it, there was a little sketch of this imitation or facsimile Sphinx, all by itself.

The large view exerted a singular fascination. The eye came back to it again and again in search of something half-glimpsed yet not really there at all—like a dim star that reveals itself only when the eye looks away from it. This was extremely puzzling. At last Richelieu began to comprehend the genius of the master artist. Leonardo must have drawn precisely what he saw in the emerald, and giving what he only half saw or imagined, as well—conveying a mood, as it were, a sense of something felt rather than seen.

The Bishop of Luçon blew a kiss in the air, perhaps to Leonardo, laid aside the sketches, and went to bed.

I T WA S on the following day that Cadillac began a series of escapades shocking to all those who knew the austere and devout lackey. He was seen in taverns instead of churches; he was observed on the street in a tipsy condition; and once he was known to have emerged from the House of the Nymphs, of which the less said, the better.

The good Bishop, however, seemed oblivious of this miscon-
duct. And it was upon the following evening that he himself
had visitors—a cloaked gallant and a lackey with a lantern. The
latter was Giles. The gallant was Marie de Rohan, who had a
liking for man's attire and could swagger like any cavalier, thanks
to specially made girdles which lessened the risk of discovery.

The Bishop of Luçon was helpless when she took him in her
arms and embraced him like an old friend and comrade. She
made a merry, laughing fellow full of oaths, but radiant with
such charm and magnetism and easy familiarity that all barriers
went down before her, especially those of a young and highly
impressionable bishop. She perched on the corner of the desk,
swung a shapely leg, and laughed gayly.

"Now we're safe and I can talk freely! You have studied the
sketches? They are said to be exact. Now, my honest Giles has
made friends with the caretaker at the church, a pliant rogue
who'll close his eyes for a pistole, and go stone-blind for a
doubloon. We can have the sacristy key at will. The tomb is
located and easy of access—"

"Good God, madame!" ejaculated the Bishop. "Would you
rob a tomb?"

"No; the stone lid is too heavy for me. You must do it," she
said gayly. "Now, I've verified the story, though it's vague in
places. King François gave the emerald to some medico from
Provence who cured him of an ailment—a Dr. Notredame or
some such name. On the way back to Provence, this physician
was followed and waylaid by a Comte de Vergy. Precisely what
happened I don't know, except that Vergy died and was buried
here. The emerald, for some reason not clear, was buried with
him. And that's the tomb from which I mean to get it, by your
aid."

"Sacrilege!" muttered the Bishop, shocked.

His impulsive words were abruptly checked. His visitor
launched into a discussion of court politics that made him prick
up his ears and listen hard. The King had said this; Prince de

Condé had said thus; Epernon and Luynes were at swords' points—and so on. Much of this information was vital; all of it was new. The young King was distracted and futile. Any man who could control the factions, restore the royal authority, and prevent the coming civil war, would save France.

"And you, M. de Richelieu, could do it," said she.

Richelieu, with no further mention of sacrilege, nodded. "Yes, I could do it—provided I got the chance."

Taking his well-kept, graceful hand, she looked at his episcopal ring.

"If you exchanged that ring for a cardinal's hat, if the King himself recalled you from exile to a seat in his council—"

Richelieu eyed her sharply. Her words were not fantastic. Bishops and cardinals were appointed by the King in those days—a matter of intrigue, not of theology.

His hand closed upon hers, gently. "Well, madame?"

Her eyes warmed upon him, twinkling softly as she returned the pressure of his fingers.

"I might arrange your recall by the King—if I thought you actually could control the nobles and factions, if I were convinced of your ability—"

"LET ME convince you," he said eagerly, as though yielding to impulse and confiding absolutely in her discretion. He kissed her fingers, rose, and went to the chessboard.

"Ah!" said she. "I've been wondering about those queer chessmen!"

She came and stood beside him, an arm about his shoulders, face close to his, as he reached out to the pieces on the board and spoke softly to her.

"For months, hour by hour, day after day, I've sat here studying these players." He touched one after another. "Here's the King—the young Queen—the Queen-mother. Here's Montmorenci, Vendome, Condé, Epernon. Here's Soissons, your father Rohan, your husband Luynes—the Archbishop of

Toulouse—the Bastille, the royal prison at Amboise, and so on. I know all these people. I form combinations of them to meet every contingency. My puppets play on this board, as upon France itself."

As the Bishop paused, comprehension flashed in Marie's face. She saw instantly how this man had schooled himself, had prepared himself for the future. He went on quickly.

"I play with these puppets, knowing what will tempt them to blunder, mindful of their characters, their ambitions, their weaknesses. And," he added, smiling thinly, "you would be astonished to see how fatal many of their weaknesses can be!"

She laughed; her bright blue eyes glittered. She broke out swiftly:

"I see, I see! Let me pose you a game. Look! Suppose the Duc d'Epernon were to release Marie de Medici from prison— suppose his army and half the forces of the kingdom were to back her, with Condé and Soissons—then what, eh? Show me!"

A startled look shot into Richelieu's face, his outstretched hand paused for an instant; her words sent a shaft of fierce and incredulous joy plunging through him.

"Very well—here, we group them like this!" He rearranged the pieces on the board with deft fingers. "Thus! Opposed to them the King and the Duc de Luynes, the court—"

"That means civil war!" she said, and caught her breath.

Richelieu smiled and moved out one of the few pawns. "No, no—look! Here comes a man who can oppose their hatreds and swords with his intellect—and beat them! The Queen-mother retires to her own estates in security; Epernon, her chief support, is bought off; Condé and Soissons are duped into a quarrel; we scatter gold, honors, titles, we make compromises— and see! The King alone remains in supreme authority."

"And the pawn, the unknown strong man, beside him!" Her quick wits leaped at the essential thing. She clapped her hands delightedly. "Who is he, this pawn?"

"That," said the Bishop of Luçon softly, "depends on whether the King recalls him from exile."

"And gives him a cardinal's hat." Her fingers caressed his cheek. "You know that I, like my husband, serve the King. Turn around. Look at me."

He obeyed. She was gripped by excitement. Her eyes were like stars; her breath came in rapid pulses that threw her bosom into tumult. She spoke jerkily.

"The King is a boy, weak, betrayed by everyone, frightened, not knowing whether to kill or to trust. Luynes is the strongest man at court. Good! I promise two things: First, that Louis himself will recall you. Second, that Luynes will propose and back you for the cardinal's hat. And this to seal the promise!"

She kissed him, lips to lips. He remained cynically unmoved. She had given him a vision of power so great, so sure, that it dwarfed all else.

"Judas got thirty pieces of silver for a kiss," he said. "What do you expect?"

The biting words frightened her. His piercing eye frightened her. She shivered, suddenly sensing the cold ambition of this man, the absolute hardness of him; perhaps she perceived that his ruling force was not intellect, but a will-power cruel and utterly inflexible and stupendous in its strength. Then she recovered.

" T H E   S P H I N X   E M E R A L D , " she said. "You must help; you must get it. I'll obtain the sacristy key, but I cannot move the stone; you must do that."

Richelieu nodded. He saw the whole trap now; it opened before him like the mouth of hell. But he merely nodded reflectively. He must have time; Cadillac must have time.

"Why not?" he said. "What waste, to bury such jewels in a tomb! It's a bargain, madame. Let us say a week from tonight—Thursday next. That gives time for a courier to reach Paris and bring back confirmation of your promises, if you send tomorrow."

Triumph lightened in her eye and he saw it, but it vanished at once.

"You don't trust me?" she murmured reproachfully. "You don't believe me?"

"I believe no one; I trust no one," replied the Bishop of Luçon. Then, abruptly, he came to life and warmth. The almost diabolic charm which he could so powerfully exert leaped into full play. He became another creature—impulsive, fascinating, intimate. His eyes softened, his voice was sheer music, his hands went out to her. "But, angelic being that you are, who could resist you? I adore you with all my heart! If you want my help, you shall have it—no matter what the cost!"

She laughed softly, deliciously. It was true—no one could resist her.

The crackling fire had died down to merest embers, the wax tapers were guttering in their *bobêches,* when she summoned Giles, who had been entertained meanwhile by Cadillac, and departed. It was arranged that on the next Thursday evening, provided that her promises received some backing from Paris, the emerald would be attempted.

The Bishop of Luçon put a fresh candle in one of the holders, sat down to the chessboard, and sipping a flagon of wine, stared at the pieces on the board.

"Either she has heard some whisper of a plot, or had the genius to invent it," he reflected. "If Epernon were to free Marie de Medici and back her against the King with an army—ah! How that one amazing stroke would simplify everything! It seems too good to be true. And afterward—let them look to it! All I want, all I need, is to be recalled from exile by the King himself. The rest is in my own head."

For a time he played with the pieces before him, then summoned Cadillac, who, though it was now late, came immediately.

"Well?" his master asked. "How goes it?"

"Excellently, monseigneur. But I have become a great sinner,

I fear. He is wavering. He has been drunk for a week. He is almost ripe."

THE DAYS flitted by with chill winds and traces of snow, until the mistral's unhappy breath blew them away. Twice, in the street, Richelieu had glimpses of Marie de Rohan in her costume of deep mourning. They had no opportunity of private speech, but on Sunday he received an unsigned note. It said: *"I shall bring full confirmation on Thursday evening. Trust me and be ready."*

Reading this, he laughed softly. As though he would trust her! The Prior of the Gray Penitents had his own couriers, and if there were anything in this strange hint about Epernon, it would come long before Thursday. Père Joseph du Tremblay, at Paris, was a true friend and a subtle worker who could discover anything.

Richelieu did not have long to wait. On Monday evening Cadillac came into the study and laid three crumpled letters on the desk.

"There, monseigneur," he said with finality. "The task is ended. He was supposed to have destroyed them. Instead, he sold them to me. And if he gets that pardon for robbing the grave, he will be a very happy man."

"He shall have it." Richelieu dismissed the lackey with another purse, and looked at the letters. All were addressed to the Duchesse de Luynes; one was from her husband, one from the young Queen, Anne of Austria, and the third from Père Arnoux, confessor to King Louis. Richelieu read the letters, then lifted his eyes to heaven as in thanks.

"Luynes hates me because he distrusts me; the Queen hates me because she dislikes me; the King hates me because he is afraid of me!" he murmured. "Ah, female Judas, false as you are beautiful—so I am to be destroyed, eh? And had you not let slip that bit of information about Epernon's plans, you might have succeeded. If that proves to be true—then, *pardieu!* France is in my hand!"

"The light—closer!" Richelieu ordered. Marie obeyed— and unexpectedly nearly went to pieces. The sacrilege of it left her shattered.

In the ensuing days it was observed that the poor young Bishop of Luçon had somewhat recovered from his melancholy. He was even seen to smile, at times. On the Thursday morning he had good reason to smile. From the Prior of the Gray Penitents came a letter just received from Père Joseph in Paris. When Richelieu had decoded it, one paragraph struck out at him with almost stunning force:

The Epernon intrigue about which you ask has been afoot for some time and may come to fruition in a month or so, I find. Your insight amazes me. I should never have believed such a thing possible, but it seems to be true.

When he read this, the exile could have shouted for joy.

That evening came Marie de Rohan, again in her cavalier's attire. She was gay, buoyant, excited, and triumphantly handed Richelieu a letter—a hasty scrawl from her husband, the Duc de Luynes, chief power at court:

Very well, madame, my utmost efforts shall back your promise;

*your bishop shall have the red hat—I swear it! As to the King, I
cannot say. If you want him to write a letter, naturally he cannot
refuse. He asks impatiently about your return.*

"You see?" she exclaimed, radiant and aglow. "It is as I said.
He will himself recall you. Now destroy that letter quickly; it
is too dangerous to be kept."

"True. We must take no risks." Richelieu, sitting at his desk, crumpled the letter into a ball and turned toward the fireplace. The top drawer of his desk stood open. For an instant his hand fell to it, dropping the letter from Luynes and catching up another crumpled ball of paper—so swift was the exchange that the substitution could not be suspected. The paper blazed up. Richelieu rose.

"Well, you wish me to keep my pledge—when?"

"Now, instantly!" she exclaimed. "I have a dark-lantern and the key to the sacristy. You and your lackey must do the work, while I hold the light and Giles keeps watch. The stone is heavy, we cannot budge it; you'll need all your strength."

The two servants were summoned. Cadillac carried a short iron bar. The four set out in company. A keen gusty wind was blowing off the Rhone, sweeping down from the Alps. The streets were dark and empty.

Reaching the desolate old shrine of St. Martial, Marie led the way around to the sacristy entrance and unhooded her lantern. The huge rusty key fitted; the door opened and they stole inside. Giles furtively swigged at a bottle and remained on guard. The other three went on into the church, with the dim beam of light showing the way; the place was cold as death itself—a still cold that ate into the bones.

Now, despite herself, Marie de Rohan was fearful, hesitant, uncertain. She pointed out a tomb built against the wall; it was not ornate—merely a marble angel showed perched on the lid. With a word to Cadillac, the Bishop attacked the lid and it moved. The cement was old and poor and broken.

"The light—closer!" he ordered.

Marie obeyed—and unexpectedly, nearly went to pieces. She was overcome by the thing they were doing. The sacrilege of it, the profane desecration of it, left her shattered, wakening all the ingrained religious fears of her nature.

RESOLUTE, COLDLY efficient, the Bishop helped Cadillac pry aside the heavy lid, slipped an arm in the tomb, and groped. The dim light showed him a chain and pendant; he removed it and slid it into a pocket.

"Now, Cadillac—close it up again. All through, madame. Lead the way."

Her teeth were chattering as she started toward the sacristy. At this instant came a scuffle of feet on the stones, a broader beam of light, a cry of warning, far too late, from Giles. Two cassocked figures, students from St. Joseph College nearby, strode into the chancel and paused at sight of the party, holding a lantern high.

Discovery! Marie faltered, came to a stop. Richelieu strode past her and went up to the intruders, facing them with calm air. He could be very arrogant, and now was.

"What means this intrusion, gentlemen?" he said coldly. "Who are you?"

"There was a light in the church," said one. "We came to investigate—"

"Then you may return," said Richelieu, holding up his hand to show his ring. "I am the Bishop of Luçon. Depart instantly, if you please."

Stammering excuses, they obeyed. The others followed outside. There, Marie took Richelieu's arm for support, gasping and trembling.

"The emerald!" she exclaimed. "Give it to me!"

"Calm yourself," said he in a troubled voice. "This discovery was unfortunate. It disturbs me. Come to my house tomorrow night, and we'll discuss things. I must have the chain and stone cleaned. It is blackened and smells of death—"

She shivered at this, and said no more. Richelieu and the two lackeys escorted her home and left her at the door; she was almost fainting when he bowed and left her.

Back in his own study, Richelieu had Cadillac build up the fire, spoke with calm authority to the unhappy man, who was overcome by the thought of sacrilege, and sent him away comforted. Then, moving the candles close, he took up a large reading-glass and began to study the emerald, on the blackened but magnificent chain made for it by the master Cellini. Since Leonardo had sketched it, he could see, the stone had been recut, and the work poorly done.

Nothing, however, could spoil the magic spell caught and held within the heart of the emerald. The sketches had warned him what to expect, but only faintly. Not even the genius of Leonardo could capture the illusive thing opening to Richelieu's eye as the lens brought it into focus. There was the Sphinx, yes; he could see it was formed by great flaws clustered within the beryl crystal. But more than this, beyond it....

His gaze became an intent, breathtaking study as fascination gripped him. Before his eye the interior of the emerald was spread out and enlarged into a landscape, as it were, a glittering, fantastic landscape of queer formations and shapes, caused by the odd bubbles characteristic of the gem—not round but angular bubbles. The field changed with every play of light. It seemed alive. It seemed instinct with motion. He could have sworn he saw moving shapes there; assuredly he could sense a mental reaction, a vibrant appeal, an upsurge of energy and puissance, a steely, dynamic ability rising within him. Fantasy he might reject with contempt; this was something more.

The Bishop of Luçon pushed away the emerald and set himself to analyze and comprehend this amazing thing, affecting him as strong drink did other men. He was well versed in the fundamentals of psychology. He perceived that this stone affected the beholder with a sort of auto-hypnosis. There was no magic about it. His own innate qualities were simply inflamed and carried to extremes; as he could solve some of his problems by gazing into the fire, just so did this green glory waken his imagination.

"So that explains it!" he murmured. He wanted to gaze into the stone anew, to satiate himself with it, to drink in these visions again; he refused. The temptation was almost unbearable; therefore he resisted with all the power of his iron will, dropped chain and emerald into a drawer, and snuffed out the candles.

Another time, yes—but he was resolute in not letting the thing master him. This was characteristic of the Bishop of Luçon. Within his purview there could be only one master—himself....

Not until the next afternoon did he permit himself to take another look into the stone. Cleaned and polished with its chain, he slipped it about his neck and for a space gave himself up to its wizardry—not blindly and fatuously, but critically, as one tastes a rare liquor. And when he finished, he knew within himself that he would never give up this marvelous thing while he lived.

Marie de Rohan arrived for dinner that evening, as bidden, and found her host the most charming of men. He agreed with her in everything; he flattered her extravagantly, he confided to her his most secret thoughts—apparently. And she, well assured that her entire game was won and in the bag, showed herself merry, affectionate and most adorable. When she mentioned the deplorable intrusion of the two seminarians, he waved his hand and dismissed it as a mere nothing—greatly to her wicked but secret delight.

Now and again she surprised an oddly sardonic gleam in the Bishop's eye. This might have disturbed her, had she not been so fully sure of her power over him. She asked about the emerald. Later, said he, with a graceful gesture toward the study, and she nodded. The meal was delicious. Cadillac served it with superb aplomb. The wines were something to astonish even a Rohan.

When they came into the study, where a cheerful fire was burning, she saw that an easy-chair had been provided; Richelieu held it for her, then seated himself at the desk facing her. The desk was littered with documents and papers. To her surprise, Richelieu regarded her without a smile; and when he spoke, his voice held a harsh crackle.

"Madame, we must discuss a certain matter very bluntly, even impolitely."

"Mercy!" A bubbling laugh broke from her. "One would

imagine that we were in a formal court of law! What is this certain matter?"

"The reason for your presence here in Avignon," he said coldly.

MARIE'S MERRIMENT vanished. Although incredulous of his attitude, she took warning.

"You astonish me, monsieur! Such a tone, between dear friends—"

"Between enemies, madame. The most bitter and implacable of enemies."

Her pride flicked on the raw, she regarded him with angry flashing eyes.

"Will you have the kindness to explain yourself, M. de Richelieu?"

There was no warmth or kindliness in his manner. For the first, and not the last time in their lives, he wore the air of a prosecutor, cold and precise.

"Certainly." He picked up a paper. "I have here a number of letters whose tenor is much the same; this one is from Her Majesty the Queen. It tells me that you are here with her knowledge and that of others, to carry out a certain design formed by them—namely, to make sure that the unhappy Bishop of Luçon shall be disgraced, deprived of his ecclesiastical honors, and prosecuted for his crimes, both by the Church and by the civil law. In short, to ruin and imprison him for life."

As she listened, the face of Marie altered. It lost its beauty. It became a mask in which glittered twin pools of blue fury. Richelieu touched others of the papers before him.

"These letters from your husband, from the King's confessor, bear out the first, madame. Lies, evasions, trickery—all are useless."

She burst into a low, vehement command. "Let me see those letters!"

"No. They are reserved for other eyes, madame."

"I understand! That vile wretch, that accursed Giles—he shall suffer for this!"

"On the contrary, I have assured him of full protection. However, you are not here to receive accusations, but orders."

SHE WAS convulsed by sudden fury, half rising from her chair, her hand sliding a dagger into view, her contorted features terrible to see. The door opened, and Cadillac appeared, his entry checking her action.

Richelieu spoke without emotion.

"Cadillac, you will be so good as to stand behind the chair of Madame and see that she does not leave it."

Cadillac obeyed. She sank back in her chair, composed herself, and spoke almost calmly.

"Very well. Play out this absurd little comedy, monsieur."

Richelieu inclined his head slightly, and produced another paper.

"I see by this letter from your husband, which did not get burned the other day as you thought, that certain promises are made. When, in compliance with these promises, I am recalled to Paris by His Majesty, I shall be very happy to return these missives to you, madame."

"That day will never come," she said with suppressed fury.

"A great pity. These epistles are somewhat indiscreet. The King, no doubt, would be displeased to learn how his actions are controlled."

She drew herself together, realizing her error in showing fury toward this dupe who had so unexpectedly become an enemy. A gleam of assured triumph in her eye, she spoke quietly, with perfect self-possession.

"We will risk all that, my dear M. de Richelieu. I gather that you wish me to manage your recall?"

"Precisely as we agreed, yes," he said, watching impassively, fully aware of her thoughts. "I, in turn, will risk the fulfillment of the promise made by M. de Luynes regarding the red hat—I believe these things will work out excellently."

"And the emerald?" she asked.

Richelieu made a gesture of regret. "Ah, that must wait upon the future, my dear lady. I trust that you will comprehend the importance of making sure about these letters, first of all."

She smiled, but her eyes were deadly.

"Have you finished, monsieur?"

"I think so, unless you find me in error."

"Very much in error." She leaned forward, and with an obvious effort held herself in restraint, launching her bolt in a voice that trembled with rage. "It is obvious that a scoundrel guilty of the vilest crimes would not hesitate to forge such letters. You cannot blackmail me, M. de Richelieu. Within three days the ecclesiastical authorities will arrest you, and you will be handed over to the courts of the King of France as a criminal. The papers are already being drawn up. It is you, monsieur, whom evasions, lies, trickery, cannot avail!" she added with a burst of triumph. "Sacrilege is a hideous sin in the eyes of the Church. A bishop guilty of sacrilege presents a scandal to the whole world. An ordinary man who desecrates a tomb is broken on the wheel—how much worse is this crime when committed by a gentleman! All France will cry out in horror!"

The Bishop of Luçon sat, chin sunken on his chest, eyes gripped to the papers before him. With keen relish, she went on:

"You have committed this crime. There is evidence in plenty to convict you. This lackey of yours must confess to the truth, under torture. The two seminarians who intruded upon the scene, and whom you dismissed with such arrogant declaration of your identity, are damning witnesses to the truth."

Richelieu sighed. "I fear, madame, that you are correct," he said in a dull voice. "I cannot evade the accusation. So you arranged for that intrusion? Cleverly done, very cleverly. It is terrible to think I am so hated by the King, by the Queen, by M. de Luynes!"

"No man in France is more hated," she said pitilessly. "You have brought your destruction on yourself. If you try to use those letters, they will be pronounced forgeries. That such a scoundrel would be guilty of forgery, is quite evident."

Richelieu lifted his head, looking at her with apparently anguished gaze.

"What do you want? What can I do to escape—"

"Nothing!" she cried vibrantly. "The accusation will be laid before the authorities in the morning. Everything is prepared, witnesses ready, statements sworn."

A faint, thin smile touched his lips.

"None the less, madame," he said quietly, "you will go to Paris, you will keep your promises to me, you will see that the King himself recalls me."

"Have you gone out of your mind?" She uttered a contemptuous laugh. "The accusation made against you in Paris—"

Richelieu lifted a document, to which were attached several imposing seals.

"There will be no accusation, madame, either here or in Paris," he said. "This document is signed by the Archbishop and other authorities here. It authorizes me, for certain purposes deemed for the best interests of both church and state, to open the tomb of one Comte de Vergy, situated in the church of St. Martial, and to remove therefrom such object or objects as I desire. I spare you the legal and ecclesiastical phrasing, which is somewhat tiresome." He set down the document, put his finger-tips together, and regarded her sharply. "It might be a mistake, madame, to make any accusations which would tend to involve you yourself in the crime of sacrilege, unless you have a similar permission from the proper authorities."

Listening to his words, the young woman went into a blaze of fury—then the blood ebbed from her cheeks, leaving her white as death. Eyes staring, lips trembling, she dropped back into her chair, beating upon the arms of it with hysterical hands.

"Oh, you devil—you devil!" she cried in a choked voice.

Richelieu inclined his head slightly. "No, madame—merely the Bishop of Luçon, at your service," he said with freezing courtesy. "You have my word of honor that these regretfully compromising letters shall be returned to you as soon as I am in Paris. And you will assure His Majesty that my sole object as Cardinal shall be to render him supreme in France. Now, Cadillac, since Giles is no longer in the service of Madame, you will have the kindness to see her safely to her home."

LATER, WHEN the footsteps and the sound of choking sobs died away, the Bishop of Luçon sat for a long while, reading-glass in hand, intently gazing into the heart of the Sphinx emerald. And what he beheld there seemed to cause him the greatest satisfaction. Presently he laid the reading-glass aside. His long, graceful fingers touched the gem almost caressingly.

"I shall never part with you," he murmured. "Decidedly, we must ever remain friends and allies! I shall have need of your helpful magic in the days ahead!"

And under his touch the emerald warmed and glowed softly, happily, as though in reassurance that everything he most desired was coming true.

But Marie de Rohan, Duchesse de Chevreuse in the future years, was to be the most deadly and implacable of all the great Cardinal's enemies.

XV

JEWELS HAVE A LONG LIFE

*Are the things we love ever ours? The old Moor
thought not: " 'I bought them! They were given me!
They are mine!' " he mocked. "Yet when you die—
what? They are just so much gravel to you, then."*

WILL PAGET paused with his host and guide, Roger Waynflete, outside the little Leghorn shop.

"This is the place," Waynflete said. "This man Hassan is the finest gem-cutter in Italy; but he's a devious rogue, an agent of the Moors, an arrant rascal who'll cheat you of your eyeteeth."

Paget smiled. "You forget, Roger, that for these many years I've been a goldsmith and jewel merchant in London town. Lead on."

Waynflete pushed into the shop and past the front attendant to the long workbench in the rear, where a man with clipped gray beard sat hunched above delicate tools and enlarging lenses great and small.

Waynflete spoke to him in Italian.

"Hassan, here's a client, Messire Paget of London. He speaks French but no Italian. Well, Paget, this is Hassan the Lapidary. Shall I wait for you?"

"No, no, get back to your counting-house, Roger. Many thanks. I'll find my way back to your house without any guide, when ready."

Waynflete departed. Paget drew up a stool, sat down, found Hassan scrutinizing him narrowly, and returned the scrutiny. Despite clipped gray beard, Hassan's lean features were smooth, unlined, ageless—a Moorish trait. His dark eyes were bright as

stars. He had a thin, satirical mouth under a hawk nose, and a
finely carven chin.

"I was expecting you, Sir William Paget," he said in fluent
English, to the surprise of his visitor. "I heard from Paris that
you had bought some gems there which would need recutting;
and you were directed there to me…. Yes, I speak your tongue.
Why not? There are English in Morocco, where I was born—or
were, until Sultan Ismail expelled them from Tangier. That is
why I am sometimes called El Maghrebi—the Moor. You are
a man of high intelligence, favored by Allah. I am humbly at
your service."

"Thank you," said Paget. He drew a packet from his belt and
set it on the bench. "Here are the stones—poorly cut, poorly
polished. Can you improve them?"

Hassan opened the packet. From wads of silk and cotton he

He wanted to take her to Adrianople as his bride....
What Tournelle wanted was not certain.

disinterred half a dozen gems—four rubies and two large sapphires. He poked them under enlarging glasses, put a jeweler's lens in his eye and examined them, with the greatest attention. Paget, himself old in the trade, which had brought him a knighthood and royal favor, watched closely. He was amazed and disturbed that this man should know so much about him and his errand, but gave no sign of it. Finally Hassan turned to his visitor and nodded.

"You are a good buyer. The sapphires and two of the rubies will be valuable gems when recut. The other two rubies will lose half their weight, but will be brilliant."

"As I thought," Paget said. "When can you do the work?"

"Within two months. I will take the smallest ruby for my pay."

"You will not," said Paget calmly, and they fell to bargaining. Hassan came at last to a decent price.

"Signor Waynflete will pay it, and will take charge of the stones for me. I shall not be here," Paget said when they had agreed. Hassan, who was no darker than an Italian, laughed softly, and his bright eyes glittered sardonically.

"For you?" he said. "I suppose you think they are yours?"

"I bought them," said Paget curtly.

"Yes. Many say the same. 'I bought them! They were given me! They are mine!' Yet jewels have long life—hundreds, thousands of years. When you die—what? Can you take them with you? They are just so much gravel to you, then."

"Too true. You're a philosopher."

"No. An exile who wants to go home." Hassan leaned forward, and spoke with an easy air of familiarity and confidence. "There is only one way I can do it—by taking the king of my country a jewel so wonderful that he will pardon my past offenses. Sultan Ismail of Morocco loves jewels. He will welcome me and restore my estates when he sees the gem I shall bring him—a gem no wealth could buy."

"I know nothing of Barbary, but you interest me. I too love jewels. Show me this gem of yours."

"Allah forbid. I have not yet secured it," said the lapidary, laughing swiftly. "To get it will take money, much money—two thousand pieces of gold, and more. But to buy it, merely to obtain it! I have chosen you to provide this gold; you see, I know much about you."

Startled and astonished, Will Paget frowned.

"I, provide you with two thousand gold-pieces—a fortune? Not likely. You jest."

"I jest not; nor has Allah touched my wits," Hassan said earnestly. He produced a folded parchment and handed it over. "Read this at your leisure. It is an attested copy. Discuss it with your friends here, and with the Venetian consul. If the original is worth two thousand pieces of gold—forty-soldi Florentine gold-pieces—come back and see me tomorrow. But I must have the money within two days. *Addio, messire!*"

Paget, who was in some haste to be gone, pocketed the parchment and walked out, not sure whether this Hassan were a jester or a madman. For the moment he left the parchment alone; he could spare time on no nonsense, having matters afoot which he deemed of more importance.

BEHOLD, THEN, Will Paget sauntering, not so aimlessly as appeared, along the colonnaded central square of Leghorn. So broad and straight were the streets that from here one could see the city gates. Paget, however, had seen Leghorn before, and now he was less intent upon the city than upon the people around. Few places on earth afforded a greater variety of types, since Leghorn was a free trade port in those days—that is, in March of the year 1694.

The Medici ruled in Tuscany, and Leghorn belonged to the Grand Duke, but was a city of absolute tolerance, where the only thing barred was politics or intrigue. Even the Turk or Moor could live and trade freely here, and did; and some queer things went on, as you might guess, within these arched colonnades where Saracen and Christian met as equals. Venetian, Spaniard, English, Fleming, Jew—every race babbled here and did business, to the profit of the shrewd and broad-minded Medici....

Will Paget, on the off side of forty, was journeying to Adrianople, there to serve as English ambassador to the Porte, but he was not hastening on his way by any means. He had a lithe, springy step, a quick smile, and his honor was as bright as his eye; momentarily, he had chucked Sir William Paget behind him and was enjoying freedom from the cares of trade and politics. To be honest about it, that romantic flowering of early middle age which drives so many a stout ship upon the shoals, had him in thrall, but Will Paget was no fool and was able to keep the helm. He had stopped over in Paris to see life, and had seen it. Now he was stopping here, with his old friend the merchant Waynflete, for private and urgent reasons not connected with his embassy.

PRESENTLY HE smiled, as the chief of these reasons appeared, seated in a light open carriage drawn by handsome grays, moving slowly along. As Will Paget stepped forth and bowed, she caught sight of him, and at her word the driver drew rein. With his handsome attire and lean, erect figure, Paget looked a dozen years younger than his age—and felt it, to boot. He advanced to the side of the carriage and took the hand she extended.

"A happy surprise, to leave you in Paris and find you here!" she said in French.

"No surprise, Contessa—you told me you were coming via Leghorn, so I came also," he rejoined. "But it is indeed a miracle, to find you alone, unescorted!"

She broke into a laugh. "Then be my escort. You shall come home with me. There is a Leone villa here, and I am occupying it for a week, before going on to Rome for the Carnival. Your friend the Vicomte is here—poor fellow, he lost everything at the gaming-table last night. So today he is making the rounds of the moneylenders."

Paget climbed in beside her with alacrity, grimacing at her mention of the Vicomte. The carriage proceeded slowly to the northern suburb of the city, called New Venice because of its canals and cleanliness and pleasant villas. And many an eye was cast at the handsome Englishman and the most famed beauty of Rome, thus riding together.

Everyone, of course, knew Flavia, Contessa di Leone, the young and beautiful owner of Rome's most renowned name and fortune; born a Colonna, wedded to the Leone heir, and now widowed, thanks to fever of the Roman marshes. Small wonder Paget had lost his heart to her in Paris, where half the court nobles had been at her feet; small wonder he had cast

*"The jewels are mine.
I intend that this
emerald shall be buried
with me, some day—"*

aside cares of state and had begun to pluck the flowers of romance! The Vicomte de Tournelle, it was rumored, had carried off this prize, but Paget had by no means given up hope.

If she was famously wealthy, as gossip reported, so was he. She liked him and treated him with cordial kindness—as indeed she did most men—and fanned his late-blooming flame till it burned high. Embassy? Embassy be damned, if he could win her by a bit of delay *en route!* He wanted, of course, to take her to Adrianople as his bride. What the Vicomte de Tournelle wanted, was not at all certain—probably her fortune. A rascal with a dark past, this Vicomte; a most engaging and charming rascal, yes, but none the less a very bad egg, by Paris report.

Having Flavia for once to himself, Will Paget now took full advantage of the opportunity. By the time they reached the pleasant little villa by the canal, the two of them were as intimate

as though parted only yesterday, and she was hanging on his
tales of jewels and monarchs—the two things went together,
naturally—with avidity. She had inherited plenty of jewels of
her own, for the Leone collection was renowned, but today she
wore nothing except an emerald pendant on a chain about her
neck—a large but rather poor emerald, Paget noted.

They went into the music-room. Flavia loved music inordi-
nately. She sat at the harpsichord and played. Paget strummed
a lute, and they sang together, until she abandoned the instrument and began to disport with the two English spaniels he
had given her in Paris. They fell into serious conversation about
themselves, Paget ardently pressing his suit the while, speaking
of Adrianople and what he could offer her there; the embassy,
he said, would ordinarily bring him a title and rank worth while.
The whole gay world would be theirs to enjoy. It was a pleasant
vista, and he kindled to it, though she did not. Then, as she
leaned over to pet the dogs, the chain and emerald fell from
about her neck. He picked it up.

"THE CLASP is worn and unsure; it needs a new one," he
said. "Why so handsome a chain for so poor an emerald?"

She laughed merrily at him. "And you a connoisseur of
jewels? For shame! This belonged to the great Richelieu. When
he died, fifty years ago, he bequeathed it to his niece, the
Duchess d'Aiguillon. She was a great friend of our family. She
was in Rome shortly before her death, in '75. I was a babe of
three then. One day she slipped this about my neck and said it
would bring me luck."

Then she must be twenty-two now, thought Paget.

"I still think it a poor stone," said he.

"Indeed? It is a most wonderful emerald!" she exclaimed
indignantly. "It is the chiefest of all my treasures. Did you never
hear of the Sphinx emerald?"

"Oh! Impossible!" said Will Paget. He had indeed heard of
that almost legendary stone. "Are you in earnest? Let me see it
again."

He took it from her. "Hold it to the light," she said. "Sometimes I sit gazing into it by the hour, with a glass. It is enchanting! Cellini, they say, made the chain; but no human hand could have made that emerald."

With keen interest, Paget went to the window, slipped from his pocket the double convex lens he always carried, and real astonishment seized him as he looked into the emerald. He had vaguely heard of this stone. He had seen sketches of it made by Leonardo da Vinci. The court painter Clouet had pictured it in a portrait of François I, who had owned it—and here in Leghorn the legend had come true!

Of good size, a wretchedly cut cabochon of only fair color, it had obviously come from the lost Egyptian mines—erroneously called the mines of Cleopatra, for this emerald had been famous long before the little queen. Like all emeralds, it was full of flaws. But unlike any other known emerald, the flaws in this one had assumed a shape, that of the Sphinx, crouching within the heart of the gem. It was not fancy, but a perfect and exact image.

What was more, the dispersal of colors was extremely odd, and since the emerald or beryl is a six-sided prism in form, the double refraction was uniaxial. Perhaps this, he thought, accounted for the singular things he saw in the jewel—things that were not there at all. His imagination was stirred uncomfortably. The Sphinx was real enough, but he fancied a grotesquerie of mocking, jeering faces in the play of greenish light, in the enlarged field of glittering green beneath the lens. Or was this caused by the bubbles? Like most true emeralds, this one contained microscopic bubbles, not round but angular in form—something that not all man's science has been able to duplicate. These, he thought, might somehow be responsible for the odd mental effect caused by the stone.

He was not aware that, while he thus stared, fascinated, Flavia di Leone was watching his face, almost with equal intentness. The look in her eyes was half amused, half sad. She fully understood the amazement, the absorbed emotion, of the man.

He had never looked at her like this, for all his passion. Here was the real man laid bare to her gaze, and it saddened her, perhaps, to read him so accurately, to know that he had all in an instant utterly forgotten her existence.

Yet when he looked up and started slightly at sight of her, she was smiling.

"You too?" she murmured. "It does that to everyone—makes them see things, some good and some bad. Some hate the stone, others would give their very souls for it."

He put away the glass and slipped the chain over her head. A lovely head it was, massy with golden glittering hair; her face was like fair satin and sweetly carven, all alight with deep allure. Yet the blue eyes were hard and cold—eyes that did not warm as a rule, or kindle to pretty words. A haughty woman, who would follow her own impulses regardless of anyone else, a woman of strange loves and intense hates. Paget wondered at himself, thus estimating her, as though weighing her for the first time. The things he saw in the emerald must have done this to him, he thought half angrily.

"A WONDERFUL gem, yes," he said quietly, "but it is poorly cut. You should—"

"No!" she cut him short. "It stays as it is. It is mine," she replied. The phrase made him think of Hassan the lapidary, and he smiled a little.

"Are the things we love ever ours, Flavia? Beautiful things— can we say beauty is ours alone, even impersonal beauty like gems?"

"Of course." Her voice sharpened a trifle. "My jewels, at least, are mine and ever shall be. I intend that this emerald shall be buried with me, some day—"

She broke off abruptly as the Vicomte de Tournelle came into the room and advanced toward her.

He was attired in cut Genoese velvet of steel blue adorned with seed pearls—a trifle worn and shabby, to a keen eye, but still magnificent. He was commanding in feature, darkly handsome, with thin, pallid lips and veiled eyes which, when wide open, revealed the whites below the pupils—sure sign, to Will Paget, of a cruelly hard and bitter dominance. And yet the man radiated charm. The very room warmed and glowed to his presence, reflecting the magic of his personality. He was the sort of man to make the sunshine brighter on a fine day like this.

For Will Paget, it was a cruel moment—as though he were still seeing unseen things and had been given an insight into realities by those visions in the emerald. Tournelle took Flavia's hand, kissed it, and stood beside her with fingers touching her gleaming hair as in quiet caress. He was sure of himself, sure of her, wearing the easy air of possession. And she reacted to it, warming and glowing like the room itself, feeling his presence happily, glad of it, rejoicing in his nearness. She loved him.

Will Paget saw all this quite clearly. Perceiving it, he knew that he would never win her, that Tournelle had already won her. A slight sigh escaped him, as he made up his mind to it. He never played a losing game.

"I must be leaving. Business awaits me," he said.

"The carriage—" she began. He checked her.

"Thanks, no. I prefer to walk." He glanced at the Frenchman. "You like Leghorn, M. le Vicomte?"

Tournelle showed white, even, pointed teeth like a cat's, as he laughed.

"Faith, monsieur, it promises to be very kind to me! I am unlucky at cards, lucky at love, and money seems easily come by here. A pleasant place indeed!"

"My congratulations," Paget said, dryly. He disliked Tournelle with all his heart, and when their eyes met, he knew the man cherished an equally vivid dislike for him. But each of them remained superficially amiable, friendly, courteous, apt at the conventions of good breeding.

They exchanged bows. Paget kissed Flavia's hand, most un-Englishly, and she bade him to an early family supper the next

*"A man was seen, but by this time he must have
passed the boundary.... It is all very puzzling."*

evening—a kindly invitation, graced with the kindliness of
dismissal. Paget sensed this in her words, her manner, her sad
cold eyes. She was letting him down easily, preparing to have
done with him and his suit. Her fingers touched those of
Tournelle and curled about them lovingly. Paget, accepting the
invitation, departed.

PAGET HAD been granted a wonderful experience and realized it; that emerald had done things to him, roused him to himself. It was characteristic of him that, as he strode the broad, straight avenue to the central square, he forgot his chagrin, forgot his dislike of Tournelle, forgot the lovely face and figure of Flavia di Leone. The Frenchman had won, and that finished it. Will Paget was too bluff and sensible a man to throw himself away on the coast of folly. His argosy was too soundly freighted for such nonsense; his grip of the helm was too firm. He felt no grief at all, and it came to him that he was not and never had been in love with her—he had merely been pursuing the wisp of an ideal.

What did grip his thought and his mind and his soul was that bit of beryl he had looked into. The emerald had completely captured his imagination. He was obsessed by it. And she thought it was hers! This made him laugh softly to himself.

Little could such a jewel belong to any woman, however beautiful. So glorious an object, an unique thing of nature's fashioning, could have nothing in common with any petty human being made for worms. It spoke with allure to mind and spirit; it was something far beyond the mere empire of the physical. Within those green depths lay all the realms of the imagination; how might any person declare this wonder his own or her own? It was absurd. That queer fellow Hassan knew what he was talking about.

"Buried with her, eh?" reflected Paget. "As though that would make her own it! Oh, plague take all such nonsense! What's this?"

Thought of Hassan the lapidary sent his fingers to the parchment in his pocket. He drew it forth, opened it, and began to decipher the crabbed writing of it.

A WHILE later, Waynflete and some of his cronies among the English merchant colony were gathered about cups of chocolate, when Will Paget broke excitedly in upon their company and flung the parchment on the table.

"Read it, Roger—read it aloud!" he cried. "Either it's some monstrous hoax or—or by gad, here's fortune within our grasp! Read it out, man—see what you think of it!"

They complied. Their first puzzled wonder became incredulity; then, when Paget told how he had come by the parchment, passed into fevered heat of cupidity. It was no hoax, no delusion. Here was a five-year concession of the whole trade of Corfu and Zante, granted by the Council of the Venetian Republic to "Hassan the Lapidary, called El Maghrebi, or to his assigns." The trade of those two Greek islands, which Venice owned, meant not one but a dozen fortunes, over a five-year period.

The chocolate-sipping assembly became a business session prolonged far into the evening. Signore Mocenigo of the great Venetian house was visiting with the Venetian consul in the city. Paget and two others were sent hot-foot to see him. The *bona fides* of the document was promptly verified by Mocenigo.

Hassan, it appeared, was really a Moroccan prince in exile, and a master genius of eastern Mediterranean trade, having friends and informants everywhere. He had rendered Venice most important services in commercial lines, and had been rewarded by the Council of Ten with this negotiable document.

The gathering at Waynflete's house canvassed the matter thoroughly. Two thousand of the Florentine forty-soldi coins for which the great Cellini had made the dies in 1535, was really something; but among so many wealthy merchants they could be supplied, even at short notice. There was sharp discussion, and the company adjourned to meet again upon the morrow, after further thought and investigation, with Signore Mocenigo.

Will Paget forgot emerald and woman alike. Here was something solid for a merchant's jaws to clamp upon, something real, with incredible profits involved! When, on the morrow, Mocenigo met with the company, he gave them full assurance that the concession, when endorsed over to them by Hassan, would be ratified by Venice. This Hassan was a person of far-reaching influence in both diplomatic and commercial quarters, an excellent man for any ambassador to know. Will Paget was glad to be deputed to see Hassan this same evening and close the deal, payment to be made on the morrow. Although exiled, Hassan was no less an agent of Sultan Ismail, it appeared.

So that afternoon the company of Zante traders was formed, each merchant sharing according to his investment. Paget, being a wealthy man, took a large share. He was in fine feather that day, talking shares and gold exchange; and upon sending a messenger to Hassan, was asked to visit the shop of the lapidary later in the evening.

Everything fitted in very neatly, and Will Paget set off for his early supper engagement with a highly contented heart. Romance was really not worth its cost. He was a methodic sort of man, and having made up his mind to the loss of Flavia, he was able to rid himself of his hapless passion with no particular difficulty. Still, as a final ember of the quenched flame, he took with him as a gift for the lady a gem that he considered a natural curiosity—a stone he had procured the previous year from a Muscovy trader. What it was he knew not, but cut and polished, it was very pleasing.

TRUTH TO tell, he was more anxious to see the Sphinx emerald again than he was to see the fair Contessa. It had been a busy day.

Bidden early, he reached the villa with daylight still in the sky, and was shown to the garden. The Contessa, said the man who admitted him, was there. Paget strolled about but saw no sign of her until he perceived one of the spaniels playing about the entrance to a little summerhouse thickly overgrown with roses, at the garden's end. He was approaching this when the sound of a voice came from it—a furious voice so charged with angry oaths and passion that it stopped him like a blow. It was the voice of Tournelle, with its usual suavity ripped away.

"But you shall and you must! I'll brook no refusal—you must!"

"Not at all, my dear Louis." This was Flavia speaking—angrily too, but quite calmly. "If you need money, I can always supply—"

"Listen to me!" Tournelle burst in upon her. "This is a fortune, do you understand? A fortune! And that cursed green jewel is worthless. You're infatuated with it, you vixen, but you're going to learn that I'm master here."

"Louis, you forget yourself." Cold was her voice now, cold with an anger greater than his, an anger deep and piercing and charged with finality. "No, now and forever! The jewels are mine, and stay mine. You ask the one thing I cannot and shall never give you. Understand it once and for all—"

Will Paget, embarrassed and scrupling to be an eavesdropper, scuffled the gravel path and whistled to the spaniels. The voices ceased.

Presently Flavia appeared. Except for her bright eyes and high color she was quite herself, greeting him with unusual pleasure and intimacy. Tournelle followed her out. He was white to the lips, and replied curtly to Paget's bow, then strode away almost discourteously. Flavia uttered a soft laugh and took Paget's arm.

"You must pardon our Vicomte. He has just received a great disappointment, and it has stricken him."

"Then I would that his chagrin spelled my happiness, dear lady," he replied gallantly, making a final futile effort despite himself. His eye went to the emerald, which she wore upon its chain. "Why not leave him to the consolations of Rome, and take the road to Adrianople with me?"

Flavia looked at him for a moment, then took his hand and pressed it. The look in her eyes was that of yesterday—half sadly compassionate.

"Because you are chasing butterflies, and take the chase to be love," she said. A sudden impetuous warmth filled her voice.

"Honest Englishman, I like you. So, for one little fleeting instant, I shall be honest too, and confide a secret to your honor—a real secret, unknown to any here. Louis and I were married just before leaving Paris. Pardon me for not telling you sooner."

Will Paget turned, looked into her eyes and saw their candor, and forced a smile. The blow hurt his pride—a trifle—but certainly not his heart. He realized how he had been swept away by passion, not by love—chasing butterflies, indeed! Still holding her hand, he bowed and kissed her fingers.

"Contessa, far from causing hurt, you can bring only joyous happiness to those around you. I respect your confidence. I felicitate you with all my heart, wishing you the greatest joy. Let me be the first to place a wedding gift in your hand."

So saying, he laid in her palm the strange olive-green stone he had bought from the Muscovite. She looked at it, turning it over curiously, and her eyes lit up.

"Thank you, indeed! It is a singular gem, like none I ever saw. What is it?"

"Nay, ask me not, for in truth I know not," he confessed. "In terms of the trade, it is doubly refractive and biaxial, and ranks in hardness above spinel. By this and its qualities of refraction, I believe it to be a species of chrysoberyl, but it has a striking and mysterious quality which you'll observe during the meal. I never before saw such a gem; like your emerald, it is unique. Therefore accept it with my humble compliments, I beg of you."

"You are kind. I shall cherish your memory in the gem," she murmured, then took her gaze from the translucent olive-green stone. "But it's growing chilly here—shall we go inside?"

THEY PASSED into the house, talking of jewels as they went, the spaniels frolicking about gayly. Tournelle met them. He was entirely himself again, witty and radiating his peculiar charm, apparently quite at ease with Flavia and the world.

Paget watched the man cynically, giving no hint of his secret knowledge. Had the Vicomte been trying to force her to hand

over her jewels? However, it was no affair of his. He seated
himself at the harpsichord, sang a tender ballad, and began to
feel extremely happy. If Flavia had chosen such a rogue instead
of him, he thought the worse of her for the choice, that was all,
and was well out of the business.

Flavia never arrived there.
Toward morning the wreckage
of her carriage had been found.

The supper was much earlier than the usual Italian custom. They sat at table with two huge silver candelabra lighting the room, and as they talked and ate, Paget indicated the Sphinx emerald on its chain.

"Will you permit me a word of advice?" he said to Flavia. "That emerald has poor color and is very badly cut. But in its heart is a spot of deeper color which a cunning craftsman could bring out, without spoiling its unique features, and thereby improve it vastly."

"Perhaps, but it shall never be done," she said, most decidedly. "It shall remain as it is; not for anything would I have it altered. I care nothing for its value. Almost all my patrimony is sunk in jewels, which will suffice me all my life. I shall never part with them—with any of them," she added. Paget fancied that for an instant her eye flicked to Tournelle with challenge. "They

are mine, mine! Mine to enjoy and keep sacredly, as I shall keep this gift of yours."

She produced the curious stone he had given her, and told the Vicomte of the gift. Then, while still speaking, her voice died away. She was looking at the stone, and her gaze widened upon it with startled fright. For the gem, which out there in the garden had been a beautiful soft olive-green, now shone in the candle-light with a rich pigeon-blood red, vivid and striking.*

Paget smiled. "The mysterious properties I mentioned, Contessa—you see? That is the peculiar and unique feature of this stone. In ordinary daylight it is a lovely green, limpid and serene. But in the sun's rays by artificial light, its color changes to a deeper red than any ruby. Why? I cannot say, alas! The Muscovite from whom I had it believed the gem to be bewitched. But beauty is never a thing of witchcraft, so wear it and fear not."

The marvel of the stone led to further discussion of gems. Tournelle, who had never previously shown much reaction to the subject, betrayed a keen interest, and made himself more than ever fascinating. At the back of his mind, Will Paget wondered. Had the Frenchman known that all the Contessa's fortune lay in her jewels? And had he been trying to get them from her, there in the summerhouse? An odd situation, thought Paget, and no promising one; he found himself cherishing a keen distrust of the Vicomte, and was rejoiced when he could take his departure.

He needed no escort, as he headed downtown, for Leghorn was the one Italian city that was well and efficiently policed. As he walked, the chill night air off the sea cleared his brain and sent him looking eagerly ahead to the important meeting with Hassan.

Flavia and her jewels were brushed out of his existence and

---

* Obviously it is a question here of the gem now called alexandrite, which at the time was totally unknown outside of Russia.

thought, and with them the Vicomte de Tournelle. Chasing butterflies, eh? A very apt figure of speech. Well, he was back to solid things again, and deucedly glad of it. Sir William Paget, egad, had better be looking to his affairs!

It was just as well for Will Paget's future peace of mind that he attained this eminently practical viewpoint when he did.

He found the little shop of the lapidary lighted but curtained from the street. Hassan awaited him, and a black Sudanese slave served them delicious mint tea. The Moor was not only affable but friendly, and showed himself amazingly frank.

"Certainly, the concession might have been sold for much more," he said. "But I was urgent for cash, and that in gold. By making it worth your while, I gain all that I desire—what more could I wish?"

The simple arrangements were quickly settled. The gold was to be delivered by noon next day; on this point Hassan was adamant.

"My word is pledged; I must have the cash by noon," he said. "You, Sir William, are an ambassador, a man of honor; you comprehend the nature of engagements which must be met on the dot. In this instance, it means a return to my own country, to life in a palace, to everything I once had and lost. True, it is the will of Allah, but this is largely dependent upon my own efforts."

Will Paget liked this sentiment. "Agreed. The gold will be here before noon."

"The concession, signed over to you and ratified by the Venetian consul, will be awaiting you," said Hassan.

Will Paget liked this, too. All clear-cut and businesslike. Sipping his mint tea, he noticed loose gold strewn along the work-bench and voiced a question.

"Are you a goldsmith also?"

Hassan laughed. "A very poor one. I have been making the setting for the great jewel to be presented to the Sultan Ismail. To please him it must be made just so. Look."

He produced a massive golden circlet, a ring designed to hold a single stone. Paget examined it critically with the eye of a master goldsmith.

"Virgin gold, and soft, eh?"

"Pure dust from the Sudan. You like the work?"

"No," Paget replied, honest as he ever was. "It is far too crude, too heavy."

"By design," said Hassan. "Ismail has no use for delicate things. He is very active, uses spear or sword every day; what is crude, impresses him. Thus, you will observe that the claws to hold the gem, seemingly so large, are meant to protect it from breakage."

"I see you know what you're about. And where is this wondrous gem?"

Hassan smiled. "It is not yet in my hands, but it will come. It must be worked over and recut before I can mount it."

PAGET INDICATED an inscription in Arabic letters, inside the circlet, asking what it meant.

Hassan chuckled.

"That means: *'El Maghrebi made me.'* It is to keep Ismail reminded whence the ring came; his favor is a fickle thing. By the way, within the next few days I expect to have some very handsome jewels, if you care to see them. The prices, to you, will not be high."

Paget was tempted, but resisted.

"I shall not be here. I have tarried too long already, and must resume my journey immediately this business of ours is closed."

The Moor nodded. "An ambassador does well to confine himself to his work. Perhaps your greater wisdom may instruct me in one or two matters."

They talked of trade and politics. Will Paget found himself utterly amazed at the shrewd conceits and deep knowledge of this graybeard Moor. He learned much regarding the Turkish policies of Adrianople and the Orient trade in general—so much, that after going home he instantly made notes of all Hassan had said and hinted. Indeed, he learned more from this half-hour's chat than from six months of big-bellied discussions with Foreign Office bigwigs in London; and these notes he made were largely responsible for the surprising address and sharpness which Sir William Paget was so soon to display in managing affairs at Adrianople for the Turkey merchants of London.

NATURALLY, WILL PAGET now had greater things to dream about than Roman blondes or emeralds; romance, in fact, was for the time being completely driven from his mind. Next morning saw the Zante Company gather and the broad gold-pieces pour in. Somewhat before noon, Paget and others of the company escorted two stout mules loaded with treasure to the little shop of Hassan the Lapidary. They were very fine white mules and therefore unusual; Waynflete had loaned them for the occasion, since such a weight of gold could scarcely be carried in one's waistcoat pocket.

The Venetian consul was waiting; the papers were duly made out and attested; and the concession became the property of the new-formed Company of Zante traders. Hassan made no count of the money, accepting Paget's word for this, but requested that the mules and treasure be left with him intact. To this Waynflete objected somewhat heatedly until Paget agreed to recompense him for the mules. The merest detail and of no importance whatever, thought Paget, but was to change his mind about this, ere long.

That afternoon Will Paget had to arrange his immediate departure for Adrianople via Venice and also had to preside over a merry banquet of the Company of Zante. Signore Mocenigo was present as a guest. Since he was leaving at noon the next day for Florence and Venice, he invited Paget to ride in his coach, promising to send him on from Venice to Stamboul by ship. Will Paget accepted this civility most thankfully, rightly counting on securing from Mocenigo, *en route,* an excellent grasp of Venetian trade affairs in the Orient.

So, what with one thing and another, we see Will Paget the gay Lothario and searcher after Continental pleasures, once more the stolid, practical London merchant bound for diplomatic triumphs and well satisfied with his lot. The morning of this his last day in Leghorn, however, he was greeted with news that left him horrified and profoundly shocked. He learned of it after breakfast, upon going with his host to the counting-house. The whole city was ringing with it by this time.

Flavia, Contessa di Leone, was dead.

Early the previous evening she had taken carriage to drive to a gambling casino in town which she had visited now and then. She never arrived there. Toward morning the wreckage of her carriage had been found on the highway north of the city. Evidently the handsome grays had run away, smashing at last into a tree. Her body was found in the wreckage; that of her coachman was strangely missing, and the man had not been found.

While Waynflete and Paget were drinking in the details of the story, an agent of police arrived. A mere conventional questioning of the English milord, he explained, Paget being known as a friend of the Contessa. Paget dazedly answered the questions asked him; he did not waken from his stupor of horror until the agent was departing, then halted the fellow.

"Where—what about the Vicomte de Tournelle?" he stammered. "Where is he?"

"That, *excellentissimo signore,* remains somewhat of a mystery, since we cannot find any trace of him," replied the police agent. "A man answering his description was seen on the highway during the night, riding a horse and leading two white mules, but by this time he must have passed the Tuscan boundary. It is all very puzzling."

So it was to Will Paget, too. Mention of the white mules plucked at his brain somewhere, but he remained bewildered.

Finally he roused from his stupor sufficiently to start his man getting packed, and while he was engaged at this, a messenger came from Hassan the Lapidary to say the expected stones had arrived and the signore might come at once if he desired to view them.

Paget jumped at the chance to get pulled out of his melancholy. It was more than an hour before Mocenigo's coach would come for him; ample time, therefore. He clapped on hat and riding-coat and walked along the colonnades to the little shop of the Moor, and went in. Hassan greeted him brightly, set aside his work, and unrolled a mat of black velvet before him. Upon this he heaped a double handful of gems.

"Most of them are unset, or were broken out of their settings," he said. "You shall see them just as I received them."

Paget began to finger the jewels, but his mind was not upon the task. Most of the stones had indeed been wrenched from their settings; to some of them still clung bits of the gold in which they had been mounted.

He was conscious of something growing within him—a certain nameless sense of horror for which he could not account. None of these jewels were familiar; yet from the mass leaped out a color, now and again—a bit of olive-green. He reached for it, lost it amid some rose-pink pearls, saw it and lost it again, then resolutely turned over the pile. There it was! He picked it up with shaking fingers, and carried it to the front window, where the sunlight struck in briefly. He held the green gem in the sun's rays; not that he did not recognize it instantly, but he was incredulous. He needed to verify the thing to his own numbed intellect.

And as he looked, the stone, limpid olive-green an instant before, turned in the direct sunlight, as it did under artificial light, to a rich red.

Horrified conjectures rushed upon him as he looked: The man with the two white mules—Hassan, who had needed the gold to pay for the gems he had expected—the woman who had died the previous night in the wreckage of her carriage! A choked cry burst from Paget. Madness burst in his brain. He turned, hurled the chrysoberyl at the Moor, and went headlong out of the shop.

There, in the street, he pulled himself together. Sanity came back to him. Tournelle was gone. He had no proof whatever of the crawling horror that seized him at thought of it. He had best get out of here, out of Italy altogether, at the first possible moment, and keep his mouth shut. For Sir William, there was no alternative.

WITHIN THE shop, Hassan stared after him, and shrugged. Going back to his workbench, the Moor seated himself and uncovered the work upon which he had been engaged. Before him was an emerald, poor in color and wretchedly cut; but when he had finished recutting the stone, its loss in weight would be nobly repaid by its gain in shape and color. He looked from it to the massive gold ring for which it was destined—the ring of Sultan Ismail—and nodded complacently.

Then, as he fell to work once more, a chuckle took hold of him, and his thin lips twisted in a mirthless grimace.

"That Englishman must be a little mad after all, like most of his race," he muttered. "Allah is great; Allah is good; He alone bringeth all things to perfection! And she thought they were hers! Blessed be Allah—she thought they were hers!"

He cackled out a laugh, and went on with his task, contentedly. And Sir William Paget, fleeing the truth he dared not face, went on to Adrianople and the high destiny there awaiting him.

XVI

LADY IN CHAIN MAIL

*From the hand of a dead Mameluke after the
battle of the Pyramids, a civilian scientist
with Napoleon's army took the Sphinx
emerald.... and though the Mameluke's militant
daughter offered to buy back the gem at a
price high indeed, swift tragedy followed.*

F ABRE TWISTED the ring from his finger and held it aloft, laughing, so that the sunset rays struck a green spark from the stone in it.

"The emerald of Ibrahim Kachef Bey, comrades!" he exclaimed lightly. "Look well at it! Today the Corsican himself offered me ten thousand francs for it. I refused."

The other two men received his careless words with grave concern. Duroc the geologist, a rocky-faced cynic of forty, spoke out in his blunt way:

"A mistake, Pierre. You might have built your fortune on that ring. Bonaparte is an Italian; he cherishes a grudge or a rebuff. And the General-in-chief of the Army of Egypt can be a bad enemy to a mere member of the Commission of Arts and Sciences."

"That's true," assented Bonnard, the historian. He was an elderly man, sad-eyed, burned-out, suffering with a liver complaint; a kindly fellow. "The ring cost you nothing. You took it from that dead Mameluke Bey at the Pyramids battle. Sell it. What good is it to you?"

"None, perhaps, but I'm fond of it." Fabre regarded them with a glint of mockery in his stubborn dark eyes. "Yes, I'm in love with the emerald. And that woman sent again to me this morning, wanting to buy it back, asking for an interview. The dead Mameluke was her father, Ibrahim Kachef Bey. I'd like to see her. Who knows? Anything's possible here, where our

*They were coming at the gallop, with
shrill cries of "Allah!" Two of the foremost
riders wore the Mameluke panoply.*

Corsican has become a sultan preaching the creed of Islam!
She may be young and beautiful, eh?"

His words drew laughter and nods of comprehension.

"I don't blame you," Bonnard said. "It's a young man's war,
so make the most of your chances, by all means."

"You're a lucky devil, and I envy you," put in Duroc, giving
his ferocious mustaches a twist. He was really the tenderest of
men, and the mustaches pleased him by lending him an entirely
false air of bloodthirsty aggression. "The stone is marvelous,
absolutely unique. And historic as well. Let me see it once more,
will you?"

The three were sitting in the coolness of sunset, in the garden
of their small requisitioned house just off the Ezbekiya, where
the palaces of the Mameluke Beys were now occupied by
Bonaparte and his various headquarters staffs. This was a

pleasant little house and garden, redolent with orange trees; and these three men, who wore no uniforms, were in luxury— the luxury of conquerors. They were not, most distinctly not, fighting men.

They were members of the Commission of Arts and Sciences, a hundred and seventy in number, summoned by Bonaparte from all the savants of France to accompany the Egyptian expedition. Pierre Marie Fabre was a minor member in the department of native manufacturers. In the fighting before Cairo was taken, when savants shouldered muskets like common soldiers, and everyone was looting the gorgeously arrayed Mamelukes, he had obtained the emerald ring from one of the dead cavaliers—no less a person than Ibrahim Kachef Bey, as he had since learned.

That had been in July. Now it was October, and easy conquest and loot had shattered the morale of the expedition. General Menou, father of the Tricolor, had turned Mohammedan and had established himself at Alexandria with a choice harem; Bonaparte purred to his native title of Sultan el Kebir. Cairo was plundered of Mameluke weapons and curios and treasures. But the emerald ring obtained by Fabre was the prize of all. The emerald was not large and was of poor color, but it was unique.

Duroc and others who knew precious stones had established that it was the Sphinx Emerald, a stone famed from ancient times, figuring in history and romance. Now, in the red sunset, the geologist took the ring, held a lens over the stone, and stared into its heart. He was openly fascinated by what he saw. His features changed and softened; his hard eyes warmed; he spoke almost dreamily.

"Richelieu, the great Cardinal, once owned this stone," he said. "He willed it to his niece, the Duchesse d'Aiguillon—and then it vanished. That was its last appearance; what became of it has never been established."

"I've read of it," said Bonnard, taking the ring and examining it with great attention. "Look! Here inside the circlet is engraving, nearly effaced!"

"I know. It's Arabic. Marcel translated it for me," Fabre put in. "It reads: *'Hasan el-Maghrebi made me'*. Some goldsmith in Morocco, evidently. The work is very crude. It's a hundred and fifty years since Richelieu died, so the stone must have gone from France to Morocco, thence here to Egypt. Pity it can't speak and tell its story."

"It does speak, though not in words," said Duroc. "A man could lose his head over the emerald. Any woman would, assuredly. No one seems to perceive the same things in the stone, either. Wonderful!"

"Not at all," said Bonnard. "I can explain it quite simply."

HE puffed at his pipe for a moment.

Then he began to speak, telling that the unique feature of this stone, which must have come in ancient times from the emerald mines in Upper Egypt, was the flaw that it contained. A flawless emerald seldom or never exists. In this stone the flaws were many; when examined under a glass, or even to the naked eye, they took on the aspect of the Sphinx in profile. It was no mere fancy but an exact duplication—startlingly exact, one of Nature's curious quirks.

"The riddle of the Sphinx is no secret," the historian related. "It represents the Mind—that unknown, wonderful, inexplicable thing we call the Mind. Here in this bit of green beryl we behold a Sphinx amid green fields and hills and landscapes. To some, it is amazing and fascinating beyond belief. Others find it repellent and repulsive. Others find in it a beauty so poignant, so exquisite, that it moves them to tears. Why is this? Because, like the Mind itself, it conveys a sense of the beautiful, the evil, the slippery and evasive—such is its appeal to the human imagination. Each one beholds in it some quality of his own mind. It speaks differently to each."

"The General," said Fabre, "declared that it spelled fame and glory."

Duroc uttered his raucous laugh. "To the Corsican, the greatest thing in the world, the only thing worth while, is glory—his own, of course. The Mameluke woman who pursues you, Pierre—why does she want it?"

"Her messenger said it was a talisman, a good-luck charm, which her father had received from his ancestors."

"Precisely! Any woman would go insane over the stone. Beware of her, I warn you! The Arabs believe an emerald renders all magic powerless. But beryl does have some curious properties—electric, for instance. The sixfold character of the crystal has an extraordinary effect on the refraction and light dispersion—"

The discussion was interrupted by the arrival of an aide from headquarters with orders for Fabre. He opened the sealed sheet,

*"Since we cannot speak as friends," she said
abruptly, "let us talk as enemies under truce."*

headed with the vignette of the Commission. He was ordered
to leave Cairo in the morning with an escort of six men of the
12th Light Foot, and to proceed to the village of El Bakri, some
miles to the east and south, there to make an exhaustive report
on the manufacture of qulla jars, for which the place was
renowned.

There was nothing unusual in this order. The Commission
was composed of writers, sculptors, mathematicians, chemists,
men of all the arts and sciences; its purpose was to prepare for
the colonization of Egypt and the utilization of all its resources.
Already the members were being scattered over the whole

country on various missions; powder factories were being started, and commercial objectives of all sorts were under way.

"Well, I'll be glad to get away for a while," commented Fabre. "But what in the devil's name are qulla jars?"

Bonnard chuckled. "They're the porous water-jars used everywhere in Egypt, made by a secret process. I believe their amazing porosity is gained by mixing certain ashes with the clay. It's an enormous traffic. The people of that village have a monopoly on the manufacture—the jars aren't made there in mass, but the villagers go out and take charge of the various factories, as experts. You're lucky to get away; things are shaping up for trouble, here in the city."

Duroc's laugh cackled, agreeing. "Didn't I say the Corsican was a bad enemy? He knows well enough a revolt is coming, and hopes for it, to establish his own authority in blood! It'll suit his purposes. What's it to him if all the Frenchmen not in barracks here get their throats cut? This is your reward for refusing him the emerald, Pierre."

"Absurd! He's too great a man to be so petty—"

"Great? Bah! You're a young idealist, full of wind and fine theories," Duroc said acidly. "The Corsican is out for himself, first, last and foremost. At Toulon, a soldier beside him was struck by a cannon-ball, drenching him with blood. It gave him the itch, and he's had it ever since. That's why he always sticks a hand inside his coat, so he can scratch his chest. It gave him an itch for glory, too, at anyone's expense—"

In a burst of laughter, the three broke off their discussion and went in to dinner. Nobody in the expedition had any illusions about their leader.

True, Pierre Marie Fabre was young, barely twenty-three, but this was an era of youth. In the six-year-old Republic, all the young men had come to the top. Darkly eager, impetuous, thin-nostriled, Fabre had plunged into the Egyptian adventure like the rest of them, careless of consequences, enthralled by the glamour of it.

His family, a wealthy manufacturing one of Lyons, had been swept away in the Revolution. At the general amnesty he had returned, alone, to build up his career anew. A friend had got him this place, as an expert in manufacturing, and he was building his hopes on the issue of the expedition, which promised fame and fortune to all concerned. But youth was a perilous thing in this army of conquest, just the same.

He had been far from frank with his two comrades. Not only had he been in touch with Amina, the daughter of Ibrahim

Kachef Bey, but he had an appointment to visit her this very evening, on the business of the emerald ring. A slave was to pick him up here and conduct him to her house. Where it was, he had no idea; not far, since it was one of the lesser Mameluke palaces, and these were all grouped nearby.

Risky, of course, and therefore all the more attractive. Hatred for the French was mounting to fever heat in Cairo, fanned white-hot by Turkish agents; tension was increasing, and Bedouins by the thousand were said to be quietly flooding into the city to augment trouble. Any revolt must be a bloody affair, since most of the army was off on detached missions or quartered in barracks outside the city.

THE SITUATION was not helped by the avidity of everyone, from the headquarters staff down, for wine and women. Blondes were no rarity here. The Mameluke ranks had for generations been recruited from Circassian, Georgian and other slaves of white skin, while the Arabs themselves were white as anyone. So the army was hugely enjoying itself, careless of any future reckoning. Yet, as Fabre well judged, a reckoning was imminent.

When, at the appointed time that evening, Fabre stepped out into the street, he was shaved and spruced up hopefully, hat pulled over eyes, and long green riding-coat buttoned to the chin, a small pistol in his pocket and a stout silver-headed cane in hand. A dark figure awaited him—the Kachef slave, a pleasant brown fellow who spoke French. They set off at once, the slave leading the way. Fabre had no fears whatever. The unknown lady had sent an oath upon the Koran that he would have safe-conduct, and he believed her.

Dimly lighted, tortuous narrow streets, strange speech and shapes on all sides, carven cedar balconies overhead echoing with voices, drunken soldiers singing, Nubian flutes and drums making unearthly noises, intent crowds around story-tellers and magicians, lighted mosque-entrances hinting at mystery; tiny open-fronted bazaars thronged with buyers—all very glamorous, no doubt, but Fabre could sense the burning hatred in Turk and Arab eyes as he passed. It troubled him little. These were the conquered; he was of the conquerors, whose artillery yawned from the towering citadel above. These people needed a hard, sharp, bitter lesson of blood that would properly cow them, and they would get it if they gave the Corsican the least excuse.

Fabre and his guide came to the house. Stables occupied the ground floor—to the now vanished Mameluke cavaliers, horses had been a large part of life. Fabre was led into a dimly lighted courtyard and garden, from which stairs mounted to the upper floors of the house, stairs with carven marble balustrades and inlaid cedar screens. On the second floor he was taken into a corridor, and on to a room of some size. The slave took his riding-coat and hat, then left him. No one else had appeared about the place.

Accustomed as he had become to Eastern luxury, Fabre found the room astonishing. Painted beams, cedar lattices, tiled floor and walls, hanging lamps of silver, Persian rugs and pillows, ivory-inlaid tabourettes the shape and size of the huge French army drums, golden dishes of cakes and of sweetmeats, Turkish water-pipes ablaze with jewels—Fabre stood gawking around until, at a slight sound, he turned to see his hostess entering. He bowed.

"Good evening, monsieur," she said in French. "I am Amina, daughter of Ibrahim Bey. Be seated; I am glad to see you."

"I am honored, Leila Amina," he replied, using the Arabic form of address.

She half sat, half reclined, among the pillows. Fabre made a pile of them for himself and sat cross-legged, native fashion. She smiled faintly, helped herself to a sweetmeat, relaxed and studied him.

IN RETURN, Fabre studied her; both of them were frankly curious. He noted her reddish hair and very white skin; a thin gauze veil half covered her face; a magnificent Kashmir shawl was looped about her shoulders; and beneath this he glimpsed, to his amazement, the links of a steel shirt that fell to her hips. Noting his glance, she touched the links.

"The daughter of Ibrahim Kachef was trained to bear arms," she said. "I was as a son to him. My great sorrow is that I was not at his side when he fell. You Franks will yet find that I can use my weapons."

"They would overcome us at the first encounter," Fabre said gallantly. "I think the name Amina means *radiance?* It was well bestowed, lady. Such eyes would put our cannon to silence."

The flattery seemed to please her. Indeed, Fabre half meant his words, for her features were surprising. Her eyes were blue, intensely sharp and bright. While not beautiful, her face, like her voice, was eloquent of strength and character; there was no Oriental languor about her. He could well believe that she could bear arms like any cavalier.

"Since we cannot speak as friends," she said abruptly, "let us talk as enemies under truce, each trusting in the honor of the other, without lies or pretense."

"As you wish, Leila Amina," assented Fabre. "You know my name. I am here as your guest. Must we indeed be enemies?"

"That is for you to choose," she rejoined coolly. "Whether you depart as you came, or stay to make this house your home, is for you to say. You know why I brought you here; it was not for yourself—though you are certainly a pleasing sort of man—but for the ring on your hand. You are here to discuss business."

Fabre blinked slightly. He had anticipated Oriental parley and evasions. He was by no means averse to a romantic adventure, and had rather taken this for granted; but her direct speech and blunt overture, her lack of any preliminaries or small-talk, quite took him aback and left him disconcerted. Duroc, he thought, would have sourly enjoyed this interview.

He put out his hand, and from his finger twisted the ring—a

massive, even clumsy circlet of gold, holding the single stone—
and held it up.

"Is this so important a thing, lady?" he demanded.

"To me, yes," came her blunt reply. "You have worn it; have
lived with it—come, be honest! Do you consider it important,
or would you part with it lightly?"

He nodded thoughtfully. "I understand. Yes, I am not anxious

*"So? The city is alive
with spies. Stores of arms
and powder have been
collected. And you imagine
all this is news to me?"*

to part with it, though many, even our General, have tried to obtain it from me. It's mine, and I keep it."

Her lips curled scornfully.

"Yours? Others have thought the same—my father thought it his. The Moor who stole it from the Sultan of Morocco and brought it to Egypt, thought it his. I say it is mine—whether in my possession or not, it belongs to me!" She checked herself.

"It is really a famous emerald, monsieur," she went on, less excitedly. "Some call it the jewel of desire. It is said that the

Prophet Mohammed—on whom be blessings!—captured the shadow of the Sphinx and confined it in the stone. One beholds things in it. The Sphinx is plainly there, other things less plainly. It is a ring of great magic power. It is worth a high price, which I am prepared to pay. I would not lower myself by cheapening it like a bazaar merchant. I must have it at any cost—and shall."

"Oh!" said Fabre. He resented the pride, the dominance of her; the force and directness of her words nettled him. She was not asking, but commanding, as though any bargaining or pleading were beneath her. An extraordinary woman, a most disturbing woman.

"Your father died under French bullets; its magic power did not save him," he said quietly. "I do not believe in magic, Leila Amina. I do like this emerald, and no one can take it from me."

"That too has been said by others," she replied significantly. "You took it as loot, and as loot it may be taken from you in turn. But let us not come to angry words. My purpose is to purchase the ring from you. I presume you're willing to sell, at a price?"

"Frankly, I'm not sure," he made slow response. "It fascinates me. I have refused large sums for it. I like it. Therefore I can understand what it means to you and why you want it." He paused. "Still, I might part with it—to you. Who knows? I don't know yet what you offer, lady."

SHE SAT looking at him in silence for a long moment; a delicate scent of perfume drifted upon the room from her. Fabre perceived that she was earnest, intent, deadly serious. Somehow the fact impressed him with singular force, made him realize that this interview was no light matter, but grave indeed, at least in her eyes.

"All you Franks, from your General down to your camp cooks, are interested in only two things," she said. "Plunder and—shall I say love? Well, here is wealth." She swept her hand around at the room. "There is more. Ask what you will, and it is yours. Here am I; ask what you will. If I do not please you, there are other women in plenty who can be provided. Your price will be paid. What more is necessary? Give me the ring. You shall have what you will."

Fabre was actually shocked in every nerve as he listened to this starkly realistic offer. Here was no spiced adventure, no glamour, no romance. This girl—for he guessed her to be young—calmly offered her wealth, herself, whatever he desired, in exchange for the ring. It was mere ugly barter; his compliance, his devotion to the grossest material things, was taken for granted.

He flushed angrily. His youthful ideals of romance, his French sense of gallantry, were offended; and in consequence he recoiled where an older man would have considered. His dark eyes sparkled angrily as he made reply.

"You have much to learn about us Franks, Lady Amina. This emerald arouses desire, emotion, makes appeal to the soul; the Sphinx crouching within its heart speaks to the mind and spirit. Can such a marvel be bought like a quarter of beef? Hardly. Beautiful as you may be, desirable as you admittedly are, tempting as might be your wealth, the exchange you propose is a shabby one."

She straightened up, staring with incredulous eyes.

"You cannot refuse! I've offered everything a man could desire!"

"Not at all," he said coldly, perceiving her utter lack of comprehension. "You offer too much, and not enough. You cannot buy things of the spirit with things material. You offer possession, but it is only love that makes possession worth while."

"You are absurd!" She flung back her veil impatiently; her blue eyes flamed. "What you say is nonsense!"

"It is what this jewel says, not I." He tapped the emerald as he spoke. "Nonsense? From your viewpoint, perhaps; not from mine, lady."

She tensed; her muscles gathered; angry passion suffused her face; and for one instant Fabre thought she was about to spring at him. Then, abruptly, she struck the cushions with her fist and relaxed, and even nodded calmly at him.

"Very well, monsieur; you speak like a fool, but I think you are an honest fool," she said, her voice restrained and quiet. "I have still another offer to make. I offer you something even greater, added to the price I have already set before you—the greatest thing of all."

"Yes?" he responded, as she paused. "And what is that?"

"Your life."

He surveyed her, puzzled. "I do not understand, lady."

"We are enemies, monsieur." She lowered her voice. "I want that ring. I must have it! Well, I might threaten you. I might say that I shall regain that ring from your dead hand, as you took it from my father's hand. Instead, I offer you your life. Under my protection it is safe. Accept, and you have nothing to fear."

Fabre smiled. "But my dear lady, as it is I have nothing to fear—"

"Oh, you imbecile!" she exploded almost frantically. "Within three days every Christian in Cairo will be dead! You Franks, all the other Christians here—not one of you remains alive! Is it nothing to you, that I offer you safety?"

He understood, and a chill went through him.

"Nothing." He rose, slipped the ring on his finger, and bowed to her. "Our interview, I think, is ended. I shall not part with the ring. I do not agree with you, Leila Amina, that we are enemies. No Frenchman can accept a woman as an enemy— much less so young and beautiful and gifted a woman. Perhaps we can meet again as friends, and I shall look forward to that happy day."

The finality of his decision was obvious. She made no response, except to clap her hands.

The slave who had conducted Fabre hither came into the room, bringing his hat and riding-coat. Amina curtly ordered him to take the Frank safely home. Fabre departed, bowing to her again from the doorway; she ignored him.

He followed his guide back to the little house he called home, fed the slave and dismissed him. Fabre found that his two comrades had gone to attend a meeting of the Institute of Egypt, Bonaparte's pet society formed from the savants and leaders of the Commission of Arts and Sciences. Both Duroc and Bonnard were members. Fabre was not.

FIVE MINUTES later Fabre was hurrying across the open square of the Ezbekiya to the palace of Elfi Bey, now occupied by Bonaparte. The corporal of the guard sent in his name, and he was conducted to the terrace above the garden. The General and a few of his chiefs were gathered here— General Dupuy, in command of the city, Murat, Dumas, Marmont, Reynier, Cafarelli and others.

"You seek me, citizen?" Bonaparte came up to him. The Republican form of address, soon to be cast aside with the Republic, was still in vogue.

"Yes, Citizen General," Fabre replied. "I learned something tonight of such urgent importance that—"

"Well, then, speak it out!" broke in the scrawny, untidy, sallow little man in his impatient way. "What is this urgent news?"

"It is that within three days the natives expect revolt. Also, a general massacre of all Christians in the city. This comes from a sure source, Citizen General."

The others had gathered around—Dumas, dark mulatto features alive with interest; Reynier, fisting the huge jeweled Mameluke saber he affected; Cafarelli and Dupuy serious and gravely intent. Bonaparte eyed his visitor frowningly.

"So? The city is alive with Turkish agents and English spies. Desert Bedouins are filtering in by the thousand. Stores of arms and powder have been collected. And you imagine all this is news to me?"

"It comes within three days—"

"How do you know this—whence comes this certain information?"

"From the daughter of Ibrahim Kachef Bey."

"She vouchsafed it for love of you, perhaps?" sneered the General.

Fabre flushed. "No, Citizen General. She let slip the words in anger. She was trying to make me part with the ring I had taken from the dead Ibrahim Bey."

"Yes, I remember you and your ring—the magic emerald, eh?" Bonaparte's scrawny features darkened with anger. "You think she let slip the words? Bah! It was done deliberately. These rascals would like nothing better than to learn my plans, my

*Fabre lifted the pistol calmly. He would
make sure of this fellow, anyhow!*

dispositions. Within three weeks, perhaps, will come the
revolt—not within three days. I thank you for the information,
citizen, but we shall not detain you."

With this cool dismissal, Bonaparte turned his back.

Fabre bowed and departed, stung to bitter anger, but word-
less. Let the cursed Corsican think what he liked! Duty was
done.

"Obviously, Bonaparte detests me," thought Fabre, hastening
home. "He's not forgotten my refusal to let him have the ring.

Duroc was right to warn me; I've made an enemy, and a bad one. Well, devil take him!"

Pierre Marie Fabre shared the opinion of many in the army about the Corsican, whose ambition had aroused the fear and hatred of the old revolutionary soldiers of '93. However, upon reaching home he dismissed the whole thing from his mind. Lighting the lamp in the living-room the three friends shared in common, he placed on the table the battered microscope Duroc had brought with him to Egypt.

Even for this day of budding science it was not much of a microscope, being of feeble power, but at least it would enlarge objects appreciably, and this was all Fabre desired at the moment. He placed it beside the light, settled down comfortably to it, took the ring from his finger and placed the emerald beneath the lens-tube.

He focused; now as always, the vision of splendor that opened to his eye made him catch his breath. This fleck of green beryl, cut *en cabochon,* became a landscape of marvel, shot athwart by the shadowy cleavage of its flaws. Those flaws rose, in the center, into the perfect image of the Sphinx seen in profile—a chance formation, of course, yet exact, even to the forepaws—a vivid green shape in a world of green mirage touched with dazzling pinnacles and points of light.

An uneven landscape it was, with clustering hills and precipices, darker depths, strange shimmering, glowing colors caused by the natural dichroism of the crystal. The minute jagged flaws and singularly angular bubbles characteristic of true emerald became monstrous shapes of dispersed radiance. With every shift of light, one beheld new vistas and glories that plucked at the imagination and swept it afar.

What Fabre saw in the stone, beyond that one stately looming figure of the Sphinx, he himself could not say precisely. Like the splendors seen in dream, these were gone as they came, and left only a sense of intense fascination and gripping illusion.

To tear himself away from the spectacle he found difficult, when Bonnard and Duroc returned.

"Hello! At it again, eh?" Duroc exclaimed. "I don't blame you. That damned stone holds a terrific fascination."

"Would you like to have it?" Fabre asked, smiling.

"Name of a black dog! Of course. Who wouldn't? But I've never tried to pry you loose from it."

"You're the only person who hasn't—except Bonnard, there."

"Bah! I wouldn't have the accursed thing; there's evil in it," said the historian, laughing. "What you people find in it, I can't see. But Duroc may cut your throat for it, some night. Well, what news?"

"None that's good. I was warned that the natives expect a revolt within three days, and took the information to headquarters. The Corsican sniffed and turned his back on me."

"Naturally," Duroc snarled. "A revolt is what he wants, to put him firmly in the saddle. He'd turn his artillery on the town, and it'd be something to remember. He'll make himself king here, as he'd be king in France if he got the chance."

"There's always the guillotine for kings, *mes amis*," put in Bonnard.

"The Corsican is too smart for any guillotine. You'll see! Are you off in the morning, Pierre?"

Fabre nodded. He liked the hard, honest, cynical geologist.

"Look, Duroc," he said impulsively. "This emerald—see? Well, if anything happens to me, you shall have it. I'll bequeath it to you, comrade. Understood?"

"Devil take you, I don't want it at that price! Anyhow, you'll outlive me."

Fabre smiled. "I expect to live a long time, but one never knows. Anyhow, remember it—if the unexpected should happen, the ring goes to you."

The three, with jests and laughter, split a bottle of wine and turned in.

THAT NIGHT Fabre dreamed of Leila Amina; at least, she figured in his dreams, but with morning he could not remember them. Her gauze-veiled features lingered in his mind; her voice, her striking eyes, her vest of steel links, combined to make her memory a vivid thing. He wakened to thoughts of her. Perhaps, he reflected, he had really been a fool to reject what she had offered! It was a chance that would never come again.

The party arrived with a spare horse for him—a sergeant and five men, a guide, an interpreter, supplies packed on lead horses, muskets and ammunition and water. Fabre swung up into the high peaked saddle, and with a gay wave of his hand to Bonnard and Duroc, rode away. It was the 29th Vendémiaire, Year VII of the Republican calendar—October 20, 1798.

Unhurried, the party followed the guide to the Bab en-Nasr gate, and out of the city past the Tombs of the Caliphs, taking the road for the Forest of Stone, as the petrified forests among the hills were called. Skirting the Mokattam plateau, they rode to the east and south, making for the hills. Here was open desert, and the sand made slow going.

Gradually they worked in among the hills, whose flanks closed from sight the dome and twin minarets of Saladin's Citadel and mosque. The soldiers, who were unused to horses, groused at everything as usual; the sun waxed high; the heat became terrific. The sense of being lost in the desert hills brought panic; but they were not lost, so the grinning native guide reassured them. Another hour, two hours, would see them at the village of El Bakri, where there was a well of abundant water.

EVENTUALLY THEY did reach the village. It was a small one with a copious well, over which leaned a few date-palms. A ruinous mud wall surrounded the place. Aside from a few naked brats, several hostile-eyed women and two old men, no one was here. Fabre put the interpreter to work and learned that most of the villagers had gone to Cairo for some celebration. Apparently the old men were entirely willing to talk, so the completion of his mission seemed assured. Not today, however. The remainder of the afternoon was given to clearing out several of the mud shacks and cleaning them for occupancy.

The place was eloquent of its livelihood, Beside every house were vats of mud or clay, with stacks of water-jars, lamps and other household articles, fired and ready for sale. Runways of water led from the well to the village street, handy for the mixing of the clay. The women and children sedulously avoided the visitors, and Fabre warned his men against molesting any of them. That evening he got out his writing-materials, ready for work. A day, or at most two, he reckoned, would see his survey completed. The two old men would be the only sources of information in the wretched place, about which sand-hills rose on every side. The loads were unpacked and stored; the sergeant arranged for a night guard over the horses; and Fabre retired to fight fleas during the night hours. He had no dreams and little sleep this night.

He was up with the sunrise, like everyone else: The lovely pure calm sunrise of the Nile valley, touched with soft lights and glowing electric air—that sunrise to which the ancient race dedicated the worship of Horus. All was secure; there had been no alarms; the grumbling of the men had subsided, and they were trying to make friends with the naked children—but unavailingly.

Breakfast over, Fabre went to work. He settled down with his writing-materials under a sunshade of dry palm-leaves; the interpreter brought the two old men, and the inquiry began. Determined to make it a thorough one, Fabre neglected no details about the mixing and baking of the clay, and information poured from the two elders. Meantime, the horses were watered and taken up the wadi to graze upon the clumps of *terfa*, the desert shrub used for fodder.

The sun rose high. Fabre wrote steadily, sending the interpreter to select jars from the village stacks, with which to

illustrate the various mixtures of ashes and clay described to
him. Absorbed in his work, he glanced up in surprise when the
sergeant, an old veteran of the Rhine fighting, came and
knocked out his pipe.

"Citizen Fabre, will you ask that interpreter what these mis-
called females are up to, with their brats?"

"Eh?" Fabre glanced around. He saw that the children were
being assembled near the well, at the other end of the village,
by their mothers. At this moment the two old men rose, gathered up their voluminous rags, and strode hastily away toward
the others. Fabre called the interpreter, who was off getting
jars—but next moment everything broke into fluid motion.
Women, naked children, and the two old men all went flowing
over the ruinous wall like so many rats, and away up the wadi
fast as they could pelt. The soldiers and the interpreter shouted
after them in vain—they only scurried the faster.

"What the devil are they up to?" muttered the sergeant,
staring after them. "Ah, plague take the lot of 'em. Look there!
Hi, you fellows! Fire over their heads, quickly!"

Too late! What happened now was swift and unexpected.
From the sand-ridges beside the wadi spurted rolling tufts of
smoke; even before the sound of the shots reached him, Fabre
saw the two men guarding the horses pitch to the sand. The
covey of women and children scattered like quail and vanished;
so did the horses. Far beyond musket-shot, horsemen appeared
rounding up the scattered beasts.

The four soldiers left in the village, seeing their comrades
thus shot down and themselves set afoot, burst into torrential
oaths and shouts of fury. The sergeant calmed them with cool,
swift orders; he seized a musket and passed it to Fabre, then
took charge. The guide and interpreter hid themselves in the
houses.

"Six of us here, guns for all.... Steady, you bastards, save your
breath! Two of you to the wall with me. The other three stay

back, hold your fire, be ready to reload fast. They'll be on us in a minute—hold your fire, damn you, till I give the word!"

Everything passed with incredible rapidity. Fabre, fumbling to load his musket, scarcely had the ball rammed down when a dozen or more horsemen appeared up the wadi; others came to join them from one side, and swept down toward the village. Thanks to the cool old sergeant, the men had recovered from their panic and fury, and stood ready. The veteran spoke again.

"Careful, now; don't waste a ball. Aim for the horses, then reload. Pay 'em for our two comrades, there!"

They were coming at the gallop, with shrill yells of *"Allah!"* Two of the foremost riders wore the Mameluke panoply—steel helmets and shirts; the others were desert Arabs. They flourished long guns and opened a furious but totally ineffective fire as they came charging. Fabre, who had brought a brace of pistols from town, hurried to get them loaded. The sergeant and his two men, at the mud wall, were aiming carefully.

Over twenty of the horsemen, and more trailing from the sandhills to join them. They came in a wild rush, sabers out, guns waving, voices screaming, evidently thinking to take the village at the first sweep. Suddenly the sergeant's long musket banged. One of the *two* Mameluke leaders plunged down. The other two muskets spoke, and two more horses fell. The sergeant, hastily reloading, waved a hand to Fabre.

"Come along, all of you! Don't waste a shot."

With his companions, Fabre ran to the wall. Several of the Arabs, afoot, were hurling themselves through the gaps; the sergeant and his two men met them with bayonets fixed. The three fresh muskets poured their fire into the huddle of figures. Fabre seized his two pistols, aimed and fired deliberately, and this broke the attack. Leaving half a dozen wounded or dead, and several horses pitching and screaming, the Arabs fled for cover. Among the dead was one of the mail-clad Mamelukes. Fabre left the shelter of the wall, darted to the glittering figure, and catching up helmet and sabre, brought them in as trophies. Two wild shots whistled overhead.

"Well, that did it," observed the sergeant. "Now things will get tough. They'll come in from all sides. Everybody scatter out along the wall, take plenty of powder and ball, and don't waste ammunition. If we're rushed, gather around the well."

Two hurt Arabs, dragging themselves away, were shot. From the *terfa* brush and sand gullies a dropping fire was opened on the village, without damage. Posts were taken, and the day that had opened to excitement of battle settled into monotony of sniping warfare, with only an occasional shot returned.

INSUFFERABLY THE sun blazed down. Noon came, passed. Fabre dragged the guide and interpreter from hiding, and put them to work as cooks. Unexpectedly, in the full afternoon heat, figures on foot burst from shelter on two sides of the village and came in with a desperate charge. Several of them were dropped, three or four gained a gap in the wall, and saber clanged on bayonet until they broke and fled again. But two of the soldiers had been wounded badly.

After this, nothing happened. The battle had settled into a siege. The attackers worked close, and their fire began to be accurate and deadly.

Fabre consulted with the sergeant, as the afternoon wore along. With the horses gone, their chance of escape was gone also; to leave the shelter of the village, with its copious well, would be madness. To judge by the figures visible beyond range, the number of the enemy was increasing; more than once, Fabre had glimpsed the glittering shape of the remaining Mameluke afar, evidently disposing his men. A messenger to bring help? Neither the guide nor the interpreter was willing to venture it; no other could regain the city.

The shadows were lengthening, and the sun was low, when everyone came to the alert at the sound of shots. They came closer. Presently Fabre discerned a horseman coming up the wadi at a gallop, while Arab guns banged at him from either side. He headed for the village at a desperate burst of speed, hanging low in the saddle, and his uniform was recognized as that of the Guides, commanded by Sulkowski.

Muskets blazed to cover his approach. His horse, streaming blood from a dozen wounds, went down thirty yards from the wall. Two men dashed out to bring him in, and he came staggering between them. Two balls had gone through his body; he was done for.

"Orders—to return!" he gasped out. "Citizen Duroc sent me—no use—all is lost! Revolt everywhere. Sulkowski is dead—Dupuy was cut to pieces—all Christians massacred—the sick and wounded killed—Arabs have the city—"

His head lolled over, in midsentence, and he died.

At this terrible information the little group looked one at another, knowing the worst. Revolt had caught the French by surprise. No help would come now; their fate was sealed. The sergeant broke in upon their frightful silence with an oath.

"Get to your places, everyone—to the walls! We're not dead yet. *Mort de Dieu,* look alive, you scoundrels! I'll arrange later for sentries to watch the night. Gather everything you can find and build fires! Quick about it, now—all the wood you can discover in this accursed village!"

They broke into action. Every scrap of wood in and about the houses was collected. With darkness, fires were lighted, sentries posted, and those off duty got some repose. No attack came; none the less, that was a frightful night. Toward dawn, one of the wounded men died.

Morning came; the sun mounted; and more natives arrived to swell the attacking ranks. A hundred or more were in full sight, sitting like vultures on the heights, while others kept up a steady fire on the village. Clouds, rarely seen here, drifted over the sky. It was mid-morning when the rumble of thunder sounded—a phenomenon almost unknown in Egypt. A peal ripped across the sky. Then a shout broke from the sergeant.

"Listen! The guns!"

Guns indeed—artillery on the distant citadel, hurling death into the Arab city, blending with and prolonging the thunder. The Corsican was at work; but what help here? None, except a furtive word that the sergeant brought to Fabre.

"Sorry, citizen. The powder's running low. Save it."

TOWARD NOON, came the attack. There must have been two hundred, pressing forward at a wild run under cover of a heavy fire. One of the soldiers was killed. The muskets smashed into them; a grenade, brought along by one of the men, exploded in the massed ranks. Again they broke and ran, while bullets hailed in from the sandy heights around.

The sergeant came to Fabre.

"Well, citizen, this looks like it. We haven't a dozen charges left."

"We've done our best," said Fabre simply.

Duroc had sent to save him—good old Duroc! He looked down at his hand. Who would get the emerald now? That Mameluke girl had spoken truly; it would be taken from him as he had taken it. The end was coming. Curiously enough, Fabre knew this, yet he could not realize it clearly; one never does.

His eye fell on one of the clay-vats nearby, and a laugh came to his lips. He took some of the clay and mixed it with water, making a firm mud. Of this he fashioned a miniature pyramid. From the ring he pried out the emerald, and thrust the green stone firmly into the heart of the little mud-pyramid, smoothing over the mud above it. When the thing was finished to his liking, he took his knife and with the point began to scratch letters in the soft mud.

"For Hector Duroc, Membre de l'Institut," he scratched, then his initials and the date. On another of the pyramid's sides he scratched the word *"morituri,"* but there was no room for the entire quotation. *"We who are about to die"*—well, that was enough! Some one would find this, and Duroc would get it

eventually, a legacy from the dead. Duroc would understand. He would look inside the pyramid for the Sphinx.

Viewing his work with satisfaction, Fabre laid it aside in the sun to dry and harden, amid a pile of the village wares. The afternoon was lengthening. Shouts and yells sounded; more Arabs had come riding up; bullets were pouring in upon the fated village; and powder-smoke drifted over the wadi. The sergeant appeared.

"Come along to the well, citizen. Only two more of us now—Lemaire just got his. Looks like a rush coming."

They ran from house to house, sheltering against the whistling balls, and reached the well. Two more men stood there; the muskets of the dead had been gathered and loaded with the last charges. The Arabs were assembling.

"Well, everybody, here's luck on the other side!" the sergeant sang out. A burst of yells drowned his voice, and the rush came—wild faces, guns and sabers waving, the name of Allah echoing to heaven.

None of the defenders uttered a word. They were too busy firing the muskets and fixing bayonets. In the forefront of the oncoming rush, Fabre discerned the mailed figure of the Mameluke, long curved saber in hand.

They were almost to the wall—they were over it, surging in at the gaps. The sergeant fired his last shot, clubbed the musket and swung into the sabers and wild faces. He was down. Fabre had his one pistol left. He saw the Mameluke coming for him and lifted the pistol, calmly. He would make sure of this fellow, anyhow!

Recognition stabbed into him; his finger slid from the trigger! That face! Those eyes! It was she, Amina herself! A smile touched his lips, and he lowered the pistol. It was his last act....

He was still smiling, faintly, when Duroc, Bonnard and their detachment of Guides found him next day. The village was deserted, save for the dead. The cursing Frenchmen collected the bodies of their own for burial. Bonnard and the geologist stood apart.

"He was no fighting man. Why did it have to come to him here?" burst out Duroc, with a volley of furious oaths. He was white and strained, almost beside himself.

"I went through his clothes," Bonnard said. "There was nothing. He left no word. Did you see the empty ring on his hand? The stone's gone—probably smashed."

"Be damned to it," said Duroc roughly. "I wasn't thinking about that. I'd give a dozen emeralds for him—to have him back. Damn it, the boy was my friend!"

"The best we can do is to see him buried decently," said Bonnard.

They did it, and rode away again, and no one noticed the little sun-baked pyramid of dried clay, shoved amid the stock of village pots.

XVII

THE BRIDE OF THE SPHINX

Now almost in our own day the Sphinx
Emerald turns up in Cairo to work its
malign magic in a memorable drama.

I FOUND THAT by any standard postwar Cairo was a tough place. It was booming with gamblers, hashish-runners, wealth, Levantine riffraff of all sorts, and hatreds. Not only the half-scotched racial and religious hatreds of the old days, but the newer hatred of Pan-Arabs for Christians, of Syrians for French, of Greeks for English, and so on. As an American, and as traffic agent for the new Consolidated Airlines, I was fairly immune to these passions; but blood was shed of nights, and the fine art of murder was being carried to a 33° peak with little pretense of concealment.

Getting the local offices established for my company was a slow business, and I had plenty of time to see the sights—which of course I had seen often enough during the war, when our first tanks dropped in to lend a hand. Running into Tom Keating in Cairo was pure accident. One morning he came walking into the hotel dining-room while I was at breakfast, and recognizing me, came straight to my table.

"Jack Hawkins! Never expected to see you here again—this is simply great!" he exclaimed heartily.

I would never have known him. We had become good friends during the final Alamein campaign, when his unrivaled knowledge of the desert had been of immense value to our tank people. Tom Keating had been doing archaeological work in Upper Egypt for some years, and in those days was a stalwart, handsome giant. Now he was a frail shadow of himself, massive frame shrunken, face deeply lined and leathery, with the rapt distance-eyes of the desert-dweller. But when he dropped into a chair and we gripped hands, his radiant smile broke out in all its old charm.

"I'm glad, glad," he said. It struck me that he was lonely—a strange thing for Sahib Keating, as his English crowd used to call him. We chatted for a bit, until I asked what he was doing now. He gave me an odd unsmiling look.

"Seeking, Hawk. Just seeking. I've been tracking down something that doesn't exist, you'd say offhand; yet I've found it. Something so fantastic that they all term me a fool. Something

I've now proved true, though I doubt if my findings will be accepted. That's one thing. Beyond it lies another search even more fantastic, for something I can't ever hope to find."

KEATING WAS very much the scholar, but he was an idealist, a bit of a dreamer, apt at strange fancies and odd imaginings. In the war days we had been quite close, and the momentary magic of this unexpected meeting drew us close again, so I did not hesitate now to put the question bluntly.

"Herodotus made no mention of
a second Sphinx," I said.

"What is it you've found, Sahib?"

He hesitated, then gave me another of his oddly intent looks. "The other Sphinx."

"What do you mean?" I suspected some leg-pulling. "Not another Great Sphinx, surely?"

"Identical. Precisely the same, built from the same plans—"

"Built? Nonsense! The Sphinx wasn't built, but carved out of rock," I broke in.

"Partly built, Hawk. And the temple between its paws was built."

"But, Sahib! As far back as history runs, the Great Sphinx has been unique, the one and only!"

"You're mistaken, old chap," he said briefly. Then I knew he was in dead earnest, and a silence fell between us. The other Sphinx? He might as well have said the other Moon!

I am pretty well read; had another Sphinx ever existed, I would have heard about it. No such thing is mentioned by Herodotus or other ancient writers; no such thing has ever been known. Of course, both Greeks and Egyptians made small sphinxes of various kinds, with different sorts of heads, but the Great Sphinx has always stood absolutely alone.

"I know." Keating spoke abruptly, with a weary air. "You're like the rest. You think I'm mad, out of my head."

I did; there was nothing else to think. But the hurt in his eyes stung me into sharp and fervent denial.

"I don't—not for a moment! I know you too well. But I don't savvy it, Sahib. If you say it's so, okay. Lay down the cards and show me."

He warmed visibly. "Thanks, old fellow. I'll do just that. Not a very simple matter, though. There are involutions and complications."

"A woman?"

"*The* woman, yes. Also, an emerald that disappeared a hundred and fifty years ago, when Napoleon's army occupied Egypt. No ordinary stone, but an historic emerald, famed in legend and story—a unique thing, a freak of nature. Surely you've heard of the Sphinx Emerald?"

Poor Keating—hipped on this Sphinx notion; must be a monomania with him, I thought. Yet during thousands of years the Great Sphinx has affected the imagination of men—even the ancient Egyptians knew little more about the critter than we do—in a vital manner; so Keating was just one more victim.

"The name of the Sphinx Emerald strikes a familiar chord, somehow," I replied, "but I can't place it. Probably read about it somewhere."

He nodded. "Probably—in the pages of Plutarch's 'Morals,' for instance. Or in Eusebius, in Agricola, in Fernand's 'Cleopatra,' in the 'Lapidarium' of Patkanov, in the travels of Tavernier. Richelieu bequeathed it to his niece; Coeur-de-Leon won it in the Holy Land; then Alexander took it from the scepter of Darius—I could go on endlessly about the thing!"

"Are you talking about an actual emerald?" I asked, staring at him.

"An actual emerald, an actual Sphinx," he replied. "I presume you know that a flawless ruby or emerald is practically non-existent?"

I nodded. "Of course; ain't no such animal in a beryl crystal. Corundum, either. Why?"

"What ruins other jewels makes this emerald unique. It has enormous flaws, even visible to the naked eye. Viewed from either side, these flaws take on the exact shape of the Sphinx in profile. The thing has an hypnotic effect."

"How do you know? Have you ever seen it?"

"I tell you it's been lost for a hundred and fifty years," he replied irritably. "I'm giving you a consensus of the reports on it—the facts. There's legend enough besides, heaven knows! It seems to have exerted a peculiar influence on the imagination, as though merely gazing on that shadowy sphinx-image in the

*The woman in the case was Linda Grey, the
English cinema star—radiantly beautiful,
with a slightly calculating eye.*

stone were enough to start a flow of the most fantastic thoughts imaginable."

"Auto-hypnosis," I suggested.

"Of course. Well, when last seen, the emerald was in a miserable little village out in the Mokattam hills—the empty hills south and east of the city. I've established this much. I have a camp near the spot, and come into town a couple of times a month for mail and supplies. If you like, I'll run you out there now, and show you my data on the other Sphinx. You can return this evening, or tomorrow."

I was delighted by his offer, and said so to him....

The village, El Bakri by name, was at some distance from Cairo, so Keating arranged to meet me in half an hour with his car, an old Army jeep that could negotiate the sandy tracks or even the open desert without trouble. Those desolate, empty hills overlooking the Nile valley from the eastward have not changed since Egypt was born. Upon this, we parted.

Keating had said no more about the woman in the case, and I was curious as to her connection with his mania, for so I regarded it. Here, as it chanced, luck popped up to assist me. I was asking for mail at the hotel *bureau* when two people paused just beside me to light cigarettes. The man was young, swarthy, rather horsy in dress and air, arrogant and with bejeweled hands. I never fancied men who wore jewels. But his companion—

If I say that she was Linda Grey, the English cinema star, it may mean little to you. Instead, I will say that she was a radiantly beautiful young woman, fresh and lovely as the dawn, with a slightly calculating eye and repulsively heavy lipstick. They passed on, and as the desk-clerk handed over my mail, I asked:

"Wasn't that the famous Linda Grey?"

"Indeed, yes," he assented. "She is occupying one of the river-suites. The gentleman with her is the big cotton broker, James Malek. His grandfather was Malek Pasha, who owned half of Upper Egypt, in his day."

I THOUGHT no more of it until, while waiting on the

hotel veranda, I saw the same couple out in front. They were getting into a huge flashy yellow Isotta, when along came Keating. He was driving a tiny, shapeless, colorless old jeep fitted with bulging low-pressure tires for desert work.

He halted beside the Isotta. Obviously all three were of old acquaintance, for Linda greeted Tom Keating with intimate cordiality; I could almost see her turn on the charm full force. Malek seemed annoyed, to put it mildly. Keating ignored him and looked ten years younger as he spoke with the girl, all his heart shining in his eyes. She broke into a gay laugh, and her voice reached me briefly.

"Very well, Sahib, if you find it for me, I'll keep my word!"

"Not much, my lady," intervened Malek, almost savagely. "I'll have a thing or two to say about that!"

Linda turned to him with cool, arrogant insolence. While I did not catch her words, her look was enough; she put him in his very sulky place, and Keating grinned amiably. After a bit more talk, Malek tooled the sporty Isotta away, and I descended the steps to save Keating the trouble of parking. The encounter had left him jubilant and enthused; he chatted brightly as the old jeep bounced us out the city streets and past the Mameluke tombs, gaining the road for the hills.

I scarcely listened to him. In that encounter the tragedy of his position had been revealed to me, merely by faces and gestures and looks. Linda Grey was the woman in the case. That he had fallen for her heart and soul was only too evident; he was that type of man. But she had not fallen for him. Her half-tolerant, half-amused manner told its own story.

PROBABLY, I reasoned, she was using him to egg on this Gippo, whose Levantine soul would be alarmed and infuriated at finding an Englishman in his path. But the Englishman was dog-poor. The Levantine was Croesus-rich, and was of course accepted in Egyptian circles as a gentleman; in the eyes of Islam, all races and colors are equal.

"I'm based at El Bakri for two reasons," Keating said, as we jounced along the road to the hills; "First, because a well at the village gives us a necessary water supply. Second, because the site of the other Sphinx was close by, and it was at El Bakri that the Sphinx Emerald was last seen."

As though to forestall any comment from me, he went on to tell about the loss of the emerald, giving it as fact.

When Napoleon's army smashed the colorful array of the Mamelukes at the Battle of the Pyramids, a dead Mameluke chief was plundered by Pierre Fabre, a junior member of the Commission of Arts and Sciences that accompanied the army; and among his loot was the emerald. It was set in a ring, which he wore. Later, one of the French savants identified the gem as the famous Sphinx Emerald, and many efforts were made to buy the ring from him, but Fabre refused to part with it. He had even refused a large sum offered by Bonaparte himself.

During the native rebellion against the French, Fabre commanded a half-dozen men stationed at the outpost of El Bakri. Attacked, they held off the Arabs for a day or two, until their ammunition ran out, then were rushed and sabered. The emerald had vanished and was not found on Fabre's body. The Arabs, who had always regarded the stone with superstitious awe, claimed to know nothing about it; and since the entire party of French had been wiped out, none remained to tell any tales.

"And that's that," Keating concluded. "I don't expect to find it, of course. It may now be on the finger of some Arab who doesn't dream what a wonder-jewel it is. It'll turn up again, as it has ere now, after a century or so, perhaps in Siam, perhaps in Russia. Well, forget it, and we'll come back to realities. The other Sphinx, at least, couldn't be lost overnight and leave no trace."

"You haven't really found it?"

He broke into a gay laugh.

"Haven't I, though—and the most wonderful woman in the world to boot! But there's El Bakri ahead. The camp is only a half-mile up the wadi."

A bullet whistled past...

I was out; and then I just ran....

Except for modern Government-enforced sanitary improvements, I suppose that mud-hut village had not changed in five hundred years. Remnants of an ancient wall could be seen surrounding it. Flies and naked brats and pottery abounded. There were vats of clay brought from somewhere, for the pottery-making, and a few scraggly trees surrounded the well. We passed without lingering, following a sandy track along the wadi, seeing nothing but patches of *terfa*, the thorny camel-fodder growth, and sand-rises.

By comparison, the tents for which we now headed looked like palatial luxury—three of them, with sunshades outspread, and a couple of deft Arab servants who knew their business. He took me to his work-tent, complete with table and camp-chairs, and we settled down. I was surprised to find how early the morning still was; and the breeze we got here put Cairo's heat to shame. Nor was any sand blowing; the day was clear.

ALONG THE line of these Mokattam hills, sand blows like a thousand devils at work; this is why the district has been an empty waste from time out of mind, afar from travel routes a bleak range of sand-blown hills overlooking the Nile valley. These hills and the savage mountains behind that run clear to the Red Sea were well known to the ancients, and sent rare stone and marble to adorn the palaces of Rome; but the wave of Arab conquest that destroyed everything in its path left them more nakedly desert than ever. Roman mines and marble quarries may still be found there, just as the workmen abandoned them.

"Now I'll give you the whole picture, Hawk." Keating slapped a dispatch-case on the table and opened it, spilling out papers, geodetic survey charts, notes and bits of papyrus in scrolls and fragments.

"About the year 1440 A.D.," he said, "the historian Al Makrizi wrote a history of the Arab conquest of Egypt; it is one of our main sources of information on the period. In it he mentions the fanatic Mahmud Saim-ed-Dahr, who hacked the features of the Sphinx to their present inept expression. He also tells how the invading Arabs found a second Great Sphinx in these hills, facing westward. The Bride of the Sphinx, they named it. Later, an emir of Sultan Ibn Kalaoun destroyed every vestige of it, seeking treasures."

He paused, got his pipe alight and resumed.

"I found these yarns in El Makrizi and believed them, and attempted to verify them, with no luck. The search became a mania with me. Then I bought from the Department of Antiquities, that oversees all the digs, this fragmentary papyrus." From the table he took the papyrus scroll and opened it. Fragmentary, yes, but silked and repaired with consummate skill.

"This," he went on, "came from the tomb of one Nefer, governor of the city of On, a highly important place in the days of Rameses the Great. They said it gave no particular information and was of negligible value. But I made my own translation."

"And struck pay dirt?" I asked.

He smiled. "It speaks of the Sphinx standing at the entrance to the hills called karath Semes—sacred to Semes. These very hills. Semes, I take it, was a primitive deity. It, like the present Great Sphinx, was built by a King Ra-nefer-ses, one of the kings who ruled before known history began."

"Herodotus made no mention of a second Sphinx," I said.

"He didn't mention any Sphinx at all. Look it up."

"Well," I ventured, "I have always thought Cheops built it."

Smiling, Keating tapped the papyrus. "He built the Great Pyramid, Hawk. The Sphinx was there long before him, but he stole the credit and left his own name as builder—a bit of larceny common to all the Pharaohs. This papyrus speaks of the Sphinx that stood here, the second one, as ruined and forgotten. Probably it was completely covered by the sand, and later, when the Arabs came along, it had been uncovered. The temple probably still exists below us," he added, pointing to the sand around.

"And the papyrus proves that a second Sphinx did exist?" I asked.

"To me, yes, but not to others. Anciently, the present or eastward-facing Sphinx was called the temple of Horus, the rising sun; this one was the temple of Horus, the setting sun —it faced westward. Remember that translations of the hiero-glyphics, like those of Chinese ideographs, may differ vastly. I'm afraid excavations must be made here before my theories are accepted. Want to visit the site?"

"Absolutely!"

"We've time to spare before our guests come," Keating glanced at his bony wrist. "Pop into the jeep, and I'll have you there in ten minutes. Did I mention that we have guests for tiffin? In order to get one, I had to invite two."

I could guess. "Linda and the Levantine?"

"Levantine!" He barked a jolly laugh. "Good name for the swine. He's thoroughly bad hat, I fear, but we preserve amicable relations. He's putting important money into her next produc-tion—they're sending a company out from Elstree to do an Egyptian picture—so she's being polite to him at the moment."

WE BUNDLED into the jeep. Poor guy! The wool was neatly pulled over his eyes, I thought. Linda Grey was playing the millionaire for bigger stakes than a mere contribution to her cinema record, if I was any judge; and I wondered why she bothered dangling a nonentity like Keating on the string. The explanation was not long delayed.

We were east and a bit south of Cairo, on the way to the Petrified Forest; presently the jeep bounced through deep loose sand around the shoulder of a wadi and halted. El Bakri was hidden from sight. The two minarets of the Cairo citadel-mosque pricked the sky, but the plateau and hills shut out the immense view of the Nile valley that could be had from the upper hills.

"The Great Sphinx is opposite, though we can't see him from here," Keating said. "The site of his Bride is thirty feet ahead of us, where those stones show; the two faced each other. It just happens that shifting sands have exposed some of the stones; no doubt the entire Sphinx was covered at times by sand. That might account for its having been forgotten in ancient days."

WE WALKED to where half-buried fragments of reddish limestone showed, wind-scooped out of the sand. A magnificent site for such an image, certainly, and well had the Arabs named it the Bride of the Sphinx. A few blocks of stone half emerging into sight—nothing else remained. Keating had found no inscriptions.

Yet he was quite jubilant. Actually he had proven nothing at all, but I refrained from saying so. Only costly excavations would afford proof that another Great Sphinx had ever stood here. To get away from the unpleasant subject, I spoke of Linda Grey, since he had already mentioned her, asking if she were interested in the discovery.

"Not in the least, but she's mad about emeralds," Keating responded, "and chiefly about the Sphinx Emerald. She's read of it and has a sketch of the gem made by Leonardo da Vinci. It came, originally, from Cleopatra's emerald mines, somewhere back in these hills. They were worked ages before Cleopatra's time, of course. Linda is convinced that I know where the stone is."

"Why, have you some clue?"

He smiled ruefully. "Not a ghost of one. I just opened my mouth too wide. You know what damned fool things a man talks when he's in love. Bits of brag and boast and so forth. Also, when I was speaking of the Sphinx, she thought I meant the Sphinx Emerald, and got all lit up about it. I didn't have the good sense to undeceive her," he added.

"Talked yourself into a jam, have you?"

He nodded. "She and Malek both believe that I know where to put my hand on the emerald, or have already located it. A sheer impossibility, of course. One thing led to another until Linda—well, she said that if I found the emerald for her, she'd take me with it. And she meant the words; she's wild about emeralds. Not very flattering, of course, but beggars can't be choosers, you know."

POOR DEVIL—HE was so infatuated that he had lost, if ever he'd possessed, all proper focus on the cinema star. I had read enough about Linda Grey—and my one glimpse of the gal had confirmed it—to know, what an utterly beautiful, but selfish, heartless angel she really was; totally self-centered, if you like to put it that way. To her, Linda Grey was the only person in the world who mattered a tinker's dam.

When we got back to camp, it was still early. So, as Keating was bound for the village to haul some fresh water in the jeep, I went along. Those natives, said he, had inherited a genius for pottery-making; El Bakri pottery had been famous through many generations.

"So are their faked antiquities," he warned. "So watch your step."

We drove back to the village. Sure enough, every house had its quota of pottery drying in the sun or stacked for sale. My romantic friend conjured up visions of Pierre Fabre and his companions making their last stand along the remains of the wall, and dying under the Mameluke sabers. Then he departed to the well with a couple of men to get his water supply, and I wandered about the place looking at the sights.

A HORDE of naked youngsters assailed me for baksheesh; whining females besought me to buy their wares. With much pretense of furtiveness, men brought out scarabs, beads, images and other "anticas"—dealing in real antiques was illegal. I was not having any of their fake bootleg relics; yet many of the things were cleverly done, and a great many of the sun-baked pottery bits looked really old. The stacks included everything from children's toys to glazed tiles.

"Veree old, veree old," droned a voice at my elbow. I turned to see a dirty-gowned old fellow holding a tray of imitation Mameluke lamps and other trumpery. But one small piece caught my eye for its very crudity. It represented a miniature pyramid, and seeing markings on the sides, I picked it up. Then, as I read the lettering that had been scratched in the soft clay before baking, my heart jumped.

"Veree old, effendi, real antica," droned the voice. "Made here long ago. Lucky charm, cheap, one piaster."

I handed over a piaster and pocketed the little pyramid, saying nothing to Keating about it till we were back at camp, where the two servants were preparing a sumptuous repast. We settled down to await the guests, and I produced the pyramid. Keating scoffed at my folly, until I began to read the scratches to *him*.

"*R. F. And VII*—seventh year of the French Republic, or 1798, eh? Here's the word '*moriturus*'—and here are initials and a name—'*Fabre, P.M.*' And—"

"My good Lord! Let me see that thing," burst out Keating, reaching for it. "Pierre Marie Fabre—that was his name, sure enough. What the devil!"

"Veree old antica, made here long ago," I mimicked, wickedly amused by the excited interest. "Apparently this relic has been under your nose all the time, Sahib."

"Good God—look at these scratches! '*For Hecter Duroc, Membre de l'Institut*'—that means the Institut d'Egypte, Bonaparte's little pet clique of savants! And this word '*moriturus*'—understand? We who are about to die—why, Hawkins, Fabre made this himself! It's been kicking around the damned village ever since!"

"So what?" I demanded.

He looked up sharply.

"He must have had a reason. Lying around, waiting for the end—taking a handful of clay, shaping it into a pyramid, scratching these things on it, putting it in the sun to dry—it may even have been fired. But why? Why?"

"And you an old soldier! Just to take his mind off his troubles and to leave some memento behind when the end came, of

*"The trouble with you, Linda," I said, "is that you
think your beauty is currency that no one can resist."*

course!" I took the relic and was inspecting it when a car honked
and the Isotta hove in sight. After that, we forgot the pyramid.

Linda Grey was quite gracious to me, deliciously *intime* with
Keating, and the old charm was turned on full flow. I fancied
a lurking mockery in her eye, and my suspicion was justified by
Malek's oily manner. He showed no trace of surliness but
chatted along eagerly, evincing keen interest in Keating's work
and displaying a dazzling gold front tooth in constant smiles.
So infinitely purring and agreeable was he, that it seemed
obvious he was now perfectly sure of Linda and no longer regarded Keating as a serious rival. She must have got down to
words of one syllable with him during the morning, I reflected
cynically.

The luncheon was enjoyable. We were nearly through the
meal when Linda mentioned cigarettes—a special Khedivial
brand that she fancied, most expensive too. Keating announced
that he had fetched a box especially for her and had left the
package in the jeep. So, being on the off-tent side of the awning,

I jumped up and went to get it. The jeep was behind the tents. I hurried to it, not without an angry thought about spoiled brats who were born to gaspers and now had to be served with Gippo brands made for royalty. Just as I came to the jeep, I turned my ankle in loose sand.

Thrown off balance, I was flung heavily against the car. My hip received a sharp bruise as something smashed in my coat pocket. Recovering, I thrust hand in pocket and swore in dismay. The miniature pyramid was now only a jumble of dust and clay particles.

Drawing out my fist, filled with the ruined handiwork of the late Pierre Fabre, I stared at the crumbled pieces. I looked again, made certain of what I had glimpsed, then hurriedly pocketed the debris. Seizing the package of cigarettes from the jeep, I strode back to the tents and, with an effort, calmly resumed my seat.

"But I say, old chap," Malek was saying in his oily way, "you promised to show us a real discovery if we ran out to tiffin! What's up, eh?"

Keating took the package, opened the tin of cigarettes, and placed them at Linda's elbow. He meant to show them the site of the other Sphinx, of course.

"Well," he began, "I've gone over the story with Hawkins, and—"

"The truth is," I cut in quickly, "he did have a big surprise to show all of us, but took it to a jeweler this morning to have it cleaned, and can't get it back until we return to Cairo later today. So we can't display it until tonight."

"A surprise?" repeated Linda, smiling at me, while Keating regarded me uncertainly. "Something he has discovered?"

"A real find," I assented. "Did you ever hear of a Lieutenant Fabre, who was killed here in Bonaparte's time—"

"Mr. Hawkins!" Linda fairly let out a whoop. "You can't mean—you're not talking about the Sphinx Emerald? It hasn't been found?"

"Oh, yes," I rejoined. "The Sahib, here, found it. You'll see it tonight if you wish."

The careless words certainly raised hell with all hands. Tom Keating was shocked and utterly aghast. Linda turned to him with a bubbly froth of excited questions, and the thing I saw unveiled in her eyes, the sharp cupidity and avid desire, was ugly. The dark features of Malek, however, became darker and flashed with sudden passion. I was amazed by the anger and suppressed fury aglow in his eyes. The active force of hatred, so vividly alive in the man, was startling to see.

KEATING WAS knocked off his pins by my words. He stammered desperately under Linda's fire of questions until I came to his rescue. I assured her that we really had the Sphinx Emerald in hand and said we would be glad to show her the stone that evening.

Malek intervened. "But we are going to the palace—King Farouk's reception, Linda! And you're to be guest of honor—"

"Bother the King's reception!" she cried. She was all on fire; the avid thing in her eyes was nakedly revealed. "That's unimportant—this is something wonderful! Oh, I know you went to a lot of trouble arranging it, James; I'm grateful, really—but this is greater than anything. What time can we get away from the palace?"

"Not before eleven," Malek said, sulky and lowering.

"All right! Sahib, where can we meet you then?"

"Wherever you say." Keating was not happy about it, and gave me a look that meant trouble. "You and Hawkins are both stopping at the Nile Palace—why not there?"

She clapped her hands. "Good! Good! We'll come right back there after the reception—meet in my suite at eleven-fifteen!"

It being thus settled, tongues clicked fast; she and Malek both wanting to hear about the discovery of the gem. On the plea that other parties must be protected and we could not talk until certain arrangements were made, I promised them the full story that evening. This was no brilliant invention but it placated them; Malek, I perceived, had a deep interest in the emerald himself.

Our excited guests departed, and no sooner had the yellow Isotta got under way than Keating charged at me in a tumult of angry dismay.

"What in hell's name d'you mean by it, Hawk? If this is your Yankee notion of a joke it's in deuced bad taste—"

FOR REPLY, I emptied my jacket pocket, dumping dust and clay fragments on the table. I stirred the pile with my finger while he looked; then, with a sharp exclamation, he swooped upon the green glitter that showed amid the dust.

"Go back to our friend Pierre M. Fabre," I said. "He knew the end was at hand, and therefore he made that little pyramid. Into the soft mud, completely hiding it, he pressed the emerald he had taken from the ring—then left the thing to dry. If he lived, he could some day regain the jewel. If not, he would keep the Arabs from getting it. He may have had further reasons, but—"

Right there, I think, a wild excitement gripped us both—for the miracle was a fact. It was true. I was looking at the jewel for the first time. Gems themselves have never meant a thing to me, but now the thrill of my own discovery was really something. I liked it.

Tom Keating produced a jeweler's glass, screwed it into his eye, examined the stone, and caught his breath. It was not a large emerald. It was a perfect cabochon the size of a small garden pea. The color was not deep, nor was the stone particularly handsome. And yet—

"My Lord!" said Keating in an awed voice.

"It's not the Sphinx Emerald?" I asked. "Looks mighty small."

"Hold it up and look at it with, not against, the light," he said.

Almost reluctantly, he handed me the emerald and the lens; his face bore a rapt, ecstatic look.

One's first glimpse into the heart of an emerald, with such a glass, is memorable. Flashing glints, odd contours, strange shapes, appear; light itself assumes form and color; a pinpoint becomes a landscape of fantasy. With the stone in my palm, I found myself viewing green fields and precipices; then the enlarged flaws loomed up. I saw the Sphinx standing there, and the wonder grew.

The perfect Sphinx in profile, yes, lit by unearthly splendor of sunlight striking across the corundum structure—a beauty uncanny and magnificent. More, the green depths suggested further things to the imagination, but I refused the tempting lure, because a sense of something repellent grew upon me.

Far from admiring the scene opening to me, I was inspired with acute dislike and even fear; why, I cannot say, but I felt a distinct repulsion that made me shiver.

"Isn't it the most marvelous thing you ever saw?" Keating demanded enthusiastically.

"No," I replied, and looked again to verify my feelings.

"Eh? What's wrong with your eyes, Hawk?"

"Nothing. The stone holds evil of some kind—that's the word for it—evil!" I removed the glass and gave it back to him, with the stone. I felt a horror of it.

"You're in earnest?" He stared at me in surprise. "That's odd; but I told you it sparks the imagination. By all reports, no two people feel the same way about it. You damned lucky beggar! What'll you do with it?"

"Me? Not a thing. It's yours, not mine."

"I say, be sensible! I've nothing to do with the stone. It's your find."

As I looked at the shimmering green thing, I shivered again.

"The hell with it, Sahib! I wouldn't have it as a gift," I retorted. "You keep it. You're welcome to it. I tell you, the devil's in it! Somehow the very feel of it's like poison—ugh! I didn't see anything special in it, yet it filled me with horror, past any explanation. Keep it, throw it away, sell it, give it to

Linda—anything you like. I never did have any feeling for jewels. They don't attract me, and this repels me."

"Here, now." From the tin of special cigarettes Keating jerked the rice-paper lining, spilling fat Egyptians all over the table. Putting the emerald on it, he twisted the paper into a knot and thrust it at me. "Take it. Keep it, look at it again and again. Take the glass too. If by tonight you don't change your mind, very well; put a price on it and I'll buy it from you. Good Lord, Hawk, don't you get my angle? I can't take advantage of a momentary whim on your part!"

"Don't you want it?" I demanded.

"Of course. More than you dream. But I want it fairly, honestly, not at your expense. The find was yours alone. It's an historic, wonderful stone. So do as I ask, for my sake. You mustn't tempt me."

I saw his point. With a nod of assent, I pocketed the paper twist.

"Very well. I'll not change my mind, so let's return to Cairo now and get it valued. After all, we may be kidding ourselves. May be just a piece of glass."

"Impossible. Anyhow, let's do it. I'm too excited to potter around here now."

He was all in a dither, certainly, and knowing the reason I did not wonder; but I did not mention Linda's name, or the thing I had seen in her eyes, or the hatred in the dark features of Malek. I was afraid and depressed. After my discovery-thrill had come reaction. There must be a curse of some kind on the stone, I told myself.

"I don't understand it at all," Keating said, while we were bouncing back on the city road, the citadel of Saladin looming against the sky ahead.

"Don't understand what?"

"The size of the emerald. It's only about three carats, I judge. Richelieu's will says it was five and a half. Da Vinci's account says it was eight. Earlier mentions make it much larger. Yet it

must be the same stone. No two could have those identical
flaws, that strange inner design and magnificent distance—"

"Probably it's been changed or recut in course of time," I
suggested, and he nodded.

"Might explain it. There'll be trouble with Malek over this.
He'll kick up a fat row if Linda—Well, never mind. He can't
force me to sell it to him, anyhow."

So Malek wanted the stone—probably wanted to give it to
Linda himself! However, we dropped the subject. Once in the
city, we went directly to a jeweler Keating knew, in the Shari
el-Majiakh.

He gave the emerald a cursory examination and smiled.

"An Egyptian stone, I'd say. Poor color and oddly cut, with
pronounced flaws. Its value? Merely nominal—a few hundred
piasters. Yet there's something fascinating about the thing. Let
me take another look—"

He once more bent over his bench with the gem, and Keating
gave me a significant glance. This man, too, felt the weirdly
compelling power of the stone, though obviously he had never
heard of the Sphinx Emerald. Indeed, he asked to keep it until
the morrow, saying he would like to make various tests, but
Keating refused and we left the shop.

WE made plans for the rest of the afternoon. Keating, who
had errands, promised to join me at the hotel for dinner, about
seven.

"You do as I asked, now," he said earnestly, before we parted.
"Don't go off half-cocked. Give the emerald a fair chance,
examine it carefully, before coming to any decision."

"All right, Sahib," I promised. "See you tonight, then."

In my own room, after a cleanup, I sat down, put the glass
in my eye, and resolved to examine the emerald with an im-
partial mind.

For a long while I searched the green depths, the curious
light-filled valleys and hills of flawed corundum which surrounded that weirdly dominant sphinx-figure. Strange fancies

drifted across my thought. The riddle of the Sphinx—was it not the mind of man, still an unsolved mystery? Hours of the sunrise, gazing eternally eastward, searching for his nameless Bride; the old primitive gods of the desert lands, spiritual forces of good and evil still at work; the strange ways of destiny that would entangle such a man as Keating with a heartless beauty like Linda Grey—such various threads of thought floated before me, with loose ends and no tieup.

But the longer I looked, the more surely returned upon me that same causeless horror and repulsion. This Sphinx among the ghostly green hills had an ethereal beauty, yes, but also conveyed a sense of intolerable depression—a nameless sadness and even loathing. Why? Impossible to say. Just a mental quirk; something wrong with me, perhaps, since others did not get the same feeling from it. Perhaps some premonition or foreboding. At all events, I laid aside the glass almost with hatred, returned the emerald to its twist of paper, and resolved definitely to be rid of it the moment Keating appeared. I was afraid of it.

SIX O'CLOCK passed, seven came and went; day darkened into night—and no Keating showed up. My watch-hands crept on, and I was hungry. When the phone rang, I jumped for it hastily. A strange voice spoke, with faint accent.

"Mr. Hawkins, sar?"

"Yes."

"I am speaking for Keating Effendi, sar. I am Inspector Ayub Hassan of the Salt Department and live in the El Faggala quarter. Mr. Keating was slightly hurt in a street accident this evening and was brought into my house. He asked me to come here and get you. I have engaged a car and am now downstairs—"

"Down in two minutes," I replied, and moved fast, spurred by alarm.

Inspector Hassan was a swarthy, suave Gippo who, as soon as we met, hurried me out to the street. He said that Keating had merely been hit by a car and knocked about slightly and was not badly injured. Before I knew it he was handing me into a smelly little Citroen, himself got under the wheel and was sending the outsize bathtub dashing forth into the night life of Cairo like an insane doodlebug.

I had not the slightest idea of where we were when my driver halted before a narrow crooked house in a crooked narrow street and said we had arrived. We piled out and the Inspector led me through a gate that opened on the street. This took us into a walled and tiled patio. On the left, stairs ascended to balconies above. Before us, orange trees grouped about a tiled fountain and paper lanterns bobbed on invisible wires. My guide vanished, and to my amazement James Malek came forward with a suave greeting. He was in evening attire and wore the ribbon of some decoration across his shirt-front.

"Good evening, Mr. Hawkins," he said, showing his gold front tooth. "I am glad to—"

"Where's Keating?" I broke in.

He looked astonished.

"Keating? How should I know?"

"But he's here—he's hurt—that's why I came! Here, Inspector—"

I turned, but there was no Inspector. I was alone with Malek, who smiled and rubbed his plump hands.

"Some mistake, what?" he said. "An odd sort of cove, Keating. He'd scarcely be here; the neighborhood is a very bad one. And now, please, the emerald. I have no desire to rob you, so name your price and there will be no trouble."

He produced a fat wad of white Bank of England notes and began to thumb them.

"You're out of soundings, Malek," I said, a trifle bewildered. "I came to get Keating. The emerald is not for sale."

"It is you who are in error, my dear sir," he rejoined pleasantly. "As they say in Chicago, give, and give fast. Come through. The emerald, and at your price!"

By this time the sense of his words, his meaning, had reached my dumb brain. I was slow to realize the fact, but I was in a jam, a bad one. I had been decoyed here by this smirking Levantine, who wanted the emerald, one way or another.

"No use," I said, thinking fast for a change. "Keating has it."

"There's no green in my eye, old chap." He lost his smile and looked ugly. "We've tried him already, so give! Loosen up, and quick about it! Here, Abdul! Yacub!"

To put it flatly, I was now scared stiff. This Gippo version of Al Capone had me on the spot. When, at his call, shadowy figures moved on the far side of the orange trees, I acted not as a hero but in sheer blind panic. He was still calling them when I slid forward on the tiles and sunk my fist into Malek's bulging cummerbund, then whirled and ducked for the gateway and the street.

A tarbooshed figure blocked my way with a mean-looking knife a foot long, but I was too frightened to take the hint and stop. So I just put down my head, butted him, a trick taught me by a disreputable pal in the tanks. He went flat and I went at the gate. A pistol barked, a bullet whistled past, and Yacub and Abdul were on my heels as I got the gate open. It slammed in their faces—I was out on the cobbles; and then I just ran like hell.

VAGUELY I remember excited Arabs, jabbering Gippos, tumultuous bazaars, kilted Scotch soldiers, and finally a room in a palatial police station. A polite, friendly official in evening dress heard my story, gave me a highball and a six-inch cigarette, and finally escorted me to my hotel room. Here he sat down to the telephone to get reports on the matter. He talked on the phone, made some notes, and turned to me.

"My dear Mr. Hawkins, I have very sad news for you," he said, with tears in his voice. "Your friend Keating Effendi, who is of course very well known, was taken from the river near the Bulak bridge half an hour ago, drowned."

"Then it's that damned Malek fellow!" I cried furiously. "He boasted to me that he had tried to rob Keating—I want him arrested at once!"

"Malek Effendi is an important man, a man of position. Let me look into it a bit," he replied, and began to jabber into the phone anew.

The shock hit me all of a sudden with numbing force—dead! Sahib Keating dead! He had been murdered when the emerald was not found on him—murdered for the damned stone, by Malek! I was getting the impact of this when my good friend the official turned from the phone again and lit one of his long cigarettes. He shook his head sadly.

"My dear sir, I cannot comprehend this murder charge, or your story of assault," he said kindly, in tones of deepest sympathy. "I have just established that Malek Effendi is now present at a reception at the palace and has been there all evening, a guest of His Majesty. Allow me to observe, Mr. Hawkins, with the greatest respect, that it is inadvisable to visit places where hashish is used—"

Well, at least I did not fly into a rage and make an utter ass of myself; we talked on, calmly. Poor Keating was dead, robbed and dropped into the river. Malek had a regal alibi, and was too respected a gentleman to be mixed up in such a crime anyway. There was no Inspector Hassan in the Salt Department, nor did any such person live in the El Faggala quarter. No one here at the hotel remembered him calling for me, either. No house, such as I described, with patio and orange trees, was known.

Yes, I got it all right, and took it standing up. It was after ten o'clock when my sympathetic and friendly police official gently patted my hand, warned me again about the delusions caused by hashish, and bowed himself out. Ferash Bey, I think his name was.

I sat down, held my head in my hands, and after a time glimpsed the twist of paper holding the emerald, on the writing-desk where I had left it. When I thought of Tom Keating my heart burned. I cursed that bit of green corundum most heartily;

then I pocketed it and the lens, brushed up a trifle, and left the room. It was a little after eleven when I reached the hotel desk and inquired whether Miss Grey had returned. She had not.

I went out on the wide veranda and waited. The hotel was a postwar luxury spot, converted from a Mameluke palace. Instead of having gardens on the river side, one wing was actually over the water when, as now, the river was at the yearly flood.

WHAT I awaited was vague; I had no particular intentions—just that deep heartburn. I had no particular animus against Malek. He was merely a Gippo halfcaste and had acted according to his nature. Linda Grey was the real murderer of Tom Keating.

My second cigarette was nearly finished when the yellow Isotta swept up to the steps. Malek accompanied Linda in, then departed at once and hastily. I left my chair and stepped in, and joined Linda at the desk. She turned to me in surprise.

"You didn't expect the rendezvous to be kept?" I said.

"I was told Sahib had left town," she rejoined, "but I'm delighted to see you, of course."

"You may well be. I've brought what you want to see. Malek couldn't get it."

She laughed. Her eyes glittered. Suddenly she was all life and animation, and swept me along to the lift with her. She knew the truth and did not care a hang. She would welcome me or Malek or anyone who brought her the Sphinx Emerald, and there would be no question of price. This was clear enough from her abrupt intimacy of manner. She put all her beauty at my disposal, and that short ascent in the lift was a passionate interlude of promise that could not be mistaken.

Her maid admitted us to her suite. Linda shed her wonderful wraps and dismissed the maid, then led me out to the balcony. It was a sweet place, directly over the river, unscreened but luxuriously furnished; the night air was cool, redolent of gardens.

Linda was ablaze with jewels. It seemed absurd that a woman wearing the gems of queens would care tuppence about the bit of green corundum in my pocket; yet there was avid expectancy in her manner, in her look, as we settled down. I sat at a small table close to the iron grille at the edge of the balcony; in the center of the table stood a lamp. I switched it on; its light was shaded but brilliant.

"Well?" she demanded without pretense.

"Better sit here where you can examine it," I said. I made no pretense either and she had to bring up her own chair to the table, opposite me.

I put the jeweler's glass before her, got out the twist of paper, and set the emerald in her palm. Then I sat back, watching her with relish.

Glass in eye, she looked into the emerald, caught her breath, then began to examine it with rapt attention. She continued to look for a long time, shifting the stone about to get different lights upon it. At last a deep, slow breath escaped her, she took the glass from her eye and set it down, and put the emerald beside it. Then she sat silently, staring down at the stone.

Her lovely features were suffused with emotion, her eyes soft and liquid; she was so deeply stirred that she quite forgot she was Linda Grey. All her heart was plain to see. When at length she spoke, the words were almost a gasp.

"Exquisite! There's nothing in the world like it. It does things to you—it speaks to the very soul!" she murmured. Indeed, she had never looked so beautiful, so abandoned to a sheer ecstasy. "Why, it's incredible! All the stories about it, even the wildest ones, are not half the truth; it simply takes possession of you!"

"Glad you feel that way about it; I don't, but I'm exceptional," I said coldly. "So you like it?"

"Like it?" She loosed her pent breath. "I adore it! I must have it. I can't live without it, now that I've seen it. It's wonderful— above words! No, I just couldn't live without it."

"You'd be surprised," I said, and got out a cigarette and lit it. As I laid down the match she put out her hand and set it on mine. Her voice came like a chord of soft music.

"And you've brought it to me?"

"No. Keating would have brought it to you. I just brought it to show to you."

She laughed amusedly, richly, but her eyes lost some of their rapt ecstasy.

"You're delightful! Well, tell me what you want for it."

"All right, let's talk business," I said, "and in plain words, no sparring. What did you promise Keating for it, if he got it for you?"

"Anything," she said simply, quietly, without evasion.

"And you promised Malek the same thing. You'd pay me the same thing. Anything. Whatever I asked."

"Yes," she breathed, her eyes on mine.

"The trouble with you, Linda," I said, "is that you think your beauty is currency that no one can resist. You're wrong. Give me what I ask, and the emerald is yours."

"Done. Name it."

"The life of Tom Keating."

She straightened up a trifle, with a shocked expression.

I went on coolly:

"He's dead. You know it. Your boy friend did for him, but you actually killed him—you and your playing around, juggling life and death and devotion. That's why I'm here. That's why I brought the stone. And you want it so badly you'd give anything for it."

"I don't know why you're talking this way," she began.

"You'll know in a minute. Hold out your hand, darling."

PERPLEXED, UNCOMPREHENDING, she stretched out her hand to me. I turned it palm up, picked up the emerald, and set it on her pink palm. It looked very lovely there. Then I caught back my second finger with my thumb, and, as one flicks away a cigarette stub, flicked the emerald from her hand—out over the balcony rail, out into the darkness and the river below us.

A cry of actual agony escaped her. Then she sat stupefied, trying to realize what had happened. I rose and bowed to her.

"Good night, beautiful; pleasant dreams," I said, and left her.

XVIII

THE PASSING OF
THE SPHINX EMERALD

*In Santa Fe, the story of this malign and
magic jewel, which began in Ancient
Egypt, comes to its strange conclusion.*

S IR EVART BUCKSON was one of those Englishmen
whom John Buchan loved to depict—a large man, powerfully built, as agile in his thirties as a boy of eighteen, and well
poised. He had calm features and keen hazel eyes. He looked
up sharply as Bill Stuart entered the room of his New York
hotel.

"I've seen you before," he observed. "How d'ye do? Stuart is
the name?"

"Yes, sir. I was in Egypt with the American Air Forces—you
had command of the field where we were putting our ships
together and making deliveries."

The calm features lighted up. "Oh, yes—I remember. You're
the chap who got hold of a mummy somewhere and dressed
him up at the wheel of a plane and raised no end of a riot! The
war seems long past now, eh?"

Stuart assented, laughing. "I saw in the papers you were
stopping here, and took the liberty of calling."

"Right. Glad you did. A spot of brandy, what?"

"Thanks, no. I didn't come to beg a drink," Stuart replied a
bit stiffly.

Sir Evart gave him another look—level, guarded.

"Aye? Sit down, lad. Let's have it."

Stuart lighted a cigarette.

"I've had an airfield job since the war—top mechanic," he
said. He too showed level-headed poise. He had a quiet manner,

but his dark eyes held a flash; his features—the right cheek lightly scarred—were crisp, his lips tight and thin. "I've a couple of sisters out West; no one else. The job folded last week. I've hung around town, hoping to get a word with you. That's the situation."

Sir Evart nodded, and wisely said nothing. Stuart went on.

"You see, I'm not too flush; but I have enough. I had a great pal in Egypt named Morrison; he was killed later over Tunis. A pilot—his sister lives here in town. She has a batch of stuff he sent home from Cairo—relics and what-not. He wrote her that some of them might be valuable. You're a world authority on Egyptian antiquities, so I wondered if I might ask you about two or three of them. You see, Miss Morrison could use money, but I haven't the faintest notion where to sell 'em. I tried the Metropolitan and got laughed at."

He leaned back, finished.

Sir Evart smiled.

"Stuart, let me be mercifully cruel. Your boys in Africa got rooked, no end. They went out and bought curiosities—knives,

"It'll be a chance shot, anyhow," said Lattimer.
Stuart's nerves leaped; he lifted the rifle.

jewels, everything, and were stuck with the finest lot of fakes ever assembled. That's one thing; here's another: My job's folded too. Our people are getting out of Egypt, or have got; my Helwan museum job was washed up with the rest. That's why I'm in your country, lecturing. Oh, I'm not broke! But we're on short commons in England, you know."

"I'm asking for advice, not help," said Stuart.

"Quite; don't flare up, my lad. You're welcome, God knows, to the advice; I'm trying to break things easily, telling you not to expect too much. Here, take one of these."

Stuart accepted one of the opulent Abdallahs offered him.

"There are several things your pal might have got hold of that'd mean a bit of luck," pursued the Englishman, "and I'm not the man to reject possibility. The mummy of Queen Hatshepsu, f'rinstance, has never been found. Or consider gems: the signet of a king might be well worth while, although the gyppies turn out some remarkable fakes. Or the Sphinx Emerald, supposedly dropped into the Nile—"

"What's that?" Stuart asked, leaning forward.

"Quite a remarkable emerald, an ancient Egyptian stone and therefore of pale color, which turns up from time to time. Some remarkable stories connected with it. One of your American magazines has printed them, I understand. This is a stone of extraordinary nature and quite large. The tale goes that it exerts a peculiar effect upon one who gazes into it. Nothing occult or that sort of thing, but psychology—I believe a kind of auto-hypnosis. The very odd thing about this emerald is that the flaws are abundant, as is usual in beryl, but come together in the center to form the perfect but tiny image of the Great Sphinx—hence the name given it."

"Morrison got that stone," said Stuart quietly.

"Eh—good God!" Sir Evart sat up as though electrified. "Did I hear you aright?"

"I said Morrison got it, yes. It's among the stuff he sent home. I thought it green glass formed about a tiny Sphinx."

"Upon my word! I—why, I can hardly believe it!" Sir Evart stared. "Where is it now?"

"Oh, Miss Morrison has it. I've met her several times and have seen the junk he collected." Stuart pulled at his cigarette. "You say it's an emerald? Has it any particular value?"

"Has it? One of the ancient Egyptian crown jewels! The factitious value is nil, owing to its poor color—but the fictitious value is anything one cares to name." The Englishman was no longer impassive. "I say, Stuart—this must be checked up at once, you know! Real beryl is readily distinguished. Not worth a farthing if it's a replica, but if real the value is colossal! Where on earth did your friend find it?"

"Some Arab fished it out of the Nile. He bought it with other things." A thrill shot through Stuart as he sensed the other's excited interest. "Look here: Miss Morrison has an apartment upon Riverside Drive—same one her brother had before the war. I can run up there in a taxi and get it—"

Sir Evart lit a fresh cigarette.

"Easy, now," he said. "Let's look at it calmly, Stuart. The original gem was lost fairly recently, just after the war—lost in the Nile. It can't be the same one your friend got, therefore. It was unset, a cabochon the size of a garden pea—"

"Hold on!" intervened Stuart. "Morrison was in Cairo after the war, too. He was killed a year or two later, not during the fighting, in an accident. And you've just described his emerald perfectly."

"Evidently I misunderstood you. But you'll not get it; I'll go with you and see it where it is." With an effort, Sir Evart regained his calmness. "Let me get my notes first. I've a description of it somewhere. Can't rush at this, you know—a famous stone and all that; must know if it's the real thing. If so, then Bernard Lattimer the collector is the man for it; his collection is world-renowned. Have a drink, compose yourself—back in a moment or so."

Left alone, Stuart scrupled not to pour himself a drink; he needed it.

Penny Morrison, he knew, needed money badly; if this yarn were true, the thing would be a godsend for her.

The Englishman came back into the room, holding a page of typed notes, and insisted on going over them aloud, in a droning voice. The stone was said to be of five carats and a fraction, of poor cut and color, its center showing the image of the Sphinx in profile, formed by flaws. That was to be expected; an unflawed emerald, like a really blue diamond, was almost unknown in the world of gems. The man was making a very real effort at self-control, fighting against credence.

"Remember, Stuart, we're dealing with a famed historical jewel," he stated, "and replicas must have been made, poor imitations; if this is beryl it will answer to simple tests. Until it does, we can't be certain. I don't want you to be misled."

Stuart laughed. "It's all new to me, Sir Evart. Are you lecturing here, by the way?"

"Not at once; my engagements begin out West; Lattimer—
the collector whom I mentioned—lives somewhere out there.
Well, if you're ready—"

They descended to the street, piled into a cab, and Stuart
gave the address of Penny Morrison. It was a fifteen-minute
drive from Park Avenue. As they rode, he told Sir Evart about

"Don't get careless or I'll put a bullet into you."
Reaching around with his free hand Stuart
began to explore his victim's pockets.

Penny—supporting herself precariously by music, with nothing except what little her brother had left her. They drew up before her apartment-building. Another two minutes saw them in her apartment.

Penny was a head shorter than Stuart; she was gowned in gold-touched maroon; her masses of brownish hair, her vivacious and alive features, her sparkling, alert eyes, were pleasing. Her voice was soft.

WITHOUT MENTIONING the emerald, Stuart told their errand.

"Sir Evart has agreed to look over the stuff," he concluded, "but he'll be brutally frank about it."

"That's very kind," said Penny. "I'll appreciate it, indeed. I'm well aware that Egyptian tourists usually get stung in their purchases, and I doubt if any of these things have much value. I have everything together—excuse me while I go after them."

She hurried from the room. Sir Evart glanced at the piano, the pictures, the worn rug on the floor, and lighted an Abdallah.

"Gad!" he murmured. "A remarkably nice young woman, Stuart. Teaches music, eh? You know, if that thing proves real, it'll positively be a wrench to sell it to Lattimer. I'd give my right arm to have it myself—but can't afford it, worse luck."

"Have you considered the difficulty of making a replica?"

"Aye; that's a sticker. You see, when the French were in Egypt around 1800 they got hold of the stone; then it vanished, went out of sight. The story says that it turned up briefly just after the war—some chap unearthed it, then dropped it into the Nile. It's known by hearsay, and figures in history and romance no end, but there are no photographs of it. Leonardo da Vinci left a drawing of it, I believe."

Stuart frowned. "Doesn't seem logical—the disappearance, I mean."

"That's Africa for you, my boy. Even people disappear. There was that young Dutch woman, Alexine Thynne—the richest woman in Europe—who vanished in the Sahara in the 1860's, supposedly killed by her own guides. Other things like that, many of them—"

He broke off and rose as Penny returned, bringing a small handbag. This she placed on a dropleaf table, whose burden of music Stuart transferred to the piano.

"Here you are," she said brightly. "Everything's unwrapped."

Sir Evart drew up his chair and opened the bag, to display a miscellaneous mass of burial beads, small images, seals and other such trinkets. He began to turn them over with his fingers.

"I thought you said there was an emerald in the lot, Stuart?"

"Oh!" A cry escaped from Penny. "I forgot all about it—that man was here only this morning! He took it to have it *expertised.*"

With a sound like a ripping balloon, Sir Evart drew back from the table.

"So! The thing we most wanted to see, is gone!"

"I'm sorry," blurted the girl, dismay in her face. "He said that if genuine it might be worth all of a hundred dollars."

"A thousand pounds—five thousand dollars, at the least!" the Englishman broke in. "Well, what's done is done. We can't help it if you've sold the stone."

"But I haven't!" she cried tragically. "He gave a receipt for it and promised he'd return in a day or two. He's a well-known person; he's just returned from a buying trip to Egypt."

"His name?"

She stared blankly and bit her lip.

"I—I don't remember. Wait! I have his card and the receipt. Let me get them for you."

She hurried out again, and Sir Evart spread his hands.

"You see, Stuart? There's a fate about this thing. The stone knocks about, over half the world, and we come to see it. A man is ahead of us by a few hours—doesn't buy it, just carries it off. Spotted it for what it is, by Jove!"

"It must have been the real thing, then," Stuart said. "But if she didn't sell it to him, then she's not lost it."

"Stuff and nonsense!" snorted the Briton. "We're not dealing with a piece of real estate, man, but with an inestimable jewel, a unique museum piece of enormous value, which can be slid into one's vest pocket—"

Penny returned, breathless, and thrust at them a receipt and a card. The receipt was for one presumed emerald of about five carats, taken on approval. The card, bearing a Madison Avenue address, was printed:

JAMES L. HARTLEY
Jewels de Luxe   *Curios*

"Good! A Madison Avenue shop!" cried Stuart. "We can go there right now. How did the man find you, Penny? Why did he come here?"

"He—he said he had met my brother in Egypt," she answered.

Sir Evart broke in: "Very well. Get your things, and we'll go see the chap."

"Ready in a moment," she replied, and hurried off. Sir Evart tapped the card and gave Stuart a beetling look.

"Rather obvious. This chap heard in Egypt about the find, about the sale to an American, obtained the address and ran the thing down—you see? Something fishy about all this. The card is not engraved, but printed; a bad sign. If this fellow Hartley knows the stone for what it is, he's no ordinary dealer."

"Do you know the man?"

"I can't say. I never heard of this name, at all events."

"You suspect something crooked?"

"I don't know. Anything is possible—any sort of fraud, rookery, or downright rascality. I may be wrong, but I'd wager pounds to dollars that your young lady does not see the Sphinx Emerald again in a hurry."

"I'll take the bet," snapped Stuart. "No crook like that is going to—"

"Easy!" The other laid a compelling hand on his wrist. "No jumping at conclusions, please; a very unwise habit. First let us gather evidence, then act upon it, my friend. Remember, Hartley must be an extraordinary person to have recognized the Sphinx Emerald or even to have heard of it. We don't know yet that he did. I am going to make a cast in the dark."

So saying, he produced his notebook, tore out a leaf, wrote down something, and folded it twice. He passed the little square to Stuart, just as Penny returned in hat and coat.

"Hold that, Stuart. Tell me, Miss Morrison: Was your visitor of this morning a very slender gentleman with a particularly large hooked nose and bushy eyebrows?"

"Yes, black brows," she said. "He wore a very large seal blood-stone ring and had fine hands. He spoke with a slight accent, but I can't say just what it was."

Sir Evart laughed.

"Come along, then, let's go to his shop, and after that to my hotel for tea."

They quickly found a taxi, and to ease the tension, Stuart spoke to Penny of her plans.

"You said that you had a chance to sublease the apartment—"

"Yes, I could step out tomorrow and turn it over to friends," she assented. "Not that I want to do so, of course. I've nowhere else to go, so it's only a temptation."

Sir Evart darted her a quick glance.

"Don't be too sure, miss. It may be a very lucky thing. Well, here we are, so out with you! And I suggest that you let me do the talking."

Before them was a shop-window glittering with jewelry and trinkets.

CHAPTER TWO

S TUART WAS prepared for black-browed rascality. Instead, the man who removed his jeweler's glass and greeted them across the counter was frail, blond, quite pleasant until Hartley's name was mentioned; then he fired up with obvious indignation.

"*Ach!* It is that man again! Look you, he has a marvelous knowledge of stones. He argued me into letting him use this address, and now I have trouble all the time. It was a big mistake. You are from the police?"

"No," replied Sir Evart. "We merely want to find Mr. Hartley."

"But there is something wrong, yes? I see it in your eyes! Well, he is gone! He took a plane this noon to fly West and said he would not be back. I have washed my hands of him."

Penny Morrison caught her breath, but Sir Evart only smiled.

"Very well, sir. Let me have his address, and we'll trouble you no more."

"Good. I can do that. For a few days only, he said, he would be at the El Portal Hotel in Santa Fe, New Mexico."

"Thank you; nothing further, then."

OUT in the street, the Englishman spoke brusquely.

"Come along—not far to my hotel. We can talk there."

To Stuart it was quite evident that, so far as Hartley went, the goose was cooked. The man had taken French leave, counting on two or three days' leeway before the police got after him. This in itself was rather conclusive evidence that the emerald was an emerald, but Sir Evart seemed to have something up his sleeve. However, the Englishman said nothing until they reached his hotel and gained his rooms. Then he ordered tea, went to the phone and spoke lengthily with the porter's office, and came back with a cheerful air to settle down at the table between his two guests.

"Now I'll trouble you for that bit of paper, Stuart—thanks."

Sir Evart spread it out. "There's our man's proper name—John Monckton. Either of you know him?"

Neither did.

"A man of prewar distinction and brilliance; a rascal of the first water, Dutch or English by birth, concerned in a number of shady transactions abroad—an international crook, and very able."

"Who's jumping at conclusions now?" asked Stuart.

"I'm talking facts, not theories, my dear fellow. Further, Bernard Lattimer lives in or near Santa Fe. The connection is quite obvious. Monckton, alias Hartley, put the emerald in the mail, addressed to himself at El Portal Hotel, then popped aboard a plane; he's quite safe, even if pursued, you see. A smart rascal."

Penny leaned forward. "Then—then you think he stole the emerald?"

"Sure of it. He'd not take such risks without a large prospective gain."

The tea arrived; also a porter with a sheet of paper for Sir Evart, who took and studied it reflectively. When they were alone again and Penny was pouring the tea, he resumed:

"You have several alternatives, Miss Morrison. It's your affair and I don't want to influence you. You may turn it over to the police, which will involve no end of publicity; you'll punish Hartley, but may not get the stone back."

"Doesn't sound attractive," she commented. "What else?"

"Hm! I must leave tomorrow to lecture in Denver; from there I can be in Santa Fe by flying, on Sunday. I know Lattimer fairly well. The porter informs me he can get one reservation for seven tonight, on a plane reaching Santa Fe early in the morning. Your American connections are rather marvelous, you know. Well, it all depends on what your wishes are. Since you've brought me into the matter—do I stay in?"

"That's up to you," Penny replied, smiling. "I think you should."

"Good. Frankly, I foresee a very active time ahead. Hartley is no fool. I fancy you'll be amazed when you learn how much Lattimer is willing to pay for the emerald."

"You say he's a friend of yours—" began Stuart.

"Friendship doesn't enter into collecting. Lattimer is a retired genius; where his collection is concerned, he doesn't regard the law. If I could steal the crown jewels out of the Tower, he'd buy 'em like a shot."

"Well, see here," broke in Stuart. "Hartley knows Penny here, by sight. You have a lecture date. I can take tonight's plane, reach Santa Fe in the morning, and grab Hartley. He doesn't know me, won't suspect me."

"Basically sound, as a proposal. What about it, Miss Penny?"

She nodded. "It's my game and I ought to play it, but I suppose—"

"Follow on by a later plane," Stuart suggested. He met her eyes and read their hesitation aright. "Sublease the apartment if you like—no, damn it! We've neither of us got the means, Sir Evart, and that's flat. Costs money to travel, you know."

The Englishman nodded, his eyes sparkling.

"Right. I've a few hundred to spare—No, Miss Penny, wait a moment! You agree to let me handle the stone—say, on commission—and I'll advance expenses. This is going to be a brisk game, I warn you; Hartley's a bad enemy to take on. I'll enjoy it no end. Yes? Then we're in alliance. Hold on a sec—I'll make sure of that reservation."

He rose and went to the telephone. Penny looked at Stuart uncertainly.

"I suppose it's the best way, really, but I don't want to trouble you—"

"Nonsense!" He broke into a laugh. "I'm tingling, for the first time in weeks! I wouldn't miss this show for anything. While not broke, I'm pretty well bent, and it's fine to have him come to the rescue; he's a grand chap, Penny. What's more, if I'm out

West I can land a drafting job with the Douglas people. Things work out, you see."

SIR EVART returned, rubbing his hands.

"All settled; reservation's in your name, Stuart. The pursuit of the Sphinx Emerald is under way! Miss Penny, you can come West with me tomorrow. At Kansas City you change to another plane that will drop you at Santa Fe while I go on to Denver. You'll join Stuart a day ahead of me, then. I'll assume your expenses and can stand Stuart a hundred dollars for expenses—his reservation is charged to me. Right?"

Stuart nodded. "I'll go as I stand; a phone call will take care of my clothes and effects."

"Then we'll toast our luck." Sir Evart lifted his cup, beaming over it. "If I were Hartley, I'd have dropped that stone in the air mail, so it should be delivered to him sometime tomorrow; mind that!"

"Which should make him liable for a Federal offense," assented Stuart.

"Careful, now, my lad! Miss Penny doesn't fancy police business. We're not out to punish anyone—we're after that emerald, and I'm trusting to your level head. A bit of beryl not as large as your little fingernail, remember."

"I get you, sir. Penny gets there sometime Saturday, you sometime Sunday. Do you want me to contact Lattimer?"

"Contact? Oh! Get in touch with him, eh? No, better not unless things go amiss. I can't tell you what to expect. You have a head—use it. Here's your hundred."

Stuart pocketed the roll of money handed him. The bus for his plane would leave downtown at six; he had time to spare.

The three sat talking. To Stuart, who knew Penny fairly well, the radiance behind her poise was a marvelous thing, like sunlight behind a chinked wall. He liked the expert way Sir Evart Buckson brought her out. He liked everything about her; he had, ever since meeting her, thought her a rare and precious thing. She was no tricky finagling female, but frank, level-eyed, genuine.

To Buckson he gave similar credit. Close to forty, Stuart reckoned, but with a youthful spring to his step, a reflective, calm eye, a lift of the spirit; one to depend upon in a pinch, for advice and for action. Practical, yes, yet not material. That reflective gaze was touched with spirituality. The man had not been knighted for making money, but for some things he had written about the Egyptian religions—Stuart could not remember exactly what. There were depths to him.

His phone call made, the safety of his few belongings assured, Stuart stepped into the bathroom and washed. He caught sight of himself in the glass. Unevenly browned by work in the sun, not by a sun lamp, his knobby features were pleasantly relieved by a hint of laughter about his steady eyes.

"No beauty prizes for you," he muttered with a sniff, "but you do get things done, old ugly-mug!"

He rejoined the others and took another cup of tea. It was a pleasant change from the universal coffee.

"Drink it fast," said Penny, glancing at her watch. "I'll walk to the terminus with you. Those buses go on the dot, remember." She turned to their host. "You've turned me topsyturvy this afternoon. I can be ready to leave with you tomorrow, by fast work, but tell me one thing: is it worth it? You mentioned a thousand pounds—"

Sir Evart took her hand. "My dear, the world I knew is all changed; institutions and men are different, values are different, nothing is the same. Yet I honestly believe that sum is the veriest minimum. You may get more."

"Thanks to you. Now, let's have all this on a business footing, please. You must have a share of all benefits—"

He laughed. "A commission, then?"

"Right. Twenty per cent is the usual art commission. Sufficient?"

"Far too much."

"Not a bit of it; so that's settled." She flung a glance at Stuart. "Ready, tea-guzzler?"

With thanks and cheery farewells to Sir Evart, they gained the street and turned toward Forty-second. Penny was brisk, cheerful, decisive.

"I like your English friend. He has an air—I think he's a magician who enchants everything around him!"

"That's the advantage of having money." Stuart spoke a trifle bitterly. "I don't like being on him for expenses. I don't like being broke. I want a stake."

Her laugh rang clear. "Bosh! So do I, but I'm not fretting over it. Don't get sour. Don't get to thinking the world's down on you!"

"I have my reasons, as you very well know," he cut in. "And to think I'm on my way West—a most amazing, incredible thing!"

"Precisely." She took his arm. "It's all out of this world. This morning I woke up sane; tonight I'll be a lunatic. And going West tomorrow—me, Penny Morrison! Oh, I just thought of something that Chuck wrote me before he died. Said he had sent an emerald, and added: *'Be careful not to look at it too long.'* What could he have meant?"

"I don't know—or yes, I do, too!" Stuart remembered what Sir Evart had said about the peculiar hypnotic effect exerted by the Sphinx Emerald, and quoted it. "Must have some reference to that quality of fancied influence. Mystics surround famous gems with all sorts of bosh, you know. Don't take any stock in it."

She laughed. "I didn't even know that was the emerald he meant; I thought it a bit of glass, really! We can be terrible fools, can't we?"

"Darling fools." Stuart had his own ideas about Penny Morrison and did not hesitate to voice them. "Wholly adorable, my dear. But if you'll accept my advice, we should have the cops step in, pinch this guy Hartley and hold him till you arrive. The emerald would be seized when delivered at the hotel there. That's the sensible thing to do."

She pressed his arm. "Stop and think, Stuart! The newspapers would be filled with the wildest sort of stories, and then questions would be asked. How did the emerald get into this country? Was it loot? Well, I don't know. Chuck got it in, and he's dead, and I don't intend to have his name dragged in the mud for a dozen emeralds. Do what our friend said—use your head!"

"Okay. Tomorrow's Friday, you'll arrive on Saturday, and I'll have the blasted thing to put in your hand when you get there! So be sure to look in your box when you reach the hotel; I'll reserve a room for you."

Their parting was lighthearted, even gay. Stuart barely had time to buy a safety razor and a tube of shaving-cream; then he was in a different world, passing through the terminus to the bus, the roaring city locked out.

On his way to Santa Fe—and what?

The future worried him little; how to get the emerald scarcely gave him a second thought. Hartley was a crook who had bamboozled Penny, that was all. Stuart vaguely reflected that he might have to knock the fellow down and take it away from him, and then dismissed the matter. He was far more concerned with the job he hoped to get in the far West; and before he leaned back in his seat that night and went to sleep, he had written the letter applying for it.

All in all, a good day's work well done, he told himself.

CHAPTER THREE

WITH SOMETHING of this same feeling, he rolled into Santa Fe in early daylight. The air was cold, high, crystal-clear; wood-smoke curled above the city; the tips of the Sangre de Cristo mountains were radiant with sunrise beams. He had a glimpse of the Plaza, of the ancient Palace of

*Coming close, Stuart
saw that this door
stood open an inch
or two. Curious,
he walked over
and knocked.*

the Governors; then the bus spewed him forth in El Portal's courtyard, in modern luxury and pseudo-Spanish surroundings.

A room, reserved from New York, was waiting. He tubbed, shaved, went down to an early breakfast and was ready for the street hours before the shops opened; he wanted a shirt, clean linen, a few odds and ends. His suit was his best, and good enough. Having mailed his letter about the job, he went to the desk and reserved a room for Penny, arriving on the morrow, and one for Sir Evart, due on Sunday.

"By the way, I have a friend who should have reached here yesterday or last night," he said to the clerk. "The name is Hartley. What's his room number?"

The clerk disappeared and came back with a shake of the head.

"No such person here at all, Mr. Stuart."

The dismayed Stuart insisted; so did the clerk, who thereupon phoned two other local hotels. No such person anywhere.

Stuffing his pipe, Stuart abandoned argument, strolled out into the morning sunlight, and made his way to the Plaza. He found an empty bench and sat down, eying the shops around the square and puffing at his pipe as he thought. Hartley had left this address in New York, but this meant little. Perhaps he did not want to be reached at all from New York. He might be using his real name of Monckton, or any other.

"Hm! First blood to the enemy," thought Stuart. "The game's not so easy. After all, it was only a guess that he had sent the stone by mail, but probably he did so. Then I'd better try the name of Monckton."

The shops were opening, now, as time passed. He stepped into a drugstore, called the hotel, and asked to speak with Mr. Monckton. No such guest was there. Stuart hung up, made the round of the shops, bought the clean linen he needed, and thoughtfully footed it back to the hotel. He bought a morning newspaper and settled down in a lobby chair, though reading was a pretense.

This was a knockout. For a little he was frightened. Hartley might not have come here at all; the proximity of Bernard Lattimer to this spot might have completely deluded Sir Evart. However, Stuart bluntly refused to accept this possibility.

Perhaps Sir Evart had gone off the deep end. Better to throw overboard all his notions and look at facts. According to the shop jeweler, he had gone to Santa Fe—no name mentioned;

and had taken a plane West. He might have stopped at a dozen places before ending at Santa Fe. He had left Penny Morrison, the emerald in his pocket, and had then wound up his affairs in New York and caught a noon plane. That was quick work.

"Registering a package by mail takes time," thought Stuart. "Why—hell's bells! He never sent the gem by mail; he lacked the time! We got off on the wrong foot. He may not be here for a week. He's far too smart to pull the obvious trick of a crook; and in fact we don't even know as yet that he is a crook."

IT WAS all very sobering; and, before Stuart had finished glancing over his newspaper, something else occurred to put a complete damper on all exuberance. A page summoned him; at the desk he was handed a telegram. He tore it open, then went back to his chair and reread it with stupefaction. It had come from New York, and read:

WIRE FROM HARTLEY CHICAGO STATES AL-
LEGED EMERALD BEING RETURNED AIRMAIL
WITH APOLOGIES. ADVISE. —PENNY

Stuart filled his pipe and lighted it. So Hartley was in Chicago! Abruptly, he caught at one word: alleged. The *alleged emerald*, Hartley called it! That was a bit of a giveaway. Had he not had Hartley described to him as a super-smart rascal, Stuart might have swallowed this; but obviously Hartley had, in using this word, implied that the stone now being returned was not genuine.

"It doesn't click, somehow," Stuart told himself, frowning at the message. "The guy is in Chicago, and therefore we're all off base. Hm! Penny wants me to advise her. I'll have to be sharp about it, time being two hours later in New York than here. No time to stop and think—"

He looked up. The desk clerk, trying to catch his eye, was beckoning. He rose and went back to the desk.

"Mr. Stuart! Weren't you asking last night about a friend named Hartley? We've just had a wire from him; he's at Chicago, and arrives here at midnight. Thought you'd like to know."

"Yes, indeed! Thanks a lot. Give me a telegraph blank, will you?"

Things were clearing, Stuart mused, as he addressed the wire to Penny. Mr. Hartley, all unwitting, had put a big spoke in his own wheel, in reserving hotel space. He had flown to Chicago—why? Never mind that. He was heading for Santa Fe right

*"I'll take this
real gem and be
responsible for it."*

enough, and using his own name. Stuart made the telegram emphatic:

CHANGE NO PLANS COME ALONG ARRANG-
ING FOR PACKAGE TO FOLLOW.   —STUART.

"Get this off immediately, please no delays. Thanks." He handed over the message, said he would later leave a note for his friend Hartley, took his packages to his own room, and after changing, went out for a walk. He did not regret his impulsive action.

"Now let's get off to a new start," he told himself, as he walked along the Plaza and the narrow streets beyond. "Hartley is a bad egg—smooth, crafty, but not brainy at all. He hears in Egypt about the finding of a certain stone or bit of glass with a tiny Sphinx inside. He traces it to New York and loses no time seeing it and grabbing it. Then what? He doesn't look for any pursuit by a woman. The chief possible purchaser lives near here, so he starts for here but makes a stop-off at Chicago. Why? For something important. I might guess why, but that's bad luck, so I won't. Meantime, I'm here. Am I going to sit around wasting my opportunity or am I going to use my head and keep my eye on the ball? Damned if I know!"

Too bad the police were ruled out; to grab Hartley and the emerald on arrival would be the sensible thing. Still, Penny had her reasons. So what? It was maddening to think of the man arriving with the jewel in his waistcoat pocket and nothing happening; something *must* happen!

Hartley, from Chicago, had wired Penny that the gem was being returned, in order to gain time and freedom from any pursuit. He must be tapped on arrival, then; he must be looted before his suspicions were aroused, and there was only one way to do it—the simplest, most direct way.

His mind made up, Stuart went back to the hotel. He left a call for eight that evening, then pulled down his blinds and got into bed. Before he knew it, he was asleep, and did not waken until his telephone summoned him.

Eight o'clock—and he felt ravenous. He bathed, dressed, got downstairs before the dining-room closed, and ordered a substantial dinner, to which he did full justice. Afterward, he went out and found a movie, which entertained him until eleven. Then back to the hotel, where he discreetly braced the night clerk about the arrival of an expected friend. The hotel bus would be in from the airport, he learned, a few minutes past midnight. Stuart settled down in a chair, his evening beginning where that of others was ending. He was alert, fresh, nimble-witted. Knowing what had to be done, he was entirely ready to do it, with no wasted effort.

The lobby emptied. Time dragged: Stuart walked about, studied the Indian sand-paintings here and there about the lobby floor, eyed the window displays of the lobby shops. His pipe was in his coat pocket. The minutes passed; twelve o'clock came and went. He lit a cigarette and took a chair near the stairs. The hotel had no elevator, being of only two rambling stories, in Spanish style.

There was a stir at the entrance; the doors swung, a bus-driver entered, carrying a bag, a man with him. Both went to the desk. Presently a bellman came toward the stairs, bag in hand, the new arrival behind him: a smallish man; under his hatbrim was a striking set of features, hooked nose, bushy black brows. "Hartley," sure enough! Stuart rose, stubbed out his cigarette, and followed them up the stairs, unhurried.

THE UPPER corridor was obscured. A door opened, lights inside were switched on. Stuart came past, noted the number of the door, went on down the corridor to the turn, waited a little, headed back. The room door was closed. He halted, pulled his hat over his eyes, and knocked.

The door was opened.

"Telegram, Mr. Hartley," Stuart said—and pushed the door with his foot so that it flew open. He stepped inside, right hand in his coat pocket gripping his pipe in ominous outline, and closed the door behind him.

Hartley stared at him.

"You can't get away with it," said Stuart. "That stop in Chicago didn't fool anybody. Turn around, face to the wall. Get your hands up—fast!"

HIS WORDS were enough to break down Hartley, who gasped and obeyed the order. Stuart came close behind him.

"Don't get careless or I'll put a bullet into you." Reaching around with his free hand, Stuart began to explore his victim's pockets, speaking the while to keep Hartley from pulling himself together. "So you mailed the imitation emerald back from Chicago, eh? Very clever bit of work. I suppose you got a bit of glass made up and sent back."

"I'll see you jailed for this!" Hartley spoke thickly, furiously.

Stuart met the threat with a laugh.

"Not likely. Hold still, now! You wouldn't like the cops to be asking you any questions, would you? Now I think we have everything—but I don't want your personal effects, so hold still while I weed 'em out. Don't move."

A small box in the waistcoat pocket—that should be it, but he could not take chances. With his one hand, he opened it, saw a pale green shimmer bedded in cotton, and pocketed it. The wallet and other items he had removed, he tossed to the nearby bed.

Then a sharp rap at the door startled him.

"Easy! Stay as you are."

With the command, he stepped back and opened the door. A stranger stood there, a man whose floppy brown hat, sprigged with a small feather, was drawn down over his eyes.

"Mr. Hartley here?" he asked.

Stuart opened the door wide.

"Sure thing. Walk in."

The other entered; as he did so, Stuart squeezed past, pulled shut the door and went down the hall fast. He ran, and no one followed. There was no outcry. His room was in the other wing of the hotel. He gained it without incident, shut the door upon himself; he was alone—and triumphant!

His writing-table had a desk light. He switched it on, and before it put the little cardboard box in which reposed the emerald. He sat down and examined this; it was the same stone he had noted among Chuck Morrison's effects—pale green in hue, an uneven cabochon in shape, with something dark in the center. At this he gazed with some interest. On holding the stone close to the light, he fancied it had the shape of the Sphinx.

"The stone's a deeper green underneath it. Hm! Should have a glass to enlarge it." He laid down the emerald, lit a cigarette,

"I just had to make you say it, Bill: 'I love you!'"

and with a smile looked at his plunder. The little box was un-marked. "Apparently I hit the nail on the head, too: the guy arranged to have a near-replica made in Chicago and sent to Penny."

Abruptly he remembered something that sobered him. That caller at Hartley's room—who had it been? Some friend who expected his arrival? Oh, the hell with it! Another crook or two mattered nothing.

"If there's any need, I can confess openly: this was stolen

property and I was recovering it," he thought. He picked up the tiny box; it seemed a bit heavy. He took out the packed cotton, and beneath it found an unrimmed enlarging-glass—evidently to assist in examining the stone.

Picking it up, he held the emerald beneath it. The Sphinx-figure leaped out; he almost gasped at sight of it, thus, perfect in form. Under the glass, too, the whole body of the gem took on new form and coloring: The minute crystalline striations, the flaws, the tiny angular bubbles—who ever heard of angular bubbles? Yet there they were!—gave him a sensation of surprise, even of delight. Instead of a dot of beryl, here he had a vista of green beneath the light, thanks to the enlarging-glass. He gazed into it for a long time, and experienced a queer upheaval of emotions. He imagined things passing before his very eyes. Astonished, he removed the glass and looked at the stone. No, nothing except a spot of greenish beryl.

Under the glass again, this expanded. Stuart wondered how the emerald could be distinguished from glass; he was ignorant of the fact that this green color, persisting true under artificial light, was one evidence. Singular fancies crept through, or came from, those green vistas. Really a double cabochon in form, this crystal had depth; the light glinted across those verdant expanses, refraction tempted the imagination, and the least change of position instantly gave birth to fresh illusions.

At the start, the sensation was not unpleasant: an uplift, a sense of power, an ecstasy such as rare old wine might engender in the spirit. But it changed. Uneasiness stole upon him, a vaguely troubling worry tormented him. He sought the cause, and there was none, visibly. Yet it remained and grew more intense. Something seemed very wrong. The sensation sharpened imperceptibly until it was acute. An odd idea took shape in his mind, as though whispers were coming to him from the emerald.

He had the stone; nor did he feel that in getting it he had acted wrongly. Yet he had taken the law into his own hands, beyond all question. His uneasiness became a definite feeling of blame, of self-accusation. This was disturbing; so was the notion of reparation, as though he had done something for which he must pay. All folly, of course. But, remembering what had been said about self-hypnosis, and Chuck Morrison's warning to Penny, Stuart abruptly tore himself from the glass and gave up his gazing. He glanced at his watch and felt a start of alarm. He had been busied with this emerald, not for a few minutes, but for two solid hours!

He dropped the stone in its bed of cotton, put down the glass, and placed them on the table. His uneasiness and troubled worry were gone at once. He locked his door, laughing at his own ridiculous notions. Thought of Hartley caused him no foreboding. Of course Hartley could discover who had been hanging about the lobby so late, and might well guess at the identity of the robber. He might even attempt some return blow—but that was nonsense. The man was in no position to strike back. Sir Evart's talk of his cleverness was bosh.

Unworried now, blissfully satisfied, Stuart disrobed, switched off his light, and stretched out in bed, feeling unaccountably tired. He fell asleep almost at once, and so profound was his slumber that nothing disturbed him until the bedside telephone rang and rang again.

This was at noon the next day.

CHAPTER FOUR

SLEEPILY, HIS head heavy and feeling like a solid marble mass, Stuart got hold of the phone. He managed to make out that the desk clerk was calling him.

"I think you reserved space for today, Mr. Stuart, for a Miss Morrison?"

"Eh? Oh, for Penny—sure thing!"

"We thought you might like to know that we just had a wire from her saying she would arrive by air at three-thirty this afternoon."

"Oh, fine! Thanks a lot."

Stuart hung up, yawned, and then glanced at his watch with incredulous horror. Noon! Impossible!

He jumped out of bed and staggered. Then he noticed an odd sort of odor in the room, sweet and sickish. He became aware of his stuffed-up head, his sluggish senses, and suddenly wanted fresh air. He had forgotten to open his window. Making his way to it, he shoved it wide open and drank in the fresh sunny air with quick relief. Almost at once his head began to clear.

Bewildered, he pulled a chair to the window and sat down. Something had happened, but he could not figure out what it was. Last thing he remembered was sitting and gazing at the emerald. He remembered the warning sent to Penny by her brother: *"Be careful not to look at it too long."* Auto-hypnosis? No, that would not cause such queer effects. Might have something to do with it, of course; but there had definitely been something in the room—

His vagrant gaze touched upon the writing-table. He blinked at it; he rubbed his eyes, got up and stared. His senses cleared. The table was empty; the little box and the glass were gone.

Now he understood. He got under the shower, his brain steadied, he came back and dressed, in a savage mood. By some odd kink, what stuck in his mind was a floppy brown hat sprigged with a red feather—a friend who had arrived to meet Hartley. A man who is not alone can manage anything.

Leaving the room, he lit a cigarette and started downstairs, suppressing a groan and an oath. Not clever, eh? He had been a fool to laugh at them. They had worked fast and efficiently, injecting through the keyhole into the room some soporific and then unlocking the door and walking in to get the emerald. By not opening his window, he had played into their hands; no doubt they had shot enough dope into the room to pretty near kill him.

At the desk, his inquiries sadly confirmed all this. Yes, Mr.

Hartley had checked out early, before five o'clock, in fact—had paid for his room and gone to visit friends. He had left no forwarding address. With this to sauce his meal, Stuart sought the dining-room and secured lunch. Nice news with which to greet Penny at three-thirty! Now he was back where he had started—except that he was a trifle wiser.

What now—the police? Definitely not. Lattimer? He had been quietly warned off by Sir Evart. Yet he felt an urgent pull toward action. Hartley had arrived at midnight and could have had no sleep since; until evening, at least, the man would be resting. This, as Stuart could see, was his only chance to get anything accomplished, to repair his own folly.

He made his way back to the desk, and there got hold of the clerk with whom he had just spoken.

"Perhaps you can help me. I missed my friend Hartley last night. He skipped out this morning before I was up—checked out about five, you said. It just occurred to me that he might have taken a taxi. If he did, and you can locate the driver, I might find my friend after all."

A bright idea, said the clerk; it might work. He summoned a bellman, telephoned, learned that a taxi had been called that morning, and set about locating it. This was not hard; calls at that hour in Santa Fe were not common. Within ten minutes a little man in a driver's cap sought him out.

"I took two men and a bag from here at five this morning," he said. "I hear you want to locate them?"

"That's right, if they're still in town," assented Stuart.

"I reckon so. I took 'em to a place on the north side."

"Got your car here? Let's go," Stuart said impulsively.

"Ain't much of a place—just a big trailer where a guy lives."

Two minutes later they were bumping toward a newly built-up section where buildings thinned and ran into brownish stretches of open country at the very edge of the city. The roads became unpaved trails. Bleak hills ran over the horizon.

"That's it," said the driver, and pointed to a reddish-brown trailer, without a car, standing in a field to the right, isolated and alone. "I'll have to stop here; can't trust my tires in that stubble."

"I'll walk over." Stuart thrust a bill at him. "Wait for me."

He left the car and started across the field toward the trailer, which was closed and apparently empty. Wooden steps mounted to the door at one end. Coming close, Stuart saw that this door stood open an inch or two. Curious, he walked over to it, ascended the wooden steps, and knocked. No answer; nothing was heard. He gave the door a push—and as it opened upon horror, his heart skipped a beat.

Directly before him, on the floor of the trailer, sat a man leaning against the far wall, holding a revolver cocked in his lap. Staring-eyed, the man had bled to death, as a blackened pool of blood on the floor indicated all too surely, from a wound apparently in his thigh or back. Beside him was a floppy-brimmed brown hat adorned with a sliver of feather; this was the man who had come to Hartley's room in the hotel.

STUART TOOK it in at a glance; the wide fixed eyes, the ghastly pallor, told of death. He caught his breath; then something white caught his eye. Beside the body, as though fallen from the lax, free hand, was the little box that had contained the Sphinx Emerald. It still contained it. In the fall, the lid had become dislodged and Stuart could see a flash of green.

The truth flashed across his brain. Hartley and this unknown had together obtained the stone from his room and had come here; then had got into a fight over the loot. This man had seized it, had been wounded, and had sunk down here. Hartley, ignorant of approaching death, had skipped out hurriedly without the emerald—and here it was!

Stuart did not stop to think. Police, investigations, folly—nothing occurred to him. He took one step forward, reached down, and picked up the stone from the little box. He touched the man, whose body was stiff and cold, then hastily drew back.

He drew the door shut and descended the steps, and strode toward the waiting taxi.

"Nobody home?" queried the driver as he came up.

"Door's unlocked, but nobody answered me," said Stuart, and climbed in. "Back to the hotel, I guess. Anyhow, I'll know where to come next time."

He sat back on the cushions and shivered. The stone was in his pocket; but realization of his own stupidity was appalling. True, no one seemed near; the bright sunlight revealed no threat in any direction; yet investigation must come, and when it came this taxi-driver would recall his name and he would be thrust into it.

Well, that could be met and faced; Stuart, with an effort, forced down his heart-hammerings. Hartley would return sooner or later, but certainly would not report the matter to the police. That would result only from curiosity of neighbors. There was no immediate menace.

Still, when he got out at the hotel he was in a sweat. He gave the driver a fat tip, and the man chuckled.

"Thanks, Mister. That brings it up to just the right figure for El Paso."

"Eh?" Stuart frowned. "What d'you mean by that?"

"I been saving up tips and so forth. I got a brother down to El Paso and I want to visit him for a month, and this is my last job for a while. Now I can get off tomorrow. I was raised down there and it'll be good to see old friends."

"Driving down?"

"When we got roads like glass, I sure ain't wasting coin on railroad fare! Well, thanks a lot."

He drove away, and Stuart turned into the hotel. A feeling of vast relief surged through him. There went his only immediate chance of being drawn into the murder mystery—for such it would be called, no doubt.

"Strictly speaking, my duty is probably to report the matter," Stuart told himself. "If the man were alive, I'd have to do it. But he's dead. I can do him no good by putting the cops on Hartley, and might do myself and Penny a lot of harm. So I'll just stand pat."

He looked at his watch—three o'clock! Procuring an envelope at the desk, he addressed it to Penny, slipped the emerald inside, sealed it, and gave it to the desk clerk to put in her box. She would find it there on arrival, as he had promised her. Somewhat tickled by this conceit, he went out to the street, stopped at the first jewelry-shop, and bought an enlarging-glass. With this in his pocket he came back to the hotel and sought his room. As he sat, lost in thought, Stuart was aware of an avid desire to have that emerald here and to gaze again into its depths. He shrugged off the desire almost angrily, and not without a trace of fear. The thing was almost uncanny—what strange sensations he had experienced from it last night!

Yet in his heart he knew it was not uncanny at all; he had simply been stirred into recognition of his own fears. In general, the close view of the stone had inspired a fine brave sensation which he craved to repeat; not hypnotic, but an awakening of his own innate consciousness. Stuart had too much common sense to credit any occult influences.

H E   W A S wakened from his abstraction by the telephone, and picked it up to hear Penny's voice.

"Hello, stranger! I'm here. And no one to meet me—not even a guy standing at the hotel door! You're a grand greeter, I don't think!"

"Hi, Penny. It's grand to hear your voice," he replied. "I left a green orchid in your box as promised."

"I got it, Bill. And I'm thrilled, honest: your crimes are forgiven."

"Thanks. Have a good trip? When do I see you?"

"Swell trip, old boy. You don't see me for the next half-hour, I hope. After that, name your time."

"Thirty-one minutes, then. Meet you in the lobby. And,

Penny— Don't leave that green thing lying around in your room. Tuck it away somewhere."

"Okay, Bill."

He hung up; the world had changed. Her voice had altered everything, and even bitter memories lessened. He was back to reality now, and before he realized, he was whistling cheerfully.

Penny was prompt to the minute. Her alive, sparkling personality was like charged wine to him; yet the eagerness in all she said and did was pleasantly restrained by an alert, hard realism; she could dream, yet kept her dreams within limits.

"I want to see everything—just walk and talk and look around!" she exclaimed. "I've never been here before, and it's interesting. You can tell me how you got the stone back, as we go."

"No." Stuart ushered her out to the street. "Let it wait. Sir Evart will be here tomorrow; then's time enough to talk about it. After dinner tonight I'll introduce you to the emerald; but now we'll just have a look at Santa Fe before the sun goes down."

Churches, *acequias,* buildings — Stuart himself had not realized what there was here to see, and "doing" the town in company with Penny made time fly. At twilight they returned to the hotel, celebrated the occasion with a cocktail, and a little later met in the dining-room for dinner.

"I'm really curious, Bill," Penny said across the table with a smile, "about how you got hold of the emerald. Do you expect me to wait until Sir Evart gets here?"

He nodded soberly as he met her dancing eyes.

"Yeah, guess you'll have to. No particular reason for secrecy— it's just that things happened pretty fast and I'm not at all sure of my ground. This business may be more risky than it appears, too."

"Okay, I'll be good. Is our friend Hartley here?"

"Not here, I trust, but he's somewhere around. I figure that he went to someone he knew in Chicago and ordered a reasonable imitation of the emerald sent you, trusting you'd accept it as the original."

"And I would have, of course, except for you and Sir Evart. I've left instructions for any airmail to be forwarded here. Tomorrow's Sunday—well, it might come any time; depends on how long it would take to make the replica and get it to me. Sir Evart will get in tomorrow, too."

Stuart again nodded thoughtfully. Before he could reply, a page appeared and gave him a card with a word.

"A gentleman gave me this for you, sir. He's waiting for a reply."

Astonished, Stuart glanced at the writing on the card, then was astonished anew. It read:

Can you give me a few moments when you finish dinner, please?
John Monckton.

Stuart blinked. He looked at the page.

"Where's this man—in the lobby?"

"Yes, sir."

"Okay. Tell him yes; I'll see him there."

THE PAGE departed. Stuart met Penny's gaze.

"You don't seem exactly enthusiastic over your visitor, Bill."

"I'm not," he replied. "It's Hartley, using his real name of Monckton. Wants to see me. Maybe he saw you dining here with me. He could easily learn my name from the hotel desk, of course. If he saw you, he'll probably be prepared for trouble."

She looked around. "Impossible. The lobby's not in view from here."

Seeing this to be the case, Stuart breathed more freely. He was in fear lest she be pulled into the affair, and said so frankly. She laughed.

"Nonsense! That man evidently takes me for a fool, and I'd like to express my opinion of him to his face. However, I'll not interfere."

"Then suppose you let me leave first. I'll draw him off into a corner so he won't notice you when you come out. Right now he probably has his eye on the dining-room entrance. You go to your room, and after a few minutes I'll come there."

She nodded assent. Dessert and coffee arrived. Stuart made no haste; he was thankful that Penny fired no questions at him. This was an amazing action on the part of Hartley and rather knocked him off balance. He wished fervently that Sir Evart were here, then could have kicked himself for the wish.

"What the hell! I'm not an idiot," he reflected. "I can handle the guy as well as anyone else could, so I'd better do it."

He called for the check, signed it, and rose, conscious of Penny's gaze.

"Well, see you later," he said, and departed.

CHAPTER FIVE

THE VISITOR was not far to seek. Stuart caught sight of him standing at the desk and talking with the clerk, and went straight up to him. Hartley saw his approach and nodded.

"Suppose we sit down and be comfortable," said Stuart, and headed for a far corner that was unoccupied. Hartley laughed slightly.

"I wasn't sure you'd know the name of Monckton, Mr. Stuart."

"Oh, I'm slightly conversant with affairs," Stuart said lightly, and switched around an armchair. He placed an ash-holder within reach, produced and lit a cigarette, and seated himself. Without doing so obviously, he now had Hartley seated with his back to the dining-room entrance.

"Well," he said, "what's the nature of your business with me?"

Hartley, in animation, was quite pleasant and perfectly calm.

"I don't think we need do any fencing, Mr. Stuart. When you stopped in at the trailer today, I was in a nearby house and saw you. I returned later to the trailer and the emerald was gone. I don't need to refer to the events of last night."

Stuart met his gaze, and smiled.

"Nor this morning. I don't think you'd better, indeed! You certainly had your nerve to go back there after I had stopped in."

Hartley shrugged. "Never mind. You came there, found what was inside, and by that fact placed yourself in what might prove a very unpleasant position."

"Nuts!" said Stuart. "You'd be in a lot worse position if I talked up."

"That might be argued. However, I'm not here in order to indulge threats. It occurs to me that you must be a practical person, and I wish to speak with you as such, without evasions or false pretenses."

"Good!" agreed Stuart cheerfully. "Threat and counter-threat really wouldn't get us anywhere—so go right ahead."

He spoke lightly; but he was conscious of danger. This man was putting a pleasant face on things, that was all. With each word uttered, Stuart was more impressed with actual peril, with craft, with weighty potentiality on Hartley's part. Behind the affable mask lurked hard, cold steel; he could feel it actively. This fellow was no lightweight; he had a lot on the ball.

"Just who you are, I don't know." Hartley spoke without haste, lighting a cigar with care and attention. "From your words to me last evening, you obviously know all about the Sphinx Emerald. How you got on to me, I don't know either, or care; that's all beside the point. The main thing is that you're here, and at this moment you have the emerald."

"You may be mistaken about that," Stuart said quietly. "I might be a detective."

The other snorted gently.

"You'd not be talking about it. I'm not a fool! You're a friend of Miss Morrison, granted. That's enough. I've made mistakes;

now I want to approach you fairly and squarely and without animosity, with a view to settlement."

Stuart was faintly amused.

"Go ahead, if you have an objective."

"Very definitely.... As a precious stone, that emerald is practically worthless. As a historical piece and a unique stone, it is priceless. I know why you're here, of course; about here live people who buy such things. That's why I'm here, naturally. In the hills about Santa Fe are millionaires, retired business men, collectors of all sorts."

As he talked, Hartley smiled thinly. "Where wealth is, the vultures gather. I can handle the stone to much better effect than can you. I'm not alone in this affair; I have friends on the way here now. I risk little in talking with you thus. Understood? Very well. I offer you half the proceeds to throw in with me and hand over the emerald. I have five hundred dollars in my pocket this minute to give you, as an advance. Yes or no, Mr. Stuart?"

No longer amused, Stuart's reaction was thoughtful. A movie hero, he reflected, would betray indignant rage at this offer of bribery, but he was not insulted; he was no hero.

"Have you an alternative?" he asked.

"Certainly; I leave that to your imagination. I'm not coming up in my offers, you know. This is your one and only chance to come in with me."

"Refused."

"Very good; that's all, then."

Hartley rose, nodded, walked away.

WITH MINGLED emotions, Stuart watched him go out of the hotel. Hartley was willing to pay five hundred to get the emerald. Then why had he not bought it in the first place? Uncertainty, of course.

"I won't get that much, even if Sir Evart does sell it," Stuart told himself. "In fact, the thing belongs to Penny—I don't want

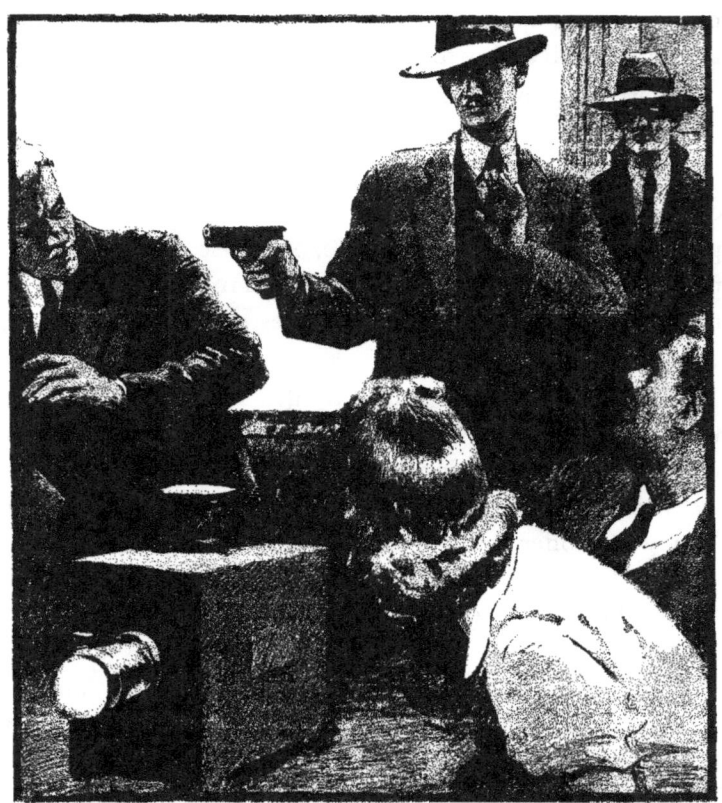

*"This stone's worth dying for—and to
you it means only money. You fool!"*

any money out of it. And now what? Of course he'll try some
other scheme. I'd better warn Penny immediately and get that
emerald into safety."

He went to the house telephone, called Miss Morrison's
room, and thrilled to Penny's response.

"Hello, Bill! Everything all right?"

"Oh, sure!"

"Good; I was anxious about it. Is our friend still there?"

"Yes; he just left. Will you come down and meet me in the

writing-room? The hotel might deem it highly improper if I came to you."

"At once, my good cautious Sir Tristram, at once!"

"And bring that green thing with you."

"Naturally; it is now my second self."

Stuart turned from the phones. He became aware of a bellboy and a man heading for him; his nerves jumped as the bellboy made an unmistakable gesture toward him. The man was a stranger—tall, of distinguished appearance, with white hair and mustache, but remarkably hale and hearty.

"Mr. Stuart?" the stranger spoke up. "My name is Lattimer. I have a wire here from Sir Evart Buckson, who arrives tomorrow, so strangely interesting that I've come to look you up. I understand that you have the Sphinx Emerald."

Mentally, Stuart drew sharply back.

"If I had, I wouldn't discuss it with you," he said. "I don't know that you're Mr. Lattimer; to me you're a stranger. You'll have to excuse me until Sir Evart is here to speak for himself."

Made aware of his ungraciousness by the other's expression, he offered a swift half-apology.

"Sorry; I don't mean to antagonize you—I've been deviled right and left. Five minutes ago a prize crook was here, bold as brass, on the same trail."

Lattimer started slightly.

"Indeed! You're quite right, Mr. Stuart. I don't blame you in the least, and I applaud your caution. I sha'n't urge you a whit. Kindly give my card to Sir Evart when he arrives, and ask him to call me immediately. It's important."

Stuart took the pasteboard handed him, and instantly repented his own lack of courtesy. He had no chance to speak further; Lattimer bowed slightly and turned away, walking swiftly to the entrance. Stuart glanced at the card: *Bernard Lattimer*, with a phone number. He turned toward the writing-room, frowning, angry at himself yet not regretting his action.

"Maybe I'm a fool, maybe not, but no harm done anyhow," he reflected.

Five minutes later, seated at a writing-room desk with Penny beside him, he told her of the two visitors.

"I don't get it—any of it," he said irritably. "I'd like to crawl in a hole and pull it in after me, until Sir Evart shows up."

"But why?" she demanded, wide-eyed.

"Too much of a squeeze—getting into murder is too much for me," he replied and confusedly broke off. "Well, let it pass. Here's an enlarging-glass. Remember what Chuck wrote you about gazing into that emerald? It says things to you. Get the stone under this writing-light and look into it."

She looked at him. "Bill Stuart, you're not washing me up like that! Murder? Well, I'll stick to my bargain and ask no questions till Sir Evart gets here; but you are certainly going to do some talking tomorrow, let me warn you, and don't try to renege then!"

She opened her handbag, took out the emerald and set it on the desk where it got the full benefit of the light. With the glass Stuart handed her, she focused on the stone and uttered an exclamation.

"Oh—the Sphinx! Why, Bill, that's wonderful—perfect as can be, too!"

"Get a good steady look—right into the heart of the stone!" he advised, settling back and getting out his cigarettes. "I'll stop chattering and let you get the full effect."

H E S AT smoking and silent, watching her, liking her capacity for silence. She had nothing to say, and did not break into unnecessary spurts of words. Also, he liked to look at her face.

That replica—if it were a replica—ought to be along pretty soon, he reflected, since speed would have been an essential part of Hartley's scheme to keep his victim satisfied and unthinking. It would be interesting to see if an exact replica had been made; one of glass could be turned out quickly, no doubt. If so, he wondered how the real could be told from the false.

Without a glass, they would probably look exactly alike. Still, the tiny Sphinx-figure could hardly be duplicated so exactly.

The girl caught her breath. She was interested now; the thing had taken hold of her. She steadied, and settled down to intent gazing. So, thought Stuart, it had not been merely his fervid imagination last night! The play of emotions in her face was fascinating to see, but he could not read them.

"I see what you mean, Bill," she murmured. "Wonderful!"

"Tell me what you get, when you feel like it," he put in, and she nodded.

Time passed; she sat entranced, and remembering how oblivious he had himself been to the passing of time, Stuart waited patiently. At length she straightened up and sighed, then turned to him, radiance in her face.

"Bill, I—I can't give this up!" she breathed. "At least, of course I must—but I'll hate to do it. Why, it seems to inspire such downright beauty—that's the only word for it: beauty! That can't be what Chuck meant."

"I didn't get that at all," dissented Stuart. "I tell you: probably it's different with everyone—causes a sort of auto-suggestion, merely wakens what's latent in the mind! That stands to reason, Penny. There's nothing eerie or occult about it; you can no doubt get the same effect by looking into any gem with a glass. In this one the flaws are so marked that it's not like an empty crystal, but a full one."

"Maybe," she agreed doubtfully. "Yet it's a lovely sensation. I'd like to go on and on looking—I'm like a child with a delight-ful new toy!"

"I know that feeling—I'd the same craving, yet I had been sitting for two hours with it last night. And that's bad, my dear; it's a yielding to the infatuation, to the dominance of the stone. You're going to put it up right now. There's only one safe place for it—in the hotel safe. And since you're the owner, come along and deposit it."

She grimaced at this, then looked at him, perplexed.

"You weren't in earnest about—about murder?"

"Absolutely. I took it out of a dead's man's hand, if you must know."

At this, she shivered, then thrust the glass at him.

"All right, take it. We'll go to the desk. I don't understand this, any of it. I think I'm a bit afraid, to be honest."

"I think you'd better be, and that's honest too," he said gravely, and rose. "I'm pretty thoroughly balled up about Hartley's words and everything; until Sir Evart comes, I'll be all at sea. You be sure to lock your door tonight. This thing has me jittery, I admit."

They sought the desk together. Here Penny wrapped the Sphinx Emerald in her handkerchief and put it into the big envelope the clerk handed her, sealed it, wrote her name where indicated, and turned to Stuart.

"A breath of this crisp, wonderful air, before turning in. Eh?"

They sauntered out to the street. Stuart kept his eyes open, saw nothing alarming, and after a turn about the Plaza they came back to the hotel. As they came in the clerk held up a hand to Stuart.

"I think you made a reservation for tomorrow—a Mr. Buckson?"

"Yes—Sir Evart Buckson."

"Just had a wire from him. He'll be here about noon. Good-night!"

Stuart saw Penny home, left her at the door, and they arranged to meet at nine in the morning for breakfast. He went to his own room, opened the window, and read himself to sleep with a magazine. Yet he slept poorly, waking often, and when he closed his eyes he dreamed unpleasantly. At a little after eight he phoned Penny.

"Good morning! How's everything?" he inquired, on getting her.

"Just lovely! No bugaboos or nocturnal prowlers, thanks."

He hung up.

"I'm a fool," he told himself happily. "Worrying over nothing. Letting a little chiseling crook throw a man-sized scare into me! Now, the hell with all that! No more nonsense. There's not a thing Hartley can do, without tying himself up even more rigidly, so I'd better forget him. And yet—that man in the trailer was certainly dead as a door-nail!"

An ugly fact; but its importance lessened with sunlight and breakfast and a radiant Penny. While they were at the table, a page fetched Stuart a yellow envelope, and he signed for it, with a grimace.

"Word that our boss won't get here," he predicted, tearing at it. "Or that his plane is down somewhere or—Whoops! Look at this—would you look at it!"

He waved the telegram at her; they read it together: a long night-letter from the Douglas people, in reply to the letter he had sent on his arrival here. Not only did it welcome his inquiry and request him to name an arrival date in California, but it was signed by one S. E. C. Bloom.

"Old Razz Bloom!" Stuart exclaimed delightedly. "He was with me in Egypt, see? And I never dreamed he was with that company! Say, this is luck of the finest kind, Penny! I'm fixed for good! Wants me as his assistant—great! Now we can eat, sure enough!"

"*We?*" she queried.

"Er—rhetorically speaking," Stuart evaded in some confusion. "Me for the West Coast, you bet! I'll wire back that I can start work the end of the week; Sir Evart should clean up the emerald business in a day or so."

Nice theorizing, anyway.

CHAPTER SIX

WHEN SIR EVART BUCKSON arrived, Stuart and Penny were at the airport to meet him. In her purse

Penny carried a tiny box that arrived by special delivery airmail, forwarded from New York to catch her here on this bright Sunday morning. In the box and carefully bedded in cotton was the replica of the Sphinx Emerald which Hartley had caused to be made in Chicago—a replica of the gem now reposing in the hotel safe, so perfect in hue and shape that it would have fooled Stuart even on close scrutiny! The tiny figure of the Sphinx was well made.

"It would have tricked me completely," said Penny. "Is it an emerald, Bill?"

"Can't be," said Stuart. "Sir Evart said that Chuck's find was a unique stone. Tuck it away. When we get back to the hotel you get hold of the real one, and we'll spring 'em both on Sir Evart at lunch."

She nodded.

The genial Briton met them delightedly and gave Stuart a questioning look.

"Everything under control, at the moment," said Stuart. "I have a taxi here, so hop in and we'll go to the hotel. Your bag can follow. I take it the first thing is a square meal."

"You're a mind-reader," said Sir Evart.

"We've a lot of talking to do, too," put in Penny. "And Mr. Lattimer wants you to call him at once. He came to the hotel last night and Bill rather shoved him off. I think Bill's been seeing things in his sleep."

"More correct than you know," chuckled Stuart. "We'll talk at the table."

At the hotel, Sir Evart checked in, got some mail that awaited him, and disappeared into a phone booth. He came out, looking grave.

"Lattimer will come here later this afternoon," he said. "So until then we can catch up on happenings."

They settled at a table a little apart from others, and when the ordering had been accomplished, Stuart went into his story. Penny laid on the table the real and false emeralds, and Sir

Evart examined them through a jeweler's glass while he listened.

"You're sure that man in the trailer was dead?" he asked then.

Stuart nodded to the sharp question.

"Cold and stiff. But that's not all. Last evening, or rather yesterday, Hartley was here openly, using his real name of Monckton—"

He went on to tell of the astonishing interview. Penny, who had been rendered speechless by his story of the trailer, watched him with anxious eyes. Sir Evart listened closely but made no comment until Stuart had finished.

"I don't pretend to understand it," he vouchsafed, with a shake of the head, "but when you monkeyed with Hartley you burned your fingers. He's hot stuff; yet I fancy we need lose no worry over him."

Stuart laughed. "I'm losing none—unless he accuses me of murdering his pal."

"Forget it! A sneak thief—that's his level. Your only danger was lest the taxi-driver talk; but the man's gone away, and I think you've nothing to fear. Hartley won't try to accuse you, since he can't stand any investigation himself. He has no doubt seen Miss Morrison here and thinks you're acting for and with her. He may have already seen and recognized me, also. Anything's possible, but don't worry."

"Just what do you propose doing?"

"First, accept your unuttered challenge to pick the true from the false." Sir Evart regarded the two emeralds with a smiling glance. "Second, unpack—or first unpack, then play with the stones. Third, meet Lattimer and get rid of responsibility and probably of the Sphinx Emerald as well. In this wild and woolly West of yours, it's a bit perilous to have the thing kicking about loose."

Stuart grinned. "You expect scalping parties to jump out from behind every bush, do you? Hardly likely, in a hotel like this!"

They all laughed together. The Briton had accomplished his

purpose of turning the subject from the gravely ominous to a lighter aspect.

After the meal Stuart accompanied Sir Evart to his room, where Penny promised to join them in five minutes. He perceived that the older man was not so carefree. Sir Evart took his arm gravely.

"Now that we're alone I can speak plainly. I didn't want to alarm Miss Penny, you see. I must tell you that our friend Hartley or Monckton is somewhat noted for his ruthless ingenuity and persistence. If the emerald were not worth a farthing he would still pursue it indefatigably. Thank heaven, we should be done with the affair today! It's a perilous business, I'm afraid."

His bluff, sturdy personality was heartening. He said what he thought, without waste of words. Stuart scarcely shared his prescience of danger—he refused to consider Hartley as a threat—yet he had a certainty that they were not through with the man.

Sir Evart emptied his single bag quickly, and Penny appeared. The early afternoon sun poured in at the window, and into the flood of light Sir Evart moved his writing-desk. On it he laid the Sphinx Emerald and its duplicate.

"Now for your challenge to differentiate these two gems!" he said cheerfully, with his best professional lecturing manner. "You'll note that they have a cabochon or round-top shape, yet there are facets visible. I'm about to impart to you an extremely simple test, most valuable to all jewelers, especially where a faceted stone is concerned, yet it can be applied even where there are no facets. The two gems are side by side in the direct sunlight."

From his pocket he took a white card.

"Now, I'll hold this card thus, a few inches from the gems, in the direction of the sun, so as to get the reflections from within the gems on the card. The reflections of certain material, such as diamond or glass or garnet, are single. Other material, beryl for example, is double-refractive—that is, the reflecting facets throw double images. Look closely as I move the card from one gem to the other. Emerald is double-refracting, though only feebly—"

He focused with the card to get the reflection. As he moved it from one gem to the other, Stuart could instantly perceive the difference in the refractions.

"IT'S CLEAR as can be!" exclaimed Penny, and touched one. "This is glass—it must be the replica!"

"Correct," said Sir Evart. "The test is quite sure. The card merely assists the eye, you see—an expert can look into the gem and examine the facets for himself, but the doubling of the lines is not always easy to perceive. I'll take this real gem and be responsible for it. In fact, I'm most anxious to examine it. Stuart, suppose you take the glass replica. We'll keep them quite separate."

With a nod, Stuart dropped the fake into his pocket, not bothering with the box and cotton. Sir Evart sat down and lengthily examined the emerald through his glass.

"Remarkable!" he said at last. "It's obvious why credulous people have credited this stone with occult powers. All rank bosh, of course! I noticed that the imitation has bubbles, too, but not angular ones. They're created by striking the material before it cools off. Quite simple; but in dealing with gems, simplicity is usually very clever. I take it, my dear, you still wish to dispose of the genuine stone?"

Penny smiled. "I do and I don't. It's a lovely plaything; but if it's as valuable as you say, I need the money. And after Bill's story, it does give me a shiver."

"Right; then we'll attend to it. Don't however, blame the stone for the things that happen," said the older man earnestly. "It, and every other famous gem, has no doubt a history passing through many phases of death and murder. After all, death is not really tragic; it's an ordinary concomitant of all life. This gem, with its microscopic Sphinx, is unique."

"What will happen to it?" Stuart queried thoughtfully. "I

mean, how will it end? An end must sometime come, whether it just drops out of sight or is crushed or falls into the ocean—"

Sir Evart smiled. "Well, it dropped into the Nile rather lately—yet here it is before us. Gems last for thousands of years, but I suppose they do some day come to an end of some sort. Lattimer will certainly be deeply interested in this stone. He's a wealthy man and can afford to pay well; so for us, I presume the gem will come to an end in his collection, at least temporarily. He lives outside the city a little way—I've never seen his house. It's said to be very fine."

Glass in eye, he bent over the stone again. His fascination was entirely understandable to Stuart and Penny.

"Do you suppose that Hartley, or Monckton, looked into it?" said Penny.

Sir Evart straightened, pushed the stone away as though repulsing it.

"Certainly. Its influence is extraordinary, he fell under it, and that would account for his mad persistence in pursuing it. This color is poor at first sight, but the stone has deeper spots and proper cutting would improve it vastly, in value. It'll be interesting to see Lattimer's reaction to the stone. Well, my friends, suppose that we settle the whole problem this afternoon. What are your plans?"

"I don't know—I haven't thought about it," confessed Penny.

"I have; you've brought me luck, Sir Evart, or the emerald has." Stuart laughed. "An old Army pal is with an airplane company on the West Coast, and I've secured a place, thanks to him, with them."

"Congratulations! You're going out right from here?"

"I think so. I may get married first."

"Eh?" Sir Evart shot him a look. Stuart was aware of Penny's gaze, but carefully avoided meeting it. "Who's the lucky girl?"

"Well, it's not settled. I haven't asked her yet. I'm merely hoping."

The Briton laughed heartily. "Well, the best luck in the world! Er, Miss Penny?"

Penny looked down. "Oh, I'm sure—yes, of course!" she said.

At this instant the telephone rang. Sir Evart answered.

"Oh, yes, yes; send him up, please!" He put down the instrument. "Lattimer. Now we'll see shortly."

"Want me to clear out?" asked Stuart. "After all, I'm an interloper."

"My dear fellow, don't be absurd!" exclaimed Sir Evart warmly. "We're all in this together. A company matter, as it were, so sit down."

Stuart relaxed.

LATTIMER ARRIVED; he and Sir Evart greeted each other warmly; he shook hands with Penny, and his eyes twinkled at Stuart, who laughed as their hands met.

"I'm frightfully sorry about my rudeness last night," said Stuart. "I was jittery, that was all."

"Don't mention it," said Lattimer. "I know just how you were feeling, Stuart. They found a dead man today on some property I own, and I had to look him over—just came from there. Some poor devil in a trailer—What's wrong? Do you people know anything about the case?"

"I do," said Stuart. "Too much, in fact. Sit down and I'll give you the yarn. Since it concerns the emerald, you're entitled to it anyhow. At least, I presume it's the same man; corpses aren't strewn by wholesale over New Mexico. A reddish-brown trailer on the north edge of town? Bled to death?"

"From a knife-wound in his hip—correct. Well, this is most amazing!" Lattimer seated himself. Despite the white hair he was vigorous and full of life, keenly alert. Well balanced, thought Stuart; an idealist, perhaps a bit ruthless.

"Yes," he went on, "the fellow was merely a transient who had camped on my land with his trailer—a guest of mine, as it were. I think the police got his name, but it meant nothing to me."

"It might have, except for Stuart, here," Sir Evart said, and got out his Turkish cigarettes. "Go ahead, Stuart, and say your say."

The latter complied, again recounting the happenings since his landing here. It seemed that Lattimer had vaguely heard of Monckton or Hartley, but did not know him; over the trailer story he evinced a keenly absorbed interest, and became wide-awake at hearing of Hartley's call at the hotel.

"Good!" he exclaimed then. "Something will come of that, I predict; there'll be some fun. This rascal is a sharp 'un. I venture that he already knows of my connection with you."

"You seem pleased," put in Penny.

Lattimer smiled, his eyes sparkling.

"I am, young lady. I enjoy life, and that means the conflicts of life. This chap Hartley sets himself against the world? Excellent! Let him make good or take the consequences! Life in these parts is raw and rich; things happen. Here's a rascal kills his pal—and that dead man in the trailer must be paid for."

Every eye was upon him. "Indeed?" Sir Evart asked. "A crime, you mean?"

Lattimer nodded. "Precisely. How or why it'll be paid for remains to be seen; I'm not speaking of the law, understand. I imagine from all you say that Hartley will act with vicious speed and precision, perhaps this very day. Good; let's leave it at that."

Stuart, wondering at the man, spoke out.

"Well, if you'll enjoy a tussle with Hartley, you're welcome to it. We'll be glad to present you with the feud."

Lattimer smiled. "Right! Look here, now. My house is empty, my servants are away till tomorrow—a Mexican couple do for me—but it's a good house, well stocked. These hillside and cañon roads are a bit ticklish at times, to strangers. I suggest that you let me run you all out there now and cook up a spaghetti supper for you, display some of my specimens, and bring you back later. Eh? Can do?"

"I fancy so." Sir Evart nodded. "It'd be a treat, for my part."

Penny nodded. "It would indeed, and I might come in handy at the supper."

"Done, then!" cried Lattimer with a lusty, hearty ring in his voice. "And if we have any interference from Mr. Hartley, we'll make him welcome also! It'll take an hour to run out there to Spider Cañon. But I'm forgetting something—I came here to look at the Sphinx Emerald, my friends. Aren't you going to show it?"

HE MOVED to the desk by the window, stuck a jeweler's glass in his eye, and proceeded to examine the stone. No one spoke. Stuart saw that the visitor had become tense, absorbed, utterly concentrated, a slow amazement growing in his manner as the stone took hold of him. Sir Evart looked on keenly, and met Penny's eye with a nod and a smile.

At length Lattimer removed the glass, and looked up.

"I'd have taken oath that no such stone could exist," he said slowly. "But it does. Here's the proof." He held a match to his pipe, puffed it alight, and leaned back. "I've heard of the Sphinx Emerald," he went on. "Fantastic little pastiches, historic tales— never believed 'em. Now I do."

"Then it's real!" exclaimed Penny.

Lattimer nodded at her.

"Yes, my dear. Real. Worthless as a gem, priceless as what it is. I congratulate you on owning such a thing. What price have you set on it?"

"That's for Sir Evart to say," she replied. "I know nothing of prices."

Lattimer looked at the Briton. "He does. What say, Sir Evart?"

"Hm! I had thought of asking a thousand pounds."

"I'll give double that—nine thousand dollars. Eh?"

"A wounded grizzly would be safer to look up,"
said Lattimer. "Give me that gun, Stuart."

"Done."

To lighten the tension that was upon the room, Stuart
reached out to the desk and laid beside the emerald its
imitation.

"I'll kick in with Hartley's contribution to the pot," he said.
"They should go together."

Lattimer unfolded a check-book and clipped a pen.

"I suggest, Sir Evart, that since it's Sunday, we might visit
the desk together with the check. The manager knows me quite
well and he'll handle it; you'll get the cash first thing in the
morning. Eh?"

The Briton nodded, not too happily.

"If I were wealthier, I'd never let the gem go to you—even
though it belongs in your collection!"

Lattimer chuckled and handed over the check. Sir Evart
endorsed it and displayed it to Penny. From his pocket the

collector produced some bits of soft tissue, in which he wrapped the Sphinx Emerald and its replica.

"My car's outside," he said. "Suppose we meet there in five minutes. Ready, Sir Evart? We'll have to locate the hotel manager."

They departed together. Penny started for the door; Stuart checked her.

"Wait; I want a word. You're a rich woman; going to buy a Cadillac with your new wealth, I suppose?"

She looked at him.

"Wealth? A few thousand dollars? Half that price goes to you, of course."

"We had no such agreement. Nix on that: nayo, hoss!"

She smiled. "Since you're dropping into groovy cat language, I'll just igg your nayo, Mr. Stuart. You've nothing to say about it."

"I control my bank account, and sha'n't take what's not mine."

"Half that money, after Sir Evart's commission comes out, goes to you," she said firmly. "You most certainly earned it, and then some! Since that is now settled, hadn't you better run along and look up the prospective bride?"

He nodded thoughtfully. "Yeah, I'm doing that—doing it right now. Okay—I'll take your money—in fact, I have to do it, since that's my only salvation."

Her brows lifted as she scrutinized him. "I don't get you—or, to keep groovy, I don't dig you. What gives?"

"Forget that stuff and be yourself, Penny," he said, regarding her seriously. "This is a new rôle for me; I had to jump at any possible approach. And the job would be impossible if you were wallowing in riches and me just a mechanic or something of the sort. That's why I must take you up and reduce your wad by half—if you agree to it."

"What on earth are you jabbering about?" she demanded, a twinkle in her eyes.

"You, darling. I'm in earnest—do I have to spell it all out? Go on my knees? It ain't done these days! Admitted, I'm no brilliant whirlwind, but I do love you. I want you to go along westward the whole way and get married with real orange blossoms in your hair. Will you do it?"

She broke into a smile. "I just had to make you say it, Bill."

"Say what?"

"'I love you'—and sure I'll do it!"

SUDDENLY PENNY tore herself free with a horrified cry.

"Bill! I must get ready—we have to meet them at the car!"

"Right," said he. "And I must see at the desk about plane reservations. Okay, dear—one more for luck—"

Another two minutes and he was making his way to the desk. At a discreet hint from the clerk he wiped lipstick from his cheek; then he found no reservations available until a three A.M. plane, which would land them in Los Angeles Monday noon. There ensued a hasty conference with Sir Evart and Lattimer and the hotel manager regarding finances. This resulted in a general exchange of checks, Lattimer's check being honored by the hotel and others issued in exchange, to the general satisfaction of everyone. Penny showed up in time to receive her money, Stuart took up his reservations for Los Angeles, and Lattimer promised to deliver them at the hotel in ample time to make the plane.

With that, they all piled out to Lattimer's big car and got off amid laughter and congratulations, a merry foursome forgetful of everything except the moment.

Lattimer, whose family was away, lived only a few miles outside the city, but the road was one of wonders. He drove past elaborate residences of millionaires and famed artists, displayed the restored ruins of cliff-dwellers along sheer rock walls, showed them scenic glories in the long sunset, and finally entered Spider Cañon. Here the road to his hillside home was narrow and required the most cautious driving, but he took it at fair speed with a laugh of unconcern.

"A road isn't dangerous if you know it, and I'm a good driver," he declared. "And no one else lives here—it's practically a private road, you see. A drop would mean a three-hundred-foot fall, but I don't intend to drop, so rest easy…. Here we are."

The house showed ahead: a huge hillside structure of timber and adobe, the walls decorated with colored tiles. They drove into a huge courtyard large enough for a dozen cars. All was spacious, and the interior of the house was softly gay with rich Chimayo and other Indian weaves.

Everything here was electric. The kitchen and dining-room were on a separate level, and with four people to take hold, supper became a joyous thing. Penny got a great caldron of spaghetti boiling; a sauce was mixed, wine was produced, and places were set in the dining-room, where Lattimer touched off a ready-laid fire in the corner hearth.

Time flew rapidly. Presently the meal was dished up; and under the soft indirect lights of the dining-room the four gathered about it hungrily. Sir Evart launched into stories, Lattimer capped them, Stuart spoke of flying in Egypt, and everyone ate enormously. Coffee and cigars for the men put an end to the meal. Penny offered to clean up, but all pitched in and lightened the labor.

At last Lattimer led the way to his "den"—a luxurious room fully thirty feet long, on the uphill side of the house. Here were more precious Indian weaves and cabinets of old silver and the now extinct turquoise of New Mexico; and against this background, gems. Precious stones, ancient and modern, beautiful and ugly, most of them in cabinets recessed in the wall and invisible until opened, when lights switched on.

Here were gems of all descriptions, from matrix to finished and polished stone; curios of form and cutting and color from every part of the world. Some were historic stones, some were priceless, many were worthless yet of intense interest as a matter of curiosity and replete with story. One cabinet of emeralds had every known variety—ancient Egyptian and Siberian, even some of the actual stones seized by Pizarro's men from the Incas, and upon these Lattimer waxed garrulous. He was a walking mine of information, for his knowledge was erudite and beyond exhaustion.

"All this is positively incredible!" exclaimed Sir Evart, lost in marveling admiration. "But isn't it dangerous for you and your family to live here in the wilderness amid a treasury of gems, unprotected?"

Their host chuckled. "Well guarded, if not protected. These cabinets are of steel. Only one at a time can be opened; the others are protected by a master switch that sets electronic devices at work. Try to break into them and your picture is taken and a general alarm is given at Santa Fe. The house is fireproof; hence, insurance is low."

"But one cabinet at a time might be looted?"

"Might be, yes: only under certain conditions, and even then every highway would be guarded by State police within twenty minutes—and hereabout there are few highways, my friend." Lattimer took the Sphinx Emerald from his pocket, placed it on the desk; beside it he put the replica.

"Actually, these two might be stolen," he went on, "yet nothing else could be touched. Once these have been photographed and placed in a cabinet, they're as safe as all the others. Here, take fresh cigars; the evening's young, and I'll show you a bit of scientific magic."

On the desk he placed what looked like a stereopticon, connecting it to a wall socket. It faced a bare spot on the opposite wall fifteen feet distant.

"This is actually an electronic enlarger of use in examining any translucent stone or crystal," he went on. "It assesses flaws, color values, and so forth; at the moment, we'll simply view the emerald, which is translucent, and the glass replica, which appears the same but is really transparent. Stuart, will you click that switch near the door, please?"

Stuart complied and the room was plunged into darkness, broken only by the glimmer of the stereopticon and the glow of light on the opposite wall. Lattimer put the replica into his machine; the glowing expanse became a soft green. This, as Lattimer focused the light, showed the flaws in the glass very faintly.

"Poor," said their host. "Obviously glass, not a crystalline structure, and no life in the color; it's artificial and singly refracting, showing little. Watch the difference when I slip in the real beryl."

The replica came out; the wall expanse showed clear white light—then, as the Sphinx Emerald went in, a murmur of astonishment and delight broke from them all.

Now the glowing expanse became alive as the light was focused. The color had depth, the flaws took on form and shape, the background stretched interminably; the stone itself, with all its magic perspective, was in this enormous enlargement. Clear stood the Sphinx, composed of the stone's various flaws. The color values blended delicately in shades of green.

One sensed patterns in the blending, exactly as when gazing into the emerald under a glass. Stuart felt the same sensations—the uplift and ecstasy, the odd uneasiness. He heard Penny's murmur about its glorious beauty; he caught Sir Evart's praise of its feeling of power and wisdom; yet he did not like it.

Lattimer shifted the stone; the whole scene changed, yet to Stuart the feeling persisted. The strange angular flaws took on new forms, the color deepened.

Lattimer's voice broke upon the darkened room with a touch of awe.

"My friends, we're seeing what no one in the world has ever before glimpsed—the living heart of this emerald! It's a thing beyond words. No wonder it takes hold of a person like a magic draught! I shall work with this stone in different degrees of light, register it in every angle, plumb all its secrets, gain from it a full and complete record of its mystery—"

In the partial darkness of the room there was movement. Lattimer's voice abruptly fell silent; feet clattered on the floor. A new voice rose, hoarse and excited, in deadly menace:

"No, you don't! Stand still—don't move—on with those lights, Jack!"

It was the voice of Hartley—or Monckton.

CHAPTER SEVEN

"QUIET, EVERYONE!" This was Hartley again. He stood beside Lattimer, an ugly automatic pistol in one hand, slowly swinging it about. He said something to Lattimer, who stepped away and disconnected his machine. Hartley, with his free hand, fumbled until he got the Sphinx Emerald free, and pocketed it.

At the doorway stood another man, a mask on his face, pistol in hand. Neither Stuart nor Sir Evart moved; Lattimer moved toward a chair and spoke composedly.

"Do as he says, please. I want no bloodshed; insurance will cover the loss of the stone."

Hartley twisted a lip at him.

"Aye, that's all you think of—*money!* This stone's worth dying for a hundred times—and to you it means only money. You fool!"

The look of him was pure tension. His features were drawn and twitchy, his eyes were wild, enlarged, showing the whites beneath the pupils, and he was livid. His companion spoke up.

"If you've got it, let's go. Don't touch a thing else here, mind."

Hartley must have witnessed the enlarged view of the stone; it had maddened him. He snarled when Lattimer said:

"I'll give you a fat sum and let you go unsought, if you'll give up that—"

"Be damned to you!" Hartley's voice bit and seared. "You and your money! As though I'd sell out to you, after trailing this thing here from Egypt!" His words shrilled with added vehemence; their slight trace of accent was intensified; he waved the pistol to and fro, almost in a frenzy, as he went on:

"Sell—buy and sell—that's all you swine know! As though I'd give up that emerald at any price! It's mine; it stays with me. One of the great things of the world! Let me go unsought, would you? That's a joke! You couldn't keep me from getting the stone—now get it back if you can! All right, Jack—get outside and start the car. I'll be along in two minutes."

Watching everyone intently, Hartley backed away toward the door; his companion turned and disappeared. Stuart made a motion as though to rise. Lattimer shook his head.

"Don't," he said quietly. "Never oppose a mad dog. Let others do it."

Stuart relaxed at the words, wondering at their meaning, but Hartley vented a snarl.

"You fool! 'Mad dog' if you like, but smarter than the lot of you! I warn you, don't start in pursuit of me, or you'll suffer. Don't stir from your chairs for a good five minutes; mind the caution, or you'll be sorry. There's blood on this stone already, and there'll be more if you force me—"

He stood glaring at them for a moment. Stuart was not minded to dare that madman's weapon, especially since Lattimer seemed to have some scheme in mind. Hartley put out his free hand to the electric switch.

"Five minutes, now," he repeated warningly. *Click!* The room went dark. Upon the sudden blackness rose the voice of Lattimer:

"Steady, everyone!"

A moment passed. Stuart came to his feet; the switch clicked again and the lights came on. Sir Evart was swearing softly. Lattimer smiled and stepped rapidly to the desk.

"Sorry you had this experience, Miss Morrison. I'll soon have the police after those fellows." He lifted the telephone and listened; his face changed. "Hello! Clever gentry; the wire's cut.... Who has the time?"

Stuart glanced at his watch. "Five to twelve."

"Hm! My car's outside—another in the garage. There's a house three miles from here where I can get a phone and rout out the State police. I can get you back to your hotel."

"Forget it!" broke in Stuart. "I'm going with you and see this thing to a finish!"

"I want to see it finished, too—after all, they got the emerald, my emerald," said Penny. "I'll wait here until you come back, Mr. Lattimer. Let our plans go; they don't matter now."

Lattimer broke into a laugh. "But you can't stay alone—eh, Sir Evart? Right; you two stop here; Stuart and I will take a flyer. You two make yourselves at home."

"BUT THEY got the emerald!" wailed Penny.

"Cheer up—we got the cash," Stuart put in. "And if Lattimer doesn't get the stone back, he'll collect insurance."

Lattimer beckoned, and Stuart followed. Lights snapped on; they went through the house to the courtyard. Lattimer opened the garage and went inside. He came out carrying a rifle and handed this to Stuart.

"Can you use it? Good man! There's a place where we can see their car, far below us; no hurry, either. No other car on this road, you know, no chance of any mistake. Cripple them if we can, then call the cops. Hop in!"

Stuart examined the rifle, then obeyed. Lattimer's door slammed, the engine roared, they were moving. The lights flung a broad beam on the turn and the road; the car slid away, the house vanished. The magazine rifle was loaded; a dropping fire would carry for an incredible distance, Stuart knew.

He felt let down, almost cheated. He realized that in this State of vast distances and few highways the State police could quickly close all roads; yet it had all been so simple, so lacking in dramatic values! Hartley was gone with the gem, but the police would collar him; another phase in the history of the Sphinx Emerald would be closed. Was that all?

The car slowed at a bend. Lattimer spoke calmly.

"Your ball, Stuart! Look down, past the right fender—you'll see the car lights down there when it comes. Better set your sights high and give 'em all you can. It'll be a chance shot, anyhow—a good half-mile below us; you'll have about ten seconds in which to fire."

Watching, Stuart steadied his rifle, cocked it, waited. Lattimer had shut off the engine; the night was quiet. A fool *thing*, he reflected; no one could hope to hit anything this way—

A THRILL seized him. Far below appeared radiance—the forelight of a coming car. His nerves leaped; he lifted the rifle. The radiance grew into a stronger light; this became two headlights. Stuart aimed as well as he could, pressed the shoulder-butt close, and fired. The weapon kicked and kicked—he got in four shots in all before the target vanished.

"Excellent!" approved Lattimer, starting the engine. "Any sort of hit, if it does nothing else, will mark their car beyond escape. Throw the rifle anywhere in back; now we'll bend all energies to getting hold of the cops. Afraid I'll have to wake up everybody in that house too, before I can get to the phone."

He had to do exactly that.

Stuart sat in the car out under the stars for what seemed an interminable time. A cautious native had let Lattimer into the house, a tiny shack above the road, and the rest was silence. Presently the glow of a cigarette announced Lattimer, who came to the car with a jovial excitement.

"Upon my word, Stuart, I believe we've got 'em!"

"You got the cops?"

"Oh, sure! And more: Headquarters had just received a

complaint by phone from old Tom Parkhurst, who lives up on Gaspar Road by the abandoned Mexican smithy, that a broken-down car had stopped by there. A shooting had taken place, and there's a dead man in the car." The engine had roared into life as Lattimer spoke, and now the lights went on and the car jumped. "We can get there ahead of the police. It's our man, no doubt of it; the two bandits had a row——"

The rest was lost in a rush of wind, as the car leaped into speed.

Stuart said nothing; he just hung on and hoped for the best, as Lattimer took the cañon curves at mad speed, evidently determined to beat the State police to the spot in question. After all, he thought grimly, the Sphinx Emerald might yet come back to its lawful owner!

The car swooped into cañon dips, took the upgrades with zooming power. If it was mad driving, it was also skillful. Lattimer grunted out scraps of speech: the abandoned smithy had been taken over by an old artist named Parkhurst, who lived in a shack nearby, and kept up the smithy for the sake of its picturesque appearance; a lonely spot and ripe for murder.

Stuart hoped that his bullets had done no murder. Not that he had the least compunction, but the idea of pouring lead into a car on the lonely highway rankled in him. Five miles had been covered, he reckoned, when a word from Lattimer told him the smithy was just ahead and warned him to have the rifle ready— needless warning! A light flickered at them—here was old Parkhurst pottering about a car that stood just off the highway. He hailed them with gleeful recognition of Lattimer.

"You beat the cops to it!" he sang out. "Look-a-here—funny how this car got crippled; looks like bullets had ripped this rear tire—"

"Never mind that," put in Stuart. "What about the dead man?"

"Shooting took place right here," said Parkhurst. "That's what woke me up. Feller's in the back seat. Here's the flashlight. You can have him; one look was enough for me! He got shot in the face at close range, like he had tried to kill the driver and got his needin's himself."

"That apparently is precisely what happened," said Lattimer, taking the light and looking into the car. "This is the man who was with Hartley, Stuart. Let the cops have him—but I want to know where Hartley is! He can't be far away. He didn't come up to your house, Tom?"

"No," said Parkhurst. "But if you ask me, the trail from here to the smithy in them trees is plain to see. The other man is liable to be hurt too; there was more'n one shot fired."

"Then a wounded grizzly would be safer to look up than our friend," said Lattimer. "Give me that gun, Stuart. You take the flashlight and throw it on the trail."

This last was no more than a path heading in among the trees toward a half-visible structure, the smithy.

"It ain't locked," sang out Parkhurst. "You fellers better wait for the cops, too. Liable to run into hot lead yonder."

Stuart disregarded him and started along the path, shooting the light well ahead. Lattimer followed closely. A wide front door of the smithy stood ajar.

Lattimer uttered a word of warning.

"He may shoot at the light. You'd better keep back."

Stuart thought so himself; however, he was not saying so.

"I'll take it edgeways," he replied. "You wait till I light up the place."

He slipped to the side of the entrance, threw his light suddenly into the interior, and followed around the edge of the door—

"Thanks for the light," said Hartley. "I need it. Don't shut it off."

The man stood there, unmasked, insolent, defiant. Beside him was the hood of the smithy; all trace of past fires was gone from the bed. Against the anvil Hartley leaned, a small sledge in his hand. Upon the flat face of the anvil was a spot of green.

THE SPHINX EMERALD

"I've got you covered, Monckton!" came Lattimer's voice.

Hartley looked up and laughed.

"Don't be more of a fool than you naturally are," he riposted. "My pal got me! Stay back, that's all! A minute more is all I need, and I'm good for that. I said you'd never regain the emerald, and you sha'n't."

Stuart saw now that there was something dark around the man's feet! Blood—a pool of it forming.

"I'm going," went on Hartley, "and the emerald's going with me, understand? Gad, what luck finding this place ready and waiting for me. The gods must have arranged it.... I'm finished; my blasted pal tried to do for me and get away with the stone, but he wasn't man enough to manage it—nor are you, damn you!"

"Stop!" cried Lattimer. "Don't be a madman! I'll make no charges against you. Turn back the stone, take the money I offered—I'll see that you're taken care of!"

Hartley laughed. "Go to hell!" his voice shrilled. "I'm done for, and I'm taking the emerald with me; that's more than you can do!"

The sledge lifted in his hand—not high—above the greenish spot on the anvil. Lattimer came forward with a rush—but too late. The sledge fell, toppled to the floor, and Hartley lost balance and sprawled forward upon it.

The green spot had gone; only a greenish dust remained.

CHAPTER EIGHT

LATTIMER WAS at the wheel of his car, heading home, Stuart was beside him. "He beat us," Lattimer said. "Poor crippled, insane devil! His mind was warped, he was crazy about that stone—and to be honest with you, I don't blame him! It was a unique stone, like nothing else in the world; and now it's gone. Nothing now but bits of green dust, and a memory."

"You regret it; I don't," said Stuart. "I think you regret even Hartley's death. I don't; he was bad medicine. It was a stone, nothing more. I'm looking ahead to life, achievement—"

Lattimer laughed.

"A bit of stone—nothing more!" he said softly. "That is one viewpoint. What an epitaph, for a wonder of the world!"

"We can't help our different feelings," Stuart replied. "There's a wonder of the world waiting for me, up at your house, that I wouldn't swap for a dozen Sphinx Emeralds."

"And perhaps you're right, Stuart. I still have the replica, remember. I think I'll present it to the young lady—as a wedding gift, eh?"

And he laughed—but his laughter still was instinct with a sigh.

H . BEDFORD-JONES

BEDFORD-JONES IS a Canadian by birth, but not by profession, having removed to the United States at the age of one year. For over twenty years he has been more or less profitably engaged in writing and traveling. As he has seldom resided in one place longer than a year or so and is a person of retiring habits, he is somewhat a man of mystery; more than once he has suffered from unscrupulous gentlemen who impersonated him—one of whom murdered a wife and was subsequently shot by the police, luckily after losing his alias.

The real Bedford-Jones is an elderly man, whose gray hair and precise attire give him rather the appearance of a retired foreign diplomat. His hobby is stamp collecting, and his collection of Japan is said to be one of the finest in existence. At present writing he is en route to Morocco, and when this appears in print he will probably be somewhere on the Mojave Desert in company with Erle Stanley Gardner.

Questioned as to the main facts in his life, he declared there was only one main fact, but it was not for publication; that his life had been uneventful except for numerous financial losses, and that his only adventures lay in evading adventurers. In his younger years he was something of an athlete, but the encroachments of age preclude any active pursuits except that of motoring. He is usually to be found poring over his stamps, working at his typewriter, or laboring in his California rose garden, which is one of the sights of Cathedral Cañon, near Palm Springs.

Bedford-Jones has written stories laid in many corners of the earth, but among his most popular tales were the John Solomon stories which started many years ago in the *Argosy*.

www.ingramcontent.com/pod-product-compliance
Lightning Source LLC
Chambersburg PA
CBHW051054030726
47504CB00006B/1621